THE SILVER LADIES SEIZE THE DAY

JUDY LEIGH

B
Boldwood

First published in Great Britain in 2025 by Boldwood Books Ltd.

Copyright © Judy Leigh, 2025

Cover Design by JD Smith Design Ltd

Cover Images: Shutterstock

The moral right of Judy Leigh to be identified as the author of this work has been asserted in accordance with the Copyright, Designs and Patents Act 1988.

All rights reserved. No part of this book may be reproduced in any form or by any electronic or mechanical means, including information storage and retrieval systems, without written permission from the author, except for the use of brief quotations in a book review. This book is a work of fiction and, except in the case of historical fact, any resemblance to actual persons, living or dead, is purely coincidental.

Every effort has been made to obtain the necessary permissions with reference to copyright material, both illustrative and quoted. We apologise for any omissions in this respect and will be pleased to make the appropriate acknowledgements in any future edition.

A CIP catalogue record for this book is available from the British Library.

Paperback ISBN 978-1-78513-251-3

Large Print ISBN 978-1-78513-252-0

Hardback ISBN 978-1-78513-250-6

Ebook ISBN 978-1-78513-253-7

Kindle ISBN 978-1-78513-254-4

Audio CD ISBN 978-1-78513-245-2

MP3 CD ISBN 978-1-78513-246-9

Digital audio download ISBN 978-1-78513-248-3

This book is printed on certified sustainable paper. Boldwood Books is dedicated to putting sustainability at the heart of our business. For more information please visit https://www.boldwoodbooks.com/about-us/sustainability/

Boldwood Books Ltd, 23 Bowerdean Street, London, SW6 3TN

www.boldwoodbooks.com

To inspirational teachers.
And inspirational pupils.

Some of us think holding on makes us strong, but sometimes it is letting go.

— HERMANN HESSE

CHARACTER LIST

Do you remember the characters from *The Silver Ladies Do Lunch*?
Here's a quick reminder.

Miss Cecily Hamilton. In her nineties, Cecily used to teach in Middleton Ferris and she still lives there.
Josie Sanderson. Ex-pupil, now in her seventies. Recently widowed. Lives in the village.
Lin Timms. Ex-pupil.
Neil Timms. Married to Lin, another ex-pupil. Lives in the village.
Minnie Moore. Ex-pupil. Lives in Oxford. Retired Classics lecturer.
Tina Gilchrist. Minnie's sister. Divorcee. Lived in the village but is recuperating from a stroke with Minnie.
Jensen Callahan. An American director who is in love with Minnie. Now living back in the States.
George Ledbury. The farmer. Ex-pupil. Virtually retired. His son is George Junior.

Penny Ledbury. His wife.
Nadine. His pet pig.
Bobby Ledbury. George's grandson, a farmer. His girlfriend Hayley and her children live with him in the farm cottage.
Natalie Ledbury. George's granddaughter.
Odile Joseph. Café owner.
'Dangerous' Dave Dawson. A mechanic.
Florence Dawson. Dave's daughter. Works at the café. Recently had a baby, Elsie.
Adam Johnson. Florence's partner.
Malia Johnson. Adam's sister, Florence's friend.
Rita and Linval Johnson. Adam and Malia's parents.
Kenny Hooper. Ex-pupil, lives in the village.
Jimmy Baker. Ex-pupil, lives in the village.
Dickie Edwards, Senior. Ex-pupil, owns The Sun Inn.
Dickie Junior. His son, runs the pub.
Darryl Featherstone. A solicitor, who used to live in the village.
Fergal Toomey. Ex-pupil, now widowed. Lives on the barge on the River Cherwell.

PROLOGUE
SUMMER, 1955. SURREY.

Cecily glanced in the mirror, swished her skirt and thought she looked a bit like Marilyn Monroe in *Gentlemen Prefer Blondes*. She showed her reflection a seductive pout and a moment's panic seized her. She hoped she didn't look too brassy. But, then again, she had no intention of being mousy. She wanted to be respectable yet pretty at the same time. Yes, she was certainly pretty. And things were changing: it wasn't the forties any more. A young woman had opportunities nowadays.

In her head, her mother's voice whined: 'You look like a tart. That red lipstick is common. Those heels are too high.'

It was only her imagination. She had no reason to assume her mother would disapprove, except that she hadn't loved her enough to stay. Cecily didn't remember the woman who had left when she was three years old, and her grandmother said little about it except that Lillian, that was her mother's name, was no better than she should be. Cecily had been born out of wedlock; her mother had run off with the next man who'd shown an interest. The neighbours all agreed it had been shameful. And

Cecily thought it was embarrassing. She certainly didn't intend to go that way.

She believed every word her grandmother told her, that her mother was not a bad person, but she'd always been easily influenced and impressionable. Emily Hamilton had brought Cecily up to be a strong, sensible girl who took pride in herself. She should wait until she was married before having – *relations*.

Her grandmother was the only one whose opinion Cecily really cared about.

As she hurried downstairs, heels clacking, she heard the wireless rattle from the living room. The BBC Home Service. As Cecily breezed in, her grandmother looked up from the armchair where she was sewing, glasses perched on the end of her nose. She murmured, 'Don't be too late back, love.'

'I won't, Nan.'

'Are you going out with Joyce?'

'Yes, we're off to The Orchid.' Cecily patted her blonde curls. She still couldn't get used to how bright and bouncy the new hairstyle was.

'Have a good time,' Emily said, smiling, briefly scanning her granddaughter's flouncy clothes. Emily always worried when Cecily went out dancing, uneasy about the attention of all those men with only one thing on their minds.

Instead, she said, 'Joyce thinks of little else but boys.'

'I know, but she's my best friend,' Cecily said loyally.

'You're not empty-headed like your mother, dear.' Emily took a deep breath. 'You're meant for more than standing at the kitchen sink washing nappies. We all are.'

Cecily knew what she meant. 'I won't stay out late. I'll only drink lemonade. And Joyce and I dance with different boys all the time, never just one. But dancing's so much fun.'

'Having a boyfriend at twenty-two is all right, Cecily, but

remember—' Emily Hamilton tugged the thread through her needle and tied a knot at one end '—you don't want to get serious yet. There's plenty of time for steady relationships. You have your future to think of.'

'I know that, Nan.'

'You're sensible.' Cecily's grandmother gave the same gentle smile she had before, and returned to the dress she was mending. 'Tomorrow morning, we'll go into town and do some shopping. We'll stop for a nice cuppa when we've finished, shall we?'

'I'll buy you a peach melba in the ice-cream bar. My treat.' Cecily rushed over and hugged her nan, feeling the scratchy silver hair against her cheek. Her grandmother was all skin and bone in her arms.

'Enjoy the dancing,' Emily said, but she didn't look up until Cecily had left the room. Her sigh was the last thing Cecily heard before she rushed outside into the last warmth of the Surrey summer.

Joyce was waiting for her at the corner, wearing an Audrey Hepburn-style cocktail dress with a swirling skirt and red high heels. Her newly blonde hair was in a high ponytail with a sweeping fringe over one eye. She waved excitedly as she saw Cecily. 'Come on, we've missed the first bus already.'

'I love the dress, Joyce,' Cecily said as she caught up with her. 'Is it new?'

'Yes. Do you think it shows off my curves?' Joyce swished her petticoat. 'I hope we meet some dreamy boys tonight.'

'I just want to dance and dance.' Cecily grinned. 'I've been learning a few songs on the guitar. I can play "Smile" by Nat "King" Cole, and I can sing it, too.'

'Oh, I'd love to smooch to that song.' Joyce glanced down the road. 'Here's the bus.'

A few moments later, the number 72 shuddered to a halt.

There were a few passengers already seated, mainly single travellers, women clutching bags of shopping, a man smoking a cigarette. The girls squeezed past the conductor, hurrying towards the back seat, flopping down as the bus jolted forward and joined the evening traffic. Joyce delved into her handbag and pulled out a quarter-pound bag of Blue Bird chocolate toffees, offering them to Cecily. Cecily unwrapped one and pushed the sweet into her mouth, biting into the chocolate, tasting the hard caramel beneath.

Joyce grinned. 'It pays to work on the sweet counter at Woolies.' She pushed an arm through Cecily's. 'Mum says come over for your tea next week. What about Tuesday? We can have ham.'

'Tuesday's my evening class. And Thursday.' Cecily glanced through the grimy window as the bus turned a corner. 'I can come on Wednesday.'

'Wednesday it is,' Joyce agreed. 'I forgot you did evening classes. You're still determined to be a schoolteacher?'

'It beats the typing pool. I've got my place to start in September. I love kids.' Cecily finished chewing. 'The little ones, especially.'

'So do I.' Joyce rolled her eyes in a mock swoon. 'I've always set my heart on two kiddies, one of each, and a dreamboat husband who adores me. We'll live in those new houses in Worplesdon. I'd be made for life.'

'Don't you want something for yourself, a career?' Cecily asked, but she knew the answer.

'I want to be a wife and a mum, have a home of my own,' Joyce said. 'Mum says you're too independent, because you never had a proper mother to bring you up.'

'Don't we all want to be independent?' Cecily thought about her mother, who hadn't wanted her, who'd left her as a child and never sent word again. Perhaps Joyce's mother had a point.

'Not me. A ring on my finger, someone to make a fuss over.' Joyce winked. The conductor was hovering nearby, so she dropped a shilling into his palm. 'Two six-pennies into town, please.'

The conductor pushed back his cap and patted thin grey hair as he looked the two girls over, taking in their bright dresses, nylon stockings, high heels. He coughed awkwardly and turned a handle to print off two tickets from the roll in his machine. 'Here you are.'

The bus rattled onwards, around a corner, down a long street. Cecily stood up. 'Thanks. This is our stop.' Joyce was on her feet, rushing towards the door.

'Off dancing at The Orchid, eh?' The conductor grumbled his disapproval. 'You want to watch yourselves, dressed like that.'

'Watch ourselves?' Joyce retorted. 'Oh no, we leave that to dirty old men like you, Daddy-o.'

Cecily grabbed her arm as they hurried off the bus and whispered, 'Daddy-o?' They burst out laughing.

* * *

The Orchid Ballroom might have been a grand place in Victorian times, but the décor was tired and worn now: the place had seen better days. The glittering chandelier still hung from the domed ceiling, a centrepiece among a swirl of red lights. The floor was already crowded with dancers; beyond was a well-lit bar, people drinking, seated around clusters of tables. Music boomed, Bill Haley and His Comets. Couples were swinging and jiving. The women's skirts swung out like bells.

Some of the men wore smart suits; others were dressed more casually. One man danced athletically, lifting his partner, a cigarette clamped between his lips.

Joyce said excitedly, 'Shall we get a drink?'

'We might have one later?' Cecily suggested.

'Come on, let's go to the bar.' Joyce grabbed her hand. 'I'll buy you a lemonade.'

'All right.' Cecily followed Joyce through the juddering crowd. Joyce leaned against the bar and waved furiously at the barman. 'Can I have two lemonades?'

The barman was busy; he ignored Joyce and turned to two men who had just arrived, who stood quietly behind them. Cecily noticed that they were smartly dressed in suits and ties. One was dark-haired, handsome in the style of heart-throb James Dean. The other man was slimmer, his fair hair too neat; he seemed hesitant, in the shadow of the first man. The good-looking one paused and indicated Joyce and Cecily. 'I think these young ladies were here first.'

'They were,' his companion agreed.

The barman seemed unconcerned. He half turned to Joyce. 'Right, darling, what did you want?'

Before she could speak, the dark-haired man said, 'What can I get you, girls?'

Joyce gave a squeal of delight. 'Oh, I'll have a snowball if you're buying.'

The man turned to Cecily. 'The same for you?'

'No, thanks.' Cecily was thoughtful. 'Just a lemonade.'

'Oh, try a snowball, Cecily. Or a gin and orange,' Joyce said.

'Have whatever you like.' The man looked into Cecily's eyes. His were dark brown, honest, kind. Cecily felt her heart bump in a new way as she said, 'Just lemonade, please.'

'Two shandies, a lemonade and a snowball,' the James Dean

lookalike said. The other man, the shyer one, said, 'I'm Albert and this is Eddie. We're brothers. Are you sisters?'

'No.' Joyce turned from Albert to Eddie. 'I'm Joyce. Cecily's my best friend.'

'Oh, I just thought, you both being blondes,' Albert said awkwardly.

'Here you are.' Eddie passed Cecily a fizzing lemonade; he gave Joyce a glass of frothy yellow liquid with a cherry on top. 'Cheers.'

'Cheers,' Joyce gushed, showing her widest smile.

'Shall we sit down?' Eddie glanced towards an empty table for four in the corner. He put an arm around Cecily's shoulders, shepherding her through the twirling dancers. Joyce was just behind, her eyes on Eddie. Albert followed a little way back, clutching his shandy as if he was worried he'd spill it. They sat down.

'So, Cecily.' Eddie leaned forward. 'Are you from this area?'

Cecily nodded, the glass to her lips, and Joyce said, 'We both live ten minutes out of town. We came here on the bus.'

'We're from Jacob's Well,' Albert explained. 'We drove here. Eddie has a car.'

'Ooh.' Joyce gave Eddie all her attention. 'What sort have you got?'

'A Morris Minor,' Eddie said, smiling at Cecily.

'What colour?'

'Green.' Eddie's eyes were still on Cecily.

'Eddie's a mechanic,' Albert explained. 'I work in a warehouse.'

'A mechanic's a great job.' Joyce leaned forward and sipped her snowball alluringly. 'I think mechanics look so nice in overalls.'

'The place I work in smells of metal and dust,' Eddie told

Cecily. 'It's not very romantic. But one day, I'll have my own garage.'

'Eddie's ambitious,' Albert explained, his face proud.

'So's Cecily. She's going to be a teacher.' Joyce gulped the last of her snowball and turned her attention to Albert. 'I want to dance.'

'Oh.' Albert stood up nervously. 'Shall I dance with you?'

Joyce grabbed his hand. 'I love Bill Haley and His Comets,' she said as she dragged him into the crowd.

Eddie's eyes were still on Cecily. 'A teacher, eh?'

Cecily realised she'd hardly spoken yet. She was watching the light in his eyes, the way his lips moved. She said, 'I'm doing evening classes to get all the qualifications. I've been offered a place for September, to train to be a primary teacher.' She wondered if she came across as dull, but Eddie's eyes gleamed.

'You've got things worked out.'

'I want to do something I love.'

'So do I.' Eddie took a deep breath. 'It's so important to follow your heart. Too many people just put up with second best. But we have one chance to grab life.'

'We do.' Cecily was thoughtful. 'My mum abandoned me when I was a child and I never knew my father. My nan brought me up and she always said that I should make the best of myself. She was a suffragette years ago.'

'Her character's rubbed off on you, I can see that.' Eddie reached out and placed his hand over hers. 'You seem so self-assured, unafraid of anything.'

'I know what I want in life,' Cecily said.

'Me too.' Eddie seemed delighted. He glanced briefly across the dance floor. 'Oh, do you want to dance? Albert and your friend seem to be enjoying themselves.'

'I love dancing,' Cecily said, looking at Eddie's earnest face, his deep-set eyes, his warm grin. 'But I think I'd like to talk a bit longer.'

'I was hoping you'd say that,' Eddie said. He reached for his shandy. He'd hardly touched it. Cecily realised her lemonade glass was almost full.

Eddie said, 'So tell me about yourself, Cecily. I want to know all about you.'

He couldn't draw his eyes away. And Cecily was still staring at his face. For a moment, time seemed to take a breath and hold it.

Cecily said mischievously, 'What do you want to know? I have to be home by ten-thirty.'

'But I'm hoping we can get to know each other,' Eddie said quickly. 'Tomorrow's Saturday. I can drive us to Winkworth. We can have a picnic.'

'With Joyce and Albert?' Cecily asked. She felt the pressure of Eddie's hand on hers.

'If you want your friend there, of course she can come. But I'd really like to be with you.'

***

At ten twenty-five, the night sky spattered with stars, Eddie stopped the car on the corner so that Albert could walk Joyce home. His arm was tentatively around her waist, but she was already being familiar, calling him Albie, clinging to him. Eddie drove the few yards to Cecily's house and, as the green Morris idled, he said, 'Can I walk you to your door?'

Cecily's breath caught in her throat. He meant that he wanted to kiss her. Her mind raced to memories of the other boyfriends she'd had, Georgie, Martin, Tommy, all nice young men she'd been friends with first, who'd all invested in her far too much, and she'd unintentionally broken their hearts, one after the other. Kissing them had happened in a spontaneous moment of affection and warmth. But with Eddie, it felt strangely different.

She said, 'I can't stay out long. My nan worries.'

'Of course.' Eddie understood at once. 'When I pick you up tomorrow, I'll meet her first, so that she knows I'm...'

Cecily finished his sentence in her mind. Respectable? Serious?

Eddie wriggled from the car, opened Cecily's door and offered a hand. When she clambered out, he didn't let go. His fingers entwined around hers and her hand felt safe, protected. It gave her a glowing feeling.

They walked to the back door and Cecily reached in her handbag for a key. She said, 'I should go in.'

'Yes.' Eddie was staring at her but neither of them moved. Cecily's gaze tangled in his; she couldn't pull away. Her heart was thudding as he pulled her close and his lips met hers.

He kissed her, tugging her against him, and straight away she was whisked into a torrent of emotions she had no name for. Attraction, love, desire? She pulled back, catching her breath. Cecily had never felt such an explosion of feelings. Eddie must have felt the same thing, like electricity.

'I'm sorry,' Eddie said quickly. 'I didn't mean to—'

'No, it's all right.' Cecily was astonished at her own words. All right? The sensation of kissing Eddie was shocking, terrifying, but it was the most incredible feeling in the world. They stared at each other again and Cecily said, 'I ought to go in.'

'Can I see you tomorrow?'

'Yes.'

'At twelve?'

'All right.'

'I'll meet your grandmother first.'

'Good.'

'Then we'll drive somewhere.'

'Eddie?' Cecily reached for his hand.

He brought it to his lips in a sudden movement and said, 'You know that you can trust me, Cecily. Since we met tonight, I—'

'You?' Cecily waited, holding her breath.

'I've never met a girl quite like you. It feels special.'

'It does.' Cecily held onto the moment a little longer, enjoying the way her skin tingled. She tugged her hand away. 'Goodnight, Eddie.'

'Goodnight, Cecily.' She heard his whisper as she closed the door behind her.

For a moment, she stood still, her mind whirling. What had just happened?

She was twenty-two years old, her life stretching before her, and until this evening everything had been ordered, predictable and stable. Now she had met Eddie Blake, it was as if still waters had been stirred up. More than stirred. It was as if she were buffeted by strong waves, powerless, lifted on a tempest of emotions. She was feverish, impulsive. She couldn't wait to see Eddie tomorrow. In one evening, everything had changed.

She would never be the same again.

Cecily took another breath and realised the word she was looking for.

Love. That was it.

She was falling in love.

1

THE PRESENT DAY

'Penny for them, Cecily?'

Cecily's hand shook as she held the china cup and brought it to her lips. Her hands always seemed to shake nowadays. She had heard Lin speak, but she'd been deep in thought. 'Pardon?'

'I said, "Penny for your thoughts."' Lin gave a light laugh. 'You were somewhere else.'

'Was I?' Cecily turned to where Lin, Josie and Minnie were watching from the sofa. 'Oh, I'm so sorry. I was thinking about...' She wondered how to explain. 'How I got to being so old. It's almost my ninety-second birthday.' She couldn't believe how time had flown. 'One minute I was twenty-two. We were quite young for our age then, but I was so hopeful for the future. I trained, and started teaching, then came to Middleton Ferris, and I met you all.'

'It was 1959,' Minnie said. 'We were desperate not to get Terrible Thomas for our teacher. Then you came into our lives, Cecily.'

'You came in and introduced yourself. You said, "My name is

Miss Hamilton. I'm your teacher for this year." We couldn't believe our luck,' Josie said. 'I remember exactly what you had on. You were wearing a fitted blue dress with a swirling skirt and blue shoes with pointed toes.'

'And you had scarlet fingernails.' Lin closed her eyes, remembering. 'And a guitar. We were all in awe. And we sang "Wake Up Little Susie" and "Peggy Sue" and "Jailhouse Rock". You were so cool.'

'You read *The Wind in the Willows* to us while we snuggled against the big hot radiators. It was heaven,' Minnie added. 'By half past three, the whole class was in love with you.'

'Ah, I remember it all.' Cecily sipped her tea again. The milkiness of it comforted her. 'I loved teaching. And you were my girls, my successes. Minnie, you went on to lecture Classics in Oxford; Josie, Lin, you stayed in the village and built your lives there. And I had the career I dreamed of.'

'You don't regret it?' Josie asked, pushing back dark hair. 'I mean, you dedicated your whole life to your pupils.'

'If you mean do I regret being a spinster, I can tell you it's perfectly all right,' Cecily said firmly.

'Absolutely.' Minnie gave a low laugh. 'I've always enjoyed the independence of life in Oxford and the whole bed to myself as and when I want it.'

Lin was about to say that she was happily married, that she wouldn't be without her beloved Neil, but she stopped herself. Josie was examining her fingers thoughtfully and Lin knew who she was thinking of.

'I had a wonderful marriage with Harry.' Josie took a shaky breath. 'But you're right. We all have to make choices. Oh, by the way—' she turned to Minnie, hunched in a long dress and Doc Martens boots '—have you heard from that American man who's besotted with you?'

'Jensen? He calls me, yes.' Minnie seemed to want to close the conversation down. 'I took Tina to see the doctor yesterday. She's making great progress. I think she'll be coming back here soon.' She pushed a hand through grey curls. 'I'm looking forward to having my own space.'

'It's kind of you to look after Tina after the stroke,' Lin said.

'Yes, but it's summertime, and summer in Oxford means parties and fun. I could do with my independence back.' Minnie thought about her words. 'I love Tina deeply, and I'm glad to help, but we're chalk and cheese.'

'I'm sure she'll be ready to come home soon,' Josie said.

'I wish she'd be quick about it.' Minnie grinned mischievously.

'You were always very different,' Cecily observed. 'Not that she didn't have your brains, Minnie, but she didn't have your drive.'

'She had drive all right, but my dad held her back. He told her that one of us going to the snooty grammar school was enough.'

'Girls have so much more opportunity now.' Cecily stared into the distance.

'I'm just happy to be at home and make the man I love an edible dinner.' Lin smoothed her blonde hair. 'I can incinerate a ping meal in seven minutes from frozen.'

'What are you cooking Neil tonight?' Josie asked.

'He's making gnocchi, I think.'

'I ought to get off to the station.' Minnie glanced at the clock. 'My train's at half two and Tina's at physio.' She turned to her friends. 'It's great to catch up though. I love our lunches.'

'Thanks for hosting, Cecily. It was lovely.' Josie smiled. 'So, we'll meet at Lin's next time?'

'Or Odile's?' Lin said quickly. 'Unless Neil bakes his lemon drizzle cake, in which case you can all come to mine.'

'I'd better be off.' Minnie stood up and moved towards her friends, arms already thrown wide. Lin and Josie joined her in a hug. Cecily was still sitting down, staring at her cup.

'Are you sure you're all right, Cecily?' Josie asked, a little anxious.

'What? Oh, I'm fine.' Cecily brought her cup to her lips again. The tea had almost all gone. 'It just seems strange that all those years ago I was your teacher and now here we are, so much older.'

'We're best friends though,' Lin said happily.

'Do you think about the old times a lot, Cecily?' Minnie asked, perceptive as ever.

'Sometimes,' Cecily said. The image of Eddie's face still lingered in her thoughts, his serious dark eyes, the way his fingers linked easily through hers, as if they fitted perfectly. 'I try to live in the present.' She brightened, changing the subject. 'In fact, I'm a modern girl now. I'm on Facebook.'

'I'm not,' Minnie said abruptly. 'There are too many people I want to avoid.'

'All your exes who are still in love with you,' Lin reminded her. 'No, I love Facebook. I keep up with the grandchildren. Melissa's always sending me photos. Selfies, mainly. And Louis is football mad – he plays in goal.'

'So what are you doing on Facebook, Cecily?' Josie asked.

'You know Jack Lovejoy, who I played guitar with last year at the fete? Your neighbour's son, Lin?' Cecily began.

Lin remembered. 'He's gone off on tour with Glyndŵr, his folk group. Janice told me they're playing up north somewhere.'

'Manchester, tomorrow night,' Cecily said. 'Jack said he

wanted to friend me on Facebook so that he could send me clips of his gigs.'

'He thinks the world of you. We all do.' Minnie reached for her bag. 'I'd better go or I'll miss the train.' She pecked Cecily's cheek. 'We'll catch up soon.'

'We certainly will.' Cecily put her cup down and eased herself up for another hug. 'I look forward to our time together.'

'What about lunch round my house tomorrow, Cecily?' Josie offered. 'It'll save one of us cooking. Come over on your little scooter.'

'Let's meet at The Sun,' Cecily said. 'It's fairly quiet on a Friday. Can you come, Lin?'

'Hairdresser's, sorry,' Lin said apologetically. 'Although I'd rather sit in the pub any day than listen to Mandy go on about her boyfriend's ingrown toenails.'

'It'll just be me and you, Josie,' Cecily said. 'I'll come down on the Flying Plum. I call it that because it's purple and I drive it too fast.' She held out her arms for one final hug. 'It's been so nice.'

'Oh, we haven't washed up. I can do that before we go,' Lin offered.

'Not at all. I'll do it,' Cecily insisted. 'Then I'll have a little nap. I'm quite fond of my afternoon naps.'

Her eyes misted over and she became quiet. Josie glanced at Minnie and Lin. 'Well, we'll be off. See you soon.'

Cecily muttered something to herself and Minnie led the way to the door.

* * *

The friends linked arms as they walked along Tadderly Road

towards the station, just as they had years ago in primary school. They were quiet, lost in thought for a while.

Minnie said, 'Our Miss Hamilton was a bit low this afternoon.'

'Do you think she's all right?' Lin looked worried.

Minnie said, 'She's tremendous for nearly ninety-two. I only hope I'm so sprightly when I'm her age.'

Lin raised an eyebrow. 'I'm not as perky as she is,' she groaned. 'The arthritis meds I'm on are better than the last ones, but there are days when I have no energy.'

'Me too,' Josie agreed. 'But in my case, it's called loneliness.'

'Oh, Josie,' Lin said sadly. 'I'm sorry.'

Josie met her eyes. 'Being a widow's hard. Even the good times are a bit empty.'

'I can't imagine what you've been through.' Lin's heart went out to her friend.

Josie forced a smile. 'Having you two and Cecily helps. It'll be nice meeting her tomorrow.'

'I wish I could be there,' Lin said sadly.

'Me too,' Minnie agreed. 'It's great to catch up.'

'You've done the best of us all, Minnie. Your life in Oxford, being an academic.'

'Retired academic.' Minnie pulled a face. 'I still get invited to the odd conference, a bit of research here and there. But, in all honesty, my days of working with the finest minds in the world are over. In short...' she laughed '...I'm defunct.'

'But we're still useful,' Lin protested as they turned into Nobb's End, the newest estate in the village.

'Useful? We're more than that. We're special,' Josie argued.

'Does Cecily seem depressed? Did you think so?' Minnie wondered.

'I did. She looked sad,' Lin said.

'Maybe we should cheer her up.' Josie was thoughtful. 'What could we do?'

'Let's think about it and text each other,' Minnie suggested.

'Definitely. Oh—' Lin paused and pointed to a sign in a garden. 'Look. The house has been sold.'

'Darryl and Charlotte Featherstone's. It's been on the market for months.' Josie frowned. 'Darryl was such a cheat. An unpleasant man.'

'He got what he deserved,' Minnie muttered. 'Charlotte's working in London now. I bet she's much happier without him.'

'I heard he's living with a nurse in Tadderly. Poor woman. After what Darryl did to that poor girl.' Lin sniffed. 'I wonder who's moving in.'

'Someone with money. These houses have all the mod cons,' Josie said. 'It'll be nice to see new faces in the village.'

'No time to linger.' Minnie leaned forward, tugging her friends towards the railway station. 'My train's due in ten minutes.'

'We'll wait till it comes.' Lin surged forward.

'Why don't you and I go to Odile's for a cuppa on the way back, Lin?' Josie said. 'We can come up with something to cheer Cecily up and text you on the train, Minnie.'

'Maybe we should ask her what's the matter,' Minnie said, ever practical.

'I'm not sure,' Lin wavered. 'She might not want to say. Oh, you don't think she's unwell?'

'I hope not. Oh, what about...?' Josie exclaimed. 'She has a birthday soon – 2 August. Let's throw her a party.'

'That's a great idea. We have plenty of time to plan it,' Minnie agreed. 'A summer party, just what she needs.'

'We all do,' Lin said, pulling an exaggeratedly sad face. 'None of us is getting any younger.'

***

Cecily shivered, although it wasn't cold. She'd tucked up in her bed for an afternoon nap, but she was still wide awake, an old photograph album on her knee. She turned the pages carefully and saw herself in a creased, grainy picture as a gawky schoolgirl, standing close to her lovely grandmother. She owed Emily Hamilton so much.

There was an old black-and-white snap of her with Joyce Perkins, her best friend; they were arm in arm, grinning. Joyce had modelled herself on Lauren Bacall, but her face held a kind of desperation, a need to be loved. Cecily wondered where Joyce might be now. She recalled her friend's dream of having an adoring husband and two perfect children. Cecily knew she had one child, Elizabeth Cecily. She wondered if Joyce was still married. If she was still alive.

With a heavy heart, she looked at the next page and there he was, Eddie Blake, staring boldly at the camera. Her heart still skipped a beat when she saw the roguish James Dean twisted grin that made a dimple in one cheek. His hair was thick, brushed back, and his dark eyes glimmered beneath strong brows. It was a rugged face, Cecily thought; he was handsome. There was another photograph below, of Cecily and Eddie together: Eddie in a jacket and casual trousers, his arm draped around her shoulders as if she belonged to him. Cecily frowned; in the picture, she was gazing up at him adoringly. It was just after they became engaged. There it was, in a click, the man she'd loved beyond words, the one who made a big mistake that changed her life forever. The one who broke her heart.

Time had passed. Eddie was probably dead now. And, Cecily thought, here she was after all these years, still in love with him.

She put a hand to her cheek and wiped away the single tear, snuggling down beneath the covers, closing her eyes. Yes, at ninety-one years of age, she was sleeping alone, as she'd done every day of her life.

It wasn't fair.

2

Lin and Josie were sitting in the café inspecting Odile's shiny menu. 'She's got new teas,' Lin said. 'Look, blackcurrant, raspberry. Hibiscus.'

'And new dishes too. That's just so Odile. Reggae-reggae nachos and Trinidadian fish stew.'

'It makes me feel hungry, even though we just ate. Oh, Josie, look.' Lin leaned forward. 'Soursop ice cream. What's a soursop, do you think?'

'I've no idea. Odile's really jazzing things up.'

Josie looked around. The café was almost empty apart from Dangerous Dave Dawson, who was chomping his way through egg and chips. He glanced over. 'All right, Josie, Lin.' He grinned. 'I had a late start again this morning.'

Josie knew why. 'Elsie?'

'It's always Elsie,' Dave said. 'Florence and Adam get up to feed her several times a night. It wakes me up and I can't get back off until seven, then I sleep like a log. I got up at nine this morning. I had an MOT to do on a Galaxy and I kept the customer waiting. She wasn't very pleased.' He made a face. 'It's a hard life, being a grandad.'

'You'll be glad when Florence and Adam find a place of their own,' Lin said.

'They were going to buy a flat in Tadderly. It fell through.' Dave's mouth was full of egg. 'To be honest, I'd miss them if they left. It'd be weird, all on my own. Florence is a princess – she makes all my meals. And Adam's a good lad. No, I don't mind the baby crying, to be honest.' He picked up a slice of bread and wiped the egg yolk across the plate. 'I can't grumble.'

'What are you grumbling about now, Dad?' Florence said as she breezed in from the kitchen, her long hair tied back in a ponytail. She paused at Lin and Josie's table. 'What can I get you?'

'Tea,' Josie said gratefully. 'Earl Grey, please.'

'I'll try a blackberry tea.' Lin looked at the menu. 'And could Josie and I share a soursop ice cream? Just to see what it's like.'

'Of course.' Florence tugged a notepad from her apron pocket. 'Odile's out back at the moment perfecting a coconut ginger slice. You'll like the soursop.'

'Florence brought some home the other night.' Dave's plate was clean. 'It's a fruit pulp, with cream and condensed milk. Lovely, it was.'

'And how's little Elsie?' Lin glanced at Florence for signs of sleepless nights. She looked tired.

'Oh, we're fine. Can you believe Elsie's nine months old already? She's trying to crawl.'

'How are you finding being a working mum?' Josie asked. 'Are you working every day?'

'I am,' Florence said. 'I miss Elsie. Geraldine looks after her – she's just the best childminder, and she only lives across the road. Right, tea and ice cream coming up,' Florence said as she hurried through the colourful plastic strips that led to the kitchen.

Dangerous Dave called after her, 'I might try one of those coconut thingies if Odile wants an opinion.'

'Coming up, Dad.' Florence's voice drifted on the air.

'There have to be some perks to being a grandad.' Dave grinned. 'Besides, that Galaxy job's going to take me all afternoon. The exhaust has a leak and the back box is gone. The owner asked me to fix it.' He glanced towards Lin and Josie and made a mischievous face. 'So I need a decent lunch down me first.'

* * *

Minnie arrived at her four-bedroomed, bay-fronted Victorian mid-terrace in Newton Road, pushed the key into the lock and stepped inside. It was far too big for one person, but she'd bought it forty years ago as a young lecturer at St Hilda's with the intention of filling it with friends, parties, and good times. And so many books. It had been the perfect base for her and it still was. It was her place of solitude, to read, to think, to be alone.

But, of course, she wasn't alone now.

'Minnie, is that you?' Tina's voice drifted from the living room. 'I got a lift back with someone from physio. You wouldn't put the kettle on, would you?'

Minnie charged in and stopped dead. Tina was wearing a tracksuit, her feet in soiled trainers up on the sofa. She was reading a comic she'd picked up from somewhere – it certainly wasn't Minnie's. The radio was blaring eighties pop music. Cushions were scattered on the floor. There was an open packet of Hobnobs on the sofa arm.

Minnie wasn't a fan of Hobnobs. Or eighties pop. The carpet was covered with biscuit crumbs. Tina said, 'Kimberley at physio said I'm improving. I've got another appointment soon.'

Minnie examined her sister. Tina, a few years younger, looked the picture of health. Over the months since her stroke, she had made a good recovery; her speech and her mobility were almost fully back. She had a slight limp when she was tired. And she'd put on weight; Minnie was only too aware that she sat around all day watching TV, eating biscuits.

'You're looking well, Tina.' Minnie believed in being direct. 'Did they say you were ready to go home?'

'Kimberley just said I was making progress.'

'So, you could go back to your place soon? Do you think you'd be up to a bit of light work on your allotment?'

'It's June.' Tina shook her head. 'I should've started earlier if I was going to plant vegetables.'

'You could plant sprouts and cabbages for the winter.'

'I let someone else take my allotment on. Kimberley said I could have a second stroke if I go home too soon.' Tina leaned on her elbow, pushing another Hobnob into her mouth.

'Right.' Minnie put her hands on her hips. 'Cup of tea, was it?' She didn't want to upset Tina. She filled the kettle full of water and shouted over the sound of it heating up. 'We had a nice lunch at Cecily's.'

'How is the old dear?' Tina called, her mouth full of another biscuit. Minnie's frown deepened.

'There's no need to be disrespectful. Cecily gets about a darn sight more than you do.' Minnie stopped herself. She'd overstepped the mark and been insensitive. Even sisters who were like chalk and cheese should be civil. 'She's ninety-two soon. A birthday party might be nice.'

'In Middleton Ferris?' Tina asked.

'Of course,' Minnie retorted.

Tina wasn't really interested. 'Nice.'

Minnie poured hot water, added milk. Tina's voice came again. 'A postcard came. From New York.'

'Oh?' Minnie knew who it was from. And that Tina would have read it. 'And what did Jensen say?'

'He's working on some play or other. And he misses you.'

'No change, then,' Minnie said, picking up two mugs. She paused, and the image of Jensen came into her mind, his cloud of hair, his inquisitive eyes behind spectacles. She missed him too. But she couldn't co-ordinate her sister's care and throw herself into the biggest romance of her life with a New York theatre director who lived across the pond at the same time. She had to admit, it had been a sacrifice. When Tina went home, they'd get together. Minnie was sure Tina was almost well enough.

She plastered a smile on her face and waltzed into the lounge. The packet of Hobnobs was almost empty. She said, 'Waitress service,' and plonked the mug in Tina's hand. Tina adjusted her position on the sofa and went back to reading her comic.

'Right, so,' Minnie said firmly. 'Let's have an honest and frank conversation. Tell me exactly what Kimberley said about your recovery. Then we can plan for the future.'

* * *

Florence opened her eyes to an ear-splitting yell. Adam's head was on the pillow next to hers. He lifted it groggily. 'Shall I go?'

'No.' Florence eased herself upright and blinked towards the alarm clock. 'It's half seven anyway. We should be getting up. I'll feed her.'

'I'll make breakfast.' Adam didn't move. 'I'll give Dave a shout too. He was late yesterday.'

Florence was already struggling into a dressing gown, on her way to the sunshine-yellow nursery that Dave had painted last year. He'd fallen from the ladder and sprained his thumb. Dangerous Dave always had accidents, she thought with a smile.

She picked Elsie up. The baby immediately stopped crying and stared up at her inquisitively. Florence spoke quietly. 'All right, sweetie. Let's give you a feed. Then we'll go downstairs and Daddy will have made breakfast.' Florence opened her dressing gown and paused. The word *Daddy* always made her feel slightly uneasy, even now, although she was determined that Adam would always be Elsie's father. She had no intention of mentioning the man who'd treated her so badly after a one-night stand. As far as she was concerned, Adam was Elsie's father, not Darryl Featherstone. The past didn't matter: she would never look backwards. That was all there was to it, despite the fact that Elsie looked nothing like Adam.

She closed her eyes and enjoyed the sensation of Elsie feeding, a special bond. Her thoughts moved to Adam, who she could hear downstairs at the front door, talking to the postie, bumping around in the kitchen. Florence wondered if she and Adam would have a child together. They'd talked about it, but it was early days.

Florence arrived downstairs with Elsie on her shoulder, now fed and nappy changed. The baby reached out a hand towards Adam, who was sitting at the table eating cereal. Wearing the smart jacket he used for work most days, his eyes dark beneath a thatch of twist curls, he looked very handsome. He'd filled a bowl of cereal for her and a mug of tea was steaming beside it. Florence knew at that moment how much she loved him.

She placed Elsie in her high chair and Adam offered her a

beaker of water. Elsie pushed it into her mouth, took two glugs and threw it on the floor. Adam eased himself from his seat and picked it up. It could stay on the table now. Elsie was playing with a colourful hedgehog toy. She began to chew its nose.

Florence reached for a spoon. 'Where's Dad?'

'In the bathroom, shaving. Apparently the Galaxy's still not finished.'

'And what are you up to in the office?'

'Busy, busy.' Adam stretched his arms over his head. 'Dad's set up a meeting with George Ledbury to talk about his farm. He's bringing invoices for me to take a look at. We're analysing financial data, helping his farm save money.'

'Why?' Florence looked concerned. 'Is everything all right?'

Adam didn't know. 'George has asked me to look at his accounts.' He lifted a pile of letters from the table. 'These just came. A bill, another bill, some sort of circular. And one for you.' He handed a pink envelope across the table.

Florence looked at the envelope and froze. Adam noticed her expression change. He asked, 'Is everything all right?'

Florence turned the letter over, examining it front and back. It was from Northampton. She kept her voice light. 'It's fine.'

'Who's it from?' Adam leaned forward. 'Florence, are you OK?'

'Yes, no. I mean, it's nothing, Adam. Just junk mail.' Florence avoided his eyes. She could tell he was concerned, but at that moment her father came in and she said, 'Morning, Dad,' relieved to change the subject.

Dangerous Dave plonked himself down. 'I could murder a cup of tea.'

Florence glanced at his chin. A ragged cut was glued together with a blob of tissue paper. He had sliced his skin shaving. She stood up quickly, shoving the pink envelope into the pocket of her dressing gown. She saw Adam's eyes follow her movements and recognised the anxious expression in his eyes. She smiled to cover her awkwardness. 'I'll make toast, shall I?'

'A fried egg would be nice, Princess. And have we got any ketchup?'

'I'm on it, Dad.' Florence stood in the kitchen, trying to catch her breath. She could hear her father chattering with Elsie, making silly noises, singing 'The Wheels on the Bus'.

Adam raised his voice. 'Can I give you a hand?'

'No, I'm fine,' Florence said quickly, reaching for a sliced loaf, pushing bread into the toaster. She tugged the envelope from her pocket. Her heart had started to bump hard.

Miss Florence Dawson,
17, Newlands,
Middleton Ferris
Oxfordshire

Florence stared at the envelope again. She recognised the handwriting. She couldn't bring herself to open it. It would only be bad news.

She shoved it back in her pocket and reached for a pan to fry her father's egg. She'd leave the letter where it was. Or she'd put it in the bin and forget about it forever.

3

Dickie Edwards Junior was drying glasses in The Sun Inn as Josie waltzed through the door. The pub was quiet; Gerald Harris — called Bomber by everyone in the village — from the immaculately tidy bungalow down the road, was treating his new squeeze, Margaret Fennimore, to lunch. Margaret was sipping gin, her voice carrying through the bar. 'Young men should be made to go. I can't see why people don't agree with conscription anyway. After all, we all have to pay our taxes. It's just the same thing, paying what's owed.'

'Exactly. It would teach youngsters discipline and respect,' Gerald said, holding her hand.

Josie smiled as she approached the bar. It was a good thing Minnie wasn't here – she'd have picked an argument with Margaret, explaining people's right to exercise free will. Josie glanced around. Kenny Hooper and Jimmy Baker were hunched over pints in the corner, gossiping. She remembered them from primary school: they'd both been in Miss Hamilton's class too. Josie was sure that as soon as Cecily walked in Jimmy and

Kenny would offer to buy her a drink. As Josie leaned on the bar, Dickie Junior gave her his best smile. 'What'll you have, Josie?'

'Cecily and I are having lunch, so I'll treat myself to a glass of wine. She'll be here any moment.'

'Do you want to sit by the window?' Dickie said kindly. 'I'll bring your drinks across. Chenin blanc?'

'Yes, please,' Josie said.

'I heard you went on a big cruise last year.' Dickie leaned forward. 'I've often thought about cruising.'

'Oh, it was wonderful.' Josie couldn't help the sigh that escaped her lips. It had been her fiftieth wedding anniversary cruise to the Caribbean, the trip she and Harry had always dreamed of. She'd gone alone to remember him. It was almost three years now since he'd passed.

Dickie looked sad for a moment. 'Of course, I've got this place to run. And Dad can't help out now.'

'How is Dickie Senior?' Josie asked anxiously.

'Not good.' Dickie Junior spoke quietly. 'The diagnosis at Christmas bowled us all over. He's gone downhill these past few weeks. The doctor says he hasn't got long.'

Josie pressed Dickie's hand. 'I'm sorry. I've known your dad all his life.'

'You were all in Miss Hamilton's class, Dad said.' Dickie gave a brave laugh. 'Dad was a bit of a tearaway when he was a kid.'

'He was,' Josie said kindly. She remembered as clearly as yesterday the time Minnie knocked his front tooth out in the rec when he attempted to bully Tina. And another time, Dickie Edwards had called Lin 'Skinny Linny' when she slipped in the mud; he'd joked to his friends she'd pooed her pants. Josie had told him to shut his cakehole and Minnie had threatened him.

But the memory made Josie sad. Dickie's time was running out now.

It was running out for all of them, Josie thought.

'Mum has COPD; she can't help. The pub keeps me in touch with people.' Dickie Junior's words dragged Josie from her thoughts. 'I was just thinking, I haven't seen Fergal Toomey for a while.'

'He's been visiting relatives in Ireland. He was going on to Appleby Horse Fair,' Josie said.

She liked Fergal. They were good friends, although village gossips said that there was much more going on between them. It made Josie feel uncomfortable and disloyal to Harry. She glanced over her shoulder as the door opened; a woman in a peach suit and crimson lipstick was making her way steadily through the pub, leaning on a stick.

Josie called, 'Cecily. What will you have to drink?'

'Wine, of course.' Cecily beamed as Dickie Junior rushed from the bar to guide her to the table by the window and settle her comfortably with cushions. She patted his hand. 'That's so sweet of you.'

Dickie blushed. 'Oh, it's no problem.'

Josie hid a smile. Cecily always had the ability to make men feel bashful around her; even now, Dickie was fawning over her, recommending the Camembert and cherry tomato tart.

Kenny Hooper and Jimmy Baker lifted their pint glasses in greeting. Jimmy shouted, 'All right, Miss? I'll buy you a wine.'

'Thank you, dear,' Cecily said warmly. 'Chenin blanc.'

Jimmy looked confused. He waved a finger towards Dickie Junior. 'Make sure Miss Hamilton has some wine, will you, mate?'

'And Josie,' Kenny added.

Josie smiled thanks and turned her attention towards Cecily.

'So, what's new?' She wouldn't talk about Dickie Senior's illness yet. Cecily would be upset. 'What have you been up to?'

'I've been on Facebook.' Cecily flourished her phone. 'Jack's sent me some footage of him playing with Glyndŵr. I was thinking I might try to video myself playing something on the guitar and send it to him.'

'Isn't that difficult?' Josie asked. 'Videoing yourself?'

Cecily winked. 'I'm getting quite adept on my iPhone.'

'What will you play?'

'I've been practising "Sultans of Swing". It's harder than you'd think, but it suits my voice. I can't croon like I used to.'

'I remember you playing Chuck Berry when we were kids.' Josie smiled fondly. 'You had a lovely voice.'

'Talking of Chuck Berry—' Cecily recalled the song 'Nadine' '—how are George and his pet Hampshire pig?'

'I saw Penny in the Co-op; she says things are tough on the farm. George's turnover isn't what it was – annual overheads have shot up.'

'Poor George,' Cecily said. 'The Ledburys are a large family too, a lot of mouths to feed.'

'George Junior manages everything. And the grandchildren are doing their best. Bobby's living in one of the cottages with Hayley and her two children, doing most of the physical work, and Natalie's taken over some of the paperwork.'

Cecily agreed. 'George should be retiring, leaving the work to his son and the rest of the family.'

'Penny didn't seem to want to rush home.' Josie lowered her voice. 'She was asking about the father of Florence's baby again. She made some comment about it not being Adam's and you could see she was desperate to know, but I told her it wasn't our business.'

Cecily frowned crossly. 'It's Florence's life and she and Adam are doing so well, bringing up the little one. Adam's always going to be a better father than that appalling waste of space whose name will never pass my lips.'

Josie agreed. Cecily's feistiness always impressed her. 'You and I and Lin and Minnie know who he is. And Adam, of course, and I'm sure the father himself must have some idea. But Florence has sworn us to secrecy. Elsie comes first.'

'Doesn't Dangerous Dave know?' Cecily asked.

'No, he doesn't – and it's best left like that.' Josie pressed her lips together. 'Do you remember the barbecue at my house? Dave picked a fight with the Toomey boys, when he thought one of them was the father. Devlin and Finn were horrified.'

'When are they all back?'

'Soon. There's no one on the barge at the moment.' Josie exhaled. 'It feels strange when I come out of the graveyard and glance over to the Cherwell, and there's no Fergal, no boys, no smell of coffee or stew drifting on the air.'

'Talking of stew, I'm hungry,' Cecily said just as Dickie arrived with plates of Camembert and tomato tart, a salad, and two glasses of wine.

'Here you are, ladies. Enjoy. The Chenin Blanc is courtesy of Jimmy and Kenny.'

Cecily glanced up and saw two faces grinning at her from a far table, two pints lifted in greeting. Cecily raised her glass graciously. 'Thank you, Kenny, Jimmy.'

'Miss,' came the chorus from the two men.

Cecily's phone pinged and she glanced at it. 'It's just Facebook,' she said as she sipped white wine. 'I'll look at it later.'

* * *

Much later, Cecily and Josie stepped out from the bar into bright sunshine. Cecily clambered onto her purple mobility scooter and said, 'Thank goodness for my trusty Flying Plum. I don't know what I'd do without him.'

'Him?' Josie asked. 'The scooter's male?'

'He whines and grumbles as I drive home, so yes.' Cecily looked sad for a moment. 'Ah, that's hardly fair. Sometimes I think it might have been nice to have, you know, a special someone to love.'

Josie understood. Her thoughts moved to her husband. 'I might pop into the graveyard on the way home and chat to Harry for a bit.'

The two women looked at each other. It was easy not to admit to loneliness, but they were both going home to an empty house. The sun warmed their faces and their eyes met. They exchanged a look of pure gratitude: good friends were a blessing.

Josie glanced towards Nobb's End. 'Do you know who's moving into the Featherstones'? It's sold now.'

'No, but it'll be nice to see new faces,' Cecily said.

'We should have asked Dickie or Jimmy. They'd have heard on the village grapevine,' Josie said. 'I hope it's a family. Those houses are nice. There's lots of space.'

'Definitely. Well, thanks for sharing lunch, Josie. We must do it again soon and bring Lin and Minnie.'

'Minnie's busy with Tina,' Josie said. 'Although Tina's better than she was. Minnie thinks she's worried about having another stroke.'

'I'm not surprised, poor thing. But Minnie likes her own company. And she's done so much for Tina. Besides—' Cecily leaned over and pecked Josie's cheek '—she has the small matter of that American to resolve. He adores her. Enjoy your chat with Harry.'

'I will.' Josie looked sad. 'I'll see you soon.'

Cecily watched Josie walk away; she pushed the key into the ignition and twisted it to turn on the battery. Accelerating along the pavement, Cecily set off down Tadderly Road as fast as the Flying Plum would allow.

Back home, Cecily tugged off her peach jacket and felt cooler. She stared around the living room of her little bungalow. She had no idea what she expected, but loneliness greeted her from each corner. Shuffling to the kitchen, she opened the fridge and poured herself some sparkling water to alleviate the fuzzy-headedness from drinking two glasses of wine. She really shouldn't have had more than one, although the journey was less than half a mile and she'd stayed safely on the pavement all the way.

Cecily took her glass to the sofa and examined her phone. Jack Lovejoy had sent her a message on Facebook.

> Hi Cecily – how do you like the new band?
> What did you think about our version of
> 'Wildwood Flower'?

She replied quickly.

> I thought it was wonderful. I loved the violin.
> Your voice is magical. I must come and see you
> play live.

Cecily sent the message and inspected her phone. A friend request had come in from someone called Sammy Pearson. She studied the face. A young woman with dark hair and eyes, a serious face. She could be in her forties, or younger – it was so hard to tell the ages of young people. Cecily wondered if they'd met before. Perhaps she was someone who lived in the village. Cecily didn't know any Pearsons. She was probably the daughter of someone she'd taught. Cecily had no idea. She had few friends on Facebook and she probably needed some.

She pressed 'Accept' and put her phone down. An early night was on the cards.

4

Two days later, Minnie sat up in bed sipping rooibos tea from her favourite cup, her laptop on her knee. The sunshine streamed through the window onto the white duvet, splashing yellow light onto a copy of *The Observer*. She glanced outside at the view of Brasenose College recreational ground, clearly visible from her bedroom. A man was crossing the grass, a miniature figure in white. She turned her attention to the laptop screen, clicked the mouse and waited. In a few seconds, Jensen Callahan's familiar face was there. He had unruly white hair, gold-rimmed spectacles and an intelligent face. He smiled, the warmth of recognition of a man who was in love.

'Hi, Dr Moore. Araminta, my darling girl.'

'Jensen.'

'Minnie. How you doing?'

'How lovely to see you.' Her voice was filled with enthusiasm. 'Happy Sunday.'

'I love our Sunday-morning chats. I look forward to them all week.'

'So, how's your work? How's the article on Tony Kushner for *Playbill* magazine?'

'Done, finished and sent.' Jensen smiled. 'And how's the *Ludi Saeculares*?'

'I read it from cover to cover again.' Minnie stretched her arms over her head. 'I desperately need a project, Jensen. Something to get my teeth into.'

'Come to New York.' Jensen arched a brow invitingly. 'I'll be your project.'

'Don't tempt me,' Minnie said. 'You know I'd be over like a shot if I could.'

'So, how *is* Tina?' Jensen asked sadly. 'I thought she was recovering, thanks to your care and attention.'

'She is. She's made so much progress. But she doesn't want to go back to Middleton Ferris.'

'She's enjoying being with you too much.' Jensen's smile was as warm as the sunshine.

'I wish I knew what the problem was,' Minnie said quietly. 'I don't know whether she needs more time or whether she's frightened of being independent again.'

'It's the same with children, I guess,' Jensen suggested. 'It's hard to know when to push and when to stand back.' His expression brightened with an idea. 'I could come over though, visit you for the summer.'

'You could.'

'I'd leap on a plane tomorrow, today. You only have to say.'

'I know, Jensen.' Minnie brought her cup to her lips. 'Just let's give Tina a bit longer, shall we? I need to be sure she's in the right place mentally.'

'Ah.' Jensen made a mischievous face. 'Are you sure you haven't taken up with one of those besotted academics who continually fall at your feet?'

'Don't even think about it.' Minnie laughed. 'I was at a dinner party last week, Wednesday, at the Jarvises' – you remember Francine and Melvyn? Anyway, there was a professor of literature sitting opposite me trying to impress me with his knowledge of Chaucer. He had dreadful breath and spent the whole evening panting over me and making suggestive remarks, mostly quoting from *The Miller's Tale*. So, when it was time to leave, he grabbed me with both hands and tried to kiss me. In front of everyone. I mean, at my age! So, do you know what I said to him?'

'What did you say?'

'I put on my best performing voice and quoted from *The Pardoner's Tale*. I said, "I wolde I hadde thy coillons in myn hond... Lat kutte hem off."'

'You didn't?' Jensen was both impressed and shocked. 'You offered to cut them off? Both of them?'

'It was a wonderful Chaucerian moment, Jensen – he knew exactly what I'd said. Everyone else around the table had absolutely no idea.'

'What a wonderful woman you are.' Jensen gazed adoringly from the screen. 'Only my Minnie would threaten to chop a man's balls off in Middle English.'

'I ought to know better, but—' Minnie stifled a smile '—he has a reputation for doing that at parties and most women are intimidated.'

'I should be more pushy,' Jensen sighed. 'I might get to see you.'

'*Mox, amans mei*,' Minnie said tenderly. 'Soon, my love.'

'Oh, I hope so.' Even with the glare of the screen, Jensen looked sorry for himself. 'I miss you more than I can say, Minnie.'

'As do I you.' Minnie sniffed the air. 'Jensen, I can smell burning. Can we speak again later? Tonight? I mean, it's not even daylight where you are. You should be asleep.'

'I set my alarm for this time every Sunday just to spend breakfast with you.' Jensen smiled.

'Let's talk later. One o'clock your time?' Minnie suggested. 'Only, that's definitely a burning smell. I have to go.'

The screen was suddenly blank. Minnie leaped out of bed and padded quickly downstairs.

Tina was in the kitchen, staring at the toaster, huddled inside pyjamas and a dressing gown. Two charred bagels stuck out of the rack, thick smoke rising. 'I was making breakfast.'

'And?' Minnie glanced around. Tina had placed marmalade and peanut butter on a tray.

'I just seemed to lose track of time.' Tina looked horrified. 'I can't even make toast now.'

'You cooked an omelette last week. And when I was at the dinner party, you heated up the lasagne I left OK,' Minnie said encouragingly. 'You're doing fine.'

'I'm sorry.' Tina's hand flew to her mouth. She seemed dazed.

'It's just toast.' Minnie hugged her sister. 'There are more bagels. I can sort it out.'

'Oh, I don't want too much for breakfast.' Tina was suddenly herself again. 'I'm going to physio.'

'On Sunday?' Minnie asked.

'Well, it's not exactly physio.'

'Then what is it?' Minnie asked gently.

'It's a gym. The gym.' Tina seemed suddenly sure. 'It's being opened for the use of stroke patients today.'

'Oh? Where?'

'In the hospital,' Tina said quickly. 'I'm getting a taxi. I have to leave at ten.' She whirled round and glanced at the wall clock. 'It's nine fifteen. I'd better get a move on.' She squeezed Minnie's arm urgently. 'I need to get dressed. Can you do me a boiled egg or something?' She kissed Minnie's cheek quickly. 'I'd better have a shower too.'

Tina whirled away, leaving Minnie staring after her. 'A shower? Before the gym?' She shook her head. 'And she's going by taxi? Oh, well.' She turned to the toaster, lifting out the blackened bagels. 'Right, boiled eggs coming up.'

* * *

A few hours later, Minnie had taken herself off for a walk beside the river towards Folly Bridge, where she paused for a moment to lean over and watch the elegant Edwardian riverboats cruising past. The sun warmed her face and she felt suddenly restless, needing a longer walk. She took the main entrance to Christ Church Meadow from St Aldate's, ambling through the War Memorial Garden, and found herself on the familiar meadow walk.

Minnie strolled along the historic pathways past Christ Church. Gazing at Oxford's famous skyline always reminded her how lucky she was, how far she had come in life. She belonged to the city now; the Isis river was in her bloodstream. It had been that way ever since she'd been a skinny student at St Hilda's. In those days, her books were all second-hand and she'd been in awe of her sophisticated fellows who had strutted around the city as if they'd owned it. She vowed she'd never forget her humble beginnings, when she'd worn cheap plimsolls and a patched skirt, when she'd sat with Josie and Lin in Miss Hamilton's class and promised herself that she'd read and read and read for the rest of her life. She had Miss Hamilton to thank for her education; Cecily had taken on her father in the battle for her future and won.

Minnie paused by the Thames to watch the boats pass. Trees dipped handspan leaves into the water, making round ripples that spread across the calm surface, then disappeared. Minnie felt the urge to linger. She put her cardigan down and sat, sticking out legs beneath a long skirt that ended in Doc Martens boots. She wanted to give herself time to think. Something was bothering her.

Of course. Jensen.

She'd love to fly off to New York and rekindle their romance. Or he'd come to Oxford and spend the entire summer with her. They'd had good times together, before Tina had her stroke. She'd found the love of her life, she was sure of it. He was the nicest, funniest, cleverest, sexiest man she'd ever known. He was her equal, and she'd never met an equal before. Not ever.

But Tina was flesh and blood; she was Minnie's priority right now.

Minnie recalled the time she'd sneaked into the Playhouse Theatre in Beaumont Street and watched Jensen at work. He'd had no idea she was there, watching him from the shadows, but he'd been advising an actor on how to play Julius Caesar and Minnie had thought it was the funniest, most inspiring thing she'd ever seen. He'd shown the actor how to understand his role by improvising as Caesar himself. Minnie could hear Jensen's voice even now, talking to Calpurnia, his wife: 'Honey, you're worrying about nothing. Nobody can touch me out there. I'm Caesar, get it? I'm the big dude, the number one, and I'm sorry for all the losers, but my IQ is the highest in Rome – and y'all know it!'

The memory made her laugh out loud and it was suddenly

followed by a moment of sadness. She should be spending time with Jensen now, but instead she was sitting on a riverbank imagining. It was not in Minnie's character to look back; it had never been that way.

A voice made her look up. A shout of excitement, two words – 'Watch out!' – and a peal of laughter. Minnie recognised that voice: it was one she'd known all her life.

Tina!

There she was, sailing past in a punt. Minnie stared as her lips moved with hardly a sound. 'Punt comes from the Latin word *pontonem*, which means flat-bottomed boat.' But her eyes were riveted on the four figures enjoying themselves. A tall woman in a green dress was seated, trailing a hand in the water and squealing with laughter as she swished it towards a man sporting a blue-and-white-striped shirt. A second man, wearing a denim jacket, was propelling the boat along – badly – while his friends teased him loudly for his lack of skill. And, her mouth open as if she was having the time of her life, there was Tina, wearing jog bottoms, lifting a glass of something.

Tina hadn't gone to a gym. So what was she doing?

Minnie watched as the four people glided past, absorbed in their fun, squealing and shouting, drinking something that might possibly have been lemonade, but might equally be something stronger. They were too busy to notice a small grey-haired woman sitting by the riverbank, her eyes narrowed.

Minnie was mystified. Why would Tina lie to her deliberately? Why would she say she was going to a gym, when really she was meeting people for a punt down the river? It made no sense.

Was she afraid to admit that she had new friends? Had she found someone special, the man in the striped top, or the one in the denim jacket? Why wouldn't she simply tell the truth?

Minnie decided there was no point guessing what she didn't know. There was an easier way to find out. She'd wait for Tina to come home later.

She'd ask her straight out what she was playing at.

5

Lin and Neil Timms were enjoying themselves, gazing through sunglasses as they drove along the Tadderly road. They'd taken the Frog-Eyed Sprite for a Sunday spin around Woodstock and Chipping Norton, stopping for a cup of tea in a little café in Bloxham. Neil wore a flat cap over his pale hair; Lin noticed with affection the same easy smile, twinkling eyes, and long curly lashes he'd had in primary school, remembering when he'd given her a Love Hearts sweet with the words 'Be Mine' on it. She'd loved him ever since: he'd been the most handsome boy in the class.

She was wearing a pretty floral dress, a silk scarf and a wide-brimmed sun-hat; as they drove towards Tadderly in their classic car, Lin felt drenched in happiness. She had her beloved husband by her side; they'd had the most fabulous day out. Neil turned to her and asked, 'Are you happy, love?'

'Oh, I couldn't be happier,' Lin exhaled. 'Fifty years of marriage and, do you know, I still love you as much as the first —' She stopped and took a breath. 'Meatballs!'

Neil was confused. 'Meatballs?'

'You were going to cook some with spaghetti. We were going to pick up some organic minced beef.' Lin lifted her tortoiseshell sunglasses. 'I'm so glad I remembered.'

'I'll stop at the supermarket in Tadderly. It's open until four, so we should have time.' Neil swung the car to the left. 'Is there anything else we need? Passata?'

Lin had no idea. She left the cooking to Neil.

'I'll fill the Sprite up too,' Neil said. 'I love our Sundays out.'

'Even if we end up at the supermarket?' Lin pulled a face as they drifted towards the car park. Neil spotted a silver Porsche Boxster and steered the car into the space next to it. Lin was puzzled. 'Why did we stop here? There are loads of spaces.'

'It's a man thing, Lindy.' Neil grinned. 'My car's nicer than his.' He clambered out and reached for Lin's hand. 'Can I buy you something?'

Lin didn't know. 'Such as?'

'Flowers? Chocolates?' He pecked her cheek. 'We've had such a lovely day.'

'Oh, I'm fine, love.'

'If you're sure.'

They walked towards the supermarket hand in hand and Lin said, 'Have you spoken to George Ledbury lately? Josie thinks the farm might be in trouble.'

'I haven't seen him since last week. He and Nadine were driving the tractor in the field.'

'The idea of a pig driving a tractor,' Lin chuckled. 'Neil, you're so funny.'

* * *

Forty minutes later, Lin and Neil pushed a trolley towards the Sprite. They'd bought much more than they needed: chocolates, flowers, biscuits to munch while watching TV. They paused by the green car and began to pack their shopping into the little boot that was only accessible from behind the seats. Lin passed groceries to Neil, who was grunting as he arranged minced beef and tea carefully into the tiny space. A cool voice came from behind them.

'You don't see many of those nowadays.'

Lin turned quickly, assuming that the man who had spoken was referring to her and Neil, then she realised that he'd meant the car. She had a smile on her face, ready to answer.

'It's a Frog-Eyed—' She paused, horrified.

The man was in his twenties, standing beside the silver Porsche, a fair-haired woman next to him, smiling for all she was worth. He was dark-haired, well-groomed and, Lin thought, more than averagely handsome. Although he was casually dressed, his jacket was expensive, his jeans were a designer brand. He smiled confidently. 'Oh, I know you. You're from Middleton Ferris.'

Lin's heart sank. 'Darryl Featherstone.'

Neil emerged from the back of the car and stood up, bewildered. He stared at Darryl for a moment. 'We met at the village fete or—' Neil stopped himself. The last time he'd seen Darryl he'd been with his wife, Charlotte. They'd been living at the house in Nobb's End.

Lin babbled, 'Where do you live now, Darryl?'

'In Tadderly, at Sophie's flat.' He smiled smoothly, not missing a beat. 'My place in Middleton Ferris has just sold. We'll be looking for somewhere to buy together.'

Sophie gazed adoringly at Darryl. 'I've heard so many good things about Middleton Ferris. Darryl says it's lovely.'

'It is.' Lin was surprised Darryl thought so: he'd hardly covered himself in glory during his time there.

'I loved the community,' Darryl enthused.

'Darryl has to pay his ex for her half,' Sophie added. 'After that, we can buy our own place. I'm a nurse. I work all over. Darryl's office is in Charlbury. So, we'd love to move to a cute little village.'

'Middleton Ferris has a lovely vibe,' Darryl explained to Sophie. 'One little pub, a garage and a café. The local people are very accommodating.'

His eyes met Lin's and he smiled. She wondered if he was referring to someone in particular. It made the skin on her neck prickle.

Sophie linked her arm through Darryl's. 'Come on, darling, we'd better get off. I'm cooking sushi.'

'It's a hard life.' Darryl winked in Neil's direction. 'It seems I'm all on my lonesome this evening. Sophie's working later. I suppose I'll stay in and watch TV.' He waved his car keys. 'Give my best to anyone at Middleton Ferris who remembers me.'

Lin watched, reaching for Neil's hand, as the couple slid into the Boxster. The engine growled and the car pulled away.

Neil said, 'I never really liked that man, Lindy. Not after what you said he did to Florence. That was disgusting, how he treated her.'

'And his wife. Poor Charlotte. No wonder she dumped him. He's a love rat, that's what he is, and now he's taken up with some unsuspecting girl who thinks the sun shines from his—' Lin took a breath – she was speaking too fast. 'Just wait until I tell Josie and Cecily.'

* * *

Cecily sat on the reclining chair in her garden, a historical romance open on her knee. She was enjoying the way the sun warmed her bare legs, but her eyes ached from reading. She took off her spectacles and rubbed the lids until they felt a little sore. She couldn't read for long periods as she used to. She leaned back. Birds were twittering not far away, swifts swooped and soared towards nests in the roof. She liked to see the mothers whirling away for food and wheeling back again to feed their babies.

Cecily's thoughts flitted towards young Florence Dawson. She'd seen her in the street out for a walk with little Elsie in the pushchair. Cecily had paused the scooter for a chat. Florence had looked tired – it was only to be expected, being a young mum, Cecily thought. Florence was well supported. Adam Johnson was a nice young man, a good father to Elsie. And his sister, Malia, was working in London now; she'd be home soon. Florence had looked delighted as she'd mentioned Malia's visit. Cecily thought the poor girl needed friends her own age. Being a young mum was difficult.

Not that Cecily knew anything about motherhood. She'd always wanted children, but the opportunity had passed her by, although she and Eddie had planned a family.

One of their own.

Cecily breathed the scent of flowers from the garden: roses, sweet peas. A sigh escaped her lips.

Eddie. He'd been everything she wanted.

She remembered the time they'd driven to West Wittering in his Morris. It had been worth the long drive. The golden sands stretched for miles, dotted with colourful beach huts. Cecily had brought a bikini – she hadn't dared to tell her grandmother that it was a two-piece swimsuit – high waisted with a halter neck. She changed nervously in a beach hut and when she came out, Eddie took one look at her and could hardly breathe. He was wearing a pair of black swim briefs and Cecily was too nervous to glance at his bare chest matted with dark hair.

They held hands and ran into the sea, squealing as the surf sprayed them. Cecily was not a strong swimmer, but she felt safe; being in the water with Eddie made her heart race. They kissed once, and Cecily tugged herself away. It was almost too much to bear.

She'd wanted Eddie more than she'd understood at the time. It had been a struggle to hold back from her desires. She loved Eddie, truly. But Cecily was sure he readily accepted what she believed to be proper, what she had been taught by her grandmother. She wasn't like her mother. She was a virgin; she wanted to wait until she was married, until the moment was right. Then – oh, she couldn't imagine the bliss of their first night together. The thought of it made her tremble. But it would be worth waiting for, she was sure of it.

Hours later beneath the stars, Eddie told her everything she wanted to hear: he loved her and he'd gladly wait until they were married. When they finally made love, it would be the most wonderful thing in the world, even sweeter for having held back, he was sure. She was a decent girl, his girl, and he respected her for that. She wasn't letting him down. She was perfect.

Cecily couldn't believe it. He'd never mentioned marriage before. Everything her grandmother had told her about making the right man wait until a ring was on her finger was true.

Cecily breathed out slowly. She was asleep, dreaming now.

Eddie stood in front of her, his hand outstretched, and she skipped forward and reached out to take it. She was no longer a silver-haired woman, slow on her feet. She was lithe and blonde, wearing capri pants, flamingo-pink lipstick. She loved the way his eyes widened when he saw her, as if he could devour her with one single kiss.

They were dancing together in a place very like The Orchid Ballroom. Pillars of light swirled overhead and she fell into his embrace. His breath was warm against her ear and she closed her eyes, taking in every sensation of being close to him, the crisp material of his shirt against her cheek, the warm scent of his body beneath it. For a moment, she felt weak with desire. Even in her dream, Cecily marvelled at how real the emotions were, how deeply she felt them.

She was aware of someone pressing on her shoulder. Her head against Eddie's chest, Cecily didn't want to move, but the tapping became more persistent. Cecily looked up, confused, and in her dream Joyce stood next to her, blonde hair over one eye, as she said sulkily, 'He wants to dance with me.'

Cecily was sure he didn't. Eddie loved her, only her. She met his dark eyes and saw sadness in them. His voice was barely audible. 'I'm so sorry.'

Something propelled her backwards and the dancing couple were far away. Joyce was wrapped in Eddie's arms, her head now on Eddie's shoulder, and she was smiling, a twist of smug satisfaction. Cecily felt the sharp pang of loss. Eddie's eyes were on Cecily, unhappy, as Joyce said, 'He's mine now.'

Cecily woke up with a jolt.

She felt cold. The sun had gone in. She'd been asleep for a while. Reaching for a cardigan from the back of her chair, Cecily tugged it on and scurried into the house. She needed a hot cup of tea.

She was shaking, as if losing Eddie were real. She was losing him all over again.

Her hand quivered as she lifted the kettle. She felt suddenly weary; life had passed her by and, now she'd woken, she had suddenly discovered that she was an old lady who lived alone, who'd missed the one opportunity to be happy.

Cecily placed a cup on a saucer and dropped a teabag inside. She was determined not to cry. It occurred to her that she had slept alone every day of her life, and she remembered Eddie's promise beneath the stars that he respected her. The thought made her sad. Her morals in those days, in the nineteen fifties, had felt so important. It was the right thing to do, it was proper. Yet, Cecily thought firmly, if she were twenty-two now, she'd hurl herself into bed with Eddie without a second thought.

Perhaps virginity had been a high price to pay. Or perhaps Eddie had been a fool.

Both.

The sour taste returned to her mouth again. Cecily poured hot water on the teabag and heard her phone ping.

She picked it up with stiff, cold fingers. There was a message from Sammy Pearson. For a moment, Cecily couldn't remember who she was; she recalled she'd accepted her as a Facebook friend. She read the text slowly.

> Can I come round to see you? Where do you live?

Cecily was still confused from the dream. She replied without thinking.

> I live in Middleton Ferris.

She pressed *send* and, with the sudden movement of her fingers, she wondered why she'd done it. She didn't know who Sammy Pearson was.

6

Florence sat on the edge of the bed in her dressing gown, thinking. She tugged the pink envelope from the pocket hurriedly. Adam was in the shower. She had a few moments before he was back in the room. Although she'd decided not to read it, she wanted to know what was inside so badly.

She could change her mind if she wanted to.

She examined the writing: she knew whose it was. Closing her eyes, she held her breath for a moment and faces came back to her from the past, voices, words, promises. For a moment, she almost tore the letter in two.

She wondered if she should read it or not. Perhaps she needed to know what lies, what excuses might be waiting inside the envelope.

What if the letter promised something good? She brought the envelope to her lips and imagined.

Adam was back in the room in boxer shorts, his hair damp. Florence was struck again by how gorgeous he was, how special. His eyes flicked to the pink envelope as Florence shoved it into her pocket.

'What's that?' Adam's voice was suspicious.

'Nothing, just a tissue.' Florence wondered why she was lying. She wasn't sure. There was no reason why she couldn't tell him about the letter. She'd been dishonest instinctively, without thinking about it. It was because she wanted to make up her own mind what to do, whether to read it or throw it away. Then she'd talk to Adam.

He looked hurt as he said, 'I popped in to see Elsie. She's fast asleep.'

'Is it too warm in her room?'

'I opened the top window just a notch to give her fresh air and I made sure she had enough blankets.'

'Thanks.' Florence slipped off her dressing gown and slithered beneath the duvet. 'Doesn't Monday morning come round quickly? I feel like we hardly had a weekend.'

'Mum said Malia's back next weekend. But I suppose you know already. My sister always texts you before anyone else.'

'She wants to come over.' Florence's eyelids felt heavy as she snuggled beneath the warmth of the cover. 'I might invite her and Natalie round and we'll chill.'

'I don't mind looking after Elsie.' Adam joined her and she reached out an arm, switching off the bedside lamp, wriggling so that her back was turned to him.

'Night, Adam.'

'Night, Florence.'

'Did you set the alarm?'

'On my phone.'

'Good.'

Silence filled the room, stretching like time.

Adam said, 'Dave's still out at the pub with his friends.' His arm circled her hip. 'It's nice to have some time to ourselves.'

'I'm tired, Adam.' Florence heard the petulance in her voice.

Adam said nothing for a while. Florence imagined he was wide awake, thinking. She could almost hear him worrying.

'Florence?'

She grunted in reply.

His voice seemed to come from far away. 'You know I love you.'

Florence wondered how to reply. She wanted to tell him she loved him back, to say something warm, something affectionate. Something. But she didn't feel like having a conversation. Looking after Elsie took it out of her. Her limbs ached. Her head had started to throb.

'Do you think we should look for a place of our own again?' Adam asked.

'Maybe.' Florence's thoughts were elsewhere. 'We're all right here for a bit. No rush.'

'I liked that place in Tadderly. It had a nice kitchen and a space for an office for when I work from home. It's a shame they took it off the market. It had a bigger room for Elsie.'

'She has a room here.'

'A place of our own, though. Just imagine.'

'Mmm.'

Adam took a breath, as if thinking how to phrase his next words. 'There's a cottage in Charlbury that's just come on the market. It's got three bedrooms and a garden. We could take a look.'

'I don't want to live in Charlbury.' Florence wished she'd said something more positive. Adam was trying so hard to reach out and she felt herself pulling away. She had no idea why she was beginning to feel irritable. It was tiredness, hormones. She closed her eyes and hoped he'd stop talking.

'George's farm's in a bad way. I had a meeting with him, and he's coming back for a financial review. He can't pay his bills.'

'I don't want to know about George, Adam.'

'Why not? Natalie's been your friend since primary school.'

'Mmm.' Florence exhaled, as if she was bored.

Florence felt Adam's hand cup the roundness of her shoulder, and he kept it there for reassurance. His palm was warm against her cold flesh. She said nothing.

His voice came again from the darkness, soft as tissue paper. 'Florence?'

'What is it, Adam?' She wished he'd be quiet.

'Can I ask you something?'

She paused. 'Whatever.'

It took him a while to speak again, as if it was difficult to find the words. 'Is everything all right?'

'All right?' Florence heard her dismissive tone and told herself sharply that she wasn't being fair.

'Between us?'

Florence sighed like a petulant schoolgirl. 'Can we do this tomorrow?'

'It's just – I keep wondering.'

'Wondering what?'

'Do you still think about him?'

'About who?' Florence knew very well who Adam was talking about.

'Elsie's real father.' Adam wasn't able to say the name out loud.

'As if.' Florence's words were muffled against the pillow, then a single angry syllable. 'No.'

'I often wonder. Do you look at Elsie and see him? Do you still have feelings...?' Adam couldn't say any more.

Florence rolled onto her back with a sigh. Adam was depriving her of sleep. 'Do we have to talk about this?'

'I just wondered how you felt.'

'I feel – I'll tell you exactly how I feel, Adam.' Florence took a sharp breath. 'I feel fed up.'

'Fed up?'

'Of you banging on.' Florence squeezed her eyes shut. A tear trickled down her cheek. She shouldn't be speaking to Adam so disrespectfully. It hurt that she was pushing him away. Her emotions were all over the place; she was angry, sad, confused, tired. Her brain ached. Her body ached more. She loved Adam dearly, so why wouldn't her mouth move to tell him that? Why couldn't her arms circle him and hold on tight? She wanted so badly to snuggle close, to cry on his shoulder, to feel some relief from all the tiredness. But she was so exhausted, she couldn't even find the energy to cry.

'Florence.'

'Can we leave it?'

'I can't help thinking—' Adam's voice was a whisper '—you don't love me.'

'Where's that come from?'

'You push me away.'

'No, I don't.'

'I feel second best. I know your priority is Elsie. She takes all your time and you're working at the café, but we need time as well.'

'I'm too tired to have this conversation, Adam.'

'I need to know.'

'You *need*?' Florence said sarcastically. 'What about what *I* need?'

'I try so hard,' Adam said. 'I'm working extra hours; I get up most nights with you to look after Elsie and—'

'Do you resent looking after her?'

'I never said that.'

'You don't need to.' Florence felt her temper rise. 'Do you

hate having to get up and change Elsie when she's crying? Is that your problem?'

'No.' Adam sounded as if he was defending himself. 'Not at all. I love Elsie as if she was mine.'

'As *if*?' Florence leaped on his words. 'But she's not yours, is she?'

'Florence.' Adam's tone held a warning.

'That's the problem, isn't it? Elsie's not yours.'

'It doesn't matter.' Adam's voice in the dark was filled with sadness.

'Oh, but it does. All these questions, all this stuff about getting our own place and do I still love you and do I still think of—?' Florence couldn't say his name either. 'That's the problem in a nutshell. You can't accept that Elsie's not your baby.'

'It's not that.' Adam's voice rose. 'I do everything I can for Elsie. I love her.'

Florence was furious. 'But it'll always be a problem, won't it, that she's another man's?' She spat the next words. 'You can't accept her. You're jealous.'

'I'm not,' Adam argued. 'Mistakes happen.'

'So now she's a mistake.'

'I never said that.'

'You did, Adam. You don't like it that Elsie isn't yours.'

'Why are you saying these things?' Adam sat up in bed. 'Florence, what's going on?'

Florence rolled over, her back to him, sulking. 'If you regret being here with me and Elsie, you can just go. If that's what you want, your own place and your own life, you can just get out.'

'Florence, stop it.'

'I don't care, Adam. You can do what the hell you like. Elsie and I don't need you.'

'Right, I'm not listening to this.' Adam was out of bed,

standing in the dark. 'I'm going down for a glass of water. I'll give you some space.'

'You can give me as much space as you like,' Florence shouted as she heard the bedroom door open. The landing light was on and Adam's footsteps could be heard padding down the stairs. Florence screamed after him, 'For all I care, you can go to hell.'

A sudden sound came from Elsie's room, a soft sob rising to a high-pitched wail. Elsie groaned. 'Adam?' She called again. 'Adam, I'm sorry.'

There was no answer. Florence struggled into her dressing gown and scrambled towards the door, already making soft sounds to calm the baby.

'I'm here, Elsie. Mummy's here. There's no need to worry.'

She picked up the tiny bundle and held her close. A tear rolled down her cheek as she murmured, 'I'm sorry I woke you. I'm sorry I was so horrible to Daddy. I'm sorry for everything, Elsie. I'm just so tired.'

7

Minnie woke early on Monday morning. She'd hardly slept. She'd spent most of the night thinking about her conversation with Jensen yesterday evening. During their Zoom call, she'd mentioned that she'd seen Tina on the river, punting along in the sunshine.

Jensen had sounded pleased. 'She's made new friends. Isn't that what you want?'

'It is,' Minnie had agreed. 'But the weird thing is, she pretended she was going down the gym.'

She'd been able to hear Jensen thinking. 'Maybe she had a good reason.'

'Do you think I'm being too protective?'

He'd given a soft laugh. 'I should come to England. Give you my take on it.'

Minnie hadn't known how to reply straight away. Jensen had carried on swiftly.

'We're good, you and I. We sparkle when we're together.'

'We do.' Minnie couldn't disagree.

'So, I want to visit you. Soon.'

'The thing is, though—'

'Minnie, I'm not a Zoom-call-twice-a-week kind of guy as far as this relationship's concerned. I'm a fly-to-Oxford-and-hold-you-in-my-arms kind of guy.'

'I know, Jensen, but Tina—'

'I'm a stay-in-the-UK-for-several-months-then-I'll-take-you-back-to-New-York-with-me kind of guy.'

'It's difficult.'

'It is, Minnie. I want to be with you.'

'Yes, but—'

'It's getting close to crunch time. You need to be straight with me. I want to book that plane ticket.'

'I'll give it some thought.'

Then he'd told her he loved her more than anything. But she had to make her mind up.

Which was why she couldn't sleep.

She'd have told any other man to go to hell. She didn't accept others' demands. But Jensen had a point. She wanted to be with him too.

But what should she do about Tina? She should have tackled her about it last night, but the time hadn't been right. Minnie felt instinctively that there was more to the situation than she was aware of and it needed approaching carefully. Sensitively.

Minnie knew what the best decision for Minnie was: she wanted her home back so that she could invite Jensen over. Perhaps now Tina had a social life, she'd feel well enough to live independently.

Then it came to her, the perfect place to talk to Tina about her future. It made total sense.

She dressed in a flowing frock and black Doc Martens. She hurried downstairs, and set about bustling around the kitchen, warming croissants, slicing fruit, making a pot of tea. She had almost finished when Tina appeared behind her in pyjamas.

'What are you up to, Minnie? I heard you bumping about.'

'I'm making breakfast.'

'It's only half seven.'

Minnie met her sister's eyes. 'Do you have any plans for today?'

Tina looked away. 'I might go back down the gym later.'

'So how was the gym yesterday?' Minnie's gaze was direct.

'Fine.' Tina changed the subject. 'Those croissants smell good.'

'I thought we'd go out. My treat.'

'Oh?' Tina hesitated. 'Where?'

Minnie looked triumphant. 'We'll get the city bus. It's a surprise.'

Tina's face wasn't wholly trusting. 'Will I like this surprise?'

'You'll love it.' Minnie placed a pot of tea on the table and a plate heaped with croissants.

They sat together downstairs on an X3 city bus that smelled of burned rubber, diesel exhaust fumes and something else. Minnie's keen nose smelled heavy perfume that had gone stale. And an old dog had probably spent a long time beneath the seat.

Tina appeared not to notice. 'So where are we going?'

'A garden centre, in Garlington.'

'Why?'

'Don't you miss your allotment?' Minnie asked pointedly.

'I've given it to someone else. I told you. The council emailed me and I told them to pass it on. A couple in Orchard Way have got it.'

'I want to buy you some plants.' Minnie was pleased with

herself. 'I thought you could have a window box or something to nurture.'

'Why?' Tina asked.

'I want you to flourish.' Minnie leaned forward. Now was the time to ask the question. 'What I'd like best is for you to make new friends, go out, do fun things like punt on the river and drink lemonade.'

'Why would I do that?' Tina didn't bat an eyelid. Minnie was impressed with her sister's ability to act innocent. It had been Tina on that punt, definitely.

Minnie changed the subject, just for the time being. 'What sort of plant would you like? Something that flowers?'

'Vegetables are my thing,' Tina said. 'I could get a few tomato plants to grow in the kitchen.'

'And herbs: thyme, parsley, basil, for the window box.'

'Basil can be hard to grow.' Tina frowned.

'Mint, then?' Minnie wrapped an arm round Tina. 'Pick whatever you like. My treat.'

The garden centre was a vast place, with a florist, a jewellery shop and a café on site. But Tina was soon knee deep in bedding plants and ornamental trees. She led the way to the fruit section and pointed to tall shrubs in pots. Minnie watched her inspect each one carefully.

'Fifty pounds for this little weaselly apple tree?' Tina was unimpressed. 'And look at this damson. There won't be much fruit off this for a year or two.' She turned to Minnie. 'You should get a couple more trees for your garden.'

'What would you get if you were me?' Minnie asked.

'A fig tree,' Tina said. 'They self-fertilise. They don't need a fig wasp to grow fruit.'

'Oh?'

'Besides, they're easy to cultivate. Did you know?' Tina's eyes gleamed. 'They're important food sources for thousands of animal species from bats to monkeys to birds.'

Minnie picked up on her sister's enthusiasm. 'Let's buy a small one. We can get it on the bus.'

Tina was delighted. 'It'll be fun to watch it grow.'

Minnie said, 'I'll get us a trolley.'

Half an hour later, Minnie and Tina stood at the checkout with a pile of plants. Minnie said, 'I hope we'll be able to get all these on the bus.'

'I'll ask for two cardboard boxes.' Tina was ever practical. 'I'll pack them carefully and we'll have one each to take home.'

'Perfect.' Minnie smiled. Then she winced and said, 'Ouch.' Someone had pushed a trolley hard into the back of her legs. She turned round sharply at the same time as Tina. A man in a cloth cap pushed the trolley again. It banged into Tina's knee. Minnie was already on the warpath.

'What the hell do you think you're doing?'

'You're just standing there gossiping.' The man wasn't apologetic. He scratched the wispy hair beneath his cap. 'Can't you get a move on?'

'We're in a queue,' Minnie pointed out calmly.

'I ent got all day to hang around and spout hot air, not like you nobby bints.'

Minnie took exception to the word 'nobby'. It reminded her of her father, how he railed against her education and tried to belittle her. She glanced over the man's shoulder. People in the queue were watching him and shaking their heads sympathetically.

The man mumbled to himself. 'Silly old women.'

'You have your entire life to be rude,' Minnie said with a smile. 'Why not take today off?'

'Bloody stupid.' The man grunted impatiently and pushed the trolley hard into Tina's legs.

Tina whirled round, her face livid. 'Stop it.' She pushed the trolley back against the man. 'I'm a recovering stroke patient. If you hit me with that trolley again, I'll hit you back twice as hard.'

'Tina!' Minnie had never heard her sister speak that way. She was trying not to laugh.

'Well done; that told him,' a woman in the queue piped up.

'He's so bad-mannered,' someone else agreed. 'And she's a recovering stroke patient too.'

'We're next.' Minnie spoke to the man gently. 'You won't have to wait much longer.'

Tina lifted her nose in the air as she turned to Minnie. 'Come on, sis, let's pay for our plants then you can buy me a cup of tea.'

'Right.' Minnie flourished her card to pay. Tina surprised her more and more each day.

* * *

They sat at a table with a pretty checked cloth, sipping Earl Grey from delicate cups. Tina had ordered herself a slice of cake with cream and jam. She had a smear on her top lip. She said, 'I took a risk when I told that old man off. Sometimes my words come out funny, because of the stroke. And I still limp a bit.'

'You've made great progress,' Minnie said. 'You're a lot better now.'

Tina reached out and patted her sister's hand. 'So, you brought me here to tell me you want me to go home, I suppose?'

'I brought you here to ask you a question. I want to know where I stand,' Minnie said truthfully.

'So do I,' Tina agreed. 'Is there space in your house for me or not?'

'We've never been as close as we are now. I like that. But to be honest, I like my independence,' Minnie answered. 'You're well now.'

'The thing is...' Tina paused, thinking. 'I don't think I can go back to my old house. I felt so isolated there.'

'I never knew that,' Minnie said.

'Nor did I, until I came to stay with you. It might sound silly, but having the stroke has opened doors for me. I'm living my best life here.'

Now was the time to get straight to the point. 'Have you met new people in the recovery group?'

'Yes.' Tina glanced away. 'I've always felt like I belonged somewhere else. Like you did, I suppose. I can see why Oxford suits you. It's vibrant.' She reached for her tea. 'Minnie, there are a few things I need to work out for myself.'

Minnie hadn't touched her cup. 'Such as?'

Tina exhaled, as if she had all the cares in the world. 'I suppose I've been avoiding this conversation. You and I are getting on so well now. I know you want your home back but please don't ask me to go, not yet.'

'Are you worried you'll have another stroke?' Minnie asked kindly.

'It's a bit of that, and...' Tina chose her words. 'I want a bit more time to decide on my next step. Do you mind?'

'No, as long as we talk it through first. How much longer?' Minnie met her eyes.

'Just another month, maybe two,' Tina began. 'Then I'll be sure.'

Tina turned her face and her cheeks were covered in tears. Minnie reached out and took both her hands. Tina was blossoming. She was becoming a much happier and healthier person. And it was entirely down to Minnie: her resilience was rubbing off.

'All right, let's keep the subject open for discussion. Of course you can stay on, Tina, for a while. But let's be honest with each other, shall we, from now on? I have a life too, you know.'

'I know you do.' Tina grinned. 'It was such a great idea to come here today. It's been brilliant. Thanks, Minnie.'

8

'The weather's been lovely this last week, but I suppose you know that, Harry.'

Josie stared up at the sky, at the looming spire of St Peter and St Paul's church. She knelt down and laid tiny flowers on the grave. 'I wish I knew if you heard every word I'm saying, or if you're just gone and I'm talking to myself.'

She took a breath. 'The Toomeys are still away. Their barge is deserted. I had lunch with Cecily. It's her birthday soon. We're going to plan a party. And Lin and Neil go everywhere in the Frog-Eyed Sprite. I'm surprised they don't sell the Sharan, but I suppose Lin's had it for years. Florence is back working at Odile's. Little Elsie is crawling now. Dangerous Dave hit his thumb with a hammer removing a wheel nut. He bruised it quite badly. Oh, and Cecily's joined Facebook – would you believe it, at her age?'

Josie glanced around. The graveyard was empty, soulless. For a moment, she expected to see Fergal Toomey. He was due back at any time. But she'd often seen him there, kneeling by a grave a few yards away, talking in monologue to his beloved Ros. It comforted her a bit; they cheered each other up.

She turned back to Harry's grave and read the inscription.

> Harry John Sanderson.
> Say not farewell.

Josie had chosen the words because she couldn't say goodbye to him. At first, it was impossible to believe he wouldn't be there, making a cuppa, sharing laughter. But now, a few years on, the stark truth was a reality. He was gone forever.

It had happened so quickly. He'd had a bit of indigestion and taken himself off to his favourite armchair in the conservatory to rest before lunch. He'd liked it there, looking out onto the garden. Josie had brought him a cup of tea half an hour later. She'd thought he was asleep.

He never drank the tea.

She kissed his photo by her bedside before she went to bed every night and again when she woke in the morning. She missed his piercing, tuneless whistle: 'Don't Worry, Be Happy'. She'd give anything to hear it now.

Josie stood up and shivered, despite the warm sunlight that illuminated each blade of grass. Even the granite of the gravestones glistened. It was hard to believe that Harry was so close, just nine feet below where she was standing.

She thought about grief, what it meant now. At first, she'd burst into tears at the thought of everything she'd lost. She'd felt angry with those people who pitied her, who offered empty words of condolence. Slowly, she'd learned to live alone, to speak to herself when there was no one else around. Silence had become normal.

But the truth was that she felt frozen. It was as if her heart had been lowered into ice. It had become numb. Or hard as a stone. That was it. She was brittle, holding herself together, empty inside. Hollow. Her emotions didn't work any more.

It was a good job that she had Lin and Minnie. And Miss Hamilton. Without them, she'd be completely alone.

She pressed her fingers against her lips and placed them against Harry's name on the gravestone. 'Goodbye, sweetheart. I'll see you soon.'

Her words took her by surprise. She'd meant she'd visit him, bring fresh flowers, tell him the village news. But the other meaning hit her bluntly. The grave had been dug double depth. There was space for her casket.

She shivered again.

Cemeteries could be windy places. The grass blew flat; flowers shuddered in memorial vases. No wonder people thought such places were haunted. But, Josie thought sadly, they weren't. They were simply desolate and empty. Harry was gone. She was fooling herself that he could hear her speaking to him.

Hands in her pockets, Josie wandered towards the gate of St Peter and St Paul's church and out onto the village green. She was surprised to see Florence Dawson sitting alone by the willow tree. She had a sandwich box on her knee.

Josie hurried over to join her. 'Hi, Florence. Aren't you working?'

Florence sniffed. Josie thought her face looked expressionless. 'I've finished my shift. It's half three.'

'Is it that late already?'

'Geraldine's taken Elsie and her little Arthur for a walk along the Cherwell. I'm meeting her here.'

Josie noticed that Florence hadn't taken a bite from the cheese sandwich. She was gazing ahead, her eyes dazed. Josie touched her arm lightly. 'You look tired.'

'I'm exhausted.' Florence closed her eyes. 'It's hard being a mum.'

'Harry and I didn't—' Josie stopped herself. 'Does Elsie keep you up at night?'

'She's a good baby,' Florence said. 'Dad never grumbles. And Adam's amazing with her. It's just...'

'Tough?' Josie tried.

Florence nodded.

Josie tried to imagine how much Florence's life had changed. A year ago she'd been single, enjoying free time with her friends. She wasn't sure how to cheer her up.

'Is Adam at work today?'

'He went into the office first thing. He must be glad to get away from me. We had the most awful row.' Florence's breath caught in her throat. Josie waited for her to go on. 'It was all my fault. I suppose I wasn't very supportive about him not being Elsie's real father.'

'It must be hard for him,' Josie said quietly.

'It is. He was upset. I apologised this morning and he said he was over it and we were fine but...'

'Do you still think about Elsie's father?'

Florence's brow puckered at the recollection. 'No. Not at all. He's not important. Adam is. He's Elsie's father as far as I'm concerned. But, Josie, I was so horrible. I don't know where all the anger came from. I just lost it.'

'You're worn out, working, looking after the baby.'

'I am.' Florence didn't move. She stared ahead. 'I hope I don't mess things up with Adam. He's special. Why did I just kick off like that?'

'Talk to him, explain that you're exhausted. He'll understand. You're both strong together.'

'I will.' Florence met Josie's eyes. 'I bet you and Harry never argued.'

A memory came back to her and Josie smiled slowly. 'We had a real bust-up once, I remember, after an anniversary, early on in our marriage. I was being silly. Harry bought me a present and I was so disappointed with it. I said, "I bet that's the nicest second-hand gift you've ever bought" and watched his face crumble with disappointment. He'd spent half a week's money on that necklace. I was so ashamed of myself.'

'Why do we do it, Josie? How can we be such bitches to the men we love?'

'We're human.' Josie took a deep breath. 'Forgive yourself. Let it go. Apologise, Florence. Tell him you love him.'

'I will.'

'Go out together. Even if it's only down the pub for a drink.'

'But who'll look after Elsie?'

'What about Dave?'

'He falls asleep in the chair as soon as he comes home.'

'I'll babysit.'

'Would you?' Florence brightened. 'Can I take you up on that?'

For a second, Josie wished she hadn't offered. She had no idea how to look after a baby. Perhaps it wasn't that difficult: Elsie would be asleep for most of the evening. And Florence and Adam could do with the break. 'I'd be glad to.'

Florence hugged her. Josie smelled the sweetness of coconut hair-conditioner. They saw a woman appear in the distance, pushing a stroller along Nobb's End. Two babies lolled to one side, both fast asleep. Florence stood up quickly.

'It's Elsie, with Geraldine and little Arthur.' She turned to Josie and her face was full of happiness again. 'Thanks, Josie. For listening.'

'Any time.' Josie offered a warm smile as Florence rushed off towards Geraldine and Elsie. She watched Florence greeting her childminder, kneeling down to kiss her baby. Josie was suddenly overwhelmed with sadness. If she and Harry had been blessed with children, she'd have a grandchild now, perhaps great-grandchildren. It would give her life meaning.

She waved as she watched Florence and her childminder disappear towards Orchard Way, deep in conversation. She felt suddenly alone. Josie stood up, wondering whether to go to Cecily's for a coffee, or text Lin and ask if she wanted to pop round. For a moment, she wished Fergal were back home. He'd drag her back to his barge for a bowl of his famous Joe Grey stew, or a strong tea. He was good company, Fergal; he always made her smile and cheered her up.

She was about to turn towards home, but the big house in Charlbury Road always felt so empty each time she'd visited Harry. She knew why. The place was full of memories.

A lorry slowed down across the road in Nobb's End, at the house with the Sold sign, and Josie paused to watch. Another car, a silver sporty model, was already parked outside. The sign on the side of the lorry said T. C. Removals, Tadderly. Two men in overalls clambered out, went round to the back and rolled up a huge door. Josie watched as a man strode out of the house and started to speak to the other two, who appeared to be unloading a leather sofa.

Josie took a step forward so that she could observe the man carefully. He was her age, probably, mid-seventies. He had tousled grey hair, a neat beard. He wore a black jacket, light jeans. There was something familiar about him. Josie stared harder.

The man laughed, a casual gesture with his hand, as if making a joke. It was a gesture she knew well, but she wasn't sure from where. The two men in overalls stopped unloading the sofa and gave the man their full attention, as if he was interesting, or commanded a level of respect.

Josie took another step forward. She wished she could see his face properly but she was too far away. There was something about the careless roll of the shoulders, the way his jeans clung to the muscles of his thighs, that was familiar and for some reason her heart had started to thump.

Josie watched for a few moments, turned and began to walk back towards Charlbury Road. She looked back once. The man had gone. The two in overalls were lugging the sofa towards the front door.

So, the new owner of the house in Nobb's End had moved in.

Josie had definitely seen him somewhere before. She just couldn't place him.

9

On Thursday morning, Cecily was sitting on the sofa, strumming her guitar, trying to perfect 'Sultans of Swing'. She wanted to video herself and send it to Jack: he'd be impressed. The phone buzzed from the table. She placed the guitar down carefully and answered the call.

'Hello?'

A woman's voice asked, 'Is that Cecily Hamilton?'

'Yes.' Cecily was a little confused. She didn't recognise the speaker, a woman with a soft voice. She thought quickly about who it might be. 'Are you Sammy, who friended me on Facebook?'

'No.' The speaker sounded baffled. 'My name is Valerie Coleman. Andrew Cooper gave me your number. He said you wouldn't mind.'

'Andrew, the vicar of St Peter and St Paul's,' Cecily said.

'Yes, I'm the chair of Tadderly WI. We have a meeting this afternoon and our speaker has had to cancel at the last minute.'

'Oh?' Cecily had no idea what the call was about.

'We were going to hear about stained-glass windows from a

lady over in Charlbury, but she has a bad cold. I spoke to Andrew by chance and he said you'd be a wonderful speaker.'

'Would I?' Cecily was still bewildered.

'Oh, definitely. You used to be a teacher in Middleton Ferris years ago, didn't you?'

'I did,' Cecily replied slowly.

'So, would you be willing to come this afternoon? I know it's a bit last minute.'

'You want me to give a talk to the WI?' Cecily asked. The penny had dropped and she began to smile. 'Oh, I'd love to.'

'We'd pay expenses, of course. And there would be refreshments.'

'What time this afternoon?' Cecily asked. 'I'd need to get transport. The Flying Plum won't make it as far as Tadderly.'

Valerie paused for a moment, as if confused. She said, 'Two-thirty. We'll have a bit of business first, then you'd speak to the group. Could you talk for about half an hour?'

'Oh, I can talk for England,' Cecily said. 'How delightful. Valerie, can you give me half an hour to arrange transport and call me back to confirm? I just need to line a few ducks up first.'

'All right,' Valerie said. 'I look forward to talking soon.'

'Indeed.' Cecily was already imagining herself addressing a huge group of fascinated women. 'Goodbye.'

Cecily smiled, turned the phone over in her hand and began to message the Silver Ladies WhatsApp group. Lin had named it because they were 'strong women of a certain age,' although Cecily was the only one with silver hair; Lin was blonde, Josie dark-haired and Minnie had a mass of grey curls. Cecily typed a message.

> The WI have asked me if I'll give a talk this afternoon in Tadderly. Can you take me there, Lin? Can you all come? Free cake.

Three replies came in within a minute.

LIN
> Of course, what time?

JOSIE
> Count me in. I'd love to

MINNIE
> I'm on my way to the station already – anything for free cake. Bonum mihi liberum crustulam.

Cecily smiled. It occurred to her that she ought to plan her speech. Teaching in Middleton Ferris in the fifties, sixties and beyond was what she knew best – she had seen many changes. It would be good to take three of her old pupils with her too. She planned to talk about how she believed that every pupil should have an opportunity, that learning should be fun but serious at the same time. She wanted to quote Malcolm X: 'Education is the passport to the future, for tomorrow belongs to those who prepare for it today.' And Benjamin Franklin: 'An investment in knowledge pays the best interest.'

Cecily was looking forward to talking about what fun she'd had as a teacher. It had been her vocation. Her life.

She wondered what to wear.

* * *

Lin parked the Sharan outside St Hugh's Church Centre in Tadderly. It had taken her ages to find the place with the confusing one-way system, despite using her phone for directions. The car park was almost full. Josie and Minnie clambered out from the back and helped Cecily ease herself from the front passenger seat. She looked wonderful in a red silk blouse, matching lipstick and black trousers. Lin and Josie were wearing jeans and jackets; Minnie wore green Doc Martens and a daisy-print dress. They sailed confidently into the church hall where a small woman with gold-rimmed glasses was sitting at a desk selling raffle tickets. She looked up quizzically, as if trying to put names to faces.

'Hello.'

'Are you Valerie?' Cecily asked.

'No. Val's over there.' The small woman pointed to the far end of the room, where a woman with white hair and spectacles on a chain seemed to be organising everyone else.

'I'm the speaker,' Cecily said proudly and Minnie tugged out her purse.

'I'll have a few raffle tickets. Is it for a good cause?'

'Charity event.' The woman smiled. '£1 per ticket. £10 for the book. The first prize is £10,000 cash, the second prize is a Baltic cruise for two.'

'I'll have a whole book.' Minnie grinned.

Val Coleman rushed over, shaking Cecily's hand. 'Thank you for coming, Miss Hamilton.'

'Cecily,' Cecily insisted. 'And these ladies are my ex-pupils. And great friends.'

Val glanced at Minnie, Lin and Josie. 'We're about to start. Can I show you where you'll be sitting? So, I'll do some WI business first, then it'll be your talk, then refreshments.'

'When's the raffle?' Minnie wanted to know.

'Oh, not until August.' Val hurried them towards the other end of the room, where her table was set up next to a wooden chair for Cecily. Another woman, called Wendy, brought three extra chairs. Cecily glanced around the hall. She'd expected there to be a dozen people, perhaps twenty, but there were at least fifty eager faces sitting around tables, some chattering, others watching Cecily. She was surprised that the women's age range was so vast: a few ladies were a little younger than she was, but there were many women in their twenties. It warmed Cecily's heart to see women congregating together as friends.

Val said, 'We will sing "Jerusalem",' and everyone stood up.

As voices were raised in song, Minnie whispered, 'You should have brought your guitar, Cecily.' But Cecily's eyes were closed and she was singing for all she was worth.

They all sat down and Val mentioned the last speaker, who'd talked about her life as an artist. Val and Wendy, who was the treasurer, spoke about a coach trip that was planned for July and how seats were filling up fast. One young woman raised a hand and said she wanted to come but was worried about being back in time to meet her youngest from school and another woman chipped in: she'd pick up the child and take him back to her house for tea. All was resolved.

Val introduced Cecily and thanked her for stepping in at the last minute. 'Miss Hamilton used to be a primary school teacher at Middleton Ferris. In fact, she's brought a few of her old pupils with her.'

'Old?' Minnie quipped. 'Gertrude Stein said, "We are always the same age inside."'

'Indeed,' Val said. 'So, she's going to tell us all about teaching in the nineteen fifties and sixties. I'm sure there are many of you here who weren't even born then.'

'I remember chocolate rationing ending in 1953.' Someone chuckled from the back of the hall.

Val continued. 'So, Miss Hamilton – Cecily – it's so kind of you to come along. Welcome.'

There was a light round of applause and Cecily heaved herself upright. She looked around at all the faces in the room and Josie, Lin and Minnie all had the same thought. It reminded them of the teacher who had sashayed into their classroom in 1959. They recalled the clack of heels, the blonde wavy hair and red lips. She'd looked like a film star.

Cecily raised a hand and the audience was held in the palm of it. Not much had changed.

She smiled, and when she spoke, as she had spoken in the classroom that smelled of stewed cabbage over sixty years ago, her voice was blanket-soft.

'It's a pleasure to be invited here this afternoon. I was moved to be able to sing "Jerusalem" with you all, with its association with the fight for women's suffrage. My grandmother was a suffragette. And in many ways nowadays, we women are still fighting. In the nineteen fifties, I gave up so much to be a teacher. Back then, a woman's place was very clearly defined. It was the age of respectability and conformity. Very few women worked after getting married; they stayed at home to raise the children and keep house. The man was considered the head of the household in all things: rent or mortgage, legal documents, bank accounts. Only the family allowance was paid directly to the mother.' Cecily smiled. 'So, my decision to be a teacher and spend my life following the vocation that filled my heart wasn't understood by everyone. But as you can see—' Cecily indicated Josie, Lin and Minnie '—my greatest wish was to give young people a chance to make a brave new world through learning.'

Minnie felt a lump in her throat. She owed everything to Cecily. Lin offered a wide smile of gratitude. She'd met her beloved husband at school and chosen her own path; she didn't regret a thing. Josie closed her eyes and listened to the rhythm of Cecily talking; she imagined she was ten years old again, leaning against the heat-belting radiators that made the room smell of the washing powder on their jumpers. Josie was there again: Miss Hamilton was reading a story about a mole, a rat, a proud toad, an elusive badger, and she dreamed of a land where animals could talk, where they were friends and had adventures.

'Teaching was my life. My pupils were everything. Watching them grow, flourish into the wonderful people they've become, was my reward. And as I look at them now, I'm reminded that Nobel Peace Prize laureate Malala Yousafzai said, "One child, one teacher, one book and one pen can change the world."'

Josie was roused from her reverie by resounding applause. Lin clapped and cheered. Minnie glanced towards Cecily, who was sipping water from a glass and smiling.

'Thank you for listening,' she said modestly.

Val took over. 'That was most informative and entertaining. Thank you, Cecily. I think we've learned a lot. And many of us have our own fond recollections.' She paused. 'Would you mind if we take a few questions?'

'Not at all,' Cecily said graciously.

Hands went up and a young woman asked, 'Cecily, you said at the beginning that the fifties was the age of respectability and conformity. I'm twenty-seven.' There was light laughter. 'Was it a good or bad thing?'

'It's simply evolution. We move forward all the time, and one period of history has an influence on the next generation,' Cecily said wisely. 'My mother gave birth to me out of wedlock, so I didn't have an auspicious start. Then she left, and my grandmother brought me up. She was wonderful and caring, but she instilled into me that sex before marriage was wrong and shameful. Of course, I believed her. I've changed my mind since.' There was a tinkle of laughter. 'Nowadays—' Cecily's eyes flashed '—we try to avoid archaic views that blame and shame women, but we still have young men who think it's their God-given right to leave girls in the family way and take no responsibility.'

Josie, Lin and Minnie exchanged glances: Cecily was talking about Florence and little Elsie.

'Cecily, you said the expectation was for women to get married when you were younger. I'm not married and I have no intention of being,' another woman piped up from the back of the room. 'My career's too important. I'm always under pressure though. I'm forty-one and people are still saying, "When are you going to settle down and get married?"' The woman met Cecily's eyes. 'Did you ever feel under pressure in the fifties as a single woman?'

Cecily paused and everyone in the room waited. She said, 'I was engaged once.' She paused again, remembering.

The woman who had spoken before called out, 'Did your fiancé get in the way of your career? Was it more important to teach?'

'Not more important, no. It was just the way things worked out.' Cecily shook her head. 'Women should be able to have everything, a career, a family, a partner; all, or some, or none of those things, just as men do. But it's their choice. We must be trailblazers for future generations. It's a woman's right to choose. If...' Her voice faltered. 'If I regret anything at all, it is the fact that my path was so narrow. I applaud women today who are unafraid to go for what they want. We have only one life. As Maya Angelou said, "Being brave is not being unafraid but feeling the fear and doing it anyway." Bravery is everything. We're all brave women.'

There was rapturous applause from the room and Cecily smiled. She sank down in her seat, feeling suddenly tired.

Later, as Lin braked outside Cecily's bungalow, stopping behind a blue Clio, and switched off the engine, Minnie said, 'You're wonderful, Cecily. I'm not surprised they've invited you back in the autumn.'

'One woman told me that you were the best speaker they'd ever had,' Lin added.

Josie agreed. 'It took me right back to the old days at primary school.'

'The home-made cakes they brought were lovely. What a spread,' Minnie said. 'Did anybody have the triple chocolate? I've got a piece in my bag to take back to Tina.'

Cecily blinked. She was exhausted. 'Does anyone want to come in for a cup of tea?'

'Do you need company, so that you can wind down?' Minnie asked. 'Or would you rather have a nap?'

'A cup of tea might be nice.' Cecily smiled. 'Although I've drunk three already this afternoon.'

'I'll make us a pot,' Lin offered kindly. Minnie and Josie clambered from the back and hurried to the front passenger seat to help Cecily out. Lin pointed towards the front door of Cecily's bungalow. 'There's a woman knocking at your door. You have a visitor, Cecily.'

'Do I?' Cecily allowed herself to be shepherded from the car. 'Who's that? Do I know her?'

'Let's find out,' Minnie said, her voice low.

They walked down the path and a woman turned to face them. She offered a smile, but something about her expression was troubled. She asked, 'I'm looking for Cecily Hamilton.'

Cecily stiffened. 'That's me.'

'What do you want?' Minnie asked, direct as ever.

The woman addressed Cecily. She was in her forties probably, with dark hair. 'You said you lived in Middleton Ferris. So, I asked at The Sun Inn, and they directed me here.'

Cecily remembered. 'Are you Sammy Pearson?'

'Yes. Can I come in?' Sammy seemed a little awkward. 'There's something I want to talk to you about.'

Minnie turned to Cecily protectively; her instincts told her that something wasn't right. 'Do you want to speak to this lady, Cecily?'

'Well...' Cecily hesitated.

'Perhaps I could explain.' Sammy took a breath. 'You used to know my grandparents.'

'Did I?' Cecily began to tremble.

'I'm sure you did.' Sammy met her eyes and Cecily knew. She'd remember those dark passionate eyes anywhere.

'My mother was Liz Blake,' Sammy continued. 'And you'll remember my grandparents, Joyce and Eddie.'

10

'You'd better come in,' Cecily said to Sammy, then she turned to Josie. 'Can you all come in? I – I'd like that.'

'Are you definitely all right with this?' Minnie asked in a low voice. She glanced towards Josie and Lin. They were all concerned for Cecily. She whispered, 'I can tell her to go, if this is too much.'

'No. I want to hear what she has to say. But please stay. I'd appreciate that.' Cecily led the way into the living room and sank into the sofa. She put her hands to her face, feeling dizzy. Lin bustled around in the kitchen, making tea. Josie and Minnie stood by the window, looking at each other.

Cecily moved her hands from her face and stared at them. Brown spots. Paper-thin skin. She whispered his name, 'Eddie.'

Sammy Pearson sat next to her on the sofa. Minnie asked, 'Where have you come from? Do you live nearby?'

'I drove here from Wallingford. The blue Clio outside is mine.'

'How long did that take you?' Josie was making conversation, but her eyes were on Cecily, who looked bewildered.

'An hour,' Sammy said. 'Thursday's my afternoon off. My husband and I run a florist's.'

'How did you find out that Cecily was here?' Minnie asked.

'My grandma mentioned her a few times. Apparently, she and Cecily were best friends years ago. I looked on Facebook, and there she was. I knew there couldn't be too many Cecily Hamiltons in their nineties. I hoped it was you.'

Cecily said nothing. She stared at her fingers. So, Sammy lived an hour away; Joyce had been talking to her granddaughter about the past, about their friendship. Cecily wondered if Joyce had told her the truth about how she had taken Eddie from her, how Cecily had moved away and refused to talk to either of them again. Seeing them with the baby had been too hard to bear. Teaching had saved her life.

But what had happened to Joyce? What had happened to Eddie? Cecily had no idea how to ask.

Minnie seemed to understand what she was thinking as she said, 'Sammy, do all your family live in Wallingford?'

'There's just me, my husband and my daughter, Lara. She's eighteen. She helps me in the shop.' Sammy looked up as Lin came into the room with a tea tray and accepted a cup. 'Thanks.' She put it down on a small side-table and flourished her phone, flicking through photographs. 'Cecily, this is my husband, Ian, and this is Lara. They're outside our florist's. She looks like Mum. Look, this one was taken of my mum last year.'

Cecily narrowed her eyes. 'Your mother looks like Joyce.'

'She does. Both fair, with blue eyes. And I look like Grandad, everyone says it.' Sammy picked up her tea.

Cecily was unsure what to say next. Minnie asked, 'Where does your mother live now?'

Sammy closed her eyes briefly. 'Mum died last year, in January. She'd been ill off and on. My dad left her when I was twelve. She brought me up. She had two jobs. It was all work and sacrifice. She never married again.'

'Were you an only child?'

Sammy nodded. 'I was. So was Mum. And so's Lara. Three generations of one female child. Funny.'

Cecily found her voice. 'Joyce didn't have any more children? Just Elizabeth?'

'That's right, just Mum. Grandma was always bubbly, and she thought the world of Grandad, although he rarely said a word to her.'

'I don't remember Eddie being quiet,' Cecily said. The room fell silent.

'Is Joyce still alive?' Minnie glanced towards Cecily to check that she was not overstepping the mark.

'Grandma died a month ago. It was awful. She was unwell for so long.' Sammy brought her cup to her mouth and took a gulp.

'Poor Joyce,' Cecily said. She shivered inside the silk blouse. Josie found a blanket and wrapped it round her.

'This must all be a shock, Cecily. Are you sure you want to have this conversation with Sammy? After all, Eddie was—' Minnie stopped herself from saying 'the love of your life'. 'Why exactly have you come here, Sammy?'

Sammy paused. 'It was something that Grandad said to me.'

Cecily looked up sharply. 'Eddie? What did he say?'

'He said, "My biggest regret in life is Cecily Hamilton."' Sammy took a deep breath. 'I knew it had to be important. That's why I wanted to find out who you were and where you lived.'

'He said that?' Cecily's hand flew to Minnie's. She closed her eyes, thinking, remembering. For a second, it was as if she could hear his voice, his promises of love. She could hardly believe this was happening. She'd wondered for so long what had become of Eddie and Joyce and, now she was finding out, the rush of emotion seemed to shake her hard. She whispered, 'Eddie.'

'Is that all he said?' Lin took over.

'He was quite secretive,' Sammy said. 'But he showed me a photograph and said it was the happiest moment of his life.'

'Have you got it with you?' Josie asked. 'Do you want to see it, Cecily?'

Cecily nodded weakly. She had to know.

'I put it on my phone.' Sammy flicked through her pictures. 'Here.' She handed the phone to Cecily, who took it in trembling fingers.

Her eyes filled with tears at the sight of them both again. There he was, in black and white. Eddie Blake, handsome, smiling, his arm around blonde Cecily. They were standing together on the beach in West Wittering. It was the day he'd talked about waiting for her until they were married. Cecily stared at it until she could bear it no longer. She handed the phone back to Sammy and placed a hand against her heart. She said his name again. 'Eddie.'

'When was that taken, Cecily?' Lin asked gently, but Cecily didn't answer. Sammy passed the phone to Lin, who inspected it before handing it to Josie and Minnie.

Lin, Josie and Minnie looked at each other. Someone had to ask the question. Minnie gave it her best shot. 'He's a handsome man, Eddie. So, when did he pass?'

'Oh, he's not dead.' Sammy brightened. 'Grandad lives in Benson, about ten minutes away from me.'

'Eddie's alive?' Cecily's eyes widened with realisation.

'Cecily, are you OK?' Minnie asked quickly. 'This man was your fiancé, wasn't he? The one you gave up?'

Cecily nodded, unable to speak. A tear trickled down her cheek and settled there.

'Grandad's good for his age.' Sammy glanced at Cecily and tried again. 'He's still independent. He reads a lot and tinkers with things – and he even goes down the bowling club sometimes, although he's not as sprightly as he was. He doesn't drive any more, mind.'

'Eddie's alive,' Cecily repeated.

'Didn't your grandparents live in Surrey in the fifties?' Josie asked.

'Grandad bought a garage in Wallingford when Mum was a child,' Sammy explained. 'Apparently, Grandma didn't want to move from Surrey – all her family lived there, but Grandad said that Oxfordshire was where he wanted to be.'

'Eddie knew I'd come to teach in Oxfordshire,' Cecily said quietly.

'Sammy, I have to ask.' Minnie took charge. 'It's very nice of you to travel to Middleton Ferris and tell Cecily all about your grandparents. But why exactly did you come?'

'I'll be honest. Grandad asked me to,' Sammy said bluntly and Cecily thought her heart would burst. She leaned back into the softness of the sofa, feeling the world whirl around her.

'He asked you to visit Cecily?' Josie asked.

'Yes. He wanted to know if she was still alive, so I friended her on Facebook and he asked me to come over.'

'He asked you?' Cecily felt weak.

'He wants to see you. He sent you his address.' Sammy tugged a piece of paper from her jacket pocket. 'His handwriting's a bit shaky now. But he asked me to give you this. And a message.'

Cecily took the paper in trembling fingers and studied the address.

Eddie Blake,
7, Woodbury Close,
Benson,
Oxon.

That was where he lived now. She glanced at Minnie and her lips moved. 'Eddie.'

'What was the message, Sammy?' Minnie asked firmly.

'He just told me to say, "Forgive me." And...' Sammy took a breath '...he would like you to visit him.'

'Visit?' Cecily's voice was a whisper.

Josie turned sharply to look at Cecily. 'You haven't heard from him for how many years?'

'You don't have to reply to him,' Minnie added.

'Unless you want to,' Lin said. 'We could all go. There are seven seats in the car and we could all help with the navigation. And we could get lunch while you meet him, then I'd drive us all home.'

'Do you want to see him, Cecily?' Josie asked. 'You've told us a little about him, but what we don't know is – how do you feel now?'

Minnie frowned, unsure. 'It was a long time ago.'

'He'd love to see you.' Sammy offered an encouraging smile. 'He's set his heart on it.'

Cecily folded the address neatly in half and dropped the paper on her knee. 'I don't think I can.'

'You don't have to,' Lin said firmly. 'You hardly know him now. So much time has passed.' She plonked herself next to Cecily and took her hand. Josie and Minnie moved to stand behind the sofa. Solidarity in numbers.

Cecily whispered, 'If I saw Eddie again, it would break my heart. I'd think of what we both missed. So, no, I won't go.

Sammy. Please tell your grandad there's nothing to forgive. I wish him all the best. I'm very sorry Joyce has gone now, and your mother, and that he's all on his own. But I won't see him. Not today. Not ever. And that's all there is to it.'

* * *

It was well after five o'clock. Sammy had gone back to Wallingford an hour before, and Minnie, Josie and Lin had made sure that Cecily was comfortable. The television was on and she was tucked up beneath a rug on the sofa, a cucumber sandwich on a plate on her knee. She was gazing at the screen, insisting that she was fine.

Minnie closed the front door with a clunk and said, 'Well.'

'Well indeed,' Josie agreed. 'We didn't see that coming.'

'Poor Cecily looks tired out. She's been through the wringer.' Lin tugged out the keys to the Sharan. 'I'll give you a lift to the station, Minnie.'

'Thanks,' Minnie said. 'I missed the last train. Tina will be able to find herself something to eat. There's another train within the half-hour.'

Josie clambered into the front of the car next to Lin. 'What do you think we should do?'

'Do?' Minnie repeated, making herself comfortable in the back.

'To help Cecily?' Lin asked. 'Do you think she ought to go and visit Eddie?'

'It might bring some closure. But she doesn't want to go,' Josie said.

'He broke her heart,' Minnie replied. '*Dormientes canes et mentior*. Let sleeping dogs lie.'

'But she's ninety-something. They might spend their last few years together,' Lin insisted. 'It's romantic.'

'Perhaps,' Josie said. 'I think she's loved him all her life.'

Lin started the engine. 'They were engaged, weren't they? How lovely if they met and fell in love all over again.'

'Really?' Minnie wasn't convinced. 'Didn't you see how she looked? The very idea of meeting him wore her out. When we left, she looked like she'd drop.'

Lin wasn't listening as she drove down Tadderly Road. 'It's only an hour to Benson. We could drop her off outside his house and pick her up late in the afternoon. What if...?' She was suddenly excited. 'What if she wanted to move in with him? What if they got married?'

'That would be a hell of a hen party,' Minnie said cynically. 'The four of us hitting the Prosecco dressed as schoolgirls in gymslips and stockings.' She took a deep breath: she was concerned about Cecily. She'd looked bulldozed by the news. 'We might be better off concentrating on making her birthday really special.'

'Oh, yes,' Lin agreed. 'Let's not forget we have her birthday bash to plan.'

'We do,' Josie remembered. 'I've had a few thoughts about the cake. And the venue.'

'The pub makes sense. It's local.' Lin turned right into Nobb's End and said, 'Oh look, the Sold sign has gone.'

'Stop here a moment,' Josie called and Lin slowed down.

'What?' Minnie asked.

'That house, number seven, where the Featherstones lived.'

'Darryl and Charlotte?' Lin recalled seeing Darryl in the supermarket. 'I didn't like him. The love rat.'

Josie frowned. 'I saw him yesterday. The new owner, not Darryl.'

'And?' Minnie wondered.

'He just seemed familiar.' Josie recalled his confidence, the roll of his shoulders. 'Just pause the car for a moment, so we can take a quick look.'

The Sharan's engine idled as three faces stared out towards number seven. Minnie said, 'Well, he's got blinds at the window and that might be a photograph we can see on the windowsill. There aren't any other clues about your mystery man.'

Lin peered over Josie's shoulder. 'He won't have done anything to the place yet. There's no car outside and no lights on. I can't see a TV flickering.'

'So the only clue we have is that he's out?' Minnie grimaced from the back seat.

'I wish I knew where I'd seen him before,' Josie said. 'It's been bugging me.'

'Is he handsome?' Lin wanted to know.

Minnie rolled her eyes. 'I might miss my train.'

At that point, a silver Audi turned the corner a little too fast, slowing down and stopping abruptly outside number seven. A man got out, reaching inside the car for shopping in a recyclable bag. He wore the same well-fitting jeans and a pale sweatshirt. He didn't notice the Sharan idling in the road opposite.

'He's good looking though. What do you reckon, Josie? Our age?' Lin said.

'I know I've seen him somewhere.' Josie pressed her lips together. She was conscious of that feeling again, her heart pumping harder than it should. She had no idea what was making her feel this way.

Lin said, 'He definitely looks familiar.'

'Oh!' Minnie exclaimed from the back seat. 'I know who that is. We all know him. I'd know that backside anywhere. It's Mike Bailey, from our class in school!'

Josie felt her skin prickle. She hadn't seen him for over fifty years. And he was the last person on earth she wanted to see now. She watched him push a key into the front door and disappear inside. She exhaled slowly to calm her thumping heart.

'It's definitely Mike Bailey. I can just see him all those years ago, longer hair, the same jeans, the same cocky walk. He was your boyfriend for a bit, wasn't he?' Lin leaned over and placed a hand on Josie's shoulder. 'He's come back to live in Middleton Ferris. Oh, Josie, are you all right? You look like you've seen a ghost.'

11

It was a beautiful evening, the last rays of sunlight glinting on the river Cherwell. Adam was pushing Elsie in the stroller as Florence walked beside him, watching her child suck the ear of a felt toy rabbit. They paused by a bench and Adam sat down. Florence flopped down beside him and stared into the river. The water was still as glass, reflecting the tall trees and dangling branches on the bank in perfect symmetry.

Florence said, 'Do you remember last summer, when I was pregnant, and we sat here and dipped our feet?'

Adam met her eyes. 'I told you I loved you then, and you said you weren't ready to make any decisions about the future.'

'I wanted you in my life, mine and Elsie's. But it was such a hard time, with being pregnant and everyone thinking: "Who's the father?" I was in a bad place. I wasn't ready.' Florence thought about it for a while. 'But we had a lovely day. The Toomeys let us use their barge for a picnic and people bought presents.'

Adam took her hand. 'Not everyone thought bad things, Florence. Most people are supportive.'

'My head was all over the place,' Florence said miserably. 'Like on Sunday night when I shouted at you. I was stupid.'

'It was our first proper row,' Adam said.

'You must think I'm awful.'

'I don't. I think you're tired. It's hard being a mum.'

'Is it hard being a dad, Adam?'

'What doesn't kill us makes us stronger.' Adam offered a brave grin. 'We're just starting out. The important thing is to be here for each other whatever comes, and to talk things through.'

Florence felt him squeeze her hand. 'Do you want to talk things through now?'

'Yes. That's why I suggested we come out and leave your dad in front of the telly.'

Florence braced herself for what was to come. She knew Adam had a right to be angry. She wanted to put things right, but it was hard finding the words. She loved Adam, she'd built her world around him and Elsie. It hurt her to see the sadness in his eyes.

'What's bothering you?' Florence asked gently. 'Is it work? Or is it us? I can tell you're unhappy. Is it because you want us to get our own place? Or how I behaved the other night? I know I was wrong. I'm really sorry.'

'It's a bit of all of those,' Adam said slowly. 'Would you mind if—? Can I talk about Elsie's father?'

'I don't like to.' Florence was tempted to tug her hand away, but she left it where it was. She loved Adam. It wasn't him she was recoiling from. 'Just remembering him leaves me with bad feelings.'

'Such as?'

'Guilt, embarrassment, shame. I feel stupid for being taken in by his lies. I love Elsie to bits, but Darryl and I both made her.

And that makes me feel horrible sometimes.' Florence's eyes filled with tears.

'In what way?'

'I don't want to think about him ever again, after how he treated me. It's not Elsie's fault, but sometimes I look at her and the memory of Darryl Featherstone is there. And I push it away. Elsie's yours, Adam. That's what I want to believe.' Florence turned to face him. His expression was so kind. A tear rolled down her face.

'Only you and I know who the father is.'

'And Josie and Lin, Minnie. And Cecily.'

'They won't tell anyone.'

'I know.' Florence took a deep breath. 'Even Dad doesn't know. I made him promise never to ask. He'd totally lose it if he found out.'

'It's our secret. Nobody else's. Florence...' Adam hesitated. 'What will you tell Elsie when she's grown up? About her dad?'

Florence wiped her eyes. 'I don't know. I've wondered about that. Your name's on her birth certificate. And maybe we'll have other children and it won't matter. You'll always be her dad. We'll cross that bridge when we have to.'

'That makes me happy,' Adam said. 'The thing is – something else is bothering me and I need to talk about it.'

'Oh?' Florence's face clouded. 'Is it something I've done?'

Adam was thoughtful. 'You got a letter, a pink one. You told me it was a tissue, but I took it off the postman and it was addressed to you. I saw it in your dressing-gown pocket.'

'Ah.' Florence shifted awkwardly. She felt a pang of regret. It was a mistake not to have confided in him. From now on, she'd tell Adam everything.

'Is it from *him*?' Adam took a breath. 'From Darryl Featherstone?'

'No.' Florence winced at the thought. 'Why would he write to me?'

'I saw you hide the letter and it's been playing on my mind.'

'I haven't opened it yet,' Florence admitted. 'But I recognise the writing.'

'Don't I have the right to know?' Adam began, his voice rising.

'It's from my mum,' Florence blurted, and she could tell that Adam was relieved. 'I can't let Dad see it. She broke his heart. You know she left when I was a kid. She went off to Northampton with the man who came round to fix the boiler. She stopped messaging me a couple of years ago. Now she's written to me.'

'I wonder why.'

'Who knows?' Florence moved her shoulders, as if she didn't care. 'She'd never win Mum of the Year award. To be honest, after what she did to Dad, I don't want anything to do with her.'

'Perhaps she's sorry? Perhaps she's sick?' Adam said, and Florence thought what a kind person he was.

'Perhaps she needs money.' Florence stared into the water again. She was glad to be confiding in Adam. He was her rock. 'I'm sorry I didn't tell you.'

'Why didn't you?' Adam asked. 'I thought the letter was from – *him*.'

'I'm so sorry.' Florence wrapped her arms around Adam and buried her face in his jacket. 'I should have told you. I thought I could handle it myself.'

'We can't have secrets.'

'I know.'

'Do you think you should read the letter?'

Florence turned to Adam again. 'Do you think I should?'

'It's the only way you'll know what she wants,' Adam said.

'Maybe I should. Or we can read it together.' Florence reached down to the stroller and tucked Elsie beneath a warm blanket. She had fallen asleep, the felt rabbit's ear still in her tiny mouth.

'Shall we talk about it another time?' Adam suggested.

Florence looked at him with shining eyes. 'Thank you.'

'And let's not keep secrets. Promise me? It's the only way. I mean that.'

'I promise.' Florence nodded, feeling foolish. 'I love you so much, Adam, and I can't believe I'd risk everything we have by...' She wiped away new tears.

'I'm not angry.' Adam touched her cheek tenderly. 'We can make this work. We can be the best little family in Oxfordshire.'

Florence took his hands in both of hers. 'We can. I'll be the best mum and the best girlfriend.'

'You're both of those.' Adam leaned over and kissed her lips. He noticed ripples forming on the top of the water. 'It's getting chilly. Shall we go back?'

'We ought to,' Florence said, and Adam turned the stroller and pushed it with one hand along the path that led to the village.

His other hand in Florence's, they walked towards home.

* * *

Lin and Neil stood in the back garden of their house in Barn Park, hand in hand, staring out across the fields. She leaned her head against his shoulder and said, 'I love this time of evening. When the sun's setting. Everywhere smells so warm, like the sun's done its job for the day.'

'It has. George's potatoes look good.' Neil cast his eyes over the crops. 'I might pop in and buy a bag of spuds off him. Mine aren't ready yet. I could make us some rosti tomorrow. They'd go nicely with a ham salad.'

Lin imagined Neil in her apron and her heart expanded with love. 'I wish I could cook as well as you.'

'You're doing all right.' Neil gave her arm a squeeze. 'The lasagne we had for dinner was lovely.'

Lin's eyes twinkled. 'You mean I didn't burn it in the microwave? Seven minutes from frozen.'

They paused for a moment, hand in hand, staring over towards the field.

'We should go to The Sun soon,' Neil suggested. 'Or drive over to Peterborough and see Debbie and Jon and the kids. We could take them all out if we go in the Sharan.'

'It'll be good to catch up with Debbie.' Lin thought of her daughter, her grandchildren. Then a thought came to her. 'We should go to see Dickie Edwards. He's poorly now.'

'He's getting worse each day. It might be goodbye.' Neil looked sad.

Lin remembered being in school with Dickie. He was a bully then, a misunderstood kid. She liked him now they were adults. But he was ill. They were all getting older. A sigh escaped her.

'Poor Dickie. It's a shame.' Lin tried her best not to feel morose. Another thought came to her. 'Do you know who we saw today at Nobb's End?'

'Who?'

'Mike Bailey.'

'Who?'

'Mike Bailey, who used to live on Orchard Way. I think he's bought the Featherstones' at Nobb's End. He was in the year above us. Cool Hand Mike. Everybody liked him. He wore a leather jacket and had long hair. He bought a Triumph

Bonneville, then he cut all his hair off when he was twenty-one and left to join the RAF.'

'Didn't he break Josie's heart?' Neil asked, finally remembering who Lin was talking about.

'He did.' Lin met his eyes meaningfully. 'That was before she met Harry. She forgot all about Mike.'

'What happened to him?'

'Mike? I did hear he got married and was living in Wiltshire. I think someone said he served in the Falklands.'

Neil wrapped an arm around Lin. 'He'd be what – seventy-seven now?'

'I'd think so.' Lin thought again how quickly time was passing. Like an egg timer. The sand running out. 'Do you think he and his wife have moved here to retire?'

'Who knows? He should have retired ages ago. Maybe he just wants to come back to his roots.' Neil made a move towards his pocket. 'Oh, I've got a text.' He tugged out his phone. 'It's from Dangerous.'

'What does he want?' Lin asked anxiously. 'He hasn't chopped his foot off or anything?'

'Don't tempt fate, Lindy.' Neil grinned. 'Oh, he says he's doing an oil change on a car tomorrow morning first thing and he wants me to pop in and take a look.'

'Whatever for?' Lin asked. 'Can't he do it himself? You gave up the garage years ago. Neil, I don't want you dragged back again.'

'Don't worry.' Neil hugged her and Lin felt that reassuring warmth of familiarity, of love. 'He probably just wants a chat. We'll stop off tomorrow morning in the Sprite, just for half an hour. Perhaps he wants my opinion on something mechanical.'

'That's what I'm worried about. Oh, look.' Lin pointed to a

figure walking across the field. 'It's George. And he's got Nadine with him.' She waved. 'Hi, George.'

George Ledbury lifted a hand as he walked between two rows of potatoes. He was wearing wellingtons and a heavy tweed jacket, a trilby hat. As he approached the fence, he turned to the Hampshire pig who was trotting behind him and reached into his pocket, offering a custard cream. The pig snaffled it.

George looked proud. 'Good girl, Nadine. Now sit down and be quiet for a minute.'

Lin watched, amazed, as Nadine flopped over by his feet. George gave a hearty chuckle. 'She's a good girl, Nadine. Good company.' He chuckled again. 'More than I can say for Penny.'

'That's not nice,' Lin said. She'd known Penny for years.

'How's the family, George?' Neil asked.

'Keeping well. How's your daughter out in Peterborough?'

'Debbie's fine,' Neil said.

'Their catering company's business is doing well,' Lin added.

'That's more than I can say for mine.' George grimaced.

'Oh? Things not good?' Neil asked kindly.

'Young George and I had a meeting with Adam Johnson and his dad at their place in Tadderly. Nope. Something will have to go.'

Lin's face was all sympathy. 'Go?'

George took a deep breath. 'The farm's a family business. George Junior looks after the sheep and cows. Natalie does the paperwork. Bobby does the grafting. He's got his partner and her two little ones living with him in the farm cottage. Mind you, she's nice, Hayley. Good baker. Makes better cakes and bread than ever my Penny did.'

Lin examined George's face. His complexion was ruddy, his ready grin with a bottom front tooth missing looked cheery enough. But there was something sad behind his eyes. She said, 'The farm will be all right, won't it, George?'

George sucked his teeth. 'Ah, it's the overheads. And farm machinery don't come cheap. No, I think something will have to go. I might have to sell off a few fields for starters.' He sniffed. 'Developers want land. There aren't enough houses being built.'

Lin and Neil exchanged glances. 'You might have to sell fields?' Lin asked. 'This potato field?'

'Who's building houses in the potato field?' a man's voice called, and Geoffrey Lovejoy popped his balding head over the fence, holding out an egg box. 'Here you are, Lin. Susan's laid some lovely ones recently. Mrs B'Gurk too.'

'What's this I hear?' Janice, a dark-haired woman with coral lipstick, was clutching a chicken. It nestled in her arms, blinking. 'Houses being built in the fields behind us? I don't like that.'

'It might come to that,' George said. 'Progress can't be stopped.'

'Young people need somewhere to live,' Neil said optimistically. 'I suppose there's space for another row of houses. Or flats.'

'Flats?' Geoffrey spat the word as if it were poison. 'We'd be overlooked. Our countryside views would go and who knows what sort of people would move in here?'

'Kids running amok, scaring the chickens.' Janice hugged the one in her arms. 'There would be more children filling the school, bigger classes, queues at the doctor's. And we're not getting any younger.'

'You can't stop expansion – it's the way of the world,' George said, but his expression told a different story. 'This land has been Ledbury land since my great-grandfather.'

'It's a shame,' Neil agreed. 'But you're right, there aren't enough homes.'

'New neighbours are always good.' Lin noticed Janice's sharp intake of breath. 'I mean, the ones we've got are nice so it follows – new ones would be.' She gave up.

'You might have to get rid of some of your animals, George. Cows. Pigs.' Geoffrey turned to the pig. 'What do you make of it all, Nadine?'

Nadine looked up through white eyelashes and wrinkled her snout. She eased herself up from the ground, turned around, wiggled her tail and peed over George's boot.

'See? That's what Nadine thinks about progress.' Geoffrey was triumphant. 'You got your answer there, George. Good and proper.'

12

It was almost dawn, but Cecily couldn't sleep. She'd been awake since midnight, worrying. She was lying in bed, staring into the paling ceiling, her head full of thoughts that collided and smashed like dodgem cars.

Eddie.

He'd sent her his address. He'd spoken to his granddaughter about their past. He had sent her a message.

Forgive me.

If that didn't mean that he still had feelings for her after all these years, what else could it mean?

He'd asked her to visit him.

Cecily blinked into swirling blackness that was becoming grainy and grey. She'd said no. She'd flatly refused.

So many feelings had surfaced and she couldn't think straight, but above everything she had to protect herself from being hurt again. But she was hurting now. What had happened was unchangeable. Eddie had married Joyce; they'd had a child, Elizabeth Cecily.

Eddie had been foolish; in a moment of weakness, he'd let

Cecily down. Joyce had betrayed their friendship. She'd set her sights on Eddie, persuaded him to sleep with her. But he hadn't exactly refused. It had changed everything between them.

But he'd never stopped loving her.

Cecily felt sorry for Joyce; if that was the case, she'd have spent her life wishing for something she could never have. Eddie's respect, his affection. But he would have done his best for her and the baby. He was that sort of man.

Another thought crashed into the previous one. Why had Eddie and Joyce had only one child? Had he turned away from his wife? Had the one mistake he'd made shaped him for the rest of his days? Cecily imagined Joyce and Eddie in a cold double bed, their backs turned against each other. It was so sad.

But what if she went to see Eddie? He'd been young, fearless, ruggedly handsome; he'd looked like James Dean. But now he was in his nineties. He would be frail. Perhaps it would be better if she remembered him as he was.

But Eddie Blake had been the man she was engaged to, the man she wanted to spend her life with. The man she loved, even now. They were both alive. He was a widower. There was time.

Cecily pushed the thought away. For a moment, she felt angry. She'd managed so well, lived independently, and now Eddie was back, wanting to see her because Joyce had died and he was on his own.

No, Cecily told herself, Eddie was not like that. He'd loved her more than anything. It was Cecily who'd told him to marry Joyce. She'd insisted it was the right thing to do – she was pregnant. He'd made a mistake and he had to pay for it for the rest of his life.

But now he was free. Cecily could visit him.

What if she did?

Cecily stumbled out of bed and flicked on the light. It was

almost five o'clock. She wanted a cup of tea, and to stretch her legs.

What if…?

She put her hands over her ears as if to stop the thought from repeating itself. She took a breath, struggled into her dressing gown and sloppy slippers and shuffled towards the bedroom door.

In the kitchen, she went to fill the kettle and there it was, a piece of paper on the worktop. Eddie's address.

Eddie Blake,
7, Woodbury Close,
Benson,
Oxon.

Cecily imagined the house in Woodbury Close. A semi. Three bedrooms. Comfortable and modest. Eddie's home. The one he'd shared with Joyce for years, the walls crammed with photos of Elizabeth, Sammy, and her daughter, Lara.

They had been his whole life.

Cecily wondered if there was an old photo of her there too. If she visited him, she'd find out. She frowned, reaching up to the cupboard to take out a cup and a saucer.

Her foot slithered inside the slipper and she faltered, stumbling to one side. Her hip hit the corner of the worktop with a sharp bump. She slipped into a heap on the floor and groaned.

For a moment she wondered what to do. She reached to a nearby chair and her fingers found a soft cushion. She pushed it beneath her head and closed her eyes to rest them. The world seemed to spin away.

* * *

The same morning, at eight-thirty, Lin tidied away the breakfast dishes as Neil tugged on his jacket. He said, 'I should walk down to see Dangerous rather than take the car. I need to stretch my legs. He'll be open at nine.'

'Hang on a minute and I'll come with you,' Lin offered. 'I want to ask him how Elsie's doing. Florence takes her to Geraldine McDermott in Newlands while she's at Odile's. Geraldine has a little boy, Arthur.'

'Right,' Neil said. 'Maybe afterwards we can walk down to The Sun and visit Dickie.'

'We should.' Lin patted his arm. 'It makes me sad to see him like that. But it's about supporting him, isn't it? He was pleased to see us last time. He's so thin though.'

'I know.' Neil held out his hand. 'Lindy, tomorrow we'll do something just for us. We'll take the Sprite out somewhere nice.'

Lin smiled. Somehow, Neil always knew the right thing to say, or the right idea to suggest. 'I hope the weather will stay like this. It's flaming June.' She slipped her hand in Neil's and they set out in the bright sunshine towards Dangerous Dave's garage.

They could hear Dave before they arrived. He was singing at the top of his lungs. Lin recognised the song: 'I'm in Love with My Car' by Queen. Lin thought it was appropriate. She turned the corner and realised why.

Dangerous Dave's overalled legs were sticking out beneath a silver Porsche Boxster. He slid out on a steel creeper and beamed. 'Oh, I thought you were the owner.' He sat up and spoke directly to Neil. 'I've done the oil change. But I had to have a look underneath. It's immaculate. I've heard these models have suspension problems and the coil springs break on them. This is the first time I've worked on this model, and I'd like to make this one a regular.' Dave turned to Lin. 'Hello, Lin. All right?'

'Fine, thanks, Dave. How's Elsie? And Florence and Adam?'

'Can't complain. Elsie pees and poos and eats and laughs. We're one happy family. It's all tickety-boo.' Dave turned back to Neil. 'Neil, you had this garage before I did. I know you like a nice set of wheels. So, this Boxster – what do you think?'

Neil smiled. 'I prefer my Sprite. I always fancied a Porsche, though.'

'I know.' Dave grinned. 'It's my dream to get a Boxster or a 911.'

Neil approached the car. 'They handle well, Boxsters. Mind you, I've never driven one. It's beautiful.'

'Sleek, good-looking,' Dave added.

'You sound like a pair of salesmen.' Lin laughed. 'I'm just going outside for a breath of fresh air.' She teased, 'There's too much gassing in here.'

'I'll be with you in a minute, love,' Neil called back. She knew he was smiling.

Lin stood on the pavement where Harvest Road became Orchard Way. Odile's café was just opening for breakfast and coffee across the road. Florence would have started work. Lin glanced towards the allotments. She thought about Tina Gilchrist and reminded herself to ask Minnie how her sister was feeling. Tina's house on Harvest Road was empty. Jimmy Baker kept an eye on it – he lived a few doors away and had a key. Lin wondered when Tina was coming home. She'd been gone since last year.

A taxi drew up to the kerb and stopped, its engine idling. Lin watched a man climb out. He was well groomed, wearing a herringbone blazer and jeans. Lin took a step backwards and said, 'Hello again.'

'Hello.' Darryl offered a charming smile. 'How are you?'

'Fine. Have you come for your car?' Lin sniffed. She didn't want to talk to Darryl. 'Dave's just finished.'

'Oh, that's good. I can drive it to the office. I work in Charlbury.'

'You're a solicitor, I know.' Lin heard her tone: it was slightly hostile. But Darryl deserved it after what he did to Florence. And here he was now, behaving as if nothing were wrong. And he had the cheek to bring his car to Florence's father's garage! Lin couldn't help what she said next. 'Your new girlfriend lives in Tadderly.'

'We both do.'

'Are there no garages there?' Lin heard her aggressive tone again.

'Oh, of course, but I miss Middleton Ferris. I'd live here again.' Darryl didn't seem to notice that Lin was being sarcastic. 'When Charlotte and I were together, we both said how charming it is. I joined the hiking group; I thought the pub was lovely.'

'Your old house has sold.' Lin frowned. 'I don't think there's anything else here now.'

'Oh, I'd love to move back. Sophie will go wherever I want.' Darryl checked an expensive watch. 'Well, it's been nice talking, but time's money. I'd better get a move on. I'll pay Dave and be on my way.'

Lin watched Darryl saunter into the garage, feeling her neck blotch with anger. Darryl had called him *Dave*. He was being familiar with Florence's father.

If Dave knew the truth about how he'd treated his daughter, he'd be furious!

Lin listened as Darryl chatted easily. Both men were laughing. Neil said nothing, of course – Lin knew why. She walked back into the garage and saw Darryl clap Dave on the shoulder.

'I love this little garage. Great rates, great service. A proper family business, Dave.'

'Well, thanks, mate.' Dave held out his hand and Darryl shook it. 'It's a lovely car to work on.'

'I'll book it in for a service next month,' Darryl said.

'It's a real pleasure.'

'I'd better be off. I've got a meeting in Charlbury at ten.'

'Nice to do business.' Dave watched Darryl leap into his car and fire up the engine. He drove off smoothly, leaving a puff of blue smoke behind.

Neil was watching. He said, 'There might be a bit of a build-up of condensation there.'

'That was what I thought,' Dave replied. 'Well, what a nice bloke Darryl is. I took to him when he lived here. Shame he and his missus broke up and he left the village. I suppose he sold that expensive house to pay her off and now he's looking for another place.'

'I can't say I took to him.' Lin thought of Florence and Elsie, and her temper exploded. 'He's all flash car and trousers. I wouldn't trust him an inch.'

Dave looked surprised. 'What's the poor bloke done to you?'

'To *me*?' Lin wished she could tell him the truth, but she couldn't. She'd promised Florence. Her lips were sealed. She tried an excuse. 'He's smug, Dave. Something about him isn't very trustworthy.'

'He's a good-looking chap. Intelligent. Well-heeled too.' Dave grinned at Neil. 'What do you think?'

Lin turned abruptly to Neil and glared. 'Neil agrees with me.'

Neil looked from Dave to Lin, his face guilty. He'd never been able to lie. 'I don't know him, Dangerous. He might be all right.'

'Neil, we should go. Dave needs to get on with his work.' Lin huffed. 'Come on.'

'There's no rush, Lin.' Dave waved a casual hand. 'I've got a Jag coming in for an MOT in half an hour. But I've got time for a coffee.'

'All right, Dangerous,' Neil said.

'We have to get on. I'm sorry, Dave.' Lin took Neil's arm firmly. 'We're going to visit Dickie. You know he's not well. Come on, Neil. You and Dave can talk about cars another time.'

'Oh, right.' Neil looked over his shoulder as Lin hurried him away.

Dangerous Dave muttered to himself, 'Women. I'll never understand them.'

Lin dragged Neil along Orchard Way, her teeth clenched. As they approached Odile's café, she hissed, 'Darryl Featherstone, a nice bloke? Really? You know what he did. He lied, made Florence pregnant and ditched her. And now he's cosying up with her father, using his garage to get his car done, calling it a family business?' Her face was livid. 'Family, indeed. And you said nothing at all to back me up. A bit of moral support might have been helpful, Neil.'

13

It was just past nine. Cecily sat up slowly. She must have dozed while she lay on the floor, her head on the cushion. Her left wrist hurt. She brought her right hand to her hip. It felt tender and bruised. She wondered if she could get up.

She took several breaths to steady herself. She was cold. Her fingers were stiff and her skin was tinged blue.

Groaning with the effort, Cecily managed to kneel; painfully, she clambered to her feet and leaned against the kitchen worktop. She glanced at the empty teacup. A hot drink would be so welcome. Her heart was thudding and she needed to sit down. She glanced down at her slippers. They were too big, they'd grown slack and she should have thrown them away ages ago. She'd slipped because they didn't support her feet.

Cecily made her way gingerly to the living room. Her phone was on the table next to the sofa. She ought to ring for help. Taking small steps, she focused on the armchair and, pausing for breath, she forced herself to move precariously towards it. She positioned herself carefully and eased herself into the seat. Leaning back, she closed her eyes and took a deep breath. She felt really cold now. Reaching behind her with her good hand, she tugged a blanket from the back of the chair and tried to cover herself with it. It extended to her thighs; if she pulled it up, her chest and stomach were covered. It would be better wrapped around her shoulders, but she couldn't manoeuvre it, so she compromised and covered her lap. She was still shivering.

Cecily reached for the phone and thought about what to do.

She paused. If she called an ambulance, one would be on its way the minute she told them how old she was. They'd dash out to Tadderly Road and whisk her into A & E. Cecily chewed her lip, thinking.

Hospitals were busy and understaffed. Tadderly General was no different. There would be needy people in the waiting room: children, people who'd had real, serious accidents, patients who needed prompt care and attention. She'd just had a silly fall, hurt her wrist, bruised her hip. She didn't want to take up the doctors' and nurses' valuable time. Besides, she might have to wait ages.

She'd sit where she was until half nine, then she'd call Dr Müller's surgery. It wouldn't be too long.

Cecily felt herself trembling with shock and cold. She moved the blanket, but she couldn't get warm. She was desperate for a cup of tea or a drink of water. Her mouth was dry as dust. For a moment, she thought about ringing Josie. She lived minutes away. She wouldn't mind coming round – she was good as gold. She'd bring a first-aid kit and bandage the sore wrist. She'd make a cup of tea and wrap her in some warm blankets.

She didn't want to be any trouble. Josie would probably be busy.

Cecily leaned her head back and decided it was time to ring

the surgery. Dr Müller would know what was best. It was only a bruise and a swollen wrist.

* * *

The digital clock in Dickie Senior's bedroom showed well past eleven thirty. He was propped up on several pillows and he was tired now. His spectacles had made a purple indentation in the skin of his nose. He smiled and Lin noticed that he only had a few teeth remaining; his false ones had been abandoned now. He lifted a shaky hand and flicked his tongue over cracked lips. 'You wouldn't get me a drink?'

Lin twisted to the bedside table and poured water from a jug. She held the glass to his lips and Dickie placed a cold hand over hers and sipped once.

'Thanks, Lin.'

'It's no trouble, Dickie.'

'You're a good woman.' Dickie glanced at Neil. 'She's a good one, Neil.'

'She is.' Neil clearly didn't know what else to say.

Dickie gave a weak chuckle as if thinking about something amusing. He said, 'You know, I was a bit of a bad lad at school.'

'You were a normal kid, Dickie,' Lin said kindly.

'My dad used to slap me round the head a lot.' Dickie tried another laugh. 'He always said I needed some sense knocking into me. So I suppose…' He paused for a moment, catching his breath. 'I suppose I passed it on to the other kids in the class, getting my own back, like.'

'You were all right, Dickie,' Neil said.

Dickie was doing his best to talk. 'Miss Hamilton sorted me out good and proper. She's a good'un.'

'She is,' Lin agreed. 'Miss Hamilton's the best.'

'She lives in that bungalow down Tadderly Road.' Dickie took a deep breath, two. 'She'll outlive me. And the missus. Gail's in her chair in the sitting room. She never moves out of it now.'

'We'll say hello to her on the way out.' Lin stood slowly. 'You need to get some rest, Dickie. We'll go now.'

'She'll outlive all of us, Cecily Hamilton,' Dickie said again as he leaned back on the pillows, closing his eyes, the spectacles still on his nose.

'We'll be seeing you,' Neil said.

'Stop by in the bar for a drink. Dickie Junior will get you one. Pop in on your way.' Dickie gasped and was silent again. His lips moved but his words weren't audible.

'We'll call in again soon, Dickie,' Lin said. She leaned over and pressed his hand gently. He seemed not to notice. He was almost asleep.

Neil led the way from Dickie's bedroom through the lounge where his wife sat in the chair, watching television. She was breathing oxygen through a nasal tube. As they passed her, Lin called, 'Bye, Gail. Take care.'

Dickie's wife lifted a hand in acknowledgement as Neil and Lin made their way outside into the gleaming sunshine. 'I fancy a drink, to be honest. Do you, Lindy?' Neil asked wearily.

'Definitely.' Lin nodded. 'Poor Dickie.'

Neil met her eyes. 'I suppose it comes to us all in the end.'

Lin took his hand and spoke firmly. 'Only once. And we shouldn't worry about it, love. Not now. It's been a hard morning, what with visiting Dickie and that unpleasant business with Darryl.'

Neil looked worried. 'You don't think he'll cause trouble?'

'It can't come to any good,' Lin said. 'If Dave finds out

Darryl's Elsie's father, he'll commit murder. Dangerous is very protective where Florence is concerned.'

'He is.'

'Remember all that fuss last summer when he blamed every young man in the village for getting Florence pregnant. What a mess. Neil?' Lin frowned. 'Do you think Darryl's hanging round the village because he wants Florence? I mean, he must know the baby is his. Do you think he's after paternal rights?'

'I've no idea. Is he the type?' Neil was puzzled. 'That would be mean. Darryl has a girlfriend. And Florence and Adam are a lovely couple.'

'You're right, love.' Lin reached for his hand. 'I need that drink. Let's go to the bar.'

The amber lights glimmered in The Sun Inn. The place was as quiet as could be expected for a Friday morning. George Ledbury and his grandson Bobby were sitting together, enjoying a well-earned pint. Adam's parents, Rita and Linval Johnson, had just arrived, Linval leaving Adam in charge at the office in Tadderly while he and Rita, who taught in the local primary school, went out for an early lunch. Rita waved when she saw Lin and called out, 'Let's catch up soon.'

'Let's,' Lin called back. 'Great to see you.' She thought again of Darryl and offered her the friendliest smile.

Neil had drifted over to the corner where Kenny Hooper and Jimmy Baker sat at a wooden table clutching pints. Another man was next to them, holding forth, while Jimmy and Kenny listened intently. Lin went over to the bar and Dickie Junior said, 'Usual, is it?'

'A pint and an elderflower pressé.'

Dickie busied himself at the pumps. 'I saw you visiting Dad earlier.'

'We probably stayed longer than we should – he fell asleep for a while, then he woke up again. He wants to chat,' Lin said.

Dickie exhaled. 'He likes to talk about the old times. I'm glad you popped in. He's hanging on by a thread.' For a moment, Dickie looked as if he'd cry. He handed the drinks over and forced a professional smile. 'Here you are. Jimmy and Kenny are over there. They've met a new friend.'

'Oh?' Lin looked over to where Neil had joined the three men and they were chatting, oblivious.

'The new bloke who's just moved into Nobb's End. He was a pilot in the RAF or something.'

'Oh,' Lin said again. 'Thanks, Dickie. I'll go and see what they're up to.' She swiped her card and carried the drinks carefully to the table in the corner and sat down.

'...only a few of us left in the village. I wouldn't be anywhere else. I was born and bred here,' Jimmy insisted.

'I likes this place. I ent going nowhere,' Kenny agreed. 'Even Miss Hamilton's come back to live here.'

'Miss Hamilton?' The man Lin knew to be Mike Bailey stretched his legs and smiled. 'She must be an age now. What is she? A hundred?'

'She's ninety-two in August and she looks very well on it,' Lin said loyally. 'We're going to plan a birthday party for her.'

Mike turned to face her slowly as if he hadn't realised she was there. He gave her a long appraising look, the scrutiny of a man who was used to judging women. He smiled. 'Linda Norton.'

'Lin Timms,' Lin said smartly.

'You were Josie Potter's best friend.' Mike held her gaze and she wondered if he still thought of Josie.

'Josie Sanderson.' Lin decided he could find out that she was a widow later. She wondered why she was being so protective, so she offered a warm smile and said, 'Have you come back here to live?'

'He's got the house in Nobb's End where that yuppy couple lived,' Jimmy explained.

'It's nice to have you back, Mike,' Neil said. 'You must be retired?'

'I left the RAF for a desk job,' Mike said smartly. 'I travelled for a couple of years after that, here and there. But I remembered the old times and I thought, let's go back to my roots.'

'So, what are you going to do with yourself?' Neil asked.

'Hiking, a bit of baking. I dabble in watercolours,' Mike said. 'I thought I might join an art class in Charlbury.'

'Does your wife like painting?' Lin asked quickly.

Mike didn't look at her. 'We aren't together.' He lifted a finger as if changing the subject. 'Of course, there are plenty more fish.'

Lin hoped he wasn't referring to Josie.

Jimmy seemed delighted. 'Me and Kenny sometimes play a bit of bowls. You could join us.'

'And I have an allotment near the rec. It ent much but I grow good spuds,' Kenny added.

'I was talking to a lovely man yesterday in the village, who invited me to dinner. His name was Gerald Harris.' Mike seemed to be settling in.

'Bomber,' Jimmy and Kenny chorused.

'You'd be welcome to come to dinner with us,' Neil offered generously and Lin imagined herself offering Neil and Mike charred spaghetti.

'Neil's a great cook,' she said with a grin.

Neil asked, 'Do you like classic cars, Mike? Lin and I've got a Frog-Eyed Sprite.'

'Nice. I'm an Audi TT sort of man, but I've always thought about getting myself a Porsche or an Aston Martin.'

'Like James Bond.' Kenny grinned.

'I'm not fond of Porsches. I always think the sort of men who drive them are lacking something. Self-esteem or manhood.' Lin wondered what was wrong with her today. She was certainly speaking her mind without a thought for the consequences. Minnie would be proud of her.

Mike looked alarmed. 'I might stick with the TT.' He turned to Neil. 'I don't remember your wife being this feisty when we were at school.'

Neil wrapped an arm around Lin. 'I like it when she's feisty.' Lin ignored him and sipped her elderflower.

'I'd like to catch up with some of the people from the old days.' Mike's eyes twinkled.

'Oh, Tina Gilchrist used to live just down the road from me. You remember, Tina Moore that was?' Jimmy said. 'She's living with Minnie in Oxford at the moment.'

'Minnie Moore?' Mike asked. 'They were a poor family, all patched clothes and headlice. I remember Minnie had an argumentative father who let his fists do the talking.'

'She's Dr Araminta Moore now,' Lin said. 'Classics professor.'

'She's done well.' Mike was impressed.

'Oh, she and Lin and Josie meet up all the time,' Jimmy began. Lin's phone vibrated in her pocket and she tugged it out.

'Excuse me.' She knew it was Josie but she wasn't going to say her name in front of Mike. She listened to her friend talking quickly, her eyes widening. 'What? How bad is it? Is she? Right. And you're with her? I'll come straight over. Can you ring Minnie? No, I'm on my way. Wait for me. I'll be right there.'

Lin stood up and Neil turned to her anxiously. 'What's happened, love?'

'Cecily's had a fall. I'm popping down to Tadderly Road.'

'Is it nasty?' Neil was concerned.

'You mean Miss Hamilton?' Kenny asked, his face troubled.

'Does she need anything?' Jimmy offered. 'I can get the car.'

'It seems she's fallen in her kitchen. Don't worry, I'll go, Neil. I'll ring you, love.' She planted a kiss on his cheek. 'I'll go straight there to see if I can do anything.'

14

Minnie was sitting in The Bear having a late lunch with Jerry Mandelbaum, a professor of Moral Philosophy, an ex who was still in love with her. They were eating steak pies with mash and red wine gravy, drinking pints of Fuller's ale. Mostly, they were talking.

'Italy's one of my favourite places in the world,' Minnie said.

'I know.' Jerry held up his fork. 'In August, a group of four of us are going to Pisa. We've planned to meet some colleagues from the Scuola Normale Superiore. It was founded by Napoleon Bonaparte in 1810, you know. Anyway, Minnie, I was hoping you might tag along.'

'Me?' Minnie was thoughtful. 'Come with you to Pisa?'

'It would be right up your street. We're being asked to contribute to conferences and summer schools. It wouldn't be hard to get you added to the list.'

'Why would I want to do that?' Minnie sipped from her pint glass.

'It's Italy. I know you've been countless times, but there's so much to see and do. You said your sister's almost fully recovered.'

'She is.'

'How about it, Minnie?' Jerry passed a hand through thick charcoal curls. 'There's wonderful wine and great food.'

'Any other time, I'd consider it, Jerry,' Minnie said. 'But I might be going to New York in August.'

Jerry was surprised. 'New York?'

'I have a lover there – Jensen. He's a theatre director,' Minnie said. 'Or he might come to stay with me. By August, I'll definitely have made up my mind to do one or the other.'

'So there's no chance of you coming to Italy?' Jerry was disappointed.

'You're a good friend,' Minnie said kindly. 'With a fine mind. And I enjoy our lunches together. But—' she placed a hand on her chest '—we know there's no time to procrastinate. We must follow our hearts. Yours takes you to the Scuola Normale Superiore, mine takes me to Jensen.'

'Well.' Jerry looked surprised. 'I never thought I'd see the day when Dr Araminta Moore's life is dictated by a man.'

'It's not dictated by a man. I decide what I do.' Minnie smiled. 'And what I intend to do is live the rest of my days with Jensen. That's all there is to it.' She finished her pint, placed it onto the table with a muffled bang, abandoned the remains of her pie and offered Jerry a wink. 'My mind's made up. It's time I settled down. Be pleased for me, Jerry.'

'I am, I am.' Jerry's face was still puzzled. 'But we're still friends?'

'Good friends. The best.' Minnie stood up and pecked his cheek. 'I have to go now. But text me and we'll do lunch again.'

She hurried on her way, towards her bicycle secured to a rack outside, clambered onto the saddle and set off down

Alfred Street towards Blue Boar Street, humming happily to herself. There was a book at home about Aristotle with her name on it.

Minnie arrived at her red-brick terraced house and tugged the bicycle into the hall. She paused and listened. Tina was in. She could hear the radio blaring in the kitchen. Tina loved rock and pop. She called out, 'Hi, Tina – are you back?' Tugging her jacket off, she dashed into the kitchen. 'Did you enjoy the Botanic Garden? It's one of the oldest scientific gardens in the world – it contains over 5,000 different plant species and—' She stopped dead. Tina was wearing a dressing gown, her hair damp, bending over, pulling clean clothes from the washing machine. 'When did you start washing your own clothes? I thought my machine was unfathomable?' She put her hands on her hips. 'You went out in that yellow sweatshirt this morning. Is everything OK?'

'I can wash my own clothes.' Tina stood up straight. 'The thing is, I fell over in the gardens and I had to get the mud off. I just had a shower.'

Minnie was immediately concerned. 'Are you all right? Did you feel dizzy?'

'No, I tripped over a tree stump. In some mud. Silly me. Ha ha.' Tina clearly wanted to laugh it off. Minnie scrutinised her sister's face; she seemed well enough.

'As long as you're all right.'

'I'm fine. Have you had lunch?'

'I went to The Bear. Are you hungry, Tina? There's ham in the fridge.'

'I've already eaten.'

'Oh? Where?'

Tina shrugged as if it wasn't important. 'I bought myself a burger.'

Minnie thought it wasn't the best food for a stroke recovery patient, but she said nothing.

Tina gave her best smile. 'What are you up to now?'

'Reading. And you?'

'I'm tired.' Tina yawned to prove it. Minnie thought she was being secretive again. 'I think I'll go up for forty winks.'

'All right.' Minnie knew there would be no mud in the Botanic Garden – it was June and the weather had been sizzling. Tina was hiding something. The phone buzzed in her pocket. 'I wonder who this is.'

It was a text, from Josie. Cecily had suffered a fall. She had a sprained wrist. Hopefully it hadn't broken. And she'd bruised her hip. Cecily was shocked and tired, but she was basically all right. Did Minnie want to pop over?

Minnie replied of course, it was only a half-hour train ride. She was on her way. She'd be there in no time. Tina could wait.

* * *

By mid-afternoon, Cecily was sitting on the sofa, surrounded by Minnie, Josie and Lin, all with the same anxious expression. Cecily gave a weak smile. 'That will teach me to wear baggy slippers.'

Lin had made everyone tea. She knelt by the tray, which was on the low table, and began to pour. 'We were all worried, Cecily.'

'Why didn't you ring 999?' Minnie asked. 'An ambulance would have taken you straight to hospital.'

'Oh, it wasn't serious,' Cecily protested. 'I'm all right.'

'You just sat here and shivered?' Lin tutted. 'You should have phoned me, or Josie. You know we'd be round, whatever the time.'

'What did Dr Müller say? She couldn't have been very pleased that you dozed off on the floor with a ballooning wrist?' Josie pretended to be stern.

'I was tired.' Cecily breathed out to calm herself. 'But yes, she told me I should have phoned an ambulance. She came round and sorted me out, and she's coming back later to check on me again. But I won't stay in hospital. I've told her that. I'm fine in my own home. She even made me a cup of tea and some toast. Imagine a GP doing that. How wonderful!'

'Dr Müller's lovely,' Lin agreed, glancing at her fingers. 'My arthritis tablets made me so tearful. She swapped my meds and I've never looked back.'

'I hate the thought of you by yourself.' Josie looked at Cecily. It must have been a shock. She needed company, someone to keep an eye on her. 'Do you want me to move in for a few days?'

'There's a nurse coming round this afternoon.' Cecily put up her bandaged hand, meaning that she wanted no fuss. 'Dr Müller said that she'd arrange for an X-ray first thing tomorrow to check that the wrist's not broken. She was asking if I had a safety net in the community. I almost invited her to join the Silver Ladies.'

'It must have shaken you,' Minnie said, watching Cecily's hand tremble as she lifted the teacup to her lips. 'It's not just that you bashed your wrist. It's the shock to your nervous system.'

'We want to help,' Lin said kindly.

'So tell us what we can do. Make your meals? Shopping?' Josie asked.

'And we can talk about anything you like.' Minnie gave Cecily one of her knowing looks.

Cecily put her cup down. 'There is something I've been worried about.'

'Oh?' The frown line between Minnie's eyes deepened.

'Ever since Sammy gave me Eddie's address, it's been playing on my mind.'

'You want to go and see him?' Lin brightened. 'I can drive you there.'

'You ought to wait and see how you feel.' Josie was still looking at Cecily's bandage.

'It's not that.' Cecily's expression was earnest. 'I just feel so sad about what happened between me and Eddie and Joyce. You know Eddie and I were making plans to marry. We had our whole lives ahead of us, then Joyce got tipsy and he offered her a lift home and she seduced him.'

'He was a stupid man,' Minnie said simply.

'He lost you because of a moment of madness,' Josie agreed.

'But Joyce was your friend. How could she do that?' Lin was horrified. 'It's so disloyal.'

'I must've told you, Joyce always had a thing for Eddie,' Cecily said sadly. 'She set her sights on him. She was determined. It was his fault though. But he would never have loved her like he loved me. He told me that at the time.'

'And you never fell in love again,' Lin whispered. 'After Eddie.'

'I loved the children I taught,' Cecily said. 'That was enough. But now, Sammy has stirred all those feelings up again. Perhaps I realise that it wasn't.'

Minnie sat on the floor next to Cecily and took her hand. Her thoughts moved from Eddie to Jensen. How important was it to seize opportunities, especially where affairs of the heart were concerned? 'Can you explain what you're feeling?'

'I'm ninety-two next birthday, Minnie. Who knows how many years I have left? And—' Cecily took a deep breath '— what the quality of those years will be like. I have a nurse coming to check on me. I have friends around me now – don't misunderstand, I'm grateful – but I feel like it's all downhill from here.'

'Oh, Cecily,' Lin said, crestfallen. She thought of Neil, how lucky she was to have him.

'We're here for you,' Josie encouraged. 'You know that. You'll bounce back; the wrist will heal. You must have tough bones.'

Cecily leaned back in her seat and closed her eyes for a moment, thinking. When she opened them, her face was etched with sadness. 'Eddie's all alone now. I live by myself. So much time has been wasted. So much loneliness when all we really wanted was each other. He threw it all away.'

'He did,' Minnie agreed. Again, she was reminded sharply of Jensen. She had no intention of throwing away what they had. It was special.

'I stood back, insisted he marry Joyce, do the honourable thing.'

'You did what was right,' Josie said.

'Did I?' Cecily's eyes glinted. 'Did I really? I should have grabbed Eddie with both hands. The two of us would have been happy. Joyce had her baby, she got the family she wanted so badly, but he never loved her, I'm sure. Three lives spoiled by Eddie's...' Cecily searched for the word. 'Eddie's weakness.'

'Hear hear,' Minnie said. 'So, what are we going to do about it?'

'Do?' Cecily said hopelessly. All the old feelings of loss had resurfaced. 'What *can* I do?'

'You can get strong. You can get better,' Josie suggested. 'Your birthday's just around the corner. We're here for you.'

'Let's have lunch somewhere soon. We'll treat ourselves.' Lin was suddenly excited. 'I know. Let's go on a picnic. I'll drive. We could go to Watlington Hill, or Woodstock, or Rollright. I haven't seen the circle of stones there for years.'

'I suppose we could.' Cecily didn't seem too sure. She glanced at her wrist. It was throbbing. And she felt confused. It was as if Eddie were slipping away from her all over again.

'Let's go to Oxford,' Minnie said defiantly. 'You can all come to me. Next Sunday. We'll sit on the grass in Christ Church Meadows. I'll bring a picnic. We'll punt down the river, glide past St Hilda's, under the miniature white bridges and back past the Botanic Garden. It'll be lovely.'

Cecily put a hand to her hip. It was tender and painful. 'I know you mean well, dear. It's just right now I'm feeling a bit low.'

'Of course you are,' Lin soothed.

'You need to rest,' Josie said. 'Maybe we should go and let you sleep for a bit.'

'I might,' Cecily said weakly. Thoughts of Eddie had disturbed her and there was little chance of rest.

'But next week, we'll have that picnic.' Minnie wasn't going to be put off. 'Lin, can you drive everyone over?'

'Of course.'

'We'll have a Silver Ladies' lunch,' Minnie insisted. 'And we'll talk about Eddie and how you feel. You'll be stronger, Cecily, and your mind will be clearer.' Minnie hugged her old teacher, turning to Josie and Lin, lowering her voice. 'Eddie's reared his head again. And I think our lovely Miss Hamilton needs her pupils to help her make a big decision. Whichever way this goes, this could change her life forever.'

15

It was a bright, sunny Saturday evening on Newlands estate. Dangerous Dave and Adam had gone down to The Sun for a drink with Adam's parents. Of course, Jimmy and Kenny were there too, so they'd be there chewing the fat until closing time.

But Florence was anticipating a better evening. She'd set the table with nibbles: tortillas, olives, bread sticks, dips, and there was wine, cider and soft drinks for herself. Elsie was tucked up in her little baby pod in the living room, sucking water from a bottle, gurgling happily. Music was playing on the smart speaker. All Florence needed now was for Malia and Natalie to arrive. She hadn't had a girls' night for a long time, and she was looking forward to it more than she could say.

Florence checked her reflection; she'd made an effort. It felt good to be wearing something nice, a pretty dress and eyeliner, even though it was just a night with her friends. Motherhood always occupied her thoughts but for a moment, she could be the old Florence again, the one who hung out with friends, who laughed, who didn't have a care in the world. She glanced at Elsie and told herself she didn't regret a thing. That was the truth: the baby and Adam were her life. But Malia had a job in London – Florence didn't even know what a Comms Officer was – and Natalie worked at her grandfather's farm full time. She'd dumped her fiancé last year.

Florence wondered fleetingly if she and her friends still had much in common.

The doorbell chimed and Florence rushed to open it. Seconds later, she was hugging Malia and they were both whooping and laughing. They stood back and examined each other at arm's length.

'Love the dress, Florence. You're looking good, girl.'

'Look at *you*!' Florence took in Malia's new hair. Gone was the long black mane, now replaced by a short stylish cut, sweeping thick curls on top, shaved at the sides. 'I love the racy hair.'

'I'm a city girl.' Malia pushed back her fringe. 'It's called an undercut faux hawk. Undercuts suit African hair. Besides, check out the ears.'

Florence noticed that Malia had more piercings, gold studs, hoops, a diamond. She suddenly felt very unfashionable. Malia kissed her cheek.

'And I have a new man.' Malia said the word 'man' as if it had three syllables. 'He's called Malik. Apparently, it means King. We work together. He's really special.'

'Malia and Malik.' Florence laughed. 'It sounds like you're meant to be.'

Malia looked round. 'When's Natalie coming?'

'She texted she's on her way.'

'She and Finn Toomey didn't last long,' Malia said.

'It wasn't serious. She's got Betsy Biscuit now.'

'Betsy?'

lorence knew what would happen next. Elsie opened her
and her mouth at the same time and began to yell. Her
face deepened in colour. Malia refilled her glass. 'I don't
how you do it, Florence. That noise goes straight through

atalie agreed. 'I had such a lucky escape with Brandon. He
lways talking about having kids.' She watched Florence
tton her dress and tuck Elsie under her arm. Elsie began to
e happily and the baby closed her eyes. Florence loved the
ent of bonding. Natalie gave her a look that conveyed
te and said, 'You're amazing, Florence. You've taken to
erhood amazingly. I can't imagine what it's like, a little
ure doing that.'

ou've done so well,' Malia agreed. 'And Adam. We're all so
d of him, how he's adapted to Elsie.' She realised what she
aid. 'He loves her.'

s if she were his own,' Natalie added and Florence thought
rink had made them both a little thoughtless.

alia leaped up. 'I'll get more nibbles and fill your glass,
nce, another juice?'

lease.' Florence touched the baby's cheek and was
ded that she was completely fulfilled. It was nice to spend
with her friends. They'd enjoyed a pleasant evening,
ing up. But she wouldn't change a thing.

o, Florence. We haven't really talked about you.' Malia
ed herself down. She seemed determined to be more
ive, as if her last careless remarks had been a bit insensi-
It must be tough, juggling childminding and the job at the
nd making everyone's dinner.'

's fine.' Florence kissed Elsie's soft hair and smelled the
ble sweetness of her baby. 'Odile's amazing and Geral-
great, Dad and Adam are really good. Adam cooks—' She

'Her four-year-old grey mare.' Florence poured wine. 'I think she's done with men.'

'Oh, I'm not surprised she wants some solo time, after being engaged to control-freak Brandon. She needs to be single for a while. Whereas I...' Malia poured herself a glass of Chardonnay. 'Watch this space.'

'Oh?' Florence tipped orange juice into a tumbler.

They moved back to the living room where Elsie was almost asleep.

'Look at this little cutie.' Malia cooed. 'Malik and I would make beautiful babies. One day, you never know.'

'It's not all cute clothes and cuddles,' Florence said. 'You should see her at three in the morning.'

'Adam's here though?'

'Oh, Adam's wonderful,' Florence said and Malia shot her an appraising look.

'I never expected him to take to it so well.'

'To what?' Florence asked.

Malia seemed to be choosing her words. 'Fatherhood.'

There was a ping on the doorbell and Florence rushed to open it. She was surprised to feel a little uncomfortable – she wondered what Malia had meant. For a second, she wondered if Adam had said something about how hard it was to be Elsie's new dad.

She was hugging Natalie, who was holding up a bottle of red wine and shrieking, 'It's been ages.' Natalie smelled gorgeous. Florence noticed she carried a cool handbag and was wearing leather trousers. Natalie breezed into the living room. 'Hi, Malia. Oh, look at your hair. That's just so stunning and—' Her voice changed to a squeaky simpering whine. 'Elsie, you're so beautiful. Look at her, Florence. She's going to be a real heartbreaker.'

'I hope not,' Florence said a bit too abruptly. 'I mean, she's pretty, but I don't want her breaking hearts. Besides, cute girls get their hearts broken.'

There was a moment's pause, when both friends stared at Florence. Natalie said, 'And how's the gorgeous Malik?'

'Oh, he's so *nice*! And special, you know what I mean?' Malia made a loved-up face. 'I've dated other men, but this one's different!'

'I can tell. That photo you sent.' Natalie grabbed Malia's hand. 'He's beautiful.'

'I must bring him next time I come. You have to meet him,' Malia gushed.

Florence watched stiffly: Natalie already knew about Malia's boyfriend; she'd seen a photo. Florence felt suddenly left out. Left behind.

'I'm done with men,' Natalie sneered. 'Up at the farm, it's nothing but Bobby and Hayley and the two new kids. You'd think Mum and Grandma Penny had never seen children before. It's nauseating. Bobby's gone from bad boy to Dad of the Year. You won't catch me with a kid, not for at least ten years.' She paused suddenly and realised what she'd said. 'Elsie's the exception though,' she enthused. 'You look so happy, Florence. And I love the dress.' Natalie turned back to Malia. 'Seriously, your hair's so *London*. Are you sure it's OK for me to come up next month?'

'You must. There's an Ethiopian place where Malik and I eat. The food's bussin', especially the spicy veggie stew and injera. We eat there all the time after work. And I can introduce you to Will, who I work with. He might change your mind about being single. We could double-date.'

'Sounds awesome. And you have to come up to the farm tomorrow and meet Betsy.' Both girls seemed to have remembered Florence at the same time. 'You mus[t] Elsie. She'd love my horse.'

There was an awkward pause. Florence s[aid] some nibbles?'

'I'm starving.' Natalie was pleased to chan[ge] move the evening on.

'I need a refill.' Malia drained her glass.

'I've brought some Merlot. I'm going to g[et] laughed. Florence inspected the glass of ora[nge] holding and Malia spoke her thoughts aloud.

'That's just the two of us, Nat. Florence's sti[ll]

'We'll drink your share,' Natalie whooped an[d] into the kitchen, still talking. Florence glanced was fast asleep, and followed them, feeling a littl[e]

* * *

It was past ten. Malia was still talking about M[alik] had been punctuated with texts from him and she was missing him and she'd soon return f[rom] they could spend Sunday evening together. N[atalie] buy another horse, or breed from Betsy; the[y] knew about and she'd asked her father to She finished the wine in her glass. 'I want to That's my ambition. Grandad gets it. He said the farm but money's a bit tight right now. On[e]

'I'll get the BF down and we'll come ridin[g]' said. 'We could all ride through Old Scra[tby] would be romantic.'

'Can he ride?' Natalie asked and Malia growled and burst out laughing. Natalie shrie[ked] frowned for a moment. There was one thing on her mind. And probably her friends were the best sounding board. In truth, she wanted desperately to share something with them and not feel excluded. 'I got a letter, though. From my mum.'

'Your mum?' Natalie repeated.

'She hasn't contacted you in ages.' Malia leaned forward. 'What did she say for herself?'

'Did you tell her about Elsie?' Natalie asked.

'Does she know you and Adam are together?' Malia wondered.

'And I bet she asked who the real dad is.' Natalie's eyes lingered on Florence's as if she wanted to know too. Natalie was tipsy now; she didn't realise that her words were insensitive.

'I haven't opened it,' Florence said simply. She lifted Elsie gently onto her knee and started to button her dress.

'You haven't opened the letter?' Malia leaned forward, swaying a little. 'How do you know it's from your mum?'

'The handwriting.'

'There could be money in it,' Natalie said.

'Or maybe she's getting married again and she wants you to be bridesmaid.' Malia clapped a hand over her mouth. 'Seriously, you should open it.'

'You should,' Natalie agreed. 'Open it now.'

'Oh, yes,' Malia urged. 'Go on. Open it.'

Florence wasn't sure. 'I don't want to upset Dad.'

'You won't,' Natalie argued. 'He needs to know what she's doing.'

'She hurt him,' Florence protested.

'But you won't know what's happening unless you read it,' Malia said logically. 'It's your right to know, Florence. Go on, open it.'

'I'll hold Elsie if you like,' Natalie added.

'I don't know.' Florence lifted the baby and placed her gently on the nest, covering her lightly. She stood up, thinking. 'I told Adam we'd open it together.'

'Where is it?' Natalie asked.

'Upstairs.'

'I can't wait to hear what she's got to say,' Malia said.

'What excuses she can come up with for all the years she's been away with her other man,' Natalie agreed.

'We're here for you, whatever she says.' Malia's face was genuinely concerned. 'I remember when she left. We were in year eight. It was so tough for you and your dad.'

'It was,' Florence said, remembering the hurt, how she'd walked around in school feeling numb inside, hollow. How her father had cried as he'd sat next to her, trying to comfort her when she woke up at midnight sobbing. Yes, Malia had a point. If Florence knew what her mother wanted, she'd be in a better position to decide what to do. She wondered whether to wait.

'I'll open it later.'

'No,' Natalie yelled. 'I have to know what's in it now.'

'I already told you – Adam and I want to look at it together,' Florence said weakly.

'Adam won't mind. Just tell him we made you open it,' Malia coaxed.

'I don't know.'

'Go on, Florence,' Malia and Natalie said. Malia added, 'All girls together.'

'What if your mum's really sick?' Natalie said.

'What if she's homeless and needs your help?' Malia added.

'All right. I'll get it now.' Florence was unsure as she moved towards the stairs. She found herself hurrying towards the bedroom. It occurred to her again that she ought to discuss it with Adam or talk to her father. But the girls were desperate for her to open it. The letter was addressed to her. It seemed OK to look at it first and talk to Adam later. He'd understand.

She reached into her dressing-gown pocket and pulled out the pink envelope. Then she was on her way downstairs, and then in the living room. Malia and Natalie hadn't moved, as if they were still holding their breath.

Florence prised the flap of the envelope open carefully and Malia said, 'Well?' Natalie's mouth was open.

Florence unfolded the paper and saw the familiar round handwriting. She read:

Dear Florence, I know it has been a long time but...

Her eyes were moving faster than her brain could take in information. She wanted to read it to herself before she spoke to her friends, although she was conscious that their eyes were boring into her face, scrutinising her expression to see if she was happy or sad, or something else.

She read on. Her mother had been looking her up on social media. She wanted to know how her girl was doing after all these years and just imagine her shock when she saw a picture of...

She knew.

Florence forced her ragged breathing to calm, her pounding heart to slow.

Her mother knew about Elsie.

She had seen a photo of the baby in Florence's arms on Facebook. She wanted to know all about her. She had a right to know.

Florence went back to the words her mother had written, examining the tone. She sounded self-righteous, left out. Moralising.

You have no idea how that felt, Florence, to find out that I have a grandchild I didn't know anything about. You could have let me know. But no, I had to find out on Facebook.

Florence felt suddenly angry. How could she write to a mother who'd left no forwarding address? And why would she even want to? Her mother had abandoned her. She hadn't contacted her or shown any interest in so many years.

Florence read the final lines.

I know I haven't been the best mum. But it's comforting to me to know that you have a beautiful child and that I'm a grandmother to little Elsie. How I wish I could have shared it all with you. It's a mother's right to be with her daughter when she has a baby. But I want to make it all up to you. I want more than anything in the world to be there for you like a proper mum should. You must need me at a time like this. So I wondered if I could visit you soon and meet Elsie...

'No,' Florence said out loud without meaning to.

Malia was on her feet, her arms round Florence. Natalie followed, both friends hugging Florence tightly. Florence heard their words muttered against her hair.

'Is she all right?'

'Are you all right?'

'What does she say?'

'What does she want?'

'How can we help?' Malia pressed a hand against Florence's hair, smoothing it, comforting her. 'We're here for you. What can we do to help?'

Their kindness was suddenly too much to bear; her friends were being so sweet. Florence wasn't ready for sympathy; she was still reeling from the shock of hearing from the mother who'd left her alone for years.

Who hadn't been there when Florence had needed her and now she knew about Elsie, she wanted to visit.

Florence couldn't speak. She handed the letter to Malia, who scanned it quickly, Natalie gaping over her shoulder.

'Your mum's found out about Elsie and so she wants to come here.' Malia was immediately furious. 'This is awful. She has no business talking about what her rights are after what she did to you.'

'What a bitch,' Natalie said.

Malia wrapped an arm round Florence. 'How can your mum be so selfish?'

'Total cow,' Natalie said.

'How do you feel?' Malia hugged Florence closer. 'What are you going to do?'

Florence felt hollow and bitter and abandoned all over again. A sense of injustice and unfairness filled her throat. She wanted to pick Elsie up and hug her, keep her safe. She didn't want to see her mother, not now, not ever, and she should just stay away for the rest of Elsie's life. And more than anything, she wished she'd opened the letter with Adam, that it were his arms around her. She needed his kindness and strength and support.

Florence knew that, right now, there was only one thing she could do.

She burst into tears.

16

'I wonder what those girls are talking about,' Dangerous Dave said into his pint glass.

'It'll do Florence good to have time with friends,' Adam replied thoughtfully.

'And it'll do you good to have time for yourself,' Rita Johnson said, tapping her son's cheek. 'You work hard, Adam. You look worn out.'

'I was worn out when the kids were little,' Linval Johnson said, in defence of his son. Rita had always been too protective of her boy.

Adam pushed a hand through his twist curls. 'Malia and Florence haven't seen each other in ages. And Natalie's there too. It'll be a riot.'

'Malia's a London girl.' Rita sighed. 'There's not much of Middleton Ferris left in her. She's a go-getter. And this new boyfriend – I'm not sure at all.'

'You were all for her getting a career in the city, Rita. You were the one who told her not to teach like her mother or be an accountant like her father and brother.' Linval shrugged expansively. 'You can't complain.'

'I'm not complaining. I'm worried,' Rita replied.

'You're always worried,' Linval guffawed and reached for his pint.

'Malia's OK.' Adam glanced around the bar and noticed Bobby Ledbury on his way in, squeezing past customers, calling to Dickie Junior, 'Pint of Hooky, Dickie.'

'There's Bobby, just come in. I expect he's taking a break from his new family,' Linval said.

'And all that hard grafting on the farm.' Dave raised an eyebrow. 'Oh, talking of grafting, I got a new customer the other day; he brought this lovely Porsche in.'

Rita smiled. 'Don't go talking about fast cars to Adam.' She gave her son a tender look. 'I was saying the other day that he needs to upgrade his old banger for a proper family car now they've got little Elsie. Get something with more space in it for a baby. Maybe two.'

Adam looked away. 'If I bought anything, it'd be a hybrid.'

'That Porsche though. What a spectacular car,' Dave continued. 'I was saying to Neil that I wouldn't mind one. I hope Darryl will become a regular customer.'

Adam winced. 'Darryl?'

'Darryl Featherstone, who lived in Nobb's End last year. His wife left him and he sold up and moved to Tadderly. But he wants to move back. He likes it here.'

'Does he?' Adam seemed to shiver.

'He's a nice bloke,' Dave said. 'I took to him straight away.'

'Oh, I met him at the fete last year. Lovely manners,' Rita said. 'He's a solicitor, isn't he? I bet he makes a good living.'

'It might be nice to have him back in the village,' Linval agreed.

'A handsome young man,' Rita observed. 'I bet he turns the girls' heads.'

'He has a girlfriend in Tadderly.' Dave seemed keen to share his information. 'I told him there's not much for sale here. Houses go quickly.'

'I don't like flash cars,' Adam said beneath his breath.

'The girls love them.' Dangerous Dave raised an eyebrow. 'I bet Darryl has no problem impressing the ladies.'

'It's a shame he has a girlfriend. We could've introduced him to Malia,' Rita said thoughtfully. 'She might settle for a nice local man.'

'She could do worse than Darryl,' Dave agreed.

'Excuse me.' Adam pushed his chair back hard. 'I need to catch up with Bobby.' He reached for his pint of Hooky, only half drunk. 'I'll see you in a bit.'

Rita, Linval, and Dave exchanged looks as Adam made his way towards the bar, where Bobby Ledbury turned and began to share easy conversation.

Linval scratched his head. 'Adam was a bit quiet.'

'Ah, he's knackered, I guess. Waking up with Elsie most nights. It's hard for those poor kids.' Dave finished his pint. 'Shall I get more drinks?'

'Pint of Hooky.' Linval proffered his empty glass.

'A G & T, please. I've earned it this week.' Rita gave her sweetest smile. She watched Dave clamber up and shuffle to where Dickie was filling pint glasses from a pump. She lowered her voice. 'I do worry about Adam, Linval. You're right. He's not been himself at all. Do you think things might be better if he and Florence had a baby?'

'Another? I remember how hard it was with one, then the second one comes along and it's double trouble.' Linval made a face. 'But you're right, Rita. He's the same at work, hardly a word all day. I think he's got something on his mind.'

'I thought that too,' Rita said slowly. 'I'm worried.'

'Right. Leave it with me.' Linval gave a cough, signifying that he was in charge. 'I'll have a proper chat with him next week at work. You know, man to man. I'll sort it out.'

***

The following day, the early morning sun streamed through the window onto Josie's face. She opened her eyes and immediately missed Harry. He was smiling from his photograph by the bedside. She kissed her fingers and placed them on his lips. 'Good morning, handsome.'

His expression didn't change, the warmth in his eyes or the creases around his smile. Josie had a sudden feeling of being empty. That hollow sense that the best days were gone.

She felt lonely.

It occurred to her to go down to the graveyard but she'd only be talking to herself. The thought made her shiver. She wished Fergal were back home; she could go to his barge and he'd offer her a mug of scalding coffee and a grin, and some sensible words about loss and love. She missed him.

It was Sunday. Lin and Neil were going to Peterborough to see Debbie and Jon and the grandchildren. Minnie would be in Oxford, meeting some of her friends for a long lunch, discussing Oedipus or Euripides or – who had she been arguing was an early Roman feminist last time the subject came up? Livia Drusilla. Apparently, in 38 BCE, she'd divorced her first husband and married her lover, who later became the emperor Augustus. According to Minnie, she was an enormously powerful woman in the imperial Roman government.

As she dressed, Josie felt anything but enormously powerful. Sunday stretched in front of her like a yawn. Even Odile's café was closed. Josie decided she'd pop down to Cecily's, make her something nice for breakfast and see how she was feeling.

In the kitchen, the tap was dripping into the sink, wasting water. Josie had no idea how to fix it. The plumber's address was in the notebook in her desk drawer. She reminded herself to give him a ring soon. She filled a basket with goodies: eggs, cheese, ham, cream, butter, sourdough bread. Not that Cecily wouldn't have groceries in her house, but Josie wanted to make it a treat. She added a box of Earl Grey tea, a packet of Machu Picchu coffee. Cecily could choose. She hoped her wrist was less painful and the bruise on her hip was fading.

Josie stepped out into the sunlight and strolled along Charlbury Road. It was a ten-minute walk past Nobb's End and along the Tadderly Road to Cecily's bungalow. As she passed the village green, she glanced beyond the willow tree to the banks of the Cherwell. She could see Fergal's barge, desolate and abandoned.

A figure was approaching, a rolling, confident stroll, and Josie's pace slowed. She knew immediately who it was and she wasn't sure whether to keep walking or – and this was her preferred choice – to turn and run back to the safety of her house, to lock the door and hide. She steeled herself, told herself that she was being stupid and that meeting the new occupant of the house in Nobb's End had been inevitable. She just didn't feel ready for it.

He was striding towards her, looking ahead. He hadn't recognised her; his face hadn't changed. Josie wondered if they'd walk straight past each other without a word, if he wouldn't know it was her. That would be a good thing. There had always been a spark between them. But the wildfire of eye contact that had defined their relationship in their late teens would have gone out. She wouldn't need to worry.

So why was her heart pounding like a drum?

He was level; she saw him glance her way, the quick appraising look of a man who knew his own mind. She was almost past him, then he said, 'Josie.'

She paused and he turned to greet her. 'Josie Potter.' He smiled and she could see the warmth in his face. 'I'd know those eyes anywhere.'

'Hello, Mike.' Josie didn't know what else to say.

'I was hoping I'd run into you.'

'You're back?'

'I am.'

'And living in Nobb's End?'

'Yes.' There was a pause. Mike said, 'It's just me now.'

'Oh?' Josie looked him over. His hair was thick, but shorter now. His beard was neatly clipped; he had put on a little weight but he was handsome in a dark jacket and jeans.

'My wife and I split up. Caroline had an affair.'

'I'm sorry.' Josie felt it was the right thing to say.

'And are you married?' Mike glanced at the wedding ring on her finger. Josie thought he wasn't wasting time finding out about her.

'I'm a widow. Harry died.' Josie forced herself to brighten. 'Well, it's nice that you've moved back, Mike. I expect you're settling into village life.'

'Oh, I am. Gerald Harris and his partner invited me round.' Mike's smile was charming. 'I've wanted to move back for a while. I was in the RAF.'

'I remember,' Josie said, recalling how he'd left her in tears, how he wrote a few times, then he didn't. He had broken her heart for a while. A year later, she'd met Harry and realised what love really was.

'I saw a lot of action as a pilot. It was tough at times.' Mike met her eyes. 'I flew a desk for a while, and after that, I retired – I travelled a bit, went away.' He gave her his most charming smile. 'I think I made the right decision, coming back.'

'Well, I hope it works out.' Josie shifted position, lifting her basket of food to signify that she was about to leave.

'Are you off anywhere nice?'

'I'm going to see Cecily; she's just down the road.' Josie felt awkward about communicating her plans. She wasn't sure why.

'Miss Hamilton. She was my favourite teacher.' Mike grinned, as if memories were flooding back. 'She's a ripe old age now.'

'She's nearly ninety-two, but she keeps herself fit.' Josie felt defensive. 'I'd better get on. It's nice seeing you, Mike.'

'It's good seeing you too,' Mike said, as if he meant it. He watched Josie walk away and called after her, 'Give my love to Miss Hamilton.'

'I will,' Josie said without looking back.

'I'll bump into you again.' Mike's voice carried a certainty: he intended to see her again. Josie hoped he didn't know where she lived. But it wouldn't be hard for him to find out.

She hurried along Tadderly Road, her head full of memories: Mike standing by his motorbike, wearing a leather jacket, his easy grin, his contagious confidence. She'd loved him for a while. It had lasted three years. He had been her first serious relationship. Her first heartbreak.

Josie didn't intend it, but as the special moments came flooding back, she felt every emotion again, as if it were happening now. How she'd clung to him when they took bends too fast on the Bonneville. The time he told her that she was the most beautiful girl he knew, that they'd be together forever. His kisses had been passionate, soft as butterfly wings. She was being silly, a foolish teenager again. Josie told herself firmly that it was all in the past.

She was a widow now. Harry's widow.

She reached Cecily's house and rang the bell. Her heart was still pounding furiously; Mike Bailey was stuck stubbornly in her thoughts.

There was no sound from inside. Josie hoped Cecily was all right. Or that she wasn't still in bed and Josie had woken her up. The door opened and Cecily appeared, a brave smile on her face. 'Josie, lovely to see you.'

'I brought breakfast. I hope you haven't eaten.'

'I haven't.' Cecily examined Josie's face. 'Whatever is the matter? You look like you've seen a ghost.'

'Perhaps I have.' Josie breathed out slowly to calm herself. 'I just bumped into Mike Bailey. He and I were...' She glanced over her shoulder as if he might be behind her. 'Can I come in, Cecily? I need a cup of tea and a chat.'

17

Florence hadn't slept well. She'd been up twice in the night to feed Elsie and change her nappy. Adam had been snoring beside her; he'd had several pints of Hooky in The Sun, and Elsie's cries hadn't disturbed him. At three in the morning, Florence crawled back into bed, snuggling against Adam's warm body, and her thoughts were filled with Malia's new job, her stylish looks and confidence, Natalie's passion for horses.

And there was that letter.

Her mother, after so long away, wanted to embrace being a grandmother. Florence felt the injustice of it all, her throat swollen with unspoken words of anger. Her mother didn't want the hard work. Florence imagined she would turn up at the door with a cuddly toy and a smile, fuss over Elsie and disappear. After one visit, Florence wouldn't see her again.

And her father would be heartbroken for a second time.

She tried to see things from her mother's point of view. Perhaps she regretted missing out on Florence's teen years. Perhaps she'd changed, was ready to make amends. Perhaps she might have so much love left over for Florence and Elsie now.

Florence rolled over and thought about leopards and spots: her mother would never change. Her mind was spinning. The cycle of thoughts started again, like a washing machine, the drum rolling round, crashing.

She fell asleep as dawn broke.

When she opened her eyes and reached for her phone it was past nine. The space Adam filled in the bed next to her was empty; his clothes were gone. She could smell cooking: toast, the aroma of coffee. She struggled into her dressing gown, gave her hair a brush and wandered downstairs.

In the living room, Adam was playing with Elsie, lifting her high, enjoying her squeals of delight. Florence watched him. He hadn't noticed her yet. His face was filled with love as Elsie's laughter bubbled. Dangerous Dave was sitting on the sofa clutching a mug that read 'Best Grandad', smiling.

Adam hugged Elsie against him. 'Morning, sleepy. I thought I'd leave you to rest.'

'Thanks.' Florence closed her eyes. 'I was shattered.'

'I made you breakfast,' Adam said, his expression mischievous and rueful at the same time. 'Dave and I have already eaten. We needed food after all the Hooky last night.'

'Give Elsie to me.' Dave reached out for the baby. 'You get breakfast.' He held Elsie against him, tickling her. 'Who's my little princess?'

Florence rolled her eyes, filled with affection for her father, and held out her hand. Adam took it and they walked into the kitchen. He began to pour coffee from the stove. 'I've got beans and mushrooms and I'll make more toast. I did spinach too – it's good for you.'

'Thanks, Adam.' Florence felt the warm rush of love. 'Did you have a nice time last night?'

'I met up with Bobby.' Adam's eyes sparkled. 'We talked

about Hayley's kids and we got onto cars and motorbikes. It was good to chat. Bobby's looking for extra work to make ends meet. He's selling his bike and getting an estate car for the family.' He was quiet for a moment. 'Do you think I should trade our car in?'

Florence shook her head. 'No. We're fine. Elsie's seat fits in the back no trouble.'

'You wouldn't like a flashier car?' Adam handed her a mug of coffee and turned his back, busying himself with heating food.

'I'm happy with what we have.' Florence didn't notice the relief on Adam's face. 'Flash cars are more Malia's style.'

Adam asked, 'Did you have a nice time?'

'It was lovely.' Florence felt hungry. 'Our lives are poles apart. But I don't think that matters, we're good friends.' She sat down at the small table as Adam passed her a plate. She noticed he'd sprinkled a bit of spice on top of the spinach. Nutmeg. 'This is nice.'

Adam's brown eyes were filled with love. 'I want to show how much I care.'

'You're special,' she whispered. As she sliced toast, she paused. 'Adam, I've got something to tell you.'

Adam's expression changed to one of anxiety. 'Oh?'

'I'm sorry. I said I'd wait, but I opened the letter.'

Adam looked hurt. 'From your mum?'

Florence nodded, fork in the air. 'I wish I hadn't. I wish I'd opened it with you.' Her lower lip quivered. 'I've let you down.'

Adam met her eyes. 'Are you all right?'

'No. I wish you'd been with me. She wants to see Elsie.'

'How do you feel about that?' Adam frowned.

'Not happy.' Florence chewed thoughtfully. 'I can imagine her coming here, being all over Elsie, taking loads of photos, then never coming back.' She reached for her coffee. 'Maybe

I'm being unfair. Maybe I should give her a chance. I don't know.'

Adam sat opposite, taking her hand. 'What does your instinct say?'

'It says stay as far away from her as possible.' Florence gave a short laugh. 'Even when she lived with us, she let me down. She was never dependable. It was always Dad who picked me up from school, took me to play netball, made my tea, washed my clothes.'

'Where was your mum all that time?'

'Bingo, with friends, shopping. But what if she's changed for the better?'

'You won't know unless you invite her round.'

Florence lowered her voice. 'But what about Dad? He'd be heartbroken if she let him down again. What if she comes here with a new bloke? That would hurt him even more.'

'And it's not fair on Elsie, to offer a relationship that your mother can't keep up. I don't want her upset. Or you.' Adam folded his arms.

Florence smiled. He was very protective, and she was glad of it. She stuck her fork into a mushroom. 'I don't know what to do. I'd love to see her, in one way, Adam. She's my mum. But I don't want to risk it going wrong. Do you think I should just throw the letter away?'

'Did she leave an address? Where does she live?'

'In Blisworth, outside Northampton.'

'I could drive you there. We could talk it over with her first, just me and you.'

'We could.' Florence hesitated. 'I don't know how I'd feel though.'

'About me being there?'

'About meeting her after so long. The last time I saw her

she was ironing her clothes in the living room and I asked her if she'd iron my school blouse. I remember exactly what she said to me. She said, "Do it yourself, Florence, or wear it creased." That was the last time we spoke.' Florence took a deep breath, feeling unwanted all over again. 'She was ironing her stuff so that she could pack a case and clear off with her new bloke.'

Adam was unconvinced. 'And you want this woman to meet Elsie?'

'She said it was her right.'

'I'm not sure it is, after how she behaved.'

'Nor am I.' Florence picked up her coffee. 'But thanks, Adam. I should have waited to read the letter with you. I'm sorry.'

'It doesn't matter,' Adam said.

'We'll decide together what's best.' Florence looked miserable. 'She broke Dad's heart. If she comes back here, she'll hurt him all over again—'

Dangerous Dave was in the doorway holding Elsie, who was reaching out her arms and grunting. He passed her to Florence. 'She wants her mummy.' He frowned, looking from Adam to Florence. 'What did I just hear you saying?' His face was filled with emotion. 'Who's going to get hurt all over again?'

'Oh, it's nothing, Dad. Just something I saw on TV.' Florence took a breath. She glanced at Adam and he nodded once. He understood. She hated lying to her father but she'd tell him another time, when she'd decided what to do.

* * *

It was almost midday as Josie stood at Cecily's front door and hugged her gently, taking care not to touch her bandaged wrist.

Cecily's eyes were filled with gratitude. 'Thank you so much for breakfast. And for spending time with me.'

'Are you sure you'll be all right?' Josie asked.

'The nurse is popping in this afternoon. The wrist's not broken.' Cecily met Josie's eyes meaningfully. 'It's you I'm worried about.'

'No need. I've seen sense, thanks to you,' Josie said. 'You're right. I won't give Mike Bailey another thought.'

'Unless you want to,' Cecily said.

'No, he and I are history. It's years ago. We're different people. And as you said, our paths are bound to cross, living in the same village, but that doesn't mean anything.' Josie was protesting far too much, in Cecily's opinion.

Cecily said, 'I know you can take care of yourself.'

'I can,' Josie agreed emphatically. 'Thanks so much for listening. I was wittering on like a schoolgirl.'

'He was handsome, as I remember.' Cecily's eyes twinkled.

'He still is—' Josie stopped herself. 'It was all a long time ago.'

'That's just years passing.' Cecily shook her head in disagreement. 'We can still be lonely and vulnerable. And being alone plays on your mind sometimes. You look back at the past and think, what if? You look to the future and think, I wonder if I should?'

Josie wasn't sure if Cecily was talking about herself. She turned to go. 'We don't need a partner. We're fine as we are.' She heard the hollow echo of her own words. 'Mike always made me smile though.'

'That's so important. I remember Eddie used to have a lovely sense of humour.'

'And Harry too. He used to whistle "Don't Worry, Be Happy" to annoy me and then he'd laugh.'

'Memories to treasure,' Cecily said.

'It's Minnie's picnic next Sunday. Do you think I should invite Florence?'

'You could. Would she bring Elsie?'

'She might leave her with Adam. Perhaps some time alone with the Silver Ladies would do her good. Oh.' Josie remembered. 'I've offered to babysit at some point. The thought fills me with horror. I'll have to get you to come with me, and Lin too. I'm terrified of babies.'

'You'll be fine.'

Josie paused. 'I'm terrified of everything at the moment. What if I bump into Mike Bailey on the way home?'

'You smile at him, you say, "Hello again, Mike" and you stroll on.' Cecily patted her arm mischievously. 'Or you invite him round for a coffee and a chat about old times.'

'Oh, I couldn't do that,' Josie said too quickly. As she turned to leave, a small cream-coloured car came to a halt by the kerb and a nurse clambered out. She was young, fair-haired, in a blue uniform, carrying a bag. As she approached, Cecily smiled and held out her good hand to shake. The nurse's lanyard carried her photo and the name Sophie Lamb.

'Thank you for coming. You're early.'

'I skipped lunch.' Sophie grinned. 'I'm out for dinner tonight. My boyfriend's taking me to a little pub at Chipping Norton. I'll be hungry by then.' She turned to Josie. 'Have you been visiting Cecily? I hope she's been taking it easy?'

'Josie cooked me breakfast,' Cecily said.

'I'm off home now. Nice to meet you,' Josie called. 'See you tomorrow, Cecily.'

Cecily waved to Josie and ushered the nurse inside. They went into the living room and Cecily sat down on the sofa. Sophie Lamb settled herself beside her.

'How are you feeling, Cecily?'

'I'm fine. I feel like a fraud, having so much attention when I don't need it.'

'You had a nasty fall,' Sophie reminded her. 'Can I take a look at that wrist?'

Cecily stuck out an arm and Sophie began to unwrap the bandage. She scrutinised Cecily's face. 'Does the bruise on your hip hurt much?'

'No,' Cecily lied, looking directly into the nurse's crystal-blue eyes. 'I've been plastering arnica on it.'

'Good,' Sophie said. 'Well, make sure you get plenty of rest. We'll keep this bandaged for a while.'

'How many more days will you need to visit?' Cecily asked. 'It's very kind of you, but I know how valuable your time is.'

'It's my pleasure,' Sophie said and Cecily thought what a sweet girl she was. 'I love Middleton Ferris. I'd love to live here.'

'Oh?' Cecily said. 'A house has just sold down the road.'

'I believe properties are snapped up in no time.' Sophie looked wistful. 'My boyfriend and I want to buy soon. He works in Charlbury and I'm based in Tadderly. It would be right in the middle for us. And it's such a nice village.'

'It's a lovely community,' Cecily agreed.

'I know we'd be happy here,' Sophie said. 'I'd love us to settle down and start a family.'

'It's a good place for children,' Cecily agreed. 'Back in the day, I used to teach at the primary school.'

'Did you?'

'Indeed. The woman you saw leave was one of my ex-pupils, Josie.' Cecily smiled. 'Yes, I love it here.'

'You're all done,' Sophie said, looking at the neat bandage. 'Can I make you a cup of tea?'

'That would be nice.'

'I'll have to rush off. I have a gentleman to see in Charlbury at two.'

'Oh?'

'But I'll be back tomorrow, same time.'

'Then you must stay for lunch,' Cecily offered kindly. 'I can't have you skipping meals.'

'That's so kind.' Sophie smiled. 'We can make it together and you can tell me all about your time as a teacher.'

'Perfect,' Cecily agreed. 'And you can tell me all about being a nurse and your plans for the future, you and your wonderful boyfriend.'

'I'll look forward to that,' Sophie said, picking up her bag. 'See you tomorrow.'

'See you then.' Cecily walked to the door with her and watched her clamber into the car. 'What a lovely young woman.'

18

On Monday morning, Minnie was sitting in the garden in a reclining chair, reading a book about Hypatia of Alexandria, a philosopher, astronomer and mathematician who was stoned to death after being accused of witchcraft. She was so immersed in her book that she didn't hear Tina wander in and say, 'I fancy a cup of tea.'

Minnie looked up. 'What was that?'

'Tea,' Tina said again. 'I'm thirsty. Then I'm going out for lunch.'

Minnie looked Tina up and down. She was wearing old denim overalls, wellingtons and a thin vest. 'Dressed like that?'

'It's a barbecue,' Tina replied quickly.

Minnie pressed her lips together. 'Let's have that cup of tea.'

'I've only got ten minutes.' Tina sounded alarmed.

'It won't take more than that.' Minnie put her book down emphatically and stood up, sweeping to the kitchen in her long dress and Doc Martens. 'What tea will you have?'

'What sort have we got?' Tina sounded sulky.

'The sort of tea that comes with sympathy,' Minnie replied

smartly. 'Because you're going to tell me what's going on and I'll be all ears. How about some rooibos?'

'Whatever.'

'Sit down,' Minnie said loftily. 'I'll make it, and while I do, have a good think about what you want to tell me.'

Tina scraped a chair. 'I don't know what you're talking about.'

'I don't think you're going to the gym every day. I think you're doing something else that you don't want me to know about, washing muddy clothes when there's no mud in the Botanic Garden and disappearing furtively all the time.'

Tina huffed. 'Are you accusing me?'

'No, I'm not.' Minnie placed a teapot and two china cups on the table. 'But I did see you punting down the river with some other people having the time of your lives.' She met Tina's eyes. 'Were you drinking champagne?'

Tina's eyes widened: she'd been caught out. 'Lemonade. I'm in recovery, remember. But it's none of your business what I do.'

'I hate to sound like Dad, but you're under my roof.' Minnie took a deep breath. 'And while I'm delighted you have new friends – and I am, Tina – I'd appreciate a degree of honesty. You've been pretending your outings are all related to your stroke recovery, and I don't know why.'

'They are,' Tina said. 'In a manner of speaking.'

'What manner of speaking?'

Tina paused. 'I don't want to say.'

'Tina.' Minnie placed her fists on the table. 'Please don't lie to me. It isn't fair. You're my sister, you're living in my house, and you don't trust me, which hurts if I'm honest. Is it a man?'

'Is what a man?'

'Are you in love?' Minnie was prepared to spell it out. 'Do

you have someone you want to keep a secret because you're feeling all fizzy and romantic?'

Tina was shocked. 'I've never been fizzy and romantic in my life.'

'Then what is it?'

Tina breathed heavily, looking nervous. 'I've met a man, yes, but—'

'He's married?'

'No.' It was Tina's turn to bang the table. 'He's a friend. He's got a house in Botley. It's only fifteen minutes away. It's a lovely place with a big garden.'

'And you want to buy it?' Minnie finished her sentence impatiently.

'No.' Tina took a breath, equally exasperated. 'I'm helping him, growing vegetables, sorting out a greenhouse.'

'Why on earth is it a big secret?' Minnie's voice was getting louder. She was feeling frustrated. Tina wasn't making this conversation any easier. 'It makes no sense.'

'Because I want to make it work. But I'm frightened of – of failing...' Tina's voice trailed off.

Minnie softened. She reached out a hand and covered her sister's. 'How can you fail?'

'It's harder now than it used to be, digging gardens, planting. I want to get my strength back but I'm not as robust as I was.'

'You're doing brilliantly.'

'I want to give myself until August. I promised Gary I'd help him.'

'Gary?'

Tina reached for her tea. 'He's a recovering stroke patient too. And a divorcee. We've got a lot in common. We met at the clinic and hit it off. He invited me round to his house and I met his friends, Sue and Mark. We all get on really well. It's not a romance though. Gary and I are friends.'

'Tina, it doesn't matter if it is a romance. Your life's your own. And I want to support you.'

Tina's expression betrayed her distrust. 'You want to get your house back so that you can move Jensen in. I know you, Minnie. I heard you talking to him on the Zoom calls.'

'I promised I'd support you,' Minnie said slowly. It was all making sense now. 'But you seem so much better. The doctor said you'd almost made a full recovery – you told me that. I just want you to be honest with me. You can stay as long as you need to, but I saw you punting down the Thames, right as rain.'

Tina looked anxious. 'Do you want me to go?'

'No. I want you to tell me what you need.'

'I'm as good as I'm going to get. I'm doing my best, but I'm often tired, Minnie.' Tina rubbed a hand over her face. 'Gary and I have planted his garden, but it's not like it would've been before we had strokes. It's frustrating. But guess what? We've got potatoes, kale, cabbages and beans coming up. There are courgettes and tomatoes in the greenhouse.'

'That's brilliant,' Minnie said encouragingly.

'I love being back in the garden, making things grow. But the other day I fell over because my body wouldn't do what I wanted it to. That's why I had to wash my clothes and have a shower. Gary and I aren't 100 per cent, and we never will be. I wanted to hang on a bit here, to see how things developed with him.'

'Is that why you didn't tell me?'

Tina nodded. 'I know you want me to go back home. But I don't want to. I thought you'd try and make me.'

'I can't make you go anywhere.'

'I want to stay here,' Tina said.

'With me or with Gary?' Minnie asked carefully.

'I don't know yet. It's early days.' Tina met Minnie's eyes. 'We aren't having a relationship. I don't know if either of us want one. But we get on, really well. And he might ask me to move in. It's a three-bedroomed house, and it's too big for him. We'd be fine there.'

'Do you need to talk to him about it?'

'I thought I'd wait until August. The veggies will be a success. And then I'll ask him straight. I've planned out what I'll say. "Shall we plant some winter stuff, Brussels sprouts, cabbages, kale, leeks and parsnips? And shall I move in?"'

'Is that what you want?' Minnie asked.

'I loved my old allotment,' Tina said. 'And now Gary's garden takes two of us to dig and plant, but, Minnie, feeling the soil beneath my fingers and watching seeds burst through gives me a reason to go on. Does that make sense?'

'It does.' Minnie finished the rooibos. 'I wish you'd told me all this earlier.'

'Well, you know now.' Tina sniffed.

'Are you going to Gary's house today?'

'I am. For lunch. We're doing some weeding. He's got a car. His GP has passed him fit to drive. He picks me up at the corner of the street.'

'Why doesn't he come to the door?' Minnie wanted to know.

'And meet you? You'd frighten him to death.'

'Tina,' Minnie said, 'I'm sorry if I'm unapproachable.'

'You're the one with the education, the one who got away.' Tina sniffed. 'I'm just thick Tina who got stuck in the mud.'

'Mud can make things grow: spinach, asparagus, celery.' Minnie offered an affectionate smile. 'Just see how things go with Gary. See what happens by August. Your veggies will burst forth, and your confidence with it. And your friendship.'

'Give me some time, Minnie.'

'You've got it.'

'Are you sure?'

'Of course.'

'And what about Jensen?'

'What about him?'

'He wants to move in, doesn't he?'

'He does. And I want him to. But we can decide about that in August,' Minnie said kindly. 'Remember, we're flesh and blood.'

'But sometimes I think that's all we are,' Tina said sadly. 'No, I'm grateful. Thanks, Minnie.' She stood up. 'I'd better go. Gary will be waiting on Chilwell Road.'

'There are two conditions.' Minnie raised a finger. 'One. Sisters don't lie to each other.'

'I thought you wouldn't understand.'

'I do understand, Tina. But we have to talk to each other honestly. I'll do my best to help you and Gary, but you have to be straight with me.'

'I promise.' Tina looked truly relieved. 'I misjudged how nice you are, Minnie. I'm sorry. It's hard being the rubbish sister.'

'You're not. Enjoy your afternoon. Have a good time.'

'And what was the other thing? You said two conditions.'

'Oh, yes. Invite Gary in for a cuppa.'

'I will. I bet he'll be scared stiff of you though. Everybody is.' Tina rushed into Minnie's arms and planted a kiss on her cheek. Minnie looked shocked. Tina hadn't done that since they were children. 'I'll see you later.'

'Oh, and, Tina, if you have any tomatoes...'

'Yes?'

'I could do with a few for next Sunday. Cecily and the Silver Ladies are coming over for a picnic.'

'Oh, right.' Tina had reached the door.

'You'd be welcome to join us,' Minnie called, but Tina was on her way through the hall. The front door banged.

Minnie stared into her empty cup. But at least she'd got to the bottom of Tina's behaviour. She filled the kettle again and reached for the tea caddy. She decided to talk to Jensen later in a Zoom call and explain how the land lay. He'd be pleased to know that they'd be together in August.

But for now, the garden was basking in sunshine and a book about Hypatia of Alexandria was waiting.

* * *

Cecily wasn't sure what Sophie ate for lunch, but she was a nurse and Cecily assumed she'd eat healthily. She laid the table with a variety of foods that she'd bought in and were easy to prepare, and then Sophie could help herself. There was a potato salad, lettuce, tomatoes, chicken, olives, wholemeal bread. Two bottles of elderflower pressé and two glasses, plates, cutlery, napkins – everything was well presented. Cecily wanted to do things properly, to say thank you. And she'd laid it all out with care, using just her right hand. She was pleased with her work.

Cecily peered through the window and saw the little cream-coloured car slowing down. Sophie clambered out with her bag, scurrying towards the house. Above, the skies had clouded. It looked as if it might rain.

Cecily let Sophie in and ushered her into the kitchen. She said, 'Shall we eat first and you can bandage my wrist later?'

'The food looks lovely,' Sophie said. Cecily noticed she had tied her fair hair back today. She looked girlish, starry-eyed. 'Can I dig in?'

'Do.' Cecily watched as Sophie filled a plate for herself.

'Can I serve you, Cecily?'

'Please.' Cecily pointed to the spread of food. 'Not too much – my appetite isn't what it was.'

'I'm always starving. I'm on my feet all day,' Sophie said. 'Last night we went to The Chequers in Chipping Norton and we had rib-eye steak and triple-cooked chips.' Sophie's eyes shone. 'My boyfriend says I could eat for England.'

Sophie carried a tray with two plates and two glasses of elderflower into the living room and Cecily followed. 'You don't mind eating food from your lap?' Cecily asked. 'I love this room. I often eat from a tray on my knee.'

'Me too. Before I met my boyfriend, I'd sit in front of the TV every evening. But now we're always out. He's got a good job, but he spends money like water.' Sophie giggled. 'How are you feeling? I should've asked.'

'Lots better. The wrist is getting stronger.'

'I'll have a look at it afterwards.' Sophie was stuffing potato salad into her mouth. 'Mmm, this is lush.'

'I'm delighted.' Cecily beamed. She didn't feel hungry, but watching Sophie eat gave her a sense of satisfaction.

'Have you always been by yourself?' Sophie asked. 'I mean, were you ever married? Do you mind me asking?'

'Not at all.' Cecily felt happier to talk than to eat. In truth, just holding the plate on her knee made her wrist ache. 'I dedicated my life to teaching.'

'That's so sweet.'

'But I was engaged once, when I was in my twenties.'

'Oh?' Sophie asked. A thought occurred to her. 'Did he die in the war?'

'No.' Cecily smiled at her naivety. 'He married someone else.'

'Oh, no.' Sophie looked really shocked. 'That must've been so hard for you.'

'It was,' Cecily said. 'But I told him to do it.'

'Why would you do that?'

'He got my best friend pregnant.'

'That's sad.' Sophie paused, fork in the air. 'Was he a scumbag?'

'No, he was weak, once.'

'Did she seduce him, then?' Sophie's eyes were wide with interest.

'She did. But he made his own mind up that evening. She didn't hold a gun to his head. Then Joyce was pregnant. She'd always wanted him. So I moved away and started my life again. I wanted to teach. I didn't want another man.'

'Oh, I can understand that. I'd do the same.' Sophie was all sympathy. 'I'd hate it if my boyfriend did something like that to me. But I don't suppose that would happen nowadays.'

'Why not?' Cecily leaned forward. 'Some men are still scoundrels with no sense of right and wrong.'

'But there's the pill, contraception,' Sophie said. 'No one needs to get pregnant.'

'Mistakes will always happen. A young friend of mine...' Cecily closed her eyes for a moment, thinking of Florence. 'She's twenty-five. She had a baby last year because some snake pretended he loved her and straight afterwards he played his trump card.'

'Oh? What did he do?' Sophie asked, horrified.

'He was married,' Cecily said simply. 'He lied to her, had sex with the poor girl in his marital bed, then he treated her like a cheap tart and threw her out. Later, when she told him she was pregnant, he didn't want to know.'

'The scumbag. I hate men like that.' Sophie was appalled. 'What happened next?'

'She had the baby. She found a much better man to be the father.'

'And what about the bastard who left her in the lurch?' Sophie whispered. 'Did he get away with it?'

'Not quite. His wife found out and she threw him out. He had to sell the house in Nobb's End. She went back to London and he found a place in Tadderly.'

'Tadderly?' Sophie put her plate down. 'That's awful.' She turned her face towards Cecily, horrified. 'And the girl had a baby?'

'She did.'

'And the wife?' Sophie was shaking now. 'The one who left him. Was her name Charlotte, by any chance? Charlotte Featherstone?'

'It was. Do you know her?'

'No. I never met her. Cecily...' Sophie stood up slowly. 'Can I —? I mean, I have to go and I'll come back later – tomorrow – I'm so sorry.' She picked up her bag. 'Thanks so much for lunch. There's somewhere I have to go – an emergency – would it be all right if I called back another time?'

'Of course.' Cecily was confused. 'Have I said something wrong? Did I upset you?'

'Not at all. No. You've done me a favour.' Sophie laughed once, a bit wildly. Her eyes gleamed with tears. One rolled down her cheek and she wiped it with her sleeve. 'I'm so sorry. Please forgive me. I'll come back and do your wrist, or I'll ask someone else to come.' She was moving towards the door.

'Sophie?' Cecily frowned. 'Are you all right?'

'Yes. No.' Sophie's hand was on the door. 'Thanks for lunch. For everything. I'm so sorry. I'll – I have to go.'

The door was open and Sophie was running towards the car.

Cecily shook her head. She had no idea what had just happened. She paused to think everything through.

She had spoken about Florence and the baby, how she was treated so badly. Sophie had reacted at that point – she had known Charlotte Featherstone. Or at least she'd known her name.

The penny dropped with a clunk. Sophie's boyfriend. Of course – it was him.

Cecily picked up Sophie's plate in her good hand, wandered into the kitchen and tipped the uneaten food into the recycling bin.

'That's the best place for rubbish,' she said to herself, and went back to sit in her chair.

19

'It's a beautiful day. We're going to enjoy ourselves,' Lin said as she drove along the A4260 towards Oxford on Sunday morning, the radio playing. She was singing along occasionally, and joining in the chatter.

'I've brought sandwiches.' Cecily sat beside her in the passenger seat. Her wrist still ached from buttering bread, but it felt better now, and the bruise on her hip had faded. She was dressed in a floral frock and a wide-brimmed hat, feeling in the picnic mood.

'I brought cake,' Josie said. She and Florence were behind Cecily, wearing dresses and summer hats, staring through the window at trees and fields and passing cars.

Cecily said, 'Adam didn't mind having Elsie for the day, Florence?'

'His parents wanted her, but Adam's arranged to take her up to Bobby's at the farm. Bobby's little ones are so excited. They're going to show Elsie the pigs and the sheep and the cows. And Adam's organised a picnic in Old Scratch's Woods.'

'Adam's the perfect dad,' Cecily said happily. She'd say

nothing about the incident with Nurse Sophie at her house last week. It was best to keep shtum. 'He loves that little girl to bits.'

'He does.' Florence closed her eyes and let the sunlight warm her eyelids. It felt strange to be away from her baby, but there was a new sensation of freedom and independence. She felt like her old self. 'Dad's gone into the garage today.'

'On a Sunday?' Josie asked. 'I thought he'd be down The Sun.'

'Oh, he will be later,' Lin replied. 'Neil's gone with him. They've got an urgent repair job on. Neil wouldn't say much about it, but apparently the owner's very anxious to have the damage repaired.'

'Oh, was it a crash?' Florence asked.

'In a sense.' Lin peered into the driver's mirror for a moment. 'It seems somebody upset his girlfriend and she keyed the side of his car. Neil says Dave's being paid double for Sunday work, and he's done a deal so Neil gets paid too. It's an important job.'

'I'm sure it is,' Cecily said to herself. She imagined the Porsche with deep score marks down the side. Sophie had clearly made her point. For a moment, she was concerned for her. 'Did the owner report it to the police?'

'I don't think so,' Lin said. 'Neil told me the man just wanted the car fixed and to put the incident behind him.'

'Local man?' Josie asked.

'No idea. Neil didn't say much. He's more concerned about Dickie Senior. Apparently, the doctor came out yesterday. Dickie wants to stay at home, at the pub, until – you know – the end, but he's very weak now.'

'Poor Dickie,' Cecily muttered. 'He was a nice boy.'

'It's tough for his wife too. Gail's been unwell for ages,' Josie added.

'It feels strange. Neil was saying.' Lin overtook a slow van.

'We all grew up together, we were all in the same class. It's come to that point in life, I suppose.'

'What point?' Florence asked.

'Where you start losing your friends.' Lin was melancholy. 'They go, one by one. Neil's quite upset.'

'Harry was the first and I didn't see it coming. Nor did he,' Josie said.

'Oh, Josie, I'm so sorry. I didn't mean—' Lin began.

'No, you're right. We're at that time when we start to think about what might be round the corner.' Josie's thoughts filled with Harry, how he'd seemed in good health.

'Nonsense,' Cecily boomed and everyone in the car sat up straight, as they did in primary school. 'We can't spend our lives fretting. Let's enjoy the bright sunshine, a glorious picnic by the river.' Her eyes glinted. She was determined to raise everyone's spirits. 'I feel sorry for Dickie, of course. He was a much-misunderstood little boy. But as for us, nothing will hold us back today. We're in our prime!'

'We are,' Lin giggled. 'Young at heart.'

'And I'm full of energy,' Florence stifled a yawn, remembering how she'd got up twice with Elsie in the early hours.

'Look at us, off to do nothing but laze by the river nibbling egg and cress sandwiches and necking Prosecco,' Lin hooted.

'We deserve it,' Josie said.

'Of course we do.' Cecily smiled. 'A bit of what you fancy does you good.'

'We're independent women of leisure now,' Lin added.

'Free and feeling fabulous,' Florence chimed in.

'Bold, headstrong and irresistible,' Cecily chuckled.

'I don't know about irresistible,' Josie said warily. 'Not at our age.'

'Oh, I do,' Cecily insisted. 'A woman's beauty isn't defined by her years.'

'Or her situation,' Florence said. 'I feel so frumpy now I'm a new mum.'

'Wait until you're older.' Lin laughed. 'In restaurants, the waiters always talk to Neil, ask him to taste the wine, give him the bill. Never me.'

'We demand change,' Cecily said. 'We shine like stars and we insist on being noticed for our brilliance.'

'Definitely,' Florence agreed. 'We do our best. We can't help it if we're not perfect.'

Lin disagreed. 'We're nearly perfect. Our men adore us. That makes us adorable.'

'Neil adores you, Lin,' Josie said.

'He does,' Lin said fondly. 'And Adam adores you, Florence.'

'Adam's special.' Florence smiled shyly. 'He's the best.'

'Aww,' Lin said. 'Young love.'

'Love might be blossoming elsewhere too,' Cecily teased. 'Apparently, Mike Bailey's still carrying a torch for Josie.'

'What does carrying a torch mean?' Florence wanted to know.

'It means he stopped to talk to me in the street once,' Josie said impatiently. 'He and I were friends when we were teenagers.'

'Friends?' Lin scoffed. 'You were the most loved-up couple in the village. Then you met Harry,' she added tactfully. 'He was the real thing.'

'He was.' Josie sounded a little piqued. 'I'm not interested in Mike.' She changed the subject. 'You're still desirable, Cecily. Eddie sent you his address.'

'Who's Eddie?' Florence leaned forward. 'Do you have an admirer, Cecily?'

'Eddie was my fiancé in the nineteen fifties. *Was* being the operative word,' she said firmly. 'We didn't marry. We lost touch seventy years ago.'

'But where does he live?' Florence asked.

'On the other side of Oxford,' Cecily said quickly. 'There's no point in seeing him now.'

'Why not?' Florence persisted. 'It might be nice after such a long time.'

'Too much water under the bridge. Best not to disturb sleeping dogs,' Cecily explained.

'It's not like you to speak in clichés.' Josie laughed. 'Is there something you're not telling us, Cecily?'

'Yes.' Lin's eyes shone. 'Perhaps love is in the air. Oh, wouldn't that be marvellous?'

Cecily coughed sharply and reached into her handbag. 'Would anyone like a Mint Imperial?' She offered the bag towards the back seat. 'I always find that too much chatter makes the mouth dry.'

* * *

Minnie was already waiting in Christ Church Meadow when they arrived. She was sitting on a rug, a wicker basket in front of her, wearing a long dress, a bucket hat and yellow Doc Martens. She was reading a book with a picture of a golden mask on the front in the ancient Greek style. She looked up with a smile. 'Ah, here you all are.'

'It took me a while to park.' Lin set down a basket. 'I think we may have brought too much food.'

'You can never have too much of something wonderful.' Minnie glanced at Cecily. 'How are you feeling?'

'Never better,' Cecily said. She was already feeling a little tired.

'And how are you all?' Minnie met everyone's eyes. 'How's Elsie, Florence?'

'We're all good,' Florence said. 'Adam's taken her out today.'

'Where's Tina?' Josie asked.

'I thought she might come.' Cecily was disappointed.

'Long story. The short version is that she has a friend with a garden and she's doing her best to grow veggies again. Anyway —' Minnie took a deep breath '—let's share this delightful spread. Then I have a surprise for you all.'

'Oh?' Lin was intrigued. 'Is Jensen visiting this summer?'

'Not that kind of surprise.' Minnie closed the conversation down. 'One we can all share.'

'I can't wait.' Florence was staring at the open meadow, the heavy trees that swept their branches across the sky, the still river. 'This place is beautiful.'

'It is,' Minnie agreed. 'It's a perfectly tranquil place. I often come here to read and think. I'm going to book Tina and her new friend a tour with the head gardener, who gives a seasonal guided tour about planting. She'd love that. And did you know the fields are managed with ecology in mind – low intensity grazing, no chemicals or artificial fertilisers.'

'That's amazing. I must tell Natalie,' Florence said.

'George told me and Neil they're having difficulty making ends meet,' Lin remembered.

'It's a hard time for some farmers. I was reading in *The Observer*.' Minnie stopped herself. 'No, let's eat. Then, the surprise.'

'I can't wait for both.' Florence plonked herself down and proffered a bag. 'Odile gave me ginger cake and banana fritters. She says they are just as nice cold.'

Minnie began to unload the hamper, placing plates and glasses, laying quiches, salads, sandwiches, Scotch eggs, bottles of Prosecco and sparkling grape juice with a green tea infusion. 'There we are. Dig in. Bon appétit!'

'It's perfect.' Lin rubbed her hands. 'Neil made a lemon drizzle for us too.' She placed her basket on the picnic rug.

'Delightful.' Cecily accepted the glass Minnie was offering and held it up. 'May I propose a toast?'

'Please do.' Minnie grinned. The Silver Ladies held up their glasses solemnly.

Cecily took a deep breath. 'To health, happiness, friendship. May we keep a little of the fuel of youth to warm our body in our old age. May we all enter heaven late.'

'And may we always be desirable,' Lin added with a wink, digging Josie in the ribs.

The glasses met in a gentle clink, reflecting the sunlight, capturing the bubbling fizz in a shard of light. Life was good.

* * *

They had finished eating. Cecily dozed for ten minutes, Minnie glanced at her book and the picnic was packed away. Everyone stood up to stretch their muscles. Minnie said, 'So, now for the surprise.'

'Ice cream?' Florence asked.

'A museum visit?' Cecily suggested.

'A cappuccino?' Josie wondered.

Lin felt she had to suggest something. 'A stripper?'

Minnie grinned. 'We're going for a boat ride.'

Florence clapped her hands as an excited child might. 'On the river. Oh, brilliant!'

'I booked it.' Minnie was pleased with herself. 'Come on,

let's go down and pick up our punt.' She threaded an arm through Cecily's and they were on their way.

Lin was a little alarmed. 'Who's going to drive the boat?'

'It's all done with a punt pole,' Josie explained.

'I've never punted before. Is it difficult?' Florence asked.

'Not once you get the hang of it,' Minnie said. 'You push off the riverbed using your pole, then you allow it to drag behind the boat.'

'I'd get it wrong and fall in the water.' Lin laughed nervously.

'Me too.' Josie peered anxiously towards the water where punts glided by, people trailing fingers in the river, laughing, chatting. It looked idyllic but she hoped she wouldn't be asked to stand in the back of the boat and propel it along.

Minnie said soothingly, 'Don't worry, I hired a punter. In fact, there he is now.' Minnie waved. 'Hello, Hugo. Here we all are.'

A young man was standing in a long boat, fair hair over his eyes. He waved back. 'Hi, Minnie.'

'Hugo's a student; he's the grandson of Francine, a friend of mine. He works on the boats at the weekends. I'll make sure he has a good tip for his hard work.'

They were standing on the end of the bank. Hugo held out a hand. 'Minnie. Welcome aboard.'

Minnie straddled the space between the bank and the boat, allowing herself to be helped aboard. Lin followed, then Hugo and Florence assisted Cecily to clamber to safety. Finally, Josie and Florence took their seats and Hugo pushed off towards a group of boats in the middle of the river.

He said, 'It's not too busy on the Cherwell today. I'll take you past St Hilda's and Magdalen Bridge. Just sit back, relax and enjoy the view.'

'Oh, this is heaven,' Josie said. The water was dappled with sunshine, sparkles of light flashing on the surface. She dangled her hand in the icy river, enjoying the strange numbing sensation of the water between her fingers.

'I'd love to bring Neil here,' Lin agreed.

'And Adam. Elsie would love it.' Florence looked at the overhanging willow branches that spread their leaves like palms on the surface of the water. 'It's so romantic.'

'It is,' Minnie agreed. 'I brought Jensen to the river the first time we met, and we went punting. I knew he was special.'

Josie imagined being in a punt with Harry, just the two of them. A pang of regret settled somewhere beneath her heart. They had never been in a small boat together. Another image took its place, Josie lying in a punt, while Mike Bailey rowed along close to the bank. She could almost smell the meadowsweet and clover.

Minnie was remembering. She said, 'Of solace, that may bear me on serene, Till eve's last hush shall close the silent scene.'

'What is that? A poem?' Florence asked.

'"The River Cherwell" by William Lisle Bowles,' Minnie said, and continued, reciting.

> *'Cherwell! how pleased along thy willowed edge*
> *Erewhile I strayed, or when the morn began*
> *To tinge the distant turret's golden fan.'*

Cecily sighed. The river was working its magic. The sunlight was warming her face as the glass-smooth water buoyed her along in its embrace. She was starting to feel nostalgic. It would be nice to come back again, to take a ride in a boat for a whole afternoon, to listen to the twittering birds as they whirled skywards, the soft gurgle of the water swirling beneath the boat.

She wanted to watch the light fade as the evening cooled the earth. She imagined a walk through the bustling city as people began to move about for the evening, their bubbling chatter. Nightfall, the stars above. A restaurant, a cosy seat in a pub, a glass of wine.

She saw herself smiling, talking, leaning towards Eddie, his hand over hers. In her imagination, she was sharing everything with him once more.

Cecily couldn't help it. The idea of seeing him again filled her thoughts and made her heart flutter. It felt a little like love, something she hadn't experienced in so many years.

She found she couldn't push the feeling away.

20

Lin dropped everyone off in turn: Cecily first on Tadderly Road, then Josie and Florence, and finally she drove back towards Barn Park. Odile's café on the left was closed but, opposite, the doors of Dangerous Dave's garage were flung wide open. She slowed the car, peering in to see if Neil was still there; he'd clearly been too busy to answer her text telling him she'd be home by six.

There he was, in the gloom of the garage, in overalls, inspecting a silver car and talking to Dave and another man.

Lin stopped the car and clambered out, feeling her anger rising. A voice in her head told her to calm down, but she'd just spent time with Florence and her closest friends, and loyalty amongst women was important. Neil had been repairing Darryl Featherstone's car all day. Had he forgotten what that man did?

She marched up to Neil, where he and Dave were laughing at some joke. She almost stamped her foot. 'I thought you'd be home by now.'

Neil offered his mild smile. 'We've just packed up, love.' He stood back to admire the car. 'You can hardly see where the damage was.'

'We did a good job.' Dangerous Dave looked pleased. 'I couldn't have done it without Neil. He's a dab hand.'

Darryl Featherstone was wearing an expensive jacket, his hands in jeans pockets. He nodded. 'Well, thank you so much. It's all been very upsetting.'

'What happened?' Lin asked.

'His bunny-boiler girlfriend,' Dave laughed. 'She lost the plot.'

Lin stared at Darryl. 'What did you do to her?'

'I've no idea.' Darryl shrugged as if it wasn't important. 'I went home a few days ago and she'd come back early and packed all my things in bin bags. She screamed at me and lost control. She was hysterical. When I started to leave, she followed me and keyed my car.' He looked at Neil and Dave for approval. 'I don't understand women at all.'

'Clearly,' Lin said sarcastically.

'I'm staying at a friend's, sleeping on the couch.' Darryl made a martyr face. 'I need a place of my own. At least Sophie won't be coming with me when I get my new pad. Do you know of anywhere in the village I could move into?'

'No,' Neil said quickly, avoiding Lin's keen eyes.

'I'd say get a room at The Sun, but Dickie's sick and Dickie Junior has his hands full.' Dave scratched his head. 'Tina Gilchrist's place is empty though. It's near Jimmy's, on Harvest Way, just down the road.'

'Oh?' Darryl was interested. 'Does she want to sell?'

Dave turned to Lin. 'Lin, do you know? You spent the afternoon with Tina.'

'No, I didn't. I was with Minnie.' Lin folded her arms. 'I think Tina's coming back here soon.'

'She had a stroke,' Dave explained.

'Well, let me know if anywhere does come up. Here's my card with my mobile number.' Darryl flourished his wallet. 'And let me pay the bill. You've been very kind.' Darryl met Neil's eyes. 'Both of you.'

'Thank you.' Dave led the way to the office.

Neil called, 'I'll get off now, Dangerous. You can settle up with me later.'

'Right,' Dave yelled back, Darryl at his elbow.

Neil followed Lin to the Sharan. She hissed, 'What on earth are you doing, working on that man's car? You know what he did to Florence, Neil!' She was exasperated as she clambered in.

'I did Dangerous a favour,' Neil said, but his face showed that he was uncomfortable with the situation. 'We sorted out the paintwork on the Porsche and Dangerous kept telling me how sorry he felt for Darryl, what with his crazy girlfriend keying his car for no reason, and I couldn't say that he probably got what he deserved, because I know about Florence and he doesn't. It got worse. Darryl turned up—' He met Lin's eyes and she felt sorry for him. 'Dave was gushing about Elsie, how he had a lovely daughter and granddaughter, and he was showing Darryl pictures on his phone. It was awful. Dangerous hasn't a clue. And I could see something on Darryl's face I didn't like.'

'Oh?' Lin started the engine and shivered.

'He was looking at Elsie's pictures. He said, "The baby doesn't look much like her mother. Perhaps she's more like her father." And he had this look on his face, a bit mean. Then Dangerous said, "She looks just like me," and he laughed. I felt really bad. I couldn't say anything.'

'Oh, Neil.' Lin pressed his arm. 'That's awful. I know you've been sweet, helping Dave. He's not an expert with paintwork, like you are.'

'I just wanted to help out.' Neil looked miserable. 'I thought the extra money would come in useful. We could have a weekend away.'

'You're so sweet.' Lin took a deep breath. She was sorry she'd felt cross with Neil now. 'Dave has no idea how Darryl lied to Florence and treated her badly. Neil, Darryl's talking about moving here in the village. I thought for a minute Dave was going to offer him the spare room in his own house.'

'Do you think he would?' Neil looked horrified. 'It doesn't bear thinking about.'

'It doesn't,' Lin agreed. She paused outside their house in Barn Park. 'Come on, love. I have some leftovers from the picnic. Let's go in. I'm really worried. Having Darryl hanging around the village can't be a good thing.'

'It isn't,' Neil agreed. 'I'm sorry, Lindy.'

'It's not your fault.' She kissed his cheek. 'But we can't have that man coming back and upsetting Florence. He'll have to get past me first. And Josie and Minnie and Cecily.'

* * *

Dangerous Dave was whistling as he pushed the front door open, looking pleased with himself. Florence was in the kitchen with a meal ready: he could smell warmed bread and quiche, leftovers from the picnic.

Elsie was settled in her high chair, chewing a piece of banana. Adam was pouring sparkling water into beakers. Dave settled himself down. 'I'm hungry. It's been a long day, but it's been a nice one.'

'For all of us, Dad.' Florence continued to lay food on the table, and cutlery. 'Elsie's had a lovely day too.'

'Oh, yes?' Dave helped himself to salad and a hunk of quiche.

Adam grinned. 'We went up to the Ledburys' and petted the animals. Bobby and I took a picnic to Old Scratch's Woods. The kids came and Hayley, his partner. She's nice, Florence.'

'I've met her in the café a couple of times bringing the kids home after school. She seems lovely. Busy all the time, like me,' Florence said.

'Bobby said we should go up there for lunch. Little Alfie and Lily were great with Elsie.'

'That would be nice.' Florence took a bowl of chunked fruit over to Elsie and was encouraging her to try bits of pear, watermelon, strawberries. The baby very quickly decided the red ones were best. Florence half turned to Dave. 'What were you up to at the garage today, Dad?'

'That bloke brought his nice car in. His girlfriend had keyed the paintwork on one side. Neil helped me retouch it. He's a good bloke.'

'Neil?' Florence asked. Dave was about to reply when she said, 'Oh, Adam, can you get me some wipes, please?'

Adam was on his feet. Dave said, 'He paid me well. He wants to get a place of his own here. He likes Middleton Ferris. He used to live—'

Florence was distracted, wiping Elsie's mouth. 'Why did she scratch his car? The girlfriend?'

Dave chuckled. 'He said she was a bunny-boiler.'

'Perhaps he did something to upset her.' Adam sat down. 'Do you want a hand, Florence? Your food's getting cold.'

'In a minute,' Florence said. 'I wonder what went wrong. It must have been bad, for his girlfriend to do something like that. It's quite spiteful.'

'Your mother would do things like that.' Dave frowned. 'I remember I had a motorbike when you were a kid. It was a Ducati Monster. I was proud of that bike – I saved up for it. Elaine got a bit jealous. I was cleaning and polishing it and she said I thought more of that bike than I did of her. I must've laughed or something. She lost her temper and pushed it over, scratched the tank. It upset me, that did. That's why I felt sorry for D—'

'Dad.' Florence sat down and glanced at Adam. She took a deep breath. 'Talking of Mum, I probably ought to tell you.'

'Tell me what?'

'The other day, I was talking and you came in and I pretended to be talking about something on telly. I wasn't. It's Mum. She wrote me a letter.'

'A letter?' Dave froze. 'What does she say?'

'She's found out about Elsie.'

'How?' Colour was draining from his face.

'Social media,' Adam said. 'Florence put pictures up.'

'She wants to visit,' Florence said flatly.

'What did you tell her?' Dave asked. His hands were shaking. 'Can I see the letter?'

'Yes, it's upstairs. I'll get it in a bit. I haven't replied, Dad. I wanted to talk to you first.'

'She wants to come here? To see Elsie?' Dave hadn't moved. 'Do you think she'll want to stay? Did she say she's left the bloke who fixed the boiler?'

'No, just stuff about being a grandmother. Nothing much about me, or you.' Florence met his eyes. 'What do you think I should say?'

'After all this time.' Dave looked at his large hands. He'd lost his appetite. 'She could come to lunch. Or we could take her out to The Sun. Perhaps she'll stay for a weekend.'

Adam asked the question that was uppermost in Florence's mind. 'Do you want her back? I mean, do you still love her?'

'I never stopped.' Dave's voice was strangled in his throat. 'From the day I met her to the day she walked out, I always loved Elaine. I know she could be a bit volatile, but I liked that about her. It showed she cared. She was the passionate one. I was always so laid-back. She brought life into my world. And her smile lit up a room. Oh, she was a good-looking woman. Any man would tell you that.' He thought about his words.

'What do you want me to do, Dad? Shall I write back?'

'I think you should.' Dave picked up his tumbler and glugged water. 'If she wants to see Elsie, that's only right.'

'What about Florence's feelings? And yours?' Adam asked gently. 'What if she lets you down?'

'I know Elaine. I bet she wants to come back. She wants to start again.' Dave pressed a fist against his chest. Florence glanced at Adam and a look went between them; they both saw how vulnerable Dave was, how he'd suddenly set his heart on a reconciliation.

Florence said, 'What if she hurts you? What if she hurts me, and Elsie?'

'She'd never hurt you,' Dave said. 'She loves you.'

'She left me when I was a teenager.' Florence struggled to keep her voice calm. 'She left us both, Dad.'

'Do you want to think about it for a while, Dave?' Adam asked sensibly. 'Read the letter. Spend time mulling it over.'

'I won't sleep.' Dave rubbed his eyes.

'Let's talk later. I'll write back to Mum tomorrow. Or I won't, depending on what you say.' Florence frowned: she'd suddenly handed over control of Elsie's relationship with her grandmother to Dave. She wished she hadn't.

'Right.' Dave had forgotten about his food. He stood up

abruptly. 'I'm going for a shower. I want to have a look at some old photos. Adam, I have to show you some of Florence when she was Elsie's age. They are up in my room. Elaine and me, we were so happy in those days.'

Florence and Adam watched Dave wander out of the kitchen. They could hear his footsteps on the stairs. Florence said, 'That didn't go as planned.'

'Poor Dave.' Adam's face was sad. 'I didn't realise he was still in love with her.'

'He always has been,' Florence said softly, moving to Elsie, picking her up from the high chair.

'What do you think about it?' Adam asked.

'It's not going to go well, is it, Mum coming back here?' Florence held Elsie closely. 'I just have this feeling.'

21

Monday morning was the last day of June. By ten-thirty, the sun was scorchingly hot and Josie felt trapped inside the kitchen, watering plants, reading a magazine. She needed to be outside. She grabbed a jacket, her keys, and closed the door behind her.

Her walk took her down to the cemetery for her regular talk to Harry. It had become a habit, sharing her secrets with him. Josie wanted to tell him about the wonderful picnic she'd enjoyed with the Silver Ladies, the relaxing boat trip down the Cherwell. But there was a sour taste in her mouth today, the taste of disappointment. She wanted to share her life with Harry, not to talk to his gravestone about it.

It occurred to her that she was alone. He wasn't there when she spoke to him. He wasn't listening.

Josie asked herself as she walked towards the willow tree on the green what she truly believed. After Harry had died, she'd spent some time with Andrew Cooper, the vicar of St Peter and St Paul's. He'd been really kind; they'd spoken about God and Heaven and the possibility of her and Harry being reunited after death. It had given Josie some comfort. After that, she'd still felt Harry was close to her; it was as if he heard her thoughts. Everything she did was for them both, the fiftieth-wedding-anniversary cruise, keeping the garden tidy, dusting his photo. Visiting his grave.

But now as she crossed the village green, each blade of grass bright emerald in the sunlight, she wasn't sure. What if he'd gone? What if that was it, forever? She didn't know any more. She wished she could believe that he was close by. But today, she felt completely alone.

An aroma met her nostrils, beans cooking, bacon and eggs frying and coffee bubbling in a pan. She glanced over towards the Cherwell and saw Fergal Toomey's barge, smoke billowing.

'He's back!'

The words escaped her lips. She found herself changing direction, wandering towards the riverbank. A cup of blisteringly hot coffee with Fergal would cheer her up. Afterwards, they'd visit Harry and Ros together in the cemetery. The morning would be much better spent in his company.

The Toomeys' red and black barge was in its usual place by the riverbank. Josie's pace quickened; Fergal was there on board, his hands on his hips, wearing cut-off jeans and a thin T-shirt. A trilby hat was at a jaunty angle, his hair curling beneath it. He was the same age as Josie, still lean and well-muscled. He waved a hand. 'Josie. How are you?'

'Fine. Hello, Fergal.' Josie stood on the riverbank, shielding her eyes from the sun. 'How was Dublin?'

'It was grand. I had a lovely time, catching up with family. Finn and Dev are still there.'

'Oh?'

'They picked up some work. They like the place.'

'So what about you?' Josie asked. 'What have you been doing?'

Fergal made a mischievous face. 'I went to the Appleby Horse Fair and had a good time. I stayed on a while, met up with some old friends and drank too much.' His eyes twinkled. 'I got more than I bargained for.'

'Oh? Did you buy a horse?' Josie teased.

'Not a horse exactly.' Fergal looked unsure of himself for a moment, gave his usual grin and stretched his arms over his head. 'Ah, but it's good to be back home.'

Josie indicated the stove, where food was cooking. 'The smell's making my mouth water.'

'I expect you've had breakfast.'

'I have. The coffee smells good though.'

'I'll pour you a cup.' Fergal lifted the steaming pot. 'It's strong, mind, and hot.' He leaned out of the barge and handed Josie a red mug with a picture of a horse on it. She took a sip. It was scalding and had an intense flavour.

'I've missed this,' Josie said honestly.

'The coffee?'

'Just spending time.'

'What's been after happening in the village while I've been away?' Fergal asked, and Josie noticed his accent had become a bit more pronounced since his visit.

'Well.' She decided not to mention Mike Bailey's return. Fergal would almost certainly remember him. 'Cecily had a bit of a tumble. She sprained her wrist. She's all right now.'

'Cecily?' Fergal lifted his trilby to scratch his curls. 'I'll call round, see if she needs any jobs doing in the garden. How's Lin? And Minnie? And how's Tina doing?'

'They're all well.' Josie took a breath. 'I was on my way to the graveyard.'

'Talking to the dead?' Fergal said. 'I think my days of talking to Ros are behind me now, Josie.'

'Oh?' Josie clutched the coffee mug, interested. 'What made you decide that?'

'I love her dearly, but it's time to let go,' he said honestly. 'I've done my time talking into the air and pretending she's listening.'

'I've been wondering about that myself.' Josie was taken by surprise. 'Not that I want to let Harry go.'

'Ah, life's for the living. Being away gave me time to think and I thought deeply. I was in a kind of lonely limbo. But now I've decided to move on.'

'That's very brave,' Josie said.

'Oh, it is,' Fergal said. 'More than you can imagine.'

'Why?' Josie was puzzled.

'I have my barge, my boys are grown. I'm fit and healthy and I have two good arms. I need someone to fill them.' He arched an eyebrow. 'It's time for me to live again.'

'I see.' Josie didn't see. She wasn't sure if Fergal was propositioning her. It wouldn't be the first time, but in the past he'd been several whiskies the worse for wear. She decided to wait for his next move. She wasn't altogether sure what she felt about it. Holding out the mug, she said, 'Good coffee, Fergal. I missed it.'

'And I've missed you too, Josie. There's something I've been meaning to talk to you about.'

'Oh?'

'It's only right I tell you. While I was at Appleby, I met up with some old friends I know from Birmingham way, the Loveridge family, and we had a few drinks, shared the craic, and in the morning when I woke up, I found my life had changed forever.'

'How?' Josie wondered if he'd found Jesus. 'What happened?'

'I wasn't alone. I discovered that the night before I'd promised—' He paused.

'Fergal? Who are you talking to?' The growling voice of a she-devil came from below deck, and a woman stomped up the stairs and stood, hands on her hips, glaring at Josie. 'Who the bloody hell are you?'

Josie noticed the woman's strong arms, her knuckles balled into fists. She was a handsome woman, tall, wearing a pale vest with a glittery design, and tight blue jeans. Her feet were in Crocs. Her hair was dark with streaks of grey and she had large brown eyes. Josie assumed she must be in her sixties.

'Josie, this is Poll.' Fergal wrapped an arm round her. 'Poll Loveridge, from Bromsgrove. Poll Toomey now.'

'You're married?' Josie didn't mean to stare.

'We are.' Poll wrapped an arm around Fergal. 'I just came up on deck to get some snap, Fergal. That Joe Grey smells bostin'.'

'Have some hot coffee, darlin'.' Fergal handed Poll a mug. 'Poll, this is my friend Josie from the village. We went to school together.'

'Nice to meet you, I'm sure,' Poll said but her face didn't match her words. 'Where do you live, Josie? In one of those posh houses in the village, I'll bet.'

'Just round the corner.' Josie didn't know what to make of this straight-talking woman. 'I often have a chat with Fergal; we used to visit the cemetery together.' Josie paused. Poll looked less than happy.

'You're a widow, then?' Poll frowned. 'Well, Fergal's married to me now. He's not footloose and fancy free any more.'

'Josie's a good friend.' Fergal was doing his best to pacify. 'I hope you two can be friends, Poll. Josie's special.'

'Is she, now?' Poll put her mug down and folded her arms.

'Well, I want some scran, Fergal. And all this chit-chat ain't gettin' the babby a frock and pinny.'

'Poll's ready for breakfast,' Fergal explained, amused. 'She's got a hunger on her this morning. How about we all meet down The Sun at some point? I'll buy you a glass of wine.' He looked from Josie to Poll and grinned. 'I'm sure you'll both get on famously.'

'I'm sure we won't,' Poll grunted and turned her back. She bent over to find a plate and cutlery.

Fergal made a 'sorry' face, shrugging. 'I'll catch you soon, Josie. She's a terror before she's had breakfast.' He grinned. 'Nice to see you.'

'You too,' Josie said, turning away. She wandered back across the village green, thinking. So, Fergal had a new wife. Poll wasn't exactly friendly. Josie wondered if she was possessive or jealous, or perhaps it was because she was new to the village and she was simply finding her bearings.

Josie smiled. That was typical of Fergal, unpredictable, letting life meander by and embracing whatever turned up on his doorstep. And now he had a new wife to embrace. She hoped he'd be happy. But a thought scratched in her mind. She didn't want to lose him as a friend. She valued his warmth and his humour more than she could say.

Josie resolved to be extra friendly next time she met Poll. She turned towards Tadderly Road. Cecily would love a cup of tea and a chat. And Josie had plenty to tell her.

* * *

'I have so much to tell you, Jensen,' Minnie said as she leaned towards the laptop screen. 'We had such a nice time in Oxford. It was good to see the girls again.'

She was in the kitchen, busying herself making a fish pie for tea. She was folding fish and prawns, capers and lemon juice into the creamy sauce she'd made. She leaned towards the screen and smiled. Jensen smiled back. She could see only his top half. He was wearing a denim shirt.

'Tell me about you, Minnie. Tell me you're missing me.'

'I am. I thought about you when I was on the punt. It reminded me of our first date.'

'I'd like to go punting with you again. Or you could come here to New York. We could stroll in Central Park, have dinner in Chinatown, hang out in the Whitney Museum. There's a whole bunch of things I want to share with you.'

'We could.' Minnie began to dice potatoes.

'It'd be more fun than making fish pie for Tina's dinner.'

Minnie stopped chopping. 'I'm sorry, Jensen.' She took a breath. 'I had a chat with her. Tina's stopping a bit longer. She's found a project, growing summer veggies. But it's only for a few weeks. So we can meet up in late August.'

'Maybe.'

'What do you mean?' Minnie moved back to the screen.

'I told you already.' Jensen grinned brightly. 'I'm a guy in love. And you're a butterfly, hard to pin down.'

'I am not,' Minnie said firmly. 'I'm helping Tina get well. She's making progress, Jensen. She's on the home stretch. Just give me a few more weeks.'

'Right. Just a couple weeks, Minnie. Then I'm going to take matters into my own hands.' His eyes twinkled.

'What does that mean?' Minnie returned to the potatoes. She loved Jensen dearly but she wasn't going to be coerced.

'I won't jump off the Brooklyn Bridge, but I won't sit around waiting. I'm an impatient man.'

Minnie put the potatoes on to boil. 'I can't help that, Jensen.'

'Come back to the screen,' Jensen begged. 'I want to pretend I'm holding you in my arms, although you're 5,487.67 kilometres away.'

'That far?' Minnie moved back to the laptop and gazed at Jensen. His face shone with love. 'I promise we'll be together soon. Tina and I have agreed.'

'Tina has agreed what?' Tina called from the hall. She rushed into the kitchen in denim overalls, carrying a basket overflowing with fresh vegetables.

'I have to call time now, Jensen.' Minnie blew a kiss to the screen. 'We'll continue this in a day or two, I promise.'

'Don't make me wait too long, honey,' Jensen called back, then the screen was blank.

Tina stood in the kitchen, her wellingtons dirty, her face glowing. 'What do you think?' She handed the basket to Minnie, who inspected the contents with interest.

'Courgettes, tomatoes, spinach, kale, beans, carrots, lettuce, a cucumber. Did you grow these?'

'In Gary's garden. He says they are his best crop ever. We're doing so well. And they're all organic.'

'Look at this courgette: it's positively bursting with health.' Minnie was impressed. 'Right, I'll do us spiralised lemon courgette and a tomato salad to go with the fish pie. That's brilliant, Tina.'

Tina looked truly happy. 'And Gary was saying what a good team we are, how we work well together, and that his house is far too big for just one person.' She took a breath. 'I think we're close to discussing me moving in.'

'That's wonderful, for us all. Can I meet him first? I mean, I'm your sister.' Minnie smiled to cover her concern. She wanted to give Gary the once-over. 'You ought really to take those wellies off in the kitchen.'

'I will.' Tina began to heave off the mud-encrusted boots. 'And guess what? I had a phone call from Jimmy.'

'Jimmy Baker?'

'Yes. I think the call came at the right time. Serendipity – is that the word? Jimmy was talking to Dave Dawson who's got a customer at the garage who's looking to buy a place in Middleton Ferris. Jimmy says he's interested in my house and I told Jimmy to show him round. Maybe there's a deal to be done if I don't need it any more.'

'You're going to sell your house?' Minnie asked.

'I might.' Tina stood in the kitchen in socks, a welly in each hand. 'I think it's time for me to make a life of my own here, in Oxford. The house will fetch a good price. And Dave told Jimmy that his customer's desperate to buy it.'

22

News came on the Saturday morning that Dickie Edwards had died in the early hours. Peacefully. Dickie Junior and Gail had been at his side.

Neil received a text at breakfast. He put his cup on the table with a dull thump and walked out into the garden, leaving Lin staring, toast in hand. She put it down and rushed out after him into bright sunshine. He was standing on the patio staring towards George Ledbury's field, holding his phone out as if it held a terrible curse. He had tears in his eyes.

Lin knew before he had a chance to tell her.

'When did it happen?'

'Half three. Dickie Junior just texted me. Dickie just breathed out and didn't breathe in again.' Neil passed a hand across his face. 'He's gone, Lindy.'

'He's not suffering any more.' Lin knew she was talking in platitudes. It didn't help.

'I've known Dickie all my life.'

'I know.'

'We played together on our trikes when we were little. He stole my Action Man.'

Lin placed a gentle hand on Neil's shoulder. 'I know.'

'We played "stretch" in the grass on the rec. He had a penknife. He threw it at me and I threw it back and I accidentally got his foot and the blade went right in. I thought he'd hit me. But he laughed and shouted, "Good shot, Nelly." He called me Nelly when we were in primary school.'

'He was a character,' Lin said. She remembered the time he'd called her 'skinny Linny' and Minnie had threatened to whack him. It seemed so long ago. 'Cecily was fond of Dickie.'

'I was fond of him. He was a good lad.' Neil's eyes filled again. 'Taking over The Sun was the making of him. Dickie and Gail. They made it like a second home to everyone in the village. Dickie would always be behind the bar, pulling a pint of Hooky, cracking a joke. We celebrated everything there: Christmases, marriages, wetting babies' heads. Remember our fiftieth anniversary do in The Sun? Dickie was well then, and that was last October. It was so quick.'

Lin sighed. 'Poor Dickie.'

'You never know.' Neil turned to her, his face filled with anguish. 'You never know what's waiting around the corner.'

Lin held out her arms. 'Come here, love.' She tugged him against her, resting her head against his shoulder. He was trembling. 'It'll be all right.'

Neil pulled away and looked at her, frowning. 'Will it, Lindy?'

'Let's concentrate on what we can do to help Dickie Junior. And Gail.'

'He's just Dickie now. There's no Senior.'

'How can we help them?'

'Dickie's closing the pub for a week from tonight, but he's

opening this lunchtime. He needs time to grieve, and to arrange the funeral.' Neil sniffed. 'He said we can go down if we want and raise a glass to his dad.'

'And we can do that again at the funeral.'

'Dickie will let us know when.' Neil took her hand. 'Can we go? Jimmy will be there, and Kenny.'

'I'll phone Cecily and Josie. They'll want to come too.'

Neil turned towards the house. 'I'd better see if I can find my black suit and tie.'

'Oh, not today, love.' Lin placed a hand on his shoulder. 'Perhaps for the funeral, yes, but today – won't everyone want to remember him with a pint and a pie?'

'I don't know,' Neil said, and wandered back into the house.

Lin watched him disappear into the kitchen and sighed. Neil had taken it very badly, worse than she had expected.

***

At lunchtime, Lin watched Neil as he stood at the bar and ordered a pint of Hooky and a G & T from a morose Dickie Junior. He glanced over to where Jimmy and Kenny were sitting, waving frantically. She took his hand. 'Go and sit with your friends, love. It might help you all to be together and talk about the old days.'

Neil met her eyes anxiously. Lin thought he looked older. 'What about you?'

Lin indicated the seat by the window. 'Cecily and Josie are over there. I'll go and sit with them. You join the boys. I'm sure you've got a lot to talk about.'

'Right.' Neil clutched his pint. 'We were in the same football team as Dickie. He played forward. He was a good striker. I remember he got a hat trick against The Blackbird in Charlbury.'

'Such lovely stories, good times. That's what we'll cling to. We all loved Dickie. We'll think of him every time we stand at the bar.' Lin placed a hand against his back and watched him go on his way. She ambled back through the crowds who had come to pay their respects and plonked herself down at the table next to Cecily and Josie. Cecily immediately raised a glass.

'To Dickie Edwards.'

'To Dickie,' Lin and Josie chorused.

'Wherever a beautiful soul has been, there's a trail of beautiful memories,' Cecily said.

Lin sniffed, her eyes filling. 'He could be a little sod at primary school.'

'I was quite scared of him at first, when we were kids,' Josie said. 'Minnie used to punch him. She was the only one who was as tough as he was.'

'Does Minnie know?' Lin asked.

'I phoned her,' Cecily replied. 'She sends love. And there's a card in the post from her to young Dickie and Gail. Minnie will come over for the funeral, of course.'

'It's a shame.' Lin glanced towards the table where Neil, Jimmy and Kenny were huddled together. Neil had almost sunk his first pint.

'Dickie was a misunderstood youngster. I had a run-in with his father once,' Cecily said.

'Oh? I didn't know.' Josie wrapped her fingers around her glass of elderflower pressé. 'What happened?'

'I was a bit suspicious. Dickie was always bruised.' Cecily glanced at her wrist. 'I don't mean just the bruises kids get from playing games and knocking about. He'd have thumbprints on his arm, fist-sized bruises. One day he came in with a black eye and told me he'd walked into the lamp post.'

'Oh?' Lin was taken aback. 'What did you do?'

'I called round his house on the pretext of bringing extra books to help him with his reading. I met Dickie's mum. She was a nervous woman, taking Valium. Of course, there was a lot of it about then, "mothers' little helpers". As if women had to be calmed down. But she had the same shiner over one eye that Dickie had. And there were three other children. One of them had bruises all up her arms. Their father came home from work, and I tackled him.'

'What did you say?' Lin asked.

'I simply stated that there were a lot of bruises on Dickie, his siblings and his wife, well above the average.'

'What did Dickie's dad say?' Josie asked.

'He called me an interfering bitch and told me to mind my own business.' Cecily raised an eyebrow. 'I often find words like that tell us far more about the speaker than the person they're aimed at.'

'Weren't you afraid?'

'I didn't think he'd hit me,' Cecily said simply. 'But I did tell him that I had several colleagues who worked for social services and a good friend who was a police officer, and I'd have no hesitation in asking them to call in if either Dickie or anyone else in his family were beaten again.'

'Cecily, you're miraculous,' Lin said, full of awe. 'I'd have been scared stiff.'

'I didn't allow myself time to think about it,' Cecily said honestly. 'But the beatings seemed to subside. Of course, the experience made Dickie a bit of a bully. I had to do something to help.'

'What did you do?'

'I was very strict with him, and I gave him extra attention. But he had to earn it. Tough love.' Cecily drained her glass. 'I might have another one, in his memory.'

'I'll get them,' Josie said, clambering to her feet just as the door opened and Fergal Toomey blustered in. Josie looked over his shoulder for his new wife, but Fergal was alone.

He said, 'I'm here to say goodbye to Dickie.'

'I'm off to the bar,' Josie said.

'I'll come with you.' Fergal shepherded her to the bar, nodded towards Dickie Junior and said, 'I've come to pay my respects.' Dickie reached for a pint glass to fill. 'I'll have a pint and a whiskey chaser, and whatever this young lady wants.'

'Same again for your table, Josie?' Dickie asked.

'Please.' Josie gave him her kindest smile as Fergal shoved a hand in his pocket and pulled out a wad of cash.

Fergal leaned against the bar and pushed back his trilby. 'I left Poll at home resting. She likes a sleep after lunch.'

'I didn't congratulate you properly on your marriage,' Josie said.

'Ah, I've known Poll's family for ages. Her dad, Bert Loveridge, was a pal of my dad's backalong. She lost her husband a couple of years ago; they were close, and she got lonely. Her kids have flown and she had a hole in her life she wanted to fill. We got talking and we hit it off all over again. There were a few drinks involved, granted. Before I knew it, we'd got married.'

Josie rested a hand on his arm. 'Are you happy?'

'I am.' Fergal grinned. 'Missing Ros was getting to me. The loneliness was changing me into a shrunken man. I needed someone. I still love Ros. I'll love that woman until my dying breath. But Poll Loveridge is some woman, I can tell you. Oh, that billow of hair in my face. And she's got a hug on her a bear would be proud of. She'll do fine.'

'And she loves you?'

'To distraction. Could you not tell the other day at the barge? She's possessive as hell, but I like that. It makes me feel manly.'

'She's nothing to fear from me.' Josie smiled.

'I told her that. But she wasn't so sure. She said, "That Josie's a bit of all right, Fergal; she's pretty, and she's well-heeled. I don't want you tempted away."'

'She said that?' Josie felt quite flattered.

'I want her to get to know you better, Josie. You'll be great friends. She's a lovely woman when you get used to her. She's a bit defensive. She comes from a large family, nine kids. Poll had to fight for her bread and butter since she was knee high.'

'And now she's got you, she knows she's onto a winner.'

'Something like that.' Fergal's eyes twinkled. Dickie placed a tray of drinks on the bar top and Fergal picked them up. 'I'll stop with you and the girls, if that's all right.' He glanced towards Neil's table. 'I think the lads are chewing the fat, remembering all the old days. I wasn't at school half the time as a kid. I'm probably better sitting with you.'

Josie and Fergal sat down and Cecily picked up her glass. 'Thank you, Fergal. We were just toasting Dickie, but I believe congratulations are due. Josie says you have a wife.'

'I do.' Fergal's face creased with a happy smile. 'I never thought I'd be happy again after Ros passed, but I am. I wasn't sure I wanted to come here today. It brings back all the memories.'

'Of Ros?' Lin's expression was sympathetic. 'It's all so sad, isn't it? Life doesn't prepare you for death.'

'It doesn't,' Josie said sadly, and Fergal patted her hand.

'We barge dwellers celebrate the passing of a loved one differently to you,' Fergal said softly. 'Death doesn't mark the end. The spirit lives on and the graveside is the place where we go to grieve and show respect.' He indicated his denim jacket. 'It's customary to wear black. I wore black for six months after Ros died, so did Devlin and Finn. I burned her clothes and bedding as a mark of respect. And I put stuff in her coffin: money, holy bracelets, tiny crosses, her wedding ring and some family photos.'

'Why did you do that?' Lin asked.

Fergal's hand gripped his chaser. 'For her to take to the afterlife.' He downed it in one. 'Ah, let them all rest in peace!'

'Harry's death was so sudden. It was a shock. At first, I trusted entirely that he was in a better place.' Josie felt sorry for him, and for herself at the same time. 'But there's a huge hole in my heart I can't fill. I envy you in a way, Fergal, to be able to marry again.'

'Ros will understand. She was the first for me, the best one.' Fergal had finished his beer and the whiskey. 'I can feel a bit of a session coming on. Death has that effect on me. I might get another round – same for you, ladies?'

Josie lifted her glass of elderflower. 'I've hardly touched mine.'

'Miss Hamilton, another gin?' Fergal asked.

'I have to drive the Flying Plum back home. I'd better not.' Cecily smiled.

'Lin?' Fergal asked gallantly.

'I won't. I'm already tearful.' Lin stared at her second glass. She'd hardly touched the first gin.

'Just me, then.' Fergal grinned. 'And I have two hands, so that's four drinks I can carry.'

Josie met Cecily's eyes, then Lin's. 'Won't Poll mind?'

'Poll? Oh, she's probably fast asleep.'

On cue, the door opened and a tall woman with billowing hair stood with her hands on her hips and snarled, 'Fergal?'

'Hello, my love.' Fergal approached her, unperturbed. 'I thought you were asleep.'

'I woke up.' Poll glanced around the bar and her eyes fell on Josie. 'I thought you'd be here. I see you're drinking with your floozy.'

Lin opened her mouth in defence.

'I'm not a—' Josie began but Fergal placed a hand on Poll's arm to calm her.

'Can I get you a drink, Poll? Come and meet my friends. You know Josie already and this is Lin and my teacher, Miss Hamilton.'

'Pleased to meet you.' Cecily stretched out a hand.

'I'll never sit down with them in a rain of pig's pudding,' Poll spat. 'Don't you come all smarmy with me, Fergal Toomey. You've been boozing here with all these women.'

Jimmy and Kenny started to laugh. Neil looked horrified. Everyone else in the pub had paused to watch.

'Oh, we're hardly jailbait,' Cecily said. 'I'm nearly ninety-two. Come on, young woman, see sense. We're here to have a drink and respect the passing of one of our friends. And you bursting in here and shouting is quite disrespectful.'

Poll met her eyes. 'Who's died?'

Jimmy's face was immediately serious. Kenny's too.

'Our friend from school, Dickie. He died this morning,' Fergal explained. 'Let me buy you a beer.'

'Someone's died?' Poll didn't move. She was shocked. 'I've come to a wake? I haven't brought any ackers, any dosh. Fergal, I can't buy anyone a drink like I ought to...'

'I'll buy you one,' Cecily said graciously.

'I've got money, Poll,' Fergal coaxed. 'Come and sit down. I'll get a round in.'

'Please come and join us,' Josie said kindly. 'What will you have, Poll?'

'Have a drink,' Dickie reached for a clean glass.

'No, I can't,' Poll said, her face horrified. 'I can't believe I walked into the middle of a wake and shouted my gob off. I'm sorry, Fergal, ladies.' She looked at Josie. 'I'll go back to the barge. I don't have any business here.' She reached out a hand as if to touch Fergal's arm, and jerked back. 'Like I said, I'm sorry, it's not my place to intrude. I'll see you later, Fergal.'

And she was gone.

'That was Poll,' Fergal said with a shrug. 'So, are you ladies sure I can't get you something from the bar?'

'Not now.' Cecily's eyes narrowed as she watched Fergal push through the crowds towards Dickie. 'That poor woman was upset. I think she needs our support.'

'Does she?' Lin asked. 'I thought she'd come to murder Josie. Or Fergal.'

'Poll thinks she doesn't fit in,' Cecily said firmly. 'So it's our job to make sure that she feels welcome. It's as simple as that. Perhaps it's time for the Silver Ladies to expand their circle.'

23

Odile's café was quiet on Monday morning, just a few diners at tables, but as lunchtime approached Odile and Florence were busy in the kitchen in anticipation of the rush. Odile was filling flatbreads with a spicy chickpea mixture. 'These doubles will bring in the punters. I was brought up on barra and roti. It's the best sandwich in the world.'

'Adam loves them.' Florence couldn't disagree. 'Me too, but you don't think it'll be a bit quiet? There was hardly anyone in for breakfast.'

'People have got to eat.' Odile sniffed. 'And The Sun's closed until Dickie's funeral so – I don't mean to be mean, but we'll pick up the business.'

'Dad said he'd be in,' Florence said. 'It's almost twelve.'

'That man keeps his own time.' Odile smiled. 'How's Elsie? And Adam?'

'Teething. Elsie, not Adam. Although he got up to change her last night at four and he looked shattered this morning.' Florence smiled, remembering. 'He's the best. I ought to buy him something, to say thank you.'

'Cook him something nice,' Odile suggested.

'I could. Or...' Florence remembered. 'I might take him out somewhere. Josie promised me she'd babysit Elsie.'

'Josie Sanderson? She's had no kids of her own.' Odile turned away from the chickpea mix. 'How's she going to cope with a yelling child?'

'I suppose Lin might come with her. She's a grandma.'

Odile laughed. 'Me too. My son has three and my daughter has two of them, but to this day the sound of a baby screaming goes right through me like a hot knife.'

Florence shuddered. 'I know what you mean. Once, Elsie had earache and she yelled and yelled, her little knees up to her chest. Adam and I were at our wits' end. I rang Dr Müller and she was wonderful.'

The doorbell tinged and Odile raised an eyebrow. 'Will you get that, Florence? My hands are covered with coriander.'

'I'm on it.' Florence adjusted her apron and scurried into the café. Gerald Harris, who lived in a large bungalow on Orchard Way, not far from the recreation ground, and his new partner, Margaret Fennimore, were sitting near the window. Gerald waved a hand as she passed. 'Can you top the coffees up, please?'

'On my way,' Florence called. But her smile was for Cecily, who'd just parked the Flying Plum and was at the door. 'I hope you brought a brolly. It looks like we're in for a downpour.' She helped Cecily to a table, sitting her with her back to the window, and gave her the menu. 'I'll just fill up Bomber—Mr Harris's coffee, and I'll be right back.'

Cecily watched as Florence drifted across the café, efficiently filling cups, offering encouraging smiles and more slices of Odile's ginger cake. Then she was back at Cecily's table. 'Do you want lunch?'

'Yes, please.' Cecily smiled through perfect lipstick.

'Are Lin and Josie coming?'

'Lin's with Neil. He's got a bit of a head cold and she didn't want to pass it on to me. I think he's a bit run-down. And Josie's at the supermarket. But I thought I'd treat myself. What specials do you have?'

'Odile's made doubles.'

'Oh, I love them,' Cecily enthused. 'Curried chickpeas between two pieces of fried flatbread, dressed in coriander sauce and mango chutney.' She smacked her lips. 'I'll have one, please.'

'Hello, Cecily.' Margaret Fennimore twisted round in her seat. 'What was it you're having for lunch?'

'Doubles. Trinidadian street food,' Cecily said.

'Are they nice?' Margaret asked.

'Try one,' Cecily replied. 'You won't be disappointed.'

'I must say I'd prefer a chicken sandwich.' Margaret made an unimpressed face.

'Or egg and mayo,' Gerald piped up, offering his opinion. He lowered his voice. 'I'm not sure I'd like – whatever it is you're eating.'

'You should give it a go,' Cecily urged. 'You know, Gerald—' Cecily put on her most innocent face '—you might be more adventurous. I always think it's a good thing to spice everything up a little.' She arched an eyebrow, smiling to herself as Gerald coughed into his handkerchief.

Margaret called, 'Florence, can Gerald and I try a couple of those doubles?' She met his eyes. 'You have to start somewhere.'

'Two more coming up.' Florence appeared from the kitchen with a plate for Cecily, piled with chickpeas on two pieces of yellow flatbread.

'Mmm – smells delicious,' Cecily said with a wink.

Florence disappeared, returning with Gerald and Margaret's food, which they nibbled tentatively, and a glass of water for Cecily, who patted the table, and Florence sat down for a moment.

'How's the family?'

'Good.' Florence leaned forward, her elbows on the table. 'Adam and Elsie are adorable. Dad's working hard.'

'And you?' Cecily's stare was piercing, as if working things out. 'Are you getting plenty of rest time?'

'Not really.' Florence grimaced, then she smiled. 'I met up with Malia recently; we text each other. Our lives are very different though. I'd visit Natalie more, but I don't think she likes babies.'

'Your friends will catch up with you eventually,' Cecily said wisely. 'But is everything all right?'

'I had a letter from my mother,' Florence blurted. 'Out of the blue. She wants to meet Elsie.' The image of her mother came into her head, holding Elsie, promising to buy her all sorts of things she didn't need, while Florence watched.

'How do you feel about that?' Cecily forked chickpeas off the plate.

Florence pushed the image aside. 'It's Dad I'm worried about.' Her voice was low. 'He's investing in it, emotionally. He wants her back.'

'So what are you going to do?'

'I wrote her a letter.' Florence tugged her ponytail over her shoulder, playing with the ends of her hair. 'I didn't say much. Just that I hoped she was all right and I was all right and Elsie was all right and Dad was fine too. I said she could write back if she wanted to.'

'You left the door open,' Cecily said.

'I didn't want to invite her round. Not yet. I need time to let Dad calm down.'

'That's wise,' Cecily said.

'Adam thinks so too.' Florence took a deep breath. 'It's hard. One minute, you're managing OK and then the past rears its head, and everything's confusing.'

'Oh, it certainly is,' Cecily said with a wry smile. 'Florence, can I ask you something?'

Florence looked over her shoulder. The café was quiet: she had time. 'Of course.'

'I'd appreciate the opinion of someone youthful.'

'That's me.' Florence grinned. 'Youthful and tired out.'

'The thing is...' Cecily dabbed her lips with a napkin '...the same thing has happened to me. Like you just said. I was managing life well enough and now the past has reared its head, and I'm not sure what to do.'

'Oh?' Florence asked.

The conversation had stopped on Gerald and Margaret's table. Either their mouths were full of spicy doubles or they were listening.

'Well,' Cecily began. 'You know many years ago, I was engaged to be married.'

A little knot appeared between Florence's brow. She'd heard the story. 'The man who got your best friend pregnant? The one you got to step up and marry her?'

'Exactly.' Cecily leaned forward. 'His granddaughter called round to see me. Sammy. She found me on Facebook, just like your mother found you.'

'Ghosting. Submarining.' Florence rolled her eyes. 'Facebook's full of that stuff.'

'I'm sure.' Cecily wasn't sure what she meant. 'Sammy gave me Eddie's address. He's still alive. He lives near Wallingford.'

'So you're going to see him?' Florence was suddenly excited. 'After all these years, you're meeting up again? Cecily, that's so romantic.'

'Do you think so?' It was Cecily's turn to frown. She hadn't expected such a positive reaction.

'I think you should go for it.'

'Why?'

Florence stared at her as if she'd lost her mind. 'He was totally hot. You loved him. You said he looked like James Dean.'

'I doubt he looks like that now.'

'That's not the point,' Florence insisted. 'It's really exciting, meeting someone after so many years. He obviously still loves you. He didn't want to marry your friend Joyce. He did it because he was honourable and kind – and because you told him to.'

'Joyce is dead now,' Cecily said sadly.

'Then what's stopping you?' Florence's eyes shone. 'It makes sense. You pick up where you left off.'

'I'm almost ninety-two.'

'All the more reason. Grab him while you can,' Florence said excitedly. 'Oh, I love a good romance. Imagine, after all those years you meet again and you know instantly that you both love each other and time and distance never kept you apart.'

Cecily was staring. 'Do you really think so?'

'You'd say the same to me,' Florence replied. 'It's Eddie. He loved you and never stopped. It's not like my mother, who dumped me and Dad for the boiler man and now she wants to be a grandma. I don't want to rush in.'

'I feel the same about Eddie. But I'm afraid I'll get hurt all over again,' Cecily said, her hand shaking. 'Once bitten.'

Florence was not deterred. 'What did you say to me once? No woman is an island. We thrive on companionship, on warmth and love. Seriously, Cecily, you should pay Eddie a visit. I mean, it's only a visit.' Florence stood up and grinned. 'If he's minging, you can always back out.'

'Thanks,' Cecily said. 'That's really helped.' She glanced at her plate. Her food was only half eaten, but she'd had enough. Her appetite was smaller nowadays. She said, 'Could you bring me a cup of tea, please? A green tea with honey might be just the thing.' She put a hand on her heart. 'I think I need those antioxidants.'

'I'm on it,' Florence called and whirled away.

Cecily sank into deep thought. What if she did visit Eddie? Getting there would be easy. Lin had offered to drive her to Benson. She'd be in a flurry about what to wear, her heart would be in her mouth for the whole journey. But, Cecily wondered, what would it feel like to see him after all this time? Could she bear the idea of meeting him, realising what they'd both missed? Or should she snatch at the last shreds of happiness life might offer them both?

She said aloud, 'I have absolutely no idea what to do.'

'You should forget him,' Gerald boomed. 'He doesn't deserve you, Cecily. He's had his chance.'

'Oh?' Cecily glanced up to see Gerald and Margaret leaning forwards, watching her.

'I disagree,' Margaret announced. 'True love is wonderful at any time of life. You and I found each other less than a year ago, Gerald, at the bridge club in Charlbury. And we haven't looked back.'

'Well, that's true, dear,' Gerald began. 'Perhaps if you were to proceed with caution, Cecily.'

'Or throw yourself in at the deep end and fall gloriously in love.' Margaret clapped her hands. 'Oh, this is exciting. And you were right – the doubles Odile made are really delicious. A bit of spice, Gerald, that's what's important.'

'I suppose it is,' Gerald agreed.

Florence appeared from the kitchen with tea and a cinnamon biscuit, which she placed in front of Cecily. 'There you go.'

'Thank you.' Cecily looked up gratefully. 'Florence, you've helped more than you know.'

'My pleasure,' Florence said. As she swivelled on her heel to go back to the kitchen to Odile, someone outside the café caught her eye. She turned back quickly. Someone was watching her a few paces away, by the kerb. Florence froze.

It was Darryl Featherstone. She was sure of it.

The door burst open and the lunchtime rush came in. Jimmy Baker, Kenny Hooper, Bobby Ledbury and, finally, Dangerous Dave in his overalls, nursing a bandaged hand. He called out, 'I burned my finger on an exhaust again. My mind was elsewhere. Florrie, get us a coffee, will you, Princess? And bring the menu. I'm half starved.'

'Right, Dad,' Florence said. Her heart was thumping. She glanced nervously through the window again, in case he was still there. There was no one outside.

She retreated to the safety of the kitchen as fast as she could.

'I think I am, although teenage years were the best. Do you remember—?' Mike chuckled. 'Do you remember the bike I had, the Triumph? The locals thought I was a bit of a tearaway. I'm sure your mother did. I had long hair and I rode the Bonneville too fast.'

'And it was before everyone wore helmets, that's why my mother worried so much. She would always stay up until I came home after we'd been out somewhere,' Josie remembered. 'She was terrified we'd fall off.'

'You wore my spare leather jacket; it was far too big for you.' Mike grinned.

'I wore sandals, though, and bare legs, and you wore shorts in the summer.' Josie shuddered at the memory. 'Imagine if we'd come off. The damage we'd have done to ourselves.'

'Oh, I fell off a few times.'

'Did you?'

'I never told you about the worst one, on Cut Throat Corner. We'd had a row. It was about me joining the RAF.'

'I didn't know you fell off. I remember you roaring away on your bike in a huff.'

'You didn't want me to join up.'

Josie sighed. 'It was a long time ago, Mike.'

'I was torn, Josie. Between you and a new career. Between staying in the village and seeing the world. It cut me up to leave you. Literally. That night, I drove like an idiot and came off on the bend. The next day I came round to see you to apologise, I could hardly move one of my legs. It was black and blue.'

'I never knew,' Josie said.

'It was the hardest decision in my life, leaving you. In fact—' Mike's eyes met Josie's '—every decision I made after that was a bad one. It was as if leaving you was the beginning of everything going wrong.'

Josie shook her head sadly. 'I'm sorry to hear that.' The mood had changed to a melancholy one, so Josie forced a smile. 'Harry and I were happy for fifty years. And I'm still happy now, remembering the good times. I suppose you've come back for the quiet life.'

'Back to where I began. I was born in the hospital in Tadderly. My parents are in the graveyard at St Peter and St Paul's.'

'Harry too,' Josie said. 'It's Dickie Edwards' funeral next week.'

'It comes to us all.' Mike put his head in his hands and Josie thought he looked depressed. She took a breath, intending to cheer him up.

'You'll settle down here, meet old friends and make new ones.' Josie did her best to sound encouraging. 'You'll enjoy it.'

'I hope so.' Mike looked up. 'That's why I came, Josie. You know, you haven't changed a bit.'

Josie forced a laugh. 'I think I have.'

'Not in my eyes. I just wondered...' Mike chose his words. 'I just wondered if we could go out somewhere.' He watched her expression change. 'As friends, for old times' sake?'

Josie wasn't sure. Mike was attractive. She'd liked him a lot, once. She glanced at the photo of Harry and his eyes were smiling. Was he giving her permission?

'Perhaps.'

'You could come round my house? We could have a housewarming, of sorts. I could cook.'

Josie shook her head. She imagined being in the house in Nobb's End with Mike. There would be music, soft lights, good food, wine. It was the same house where Darryl took Florence, where he lied to her.

'Maybe some other time.'

'There's a lovely inn in Charlbury, The Rose and Crown. We could go there. I've heard they do great steaks.'

'That sounds nice. Or...' Josie wondered if she'd be safer going to The Sun, where she knew everyone. It would be closed until the funeral. She was playing for time.

But if she and Mike were seen in the village together, tongues would wag. Once Jimmy Baker knew, he'd have to blab. And Penny Ledbury would mention it to everyone who came into the Co-op.

She said, 'The Rose and Crown might be nice.'

'Tomorrow? Friday?' Mike leaned forward. 'I'll drive us there.'

'Can I think about it?' Josie said, trying to be firm. 'I'm meeting with the girls. We do lunch a lot. Lin and Minnie.'

'Minnie Moore?' Mike made a face. 'She was fierce. She scared me a bit. Didn't she leave for university, Cambridge or Oxford? Lin's nice though. She and Neil are a lovely couple.' An idea occurred to him. 'We could make a foursome. We could have days out.'

'We could.' It was all going too fast for Josie. 'Just give me a day or so, and I'll come back to you.'

'All right.' Mike sat up straight. 'Well, I've enjoyed spending time, Josie. You know, I regret losing touch. Things would have been very different if I'd stayed.' He paused, as if he couldn't finish his sentence. He forced a smile. 'But the chance of meeting you again, it's a lifesaver, do you know that?' He rose to his feet. 'I really enjoyed catching up. We must do it again soon.'

'We must.' Josie put a hand to her mouth. 'Oh, I forgot the biscuits.'

'Next time,' Mike said, as if he was sure there would be a

next time. He made a move towards the door and Josie followed him. 'It's been lovely.'

They paused at the door. 'It has,' Josie agreed, although her mind was still whirling. She had no idea what it had been: confusing, unexpected. Strange. Awkward.

Mike lurched forward, a swift move like a pecking bird, and kissed her cheek. Josie felt her spine stiffen.

'So, Josie, I'll see you soon.'

'Great to see you, Mike.' Josie found herself smiling. She wasn't sure what else to do. She tugged open the door. 'Take care.'

'Let's stay in touch,' Mike called. She watched him walk down the path towards the gate, turn and wave a hand.

Josie waved once and closed the door. Then she sighed.

She returned to the living room, collected the cups and put them in the sink, leaving one beneath the dripping tap to collect water. She'd wash them later.

With a heavy heart and a great deal of confusion, she returned to the sofa and plonked herself down. She reached out and picked up a photo of Harry. He was standing in the garden in the sunshine, smiling. It must have been ten years ago. Happy times.

Josie looked into his warm eyes. 'What shall I do, Harry? Should I go out with him? Would it be all right?'

Harry continued smiling, as if he wanted her to be happy. Josie put the photograph back. She stared at her hands, at her wedding ring.

She wasn't sure. A date might be pleasant. More than pleasant. She liked Mike. He was good-looking. He still made her heart thud.

But there was something about him now. Was he depressed? Moody? No, it was something else.

Josie couldn't put her finger on it. But it unsettled her and made her feel nervous.

Mike Bailey had always had this effect on her. Now he was back, and living around the corner, she had no idea what to do.

25

The letter arrived on Monday, the day before Dickie Edwards' funeral. It was a pink envelope again. The round handwriting looked innocuous enough, but Florence felt as if her skin were covered in ants. She sat at the breakfast table with Dave and Adam, looking at the letter, fear in her eyes.

Elsie was lying on a baby gym mat that Bobby Ledbury had passed on from Hayley's children. She was playing with the activity toys, making gurgling noises. Florence wondered what the letter contained.

Dave said, 'Are you going to open it?' He reached for more toast.

'I ought to,' Florence said.

'It's addressed to you.' Adam stated the obvious. 'It's yours to find out.'

'I wonder if Elaine wants to come back.'

'Dad, you can't think that,' Florence said determinedly. 'It's Elsie she wants to meet.'

'But once she meets Elsie, she'll want to move back, won't she?'

'Perhaps she's settled, Dave,' Adam said carefully. 'In Blisworth.'

Dave was hopeful. 'Perhaps she's lonely. Perhaps she regrets leaving us.'

'Perhaps she'll breeze in, upset the applecart and clear off again, just like she did before,' Florence said bitterly. 'Dad, please don't get carried away. She might break your heart over again.' She reached out and lifted the envelope as if it were a bomb, opening it carefully. 'I'd better have a look.'

Dave's eyes didn't leave Florence's face. He was searching for a clue; for a hint of what was in the letter.

'Florence.' Adam touched her arm. 'What does she say?'

'It's just a short note.' Florence was reading. 'Oh my!'

'What?' Dave's eyes widened. 'Is she all right?'

'She's coming here.'

'When?' Dave couldn't contain himself. 'Does she say she might stay?'

'No, she just says, "Dear Florence. Thank you for your letter. I can't wait to meet Elsie. I'm getting a train ticket to come on Friday so can you meet me at the station? The train comes in at two-thirty."' Florence frowned. 'I'll be at work on Friday.'

'Does she mention me?' Dave asked.

'That's all she wrote,' Florence said tactfully.

'And she expects you to be there when she arrives? With Elsie?' Adam said.

'I suppose she didn't think that I had a job,' Florence said quietly. 'That's typical of Mum. She doesn't think of anyone.'

'I could meet her,' Dave said eagerly. 'It would be no trouble. I could take Elsie.'

'There's no need, Dad.' Florence looked suddenly cross.

'How did she sign the letter?' Adam asked.

Florence passed the letter across. 'See for yourself.'

Adam scanned the letter. '"From Elaine".' He was unimpressed. 'Not "love, Mum", or "looking forward to seeing you".'

'And nothing about me?' Dave was disappointed.

Florence sniffed angrily. 'I've a good mind to tell her not to bother. I'll be working. Why couldn't she come on Sunday?' She reached for her coffee mug. 'I've got no way to put her off. She hasn't given her number.'

'You have to meet her,' Dave said quickly.

'I don't *have* to,' Florence countered. 'Dad, she wants to meet Elsie. And who knows how long that novelty will last?'

'Perhaps you're being unfair, Princess,' Dave said. 'You should give her a chance.'

'I'm not. I'm protecting us all,' Florence argued. 'What do you think, Adam?'

'It's not about me. Your mum doesn't even know I exist,' Adam said sadly. 'I want you and Elsie and Dave to be OK. In truth, what I've heard about your mum, I don't think you should invest too much emotionally yet.'

'She hasn't asked anything about me.' Florence's face was troubled. The image of Darryl Featherstone watching her, standing outside Odile's café, came back to her for a moment and she shivered. She glanced towards Elsie, who was chewing a soft felt hedgehog. 'I don't know what to do.'

'Perhaps you'll know, once you've met her?' Adam suggested. 'I've got a big meeting with the Ledburys and Dad on Friday, or I'd take time off.'

'Perhaps when she comes here, we won't be able to get rid of her,' Florence said.

'Perhaps we won't want to.' Dave helped himself to more toast.

'No, Dad.' Florence felt her face reddening with temper.

'She'll start telling me how I should bring Elsie up, or she'll come here once, look around, then disappear and we won't see her again.'

'Meet her on Friday, see what happens,' Adam said thoughtfully.

'Right,' Florence said, folding her arms. 'But I won't allow Mum to let us all down again.'

* * *

That afternoon, Lin stood in the Co-op on Orchard Way looking for ingredients. Neil wanted to make a cake. Lin paused in the baking aisle, trying to remember if baking powder was the same as bicarbonate of soda, and if it mattered which one she bought. There were lots of interesting things: coloured icing, silver bauble decorations, almond extract, food colouring. She wondered whether to buy a stock of baking ingredients. Perhaps she and Neil could make cakes together. She imagined them in the kitchen, a blob of pink icing on her nose, Neil holding a wooden spoon, laughing.

A voice brought her from her thoughts. 'Penny for them, Lin?'

She turned to see Janice, her neighbour, coral lipstick gleaming. She was wearing high-heeled shoes that clack-clacked on the floor. Her shopping basket was full of tea. 'I'm going to try all these flavours,' she said with a flourish. 'Peppermint to calm me and raspberry to pep me up. Oh, to be honest, I don't know what they all do.' She lowered her voice. 'Are you going to the funeral tomorrow?'

'Yes, it's at the crematorium in Tadderly.' Lin felt sad. 'Then back to The Sun.'

'Geoff and I thought we'd just go to The Sun.' Janice made a face. 'The crem depresses me. The last time we went there was for Geoff's dad.'

'I understand.' Lin patted her arm. 'Neil and I knew Dickie all our lives. Poor Neil's dreading it.'

'Is he?' Janice hesitated. 'Why's that?'

'He'll be really upset. We both will.' Lin exhaled slowly. 'It's the end of an era.'

Janice misunderstood. 'His son, Dickie Junior, will still run The Sun, though.' She thought for a minute. 'Gail Edwards isn't well either, is she?'

Lin tried to change the subject. 'Neil asked me to get baking powder. I wondered if I should get bicarb?'

'Bicarb's stronger. Doesn't one of them have cream of tartar in it?' Janice asked.

'I don't know.' Lin was confused.

'By the way,' Janice said, 'I heard the other day. George Ledbury's going to sell the field behind us. He's virtually penniless.'

'Oh, poor George.'

'Poor George my foot. What about us? Apparently, George has three people interested in buying the field. And none of them is any good.'

'Why? Don't they want to pay him a fair price?'

'No, it's not that,' Janice said. 'One lot are property developers who want to build 400 houses.'

'Houses are important. Young people need them,' Lin said.

'And another one is some sort of excavator. They want to turn the field into a quarry.'

'Oh, I can't imagine that.' Lin tried to picture diggers behind their house, dynamite. 'That might not be good.'

'And Farmer Henry Turvey from Charlbury wants to put his pigs in there.'

'Oh, that's nice. Nadine might have company.'

'Imagine the smell.' Janice was horrified. 'Before long, he'd have a silo. Just think of the stink in the summer.'

'I'm sure there are laws against—'

'Penny said George has a meeting with Linval and Adam at the end of the week. They're going to decide what to do.' Janice leaned forward like a spy sharing a secret. 'I think the Ledburys are broke. It'll all have to go, the whole farm, the lot.'

'Oh, I hope not.'

'Everything's changing.' Janice shook her head. 'Soon there will be drones delivering parcels and we'll all be chipped at birth. Geoff thinks so.'

Lin shuddered. 'I'll buy baking powder and bicarb. Neil will have both options.'

Janice indicated the tea. 'I need this chamomile to calm my nerves. Well, I'll see you at The Sun tomorrow afternoon. Are you wearing black?'

'Dickie Junior wants cheery colours. He wants to celebrate Dickie's life.'

'I'll wear a frock and these shoes.' Janice hurried away, her heels clacking. Lin put the baking powder and the bicarb into her basket, some almond essence and a tube of pink icing. Neil needed cheering up.

She walked home briskly, thinking about a nice pink sponge filled with cream, topped with swirls of sugary icing. She could imagine Neil making one. She paused outside Tina Gilchrist's house in Harvest Road. The front door was open and two men were standing outside, talking and laughing. She recognised Jimmy Baker and Darryl Featherstone. His Porsche was parked by the gate.

Jimmy waved a hand. 'Hello, Lin.'

'Jimmy.' Lin had no intention of stopping. His sharp cologne wafted towards her and Lin remembered how he'd been teased in primary school for his sweaty smell. Stink bomb, the girls had called him. Except Minnie. She'd always been far too wise and kind.

'Hey.' Jimmy wanted a chat. 'I might be getting a new neighbour, Lin.'

'Oh?' She paused. Jimmy's words were enough to make her put her basket down. 'Isn't Tina coming back?'

'She wants to stay in Oxford.'

'At Minnie's?' Lin couldn't believe it: Minnie wanted Jensen to come over.

'Tina's thinking of settling there. She likes it.'

'Really?'

'So she's selling her house.' Jimmy was full of himself, the bringer of good news. 'And Darryl's thinking of buying it. You'd love it here, Darryl. We're a welcoming community.'

'Oh, I know.' Darryl looked smug. 'There's a deal to be done.'

Lin couldn't believe it. 'You want him to buy Tina's house?'

'I just gave him the full tour,' Jimmy said proudly. 'Tina said I could. I've got the key.'

'Does Minnie know he's looking round her sister's house?' Lin spoke directly to Jimmy.

'Well, I don't know. I just asked Tina if I could show the place to someone who knows the village well.'

'Too well, if you ask me.' Lin turned to Darryl and her lip curled. 'I wouldn't have thought this was your sort of house.'

'It does need a bit of TLC, to be honest,' Darryl said, with a short laugh. 'I'd rip the old kitchen out and make it open-plan. Some quartz worktops and a modern range would help, a TV on the wall, a white three-piece suite. And I'd knock two of the bedrooms into one. I need space.'

'I can't imagine why,' Lin said sarcastically. 'There's only one of you.'

'Ah, but not for long,' Jimmy piped up. 'He'll have the girls falling at his feet.'

'Really?' Lin said. 'How many girls does he intend to drag into Tina's house?'

'Only one at a time,' Darryl joked and Lin scowled, but he wasn't put off. 'It would be lovely to live just down the road from you and Neil.' He gave her his most charming smile. 'We'd be neighbours. I could call in for a cuppa. You could give me decorating tips.'

'The best tip I can give you is to move somewhere else.' Lin was amazed how hostile she sounded.

'Now there's no need for that, Lin.'

'I'm sure Darryl takes my meaning, Jimmy.' Lin met Darryl's eyes. 'Wouldn't you be better living in Tadderly?'

'Oh, I can't go back to Tadderly,' Darryl joked. 'Besides, I like this village. I feel connected to it.'

'I think there's a woman in Tadderly who wants his guts for garters,' Jimmy laughed.

'A woman in every town, eh?' Lin said dismissively. 'You'll have to excuse me, Jimmy, I haven't got time to waste. Neil's making a cake.'

'We'll have to call round for a slice, eh, Darryl?' Jimmy was behaving as if he had a new best friend. 'I'll be seeing you, Lin. Tomorrow. At Dickie's.'

'Right.' Lin was almost out of earshot.

She was annoyed with herself for not being cool and calm and giving herself time to think. She couldn't wait to tell Neil that Darryl was looking around Tina's house with the intention of buying it. Tina clearly had no idea she was selling it to the man who had fathered Florence's baby.

Minnie would be furious. Lin would have to tell her.

Darryl returning to the village could only spell trouble for Florence, Elsie and Adam. And Lin had the strangest feeling that was exactly what Darryl wanted.

26

Tuesday was a wet, cold day. The rains came in from the west. A cold wind blew through the crematorium as Dickie Junior gave a speech about his father; when he finished, speakers boomed Baddiel & Skinner & The Lightning Seeds singing 'Three Lions'.

Dickie had been a great football fan. He'd loved to watch England play. He had been to see them play Italy at Wembley in 2023 in the Euro qualifiers. They had won 3-1. Dickie had been well then. He'd had no idea that, just around the corner, they'd be playing the song at his funeral. The thought made Lin cry, and as she glanced to her left, Neil's face was covered in tears. They left the crematorium hand in hand and grouped together in the drizzle.

Minnie, Josie and Cecily shivered inside thin frocks. Most of the men wore white or red football shirts; Dangerous Dave wore the full kit. Kenny Hooper was the only one in a suit and tie. Lin said, 'Shall I drive us to The Sun?'

Neil looked forlorn. 'I suppose so. We could all do with cheering up a bit. That was awful, listening to the happy music, watching the coffin go through those curtains.' He shivered again. His hair was plastered to his head and his skin was grey. He shoved his hands in his pockets.

Feet away, Jimmy Baker and Dangerous Dave were making jokes to lift the mood.

'I'm going to get them to play "Overkill" by Motörhead when I'm gone,' Jimmy joked.

'I already said, when I'm cremated, I want them to play that Crazy World of Arthur Brown song.'

'What song?' Jimmy asked.

'"Fire".' Dave laughed.

'That ent funny,' Kenny Hooper said.

'We should go.' Cecily glanced at Neil. 'I need to collect some flowers I bought for Gail and Dickie Junior. Lin, could you drop me off at the bungalow and I'll come up to the Sun on the Flying Plum.'

'We'll wait,' Lin offered.

'No, you go on. Neil will wait with me,' Cecily said firmly.

'Right,' Lin said.

'No problem,' Neil agreed. So many years had passed but they still obeyed their teacher.

Half an hour later, in her kitchen, Cecily made two strong cups of tea. She put one in Neil's hands and noticed they were shaking. She said, 'We'll take this in the living room.'

'OK.' Neil took his tea and sat down dutifully on the sofa. Cecily perched next to him and took a sip. She was quiet for a moment.

He said, 'How are you feeling since your fall?'

'I'm fine. Don't you think that's miraculous for someone who's nearly ninety-two?'

'Everyone thinks you're miraculous.' Neil tried a smile.

'Life's a miracle,' Cecily said.

Neil nodded and sipped his tea again.

Cecily continued. 'Dickie had a good life. He did exceptionally well, coming from a tough background. He and Gail were happy. They had Dickie Junior. He's a good man.'

A sob escaped Neil's lips. 'It doesn't seem fair.'

'What doesn't?'

Neil sniffed again. 'Death. It's so cruel.' He wiped a hand across his face. 'I mean, why, Cecily? We're born and we live our lives and we all think we're fine, then suddenly, out of nowhere, we're gone.'

'Some people have faith. Some have different beliefs.'

'I don't know what to think,' Neil said.

'No one knows for sure.' Cecily felt the warmth from the cup against her cold hands. 'We can only do our best to make today wonderful.'

'But when I think about losing Lin, it terrifies me.' Neil gulped.

'That's natural. And you're a better man for thinking it.' Cecily looked at him fondly. 'You were always one of the nicest boys in the class.'

Neil gave her a look of admiration. 'You were the best teacher.'

'You and Lin have a special relationship.'

Neil was close to tears again. 'We do.'

'It's all about making today wonderful. Make memories. But don't worry.'

'How can I not think about it? Dickie's gone. What if I'm next? Or Lin?'

Cecily smiled. 'Statistically, it's my turn.' She put her hand on his kindly. 'Do you know what Lorca said? It's a comfort to me, his words.'

'Lorca?'

'The Spanish playwright.'

'No.'

'He said, "Those who are afraid of death will carry it on their shoulders." Concentrate on having fun now. Live today.'

Neil smiled slowly. 'You're right.'

'I am,' Cecily agreed. 'You have a wonderful woman, a wonderful life, so much love. You have laughter, a family, a Frog-Eyed Sprite.' She squeezed his arm. 'Enjoy them all.'

Neil met her eyes. 'Is that what you do? Enjoy everything?'

'It is.'

'But you're on your own,' Neil said. 'Don't you get lonely?'

'I have friends, I have books, music, memories.' Cecily paused. 'Neil, I have a question for you. Do you think being ninety-two is too old to find happiness?'

'No. Why should it be?' Neil said. 'You told me to enjoy everything. You should do the same.'

'Ah.'

'Why?'

'Just something I've been thinking about recently. A decision I need to make. Do I take a chance or do I spend the rest of my life wondering what might have happened?'

'That's a no-brainer, isn't it, given what you've just said?'

'I think it is.' Cecily smiled slowly. 'Thank you, Neil.'

'What for?'

'Let's go down to The Sun and celebrate Dickie's life. Afterwards, we'll start celebrating our own.' Cecily stood up purposefully. 'I'm going to contact someone I loved very dearly. And I'm going to find out what he has to say for himself after almost seventy years.'

* * *

Minnie, Lin and Josie sat at the table in the window of The Sun, glasses in their hands. The pub was packed – everyone had just chorused another toast to Dickie Senior. Minnie took a gulp from her pint. 'I'm furious, Lin. That man can't buy Tina's house and move to the village. Not after what he did to Florence.' She glanced across the bar. Dangerous Dave was sitting with Jimmy, Kenny, Fergal Toomey and Mike Bailey.

'Dave has no idea,' Lin whispered. 'He'd kill Darryl if he knew what he'd done to his princess.'

'We are the only ones who know, apart from Adam. It's best kept that way,' Josie said.

'I may have to tell Tina,' Minnie mused. 'Just to prevent that man from buying her house.'

'Is she going to buy somewhere in Oxford?' Josie asked.

'I'm not sure. She has a friend she might move in with. They share a love of gardening.'

'Oh, that's good,' Lin said. 'So Jensen will be able to visit you this summer.'

'Jensen's being cryptic,' Minnie sighed. 'I spoke to him last night and he said he'd had enough of my procrastinating and was going to take matters into his own hands.'

'What will he do?' Lin asked.

'He's been reading a lot about early Indian theatre.' She was thoughtful. 'It wouldn't surprise me if he took off there to do some research.'

'How would you feel if he did?' Josie asked.

'Devastated by the timing,' Minnie said honestly. 'I think Tina's ready to move out.'

'Speak to Jensen,' Lin urged. 'Tell him to visit you. Or leap on a plane and throw yourself in his arms.'

Minnie said, 'I've asked Jensen to give me a bit more time. Tina and I are bonding.'

'And Jensen?' Josie asked fondly.

'He's a big part of my future,' Minnie said. 'And what about you, Josie?'

'Me?' Josie felt her skin prickle with heat.

'Mike Bailey hasn't stopped looking at you since we came in the pub,' Minnie said matter-of-factly. 'And you've been peeking at him.'

'I noticed that too,' Lin said. 'What's going on, Josie?'

Josie waved her hand in front of her face to cool her skin. 'He came round with flowers and asked me out.'

'What did you say?' Lin shrieked and Josie gestured for her to keep her voice down.

'I put him off a bit.'

'Do you like him?' Lin whispered.

'I don't know,' Josie whispered back. 'I used to like him a lot. I've been thinking about it. I said there would never be anyone after Harry, and I still think that, but—'

'*But* is an interesting word.' Minnie smiled.

'I just wonder if I went out with him just once...'

'You might rekindle the old romantic feelings?' Lin suggested.

'That's not what I want,' Josie said awkwardly. 'That's what I'm worried about. He still has the ability to make me feel – something I don't want to feel.'

'So it's safer if you don't go,' Minnie said practically.

'But if you don't go, you'll never know,' Lin added.

Josie's face was troubled. 'What do you think I should do?'

Minnie glanced over towards the table where Jimmy was toasting Dickie again. Mike glanced over to her and smiled. Fergal did the same, raising his glass.

'I think you need to go with what makes you happiest,' Minnie replied.

'Fergal has a new wife,' Lin said. 'She's made him happy.'

'Isn't she here?' Minnie asked.

'She didn't know Dickie, so she wouldn't come,' Josie said by way of explanation. 'It must be hard being new to the village. I'm going to invite her over for lunch.'

'Oh? When?'

'This weekend.' Josie raised a glass back towards Fergal, noticing Mike's eyes on her. 'I arranged it with Fergal. He says she's shy but he'll get her to come round. Although when I met her at Fergal's barge, she wasn't shy then.'

'I thought she was a bit blunt,' Lin said anxiously.

'Fergal seems happy with her. She's probably got a heart of gold,' Josie said. 'I want to get to know her. She must feel isolated.'

'I think that's a great thing to do,' Minnie said. 'We'll take her to Odile's café for tea and cakes.'

'Small steps,' Josie said.

'So...' Minnie leaned forward confidentially. 'I know we're here to remember Dickie, and celebrate the man he was, but there are other things on the Silver Ladies' agenda too this afternoon.'

'Are there?' Lin asked.

'Oh, yes.' Minnie finished her pint. 'Josie's love life, for one thing. Well, here's my considered opinion. I think you should go out with Mike once, Josie, see how it goes. We're here for you. And I need to talk to Tina and make sure she doesn't sell her house to Casanova Darryl.' She placed her glass down firmly. 'He can't come here to live. It doesn't bear thinking about.'

'Does Darryl know the child is his?' Lin asked.

'He'd be a fool not to. Charlotte knew. She found Florence's earring in their marital bed,' Josie recalled.

'She'll have cited his adultery in their divorce,' Minnie said grimly. 'He'll know.'

'So why does he want to live here?' Josie asked.

'Your guess is as good as mine, but I don't trust his motives.' Minnie stood up to go to the bar.

'What a rat,' Josie added.

'And we've Cecily's birthday to plan. We need to organise a big bash, once Dickie's ready to think about it. And what about Eddie?'

'Eddie?' Lin clapped her hands. 'Yes. I think Cecily should meet him. It could be wonderful.'

'It would, to see each other after all these years. It might bring some sort of closure,' Josie said.

'If anyone can help her, we can.' Minnie pressed her lips together. She glanced over her shoulder. 'Oh, here's Cecily now, with Neil. She's parking the Flying Plum. I'll get drinks.'

'Shall we keep her party details a secret?' Lin suggested. 'She knows when it is, but not where and how. We could make it a surprise.'

'We could.' Minnie's eyes glittered with mischief. 'We owe Cecily so much. Her happiness is our priority. And we all agree, there's unfinished business with Eddie. We have to get them together.' Minnie waved as Cecily and Neil came in together, and whispered, 'Just imagine if he was the ultimate birthday present...'

27

The kitchen clock in Odile's café showed that it was half past one. As Florence took her apron off, Odile placed her hands on her hips and said, 'Friday lunchtime, our busiest time, and your mother has to show up at the station.'

'I'm sorry,' Florence said.

'Not at all. Take the time,' Odile replied. 'I'll cover. The point is that your mother thinks she can swan back into your life whenever it suits her.'

'I know,' Florence said sadly. 'I hope it goes all right.'

'You mean you hope she behaves herself and leaves without upsetting anyone.'

'My dad's ready to forgive her.' Florence tugged on her jacket and swung her handbag over a shoulder. 'She didn't think twice before leaving me when I was a teenager. She doesn't contact me for years, then when she finds out about Elsie she's all over the idea of being a grandma.'

Odile folded her arms. 'I hope she realises what she's got. A grandchild is for life. I know. I got five of them.'

'Dad's been told to stay in the garage. I'll bring Mum up to the house for a cup of tea and message him. He can come back and join us.'

'And Adam?'

'He's got a meeting with the Ledburys.'

'I was talking to Penny yesterday,' Odile said. 'She thinks they may have to sell everything.'

'Adam's working late tonight, going through the farm books.' Florence turned to go. 'To be honest, I think he's giving us space to spend time with Mum.'

'He's a good man,' Odile said. 'Your mother doesn't know about him yet?'

'She hasn't asked.'

Odile made a tutting noise. 'That boy needs to be included.'

'I know,' Florence agreed. 'I'll talk to Mum.'

Odile met her eyes and Florence imagined that she was wondering who Elsie's father was. Florence knew that every eligible young man in Middleton Ferris had been suspected at one time or another, the Toomey boys, Bobby Ledbury, Jack Lovejoy. But not Darryl.

She never wanted to see Darryl again. Natalie had heard he'd shacked up with a nurse in Tadderly. Florence hoped he wasn't going to make a habit of coming to the village. It petrified her to think he'd come to the café. She was sure it was him she'd seen outside. And she had no intention of ever letting him near Elsie.

But it was time to deal with different ghosts.

She hugged Odile. 'Thanks. I'll see you tomorrow morning.'

'Good luck.' Odile slipped a bag of biscuits into her hand. 'Your mother will want something sweet with her tea. Dave too, when he comes home a-wooing.'

'I hope he doesn't,' Florence said with a brave smile, grateful for Odile's thoughtfulness.

She was on her way down to Geraldine's in Newlands, where Elsie would be waiting in her stroller, dressed in a clean frock. It wouldn't take long to get to the station for the two-thirty train. Florence hoped she looked all right in her summer work dress, her hair brushed and loose. She wondered if her mother had changed. What would she look like now? Would they recognise each other?

* * *

At two-twenty, Florence stood on the platform, gazing down the line. Her mother would probably have to go to Northampton to get the train to Middleton Ferris. It was a long journey, an hour and three quarters. She glanced at Elsie, completely oblivious that her grandmother was coming to visit. She was kicking her legs, chewing a toy donkey.

Florence's heart suddenly ached for her daughter. She'd never abandon Elsie; she'd always put her first. She felt a momentary pang of anger – her mother wouldn't be allowed to promise the earth and then let the child down.

A text came in from Adam.

> Good luck with meeting your mum. xx

Florence wondered if her mother would be sitting at the kitchen table when Adam came home. She imagined her drinking tea, eating Odile's biscuits, flirting with Dave. Flirting with Adam. Florence was filled with apprehension.

The platform was quite busy; there were people with cases, probably on their way to Oxford. There was a man with a beard and round glasses; a woman with a toddler who was hugging a baby laptop, two men who might be father and son, a bunch of teenagers who ought to be at school. Florence stared along the line again into the distance. The train was due at any moment.

Her heart was thudding.

A crackle from the speaker and a nasal voice announced that the train would arrive in one minute, before stopping at Bicester, Bicester North and Oxford. Florence found a fixed point in the distance and watched. The train appeared, hurtling along the rails, rolling, slowing and finally stopping. A dozen doors hissed open, and people clambered out. A couple holding hands. A blonde woman carrying a handbag, wearing a suit. Florence's mind raced as she inspected the woman for signs of the mother she remembered. The woman walked past. It was not her. She was probably in her thirties, much younger than Florence's mother would be now. Florence looked round.

There was no one else. The platform was empty.

A whistle blew a piercing shriek. The train shambled away from the platform, picking up speed, until it rattled into the distance and became a speck.

Elsie was asleep now, her little mouth open, still hugging the toy donkey.

Florence didn't move. Her mother had let her down again. She hadn't turned up. She wasn't coming.

Why had Florence expected her to? She should have known.

Of course, if Florence and her mother had exchanged phone numbers, perhaps she'd have received a text. But she could have phoned on the old landline. The number hadn't changed. Something must have happened. But Florence had no intention of giving her mother access to her phone. Who knew how often her mum might ring or text? There would be no boundaries. She'd already stalked her on Facebook.

With a sigh, Florence turned the stroller around and pushed Elsie towards the gate. All she could do now was head home.

Her father had been on edge all week. Right now, he'd be thinking of nothing else but the woman he believed was on her way to his home, who he wanted to meet again more than anything.

Florence knew how disappointed he'd be. But she wasn't disappointed. She felt angry. And, what was worse, she wasn't the least bit surprised.

* * *

The same afternoon, Minnie watched, frowning, as Tina stood in front of the living-room mirror in denim dungarees and a vest, applying mascara. Tina said, 'Are you in a bad mood?'

'No. What?' Minnie heard the defensiveness in her voice.

'You've been grumpy all morning. You're still grumpy.'

Minnie avoided the conversation. 'Why are you putting make-up on to work on the garden?'

'It's just mascara.'

'I can see that.' Minnie noticed there was a slight tremor in Tina's arm. 'When can I meet Gary?'

'You want to meet him?'

'He's got you putting make-up on.'

Tina turned and sighed dramatically. 'I want to look my best.'

'To weed cabbages?'

'Gary and I are just gardening. Afterwards, we're off to the garden centre that you and I went to. We're looking at stuff to plant for the winter.'

'Planning,' Minnie said with a half-smile. 'For the future.'

'He's hinted again about me moving in.'

'What did he say?'

'That it was nice to spend time working with me, so much so

that...' Tina smiled, remembering '...it might be good to have me on the plot full-time. I'm so useful.'

'Useful? Like Thomas the Tank Engine?' Minnie was appalled. 'That's not romantic.'

'He's not a man of words, like Jensen.'

'Jensen.' Minnie made a low sound. 'The less said about Jensen, the better.'

'Is that why you're grumpy?'

'He stood me up.'

'He's in New York, Minnie. How can he stand you up?'

'He was due to call me this morning and he hasn't.'

'I thought you were both loved up.'

'We are.' Minnie's mouth became a straight line. 'Last time we spoke, he said he'd take matters into his own hands. And now he failed to call this morning. *Ergo*, he's probably losing patience with me.'

'Can't you call him?'

Minnie was horrified. '*Me* call *him*? I've never chased after a man in my life.'

'Perhaps he's had a fall. Perhaps he's had a—'

'Better offer?'

'A stroke.'

For a moment, Minnie looked worried. She said, 'You're right. I'll text him later.'

'You should.' Tina turned from the mirror. 'How do I look?'

'Like a glamorous Gertrude Jekyll.'

'Who?'

'A British horticulturist, garden designer, writer and artist. She lived a century ago.'

'Oh.' Tina shrugged. 'Well, can't you ring Jensen and say you're getting your house back and to come over next month?'

'Is that a non sequitur?'

'It's a fact. I'm going to sell my house. The Featherstone man's going to make me an offer. Jimmy Baker said. Then I'll be independent.'

'You can't sell your house to him.' Minnie remembered the last call she'd had with Lin. She'd told her all about it. 'He can't move to Middleton Ferris.'

'But he's well off. He's keen to buy. I'd save on estate agents' fees.'

'Tina, he's a love rat.'

'In what sense?'

Minnie took a deep breath, choosing her words. She remembered Florence, distraught, pregnant, how much she'd suffered as Darryl paraded through the village, smug, hand in hand with his wife. She'd heard how Darryl had lied to Florence to get her into his bed, how he'd ignored her straight afterwards as if their encounter had been nothing. The injustice made her blood boil. It could only do some good if Tina knew what sort of man she wanted to sell her house to. 'In the sense that he coerced Florence Dawson into having sex with him and he left her in the lurch and pregnant.'

'Oh.' Tina's mouth twisted in thought. 'So he wants to come back and claim the baby?'

'Who knows? He might. So he can't buy your house.'

'He can't, you're right,' Tina said. 'But if I'm moving in with Gary, I need to sell it to someone. I can't turn down a good buyer and freeload off Gary forever, can I? We could do his place up, get an allotment.'

'Big plans.' Minnie grinned. 'Back to my original question – when can I meet Gary?'

'Soon.'

'Let me take you both to lunch in The Bear.'

'I'll ask him.'

'Is he shy?'

'He will be when he meets you.'

'Why?'

'Because you're intimidating, Minnie.'

'I am not.'

'I bet that's why Jensen hasn't called you. I bet he's frightened of getting another knock-back.'

'Do you think so?'

Tina didn't know, but she seemed to be relishing a moment's triumph over her sister. It had been all cut-throat disputes when they were teenagers. Minnie decided this must be the geriatric version of teenage banter. The thought made her smile. She said, 'You don't want to be late for Gary.'

'I'll ask him about lunch at The Bear.'

'I'd like to meet him.'

'Oh, I forgot my earrings.' Tina was suddenly flustered. 'I ought to put some in.'

'You're going gardening. It's hardly a catwalk.' Minnie grinned, but Tina was on her way upstairs.

The tinkle from the coffee table alerted Minnie and at first she thought it might be her phone, but the purple case was Tina's and her own phone was in her pocket. Minnie wondered if it was Gary, cancelling, or if it was an important call from the hospital. She picked it up and noticed the unknown caller. She said, 'Hello?'

'Hello. Is that Mrs Tina Gilchrist?'

Minnie registered the smooth, male voice. Her instinct kicked in and she said, 'Yes, speaking. Who are you?'

'You don't know me. My name is Darryl Featherstone.'

Minnie arched an eyebrow. She knew only too well who he was. 'How can I help you?'

'Jimmy Baker took me on a tour of your house in Harvest

Road. I've had a think about it. It's very convenient and just where I'd like to live. Of course, there are a few things I'd like to do to it, to bring it up to scratch. But I'd like to make you an offer.'

'Really?' Minnie's mind moved quickly. 'That's very kind of you, Mr Feverstein.'

'Featherstone.'

'Indeed. But I have someone else who's interested in it.'

'Oh. Who?'

'A local person.' Minnie was improvising. 'They're inspecting the property this week. So come back to me next weekend and we can discuss it.'

'Well, whatever they offer, I'll beat it,' Darryl said confidently.

'I want to sell to the person who will benefit from it most.' Minnie put a hand over her mouth to suppress a laugh.

'Oh, I have very close connections to the village.'

'Really?' Minnie held her breath. 'What connections?'

'Dave Dawson's a friend of mine. I know his family well.'

Minnie's teeth clacked together. 'Do you?'

'Look, Tina – can I call you Tina? Why don't I take you to dinner somewhere? The Rose and Crown in Charlbury? Or I can drive to Oxford and we'll have lunch. I'm sure I can convince you.'

Minnie laughed, a tinkling, dismissive sound. 'Look, Mr Feathergill, let me show the other interested party around the house. Then we'll talk about it.'

'I'm a cash buyer.'

'I don't see the need to rush. Is there one?'

'Well, no, but—'

'Ring me next weekend, there's a good man.' Minnie heard

Darryl catch his breath. He'd clearly never been spoken to that way. She smiled. 'Thank you for calling. Goodbye.'

Minnie placed the phone back on the table just as Tina came in, wearing dangly earrings. 'Was that my phone? Who was it?'

'A nuisance caller.' Minnie felt a pang of guilt. She probably should have told Tina about the offer on her house. But she'd tell her later.

Tina was loitering at the door. 'Well. Bye, Minnie. Don't wait up.'

'Oh? Are you spending the night?' Minnie asked. 'Mascara, dangly earrings. Gary won't be able to help himself.'

Tina laughed, blew a kiss and was gone.

Minnie sat down, thinking of Darryl Featherstone. She'd never really spoken to him before. Now she'd had a conversation, she thought he was arrogant, conceited, smug. She'd need to find a way to stop him buying Tina's house without Tina losing out.

Minnie was lost in thought. The simple answer was to put the house on the market and let an estate agent deal with it. But that might not stop Darryl.

Her phone buzzed and she tugged it from her pocket. It was a text from Jensen. She scanned the words quickly. 'Aha.'

> Minnie, my love. I'm going to India for ten days to research theatre. I have been offered the chance to meet Makarand Deshpande and I can't turn it down. But I'll be back soon. Then you and I have a big decision to make. Amor aeternus, J. xx

'Indeed we do,' she said aloud.

He was going to India. But what if he was also giving himself thinking time? Perhaps she'd put him off once too often, blowing hot and cold. Minnie wondered if he was finally going to give her the brush-off. She'd hardly blame him. But it would break her heart.

No, Jensen loved her. He'd written *amor aeternus* – eternal love. Perhaps it was time for her to put her cards on the table. She missed him. She craved his company more than she'd admitted. She'd been looking forward to the time they could be together again. In quiet moments, she found herself dreaming of their sweet reunion. Feeling romantic, even.

Jensen was her equal, her soulmate. The only man she'd ever truly loved.

She needed to tell him that once and for all.

28

On Saturday morning, Cecily sat at a patio table in the warm sunshine of her garden, a blank card in front of her, a pen poised between her fingers. She had no idea where to start.

'Dear Eddie,' she said aloud.

She couldn't write that. It wasn't a normal letter. It wasn't easy to use the word 'dear' without so many emotions flooding back.

'Hello, Eddie.'

No, that didn't sound right.

'Eddie. I decided to contact you after all this time.'

Still not right. Cecily wasn't sure what to put. He wasn't the same person as he'd been in his twenties. She didn't know him any more. How could she write to someone she didn't know?

But what if he was the same person he'd always been, warm, passionate, in love with her? What would she write then?

Cecily lifted the pen and whispered, 'My darling Eddie.' She caught her breath. That was what she really wanted to say.

Cecily picked up a piece of paper and started to write down what was in her heart. Her hand shook with emotion.

My darling Eddie. Not a day has gone by when I haven't thought of you. I believed once that we did the right thing to go our separate ways. You and Joyce

Cecily closed her eyes. Eddie and Joyce. That was the barrier. That was what kept them apart. And the baby, Elizabeth, Sammy's mother. She took a breath and started again.

She wrote more, her thoughts coming quickly.

I want to say that I know Joyce seduced you and I never really acknowledged her part in splitting us up. I blamed you. It was easy to do that because you let me down. But how could you sleep with Joyce when you loved me? Did I matter so little that you could forget how you felt about me, even for a moment?

Cecily paused. Could she really forgive that betrayal?

It was easier to forgive Joyce now she was dead. Besides, Joyce's desperate tipsy attempt to seduce Eddie had never surprised Cecily. Joyce had never made a secret of how attractive she'd found him. No, Eddie was to blame. She couldn't forgive his lack of loyalty. His lack of true love.

For a moment Cecily put herself in Eddie's position. Joyce had offered him something Cecily held back. It had been important to Cecily to remain a virgin until she married. Eddie had respected that. He'd said he did. But he'd taken advantage of Joyce without a moment's thought.

Cecily made a low sound of contempt. Eddie had been an opportunist. He'd slept with Joyce for the same reason that George Mallory had climbed Everest. Because it was there. He'd simply used her. And she'd had a few drinks. Eddie's behaviour was unforgivable.

Cecily wriggled the pen in an attempt to think things through, trying to consider Eddie's side of the story. It was only fair. She hadn't been there. Joyce would have been persuasive. Eddie had been weak.

He'd still betrayed her though, and there was no excuse for it. He had ruined so many lives with one selfish act.

No, she wouldn't contact him or send him a card. She wasn't sure she wanted to see him or speak to him again. Because of his recklessness, he'd changed the course of her life, Joyce's, his own, forever. Cecily was still reeling from it even now, in her nineties.

Her hand shook with fury. Eddie was a fool.

She stared out at the garden, the nodding roses, the sweet peas that twirled in the light breeze. She had no idea what to do. Contacting Eddie would swirl all the old hurt in her heart. But not contacting him left so many questions unanswered.

She felt her heart ache in her chest. Her cheeks were damp with tears.

The brave thing to do was to walk away. Or, the brave thing was to contact him and give him a chance to explain.

Cecily threw the pen onto the table. She had no idea which way to go.

* * *

Josie's large house in Charlbury Road was sparkling clean. She had vacuumed, plumped cushions, dusted. The scent of the Tropical Blossom plug-in was so overpowering, she'd had to open two windows, but she wanted the place to smell nice for Poll Toomey. She'd be here at half twelve, and that was twenty minutes away.

Josie was surprised she felt a little nervous. She wanted the lunch to go well. She'd spread all sorts of dishes on the table in the hope that Poll would be able to pick some she liked. There was salad, chicken, bread. Josie wondered if Poll was vegetarian – she should have asked. It would be embarrassing if Poll didn't like any of the dishes. Surely Fergal would have said. Josie was beginning to wish she'd spoken to Poll directly. Or she should have asked Lin to come along. She was easy to get on with. Poll would love her and it would have taken some of the stress from Josie. But Lin and Neil had gone off in the Sprite somewhere.

There was a rap on the front door. Josie glanced at the clock. Poll was early. Perhaps she didn't own a watch, or there were no clocks on the barge. She'd have a phone though, surely? Such thoughts were silly. Josie realised how little she knew about Poll.

Lunch would be an opportunity to find out. She took a breath and hurried to the front door.

She was surprised to see Mike Bailey there. He looked gorgeous in a smart jacket. Josie peeked at his jeans, which were tight and clung to his muscular thighs. He smelled of something musky, with vanilla notes, a warm, inviting scent.

Sexy.

Josie told herself to calm down. He handed her a red rose.

'Thanks, but—'

'For you,' Mike said, his eyes twinkling. 'Are you busy?'

Josie didn't invite him in. 'I have a friend coming for lunch.'

'A man?'

'Fergal's wife, Poll.' Josie smiled awkwardly.

'Good.' Mike looked pleased with her answer. 'I wanted to ask. What are you doing on Tuesday?'

'Tuesday? I'm not sure.' Josie twirled the rose between her fingers.

'I'll take you out for a drive, buy you lunch.' Mike raised an eyebrow. 'If that's all right?'

'Yes.' Josie had no idea what else to say. He'd caught her completely off guard.

Mike beamed. 'Shall I pick you up around ten?'

'Yes, I suppose.'

'Excellent.' Mike leaned towards her and pecked her cheek. Her nose filled with the strong scent of musk. 'It promises to be a beautiful day. And you and I...' His eyes twinkled and Josie felt a little unnerved by his easy confidence. 'We'll have a wonderful time. I look forward to it.'

Josie watched as he sauntered down her path. At the gate, he was met by Poll Toomey coming the other way. She eyed him suspiciously as he said something that sounded like, 'Enjoy lunch.'

Poll reached the door and frowned. 'He was smarmy. Oh, he's not your boyfriend, is he?'

'Mike?' Josie wasn't sure how to answer, so she said, 'We sort of know each other.' She held the door wide. 'Come in, Poll.'

Poll stayed where she was. She handed Josie a pack of six beers. 'I brung these, just in case. I'm partial to stout.'

'Thanks.' Josie ushered her inside. 'Come into the living room.'

Poll stood in the hall and sniffed loudly. 'What's that stink? Oh, you've got one of those plug-ins on the go. They give me a headache.'

'Shall I open the window?'

'It's no problem, we can eat outside.' Poll walked up to the table of food. 'Look at all this bostin' fettle. It looks scrumptious. You've pushed the boat out.'

'Thank you.' Josie was relieved. 'I hope you enjoy it.'

Poll stuck out a hand. 'Now let's do things proper and get introduced. My name's Pollyanna Esmerelda Brittanica Loveridge. My dad was Bertrand Samson Loveridge and my mother was Margaret Charity Loveridge. My husband who died – ah, let them all rest in peace! – his name was Silvanus Goliath Lee. So, now it's your turn to say where you come from, and then we'll know each other.'

'Josie.' Josie shook Poll's hand. She'd never met anyone so forthright. But there was something about Poll she liked instinctively. She was honest: what you saw was what you got. Behind the brusqueness, she probably had a heart of gold. 'Sanderson. My husband was Harry. My mum and dad were Doris and John Potter.'

'That's good, now we're friends.' Poll folded her arms. 'That man who was calling on you – Mike. Is he giving you any trouble?'

'No,' Josie said hesitantly.

'It's just if he is, now we're friends, I'll sort him out for you.'

'Sort him out?' Josie was worried.

'Tell him to shove off. If he lays a hand on you, I'll knock him into next week with one bomb.' Poll showed a fist proudly. 'Not that I like fighting, mind. Not since I grew up. The road of peacefulness is always better.'

'Right, er, I think I'll be safe with Mike. He's new to the village.'

'Same as me,' Poll said. 'I just wanted to say, Josie, thanks for your hospitality. That's proper kind of you.'

'My pleasure.' Josie indicated the table. 'Shall we eat?'

'Oh, no, not yet. I have to work for my bread and butter first.' Poll winked. 'Let's sort out that annoying drip and afterwards, we'll tuck in.'

'Annoying drip?' Josie wondered if Poll was still talking about Mike.

'I can hear it going plip! plip! in your kitchen. You've got a leaky tap.'

'I don't know how to fix it.'

'I do.' Poll grinned. 'I'm a dab hand. Just you leave it to me, Josie. And while you're at it, if there's anything else needs sorting out around the house, I'm your woman.'

'Well, there's a cracked tile in the bathroom.' Josie was filled with admiration. She'd never met anyone like Poll before.

'Easy as pie. Just let me have a look. I'll need a spanner, a chisel, some grouting and a spare tile – oh, and a bucket.'

* * *

At four-thirty, Josie and Poll were sitting in the garden, their plates empty. Cans of beer had been drunk, and several glasses of Cava were all but empty. Poll smacked her lips. 'That was scrumptious, Josie.'

Josie was delighted. 'I can't believe you fixed the tap.'

'Your Harry had left everything in the box beneath the sink to do the job. I just put the replacement O-ring in position and put the valve back on. Simple.'

'And that chipped tile looks so much better.'

'Your Harry loved you,' Poll said, meeting her eyes. 'He had everything so well organised, so that if something happened to him, you'd be able to find everything.'

'And it did happen.' Josie exhaled. 'Poll, did you find it hard being a widow?'

'I married my Silv for love, Josie.' Poll was quiet for a moment. 'The more you love someone, the more it hurts when they've gone. But I have Fergal now. He lost his Ros. So we're good for each other.'

'Do you love him?' Josie asked and Poll gave a low cackle.

'Do I? Look at him. I mean, Josie. He's in his seventies but that bod still turns heads. He has lovely hair and a voice that would melt your heart. He's twelve years older than I am, but what's twelve years when you're lying in a man's arms beneath the stars at night and he's whispering in your ear?' Poll took her hand. 'You know, my heart broke when my Silv died. But Fergal has stuck it back together with Sellotape. I'll be all right now. And I did the same for him, so he's happy too.' She stared at Josie, watching her face change. 'I think you want to go out with that man who was at the door, the one who smelled like a madame's boudoir. Am I right?'

'I'm thinking about it.'

'But you're worried because of how much you loved your Harry?'

'That's about the size of it,' Josie said quietly.

'Give him one chance. Just one. And if he doesn't blow it, give him another one. Just go out with him and see how it goes. Like a trial-size packet of washing-powder. And if you like the product, eventually you can buy it. If you don't like it, bin it off.'

Josie thought she understood what Poll was saying. 'You mean I don't have to decide after the first date, or the second.'

'As long as he shapes up, he gets another chance.' Poll winked.

'You're going to make an incredible Silver Lady.' Josie smiled.

'What's one of them when it's at home?' Poll shook a beer can to check it was empty. It was.

'My friends and I meet for lunch every so often. Minnie, Lin and Cecily. Lin called us the Silver Ladies because we are all of a certain age. The name stuck.'

'But you haven't got silver hair.' Poll fluffed her own billowing mane. 'I keep mine long, that's tradition. I might do what my grandmother Clementina Loveridge used to do back in the day. She'd stew some elderberries over a fire and make hair dye out of the liquid. It gives a lovely colour to grey hair and makes it shine.' She laughed. 'We could be the Burgundy Ladies.'

Josie giggled. 'Will you come to our next lunch?'

'What if I don't fit in?' A look of mistrust passed across Poll's face. 'What if they don't like me?'

'They'll love you,' Josie said.

'Well, I won't know if I don't try, will I?' Poll replied. She gave Josie a meaningful stare. 'It's just the same with you and that bloke you fancy who smells of moth repellent. You've got to go out with him and see what happens.'

'I suppose I ought to,' Josie said. She smiled. Poll was right.

She was already planning what to wear for the date on Tuesday.

29

It was Saturday evening, six-thirty. Adam was folding clean baby clothes and Dangerous Dave had his feet up, reading the newspaper. Florence sat at the kitchen table, her head on her arms, and groaned. 'I suppose I'd better make something to eat. Elsie will wake up in a minute. I'll bring her down here and we'll keep her up as late as we can. Or she'll wake up three times in the night again.' She closed her eyes briefly. 'I'm tired.'

'Nothing for me, Princess.' Dave's nose was in the newspaper. 'I promised Jimmy and Kenny I'd go down The Sun tonight. I might get a bite down there.'

'Josie said she'd babysit at some point, Adam,' Florence said. 'I'd ask her to come round, but I'm too tired to go out.'

'You deserve a night off.' Adam kissed the top of her head. 'Why don't you go up to see Natalie at the farm, and I'll stay with Elsie?'

'Natalie will be out. She goes clubbing in Tadderly on Saturdays.' Florence reached out and grabbed Adam's hand. 'Besides, I want to spend time with you.'

'I'll babysit if you like,' Dave said. 'I don't mind giving the pub a miss. Adam, you and Florence go down The Sun.'

'No, Dad,' Florence said quickly. 'You have a night out with Jimmy and Kenny.' She remembered the last time Dave had babysat Elsie. He'd fallen asleep in front of the TV; the baby had been crying in the nursery upstairs. Florence had heard her wails before she'd opened the front door. And another time, Dave had tried to feed Elsie yogurt and left her alone with the bowl. When Florence had come home, both Elsie and her grandfather had been plastered in yogurt. The table, Elsie's high chair, her clothes and the floor. Florence had decided it was easier not to leave Dave in charge.

'I'll cook,' Adam said. 'I can make pasta.'

'You could.' Florence wasn't inspired. Adam made great pasta, but she was just not in the mood for it. She needed something to lift her spirits. She knew what was troubling her. She said it out loud. 'I wish Mum hadn't let us all down.'

'You should have given her your phone number, Florence.'

'I don't want her to have my phone number, Dad.' Florence heard the petulance in her voice.

'You could've given her mine.' Dave looked hopeful. 'That way, we'd know why she didn't come. I expect something came up at the last minute.'

Florence caught Adam's eye and a look passed between them. Florence's mother was unreliable.

But Dave was still hopeful. 'She'll write again. There'll be a letter in the post on Monday, you'll see. She'll have a good reason. She'll make another date and come and see us.'

Florence wasn't sure she wanted her mother to make another date. Life had been easier before she'd come back into their lives.

'What about if I—?' Adam took Florence's hand. 'What if I

go to the takeaway and get us something? We won't need to cook.'

'Great.' Florence met his eyes. 'That would be really nice, just for a change.'

'Let's make it date night, since your dad's out.' Adam's eyes shone. 'Candles, soft music, just me and you and Elsie. I've got some things I want to talk to you about.'

'Oh?' Florence was interested. 'Yes, let's do that.'

'Right.' Dave put the paper on the table. 'I'd better get changed, have a shave.'

He was on his way out when Florence shouted, 'Try not to cut yourself again, Dad – I left the first-aid kit out just in case.'

'Yeah, yeah,' Dave laughed and was gone.

Florence stood up and went over to Adam, leaning into his embrace. 'What did you want to talk about?'

'Just ordinary stuff. Me and you. Elsie. Work.'

'How did the meeting go?'

'The Ledburys?' Adam brightened. 'They need to think outside the box. They aren't making enough profits to match overheads, running a loss. But I sent them away with a business plan and a couple of things to think about.'

Florence wrapped her arms around his neck. 'Natalie texted. Bobby's looking for extra work. Builders' yards. She said she needs to find a new job too.'

'It might be OK. George and Penny and George Junior are going to talk to the bank, then we'll meet again.'

Florence leaned her face towards Adam's for a kiss. 'I'm proud of you.'

'I'm proud of you too,' Adam murmured into her hair. 'All this business with your mum and Elsie and Dave. It's been tough.'

'It really got to me, Adam. I'm trying not to get angry. But she let me down again.'

'We've got each other,' Adam said, touching her cheek. 'We're solid. Nothing's going to spoil that.'

'I know,' Florence said, her voice tender with emotion. 'Me, you and Elsie. I've been a bit wobbly lately, but we're stronger than ever.'

'You've been really tired. We both have.' Adam kissed her. 'What if I ask Mum to take Elsie tomorrow? We can go for a ride in the car. It'll give us a break. And Mum loves to fuss over Elsie.'

'At least one of us has a mother we can depend on.' Florence exhaled frustratedly. 'Oh, I just need to forget her and think of something else.' She paused for a moment. 'Kung Pao chicken.'

Adam laughed. 'What?'

'That's what I'd like from the takeaway. And some dim sum.'

'I'm on it.' Adam grinned. 'I'll get chow mein and spring rolls and crispy seaweed. We can have a proper feast.'

'Saturday night in, with the man I love.' Florence kissed him. 'I'll put your favourite music on.'

'I'll get going.' Adam reached for his jacket and tugged it on, checking he had his phone in his pocket and his cards. He kissed Florence briefly. 'You could warm plates and get something to drink.'

'Once I'm not feeding Elsie, I'm having wine with everything.' Florence grinned. 'Shall I get you a beer?'

'Yes, please, lager.' Adam was already at the door. 'I won't be long.'

'Don't be.' Florence blew him a kiss. 'This is our time.'

'It is. Love you,' Adam said, and was gone.

The door behind him closed with a crisp click, and Adam was on his way up the Newlands estate hill towards the parade of shops, with the takeaway in the middle. It had been called

The Golden Dragon since Adam was a boy, but new owners had taken it over recently and renamed it Thai Tanic. Adam grinned. The menu was the same and the prices had gone up.

Money made the world go round. Pushing his hands in his pockets, Adam thought back to his meeting with the Ledburys. His plan was a good one. It would be a new venture that involved Natalie and Bobby – who had seemed far more keen on the idea than George and Penny – and young George, Bobby and Natalie's dad.

Adam wondered how it would all turn out. He'd already heard rumours that some of the villagers were grumbling about the possibility of change. Dangerous Dave had been talking to Geoff Lovejoy, who lived next to Lin and Neil Timms. Geoff and Janice insisted that everyone else they'd spoken to was dead set against the fields being used for development.

Adam's mind drifted to Florence. There were things he wanted to discuss with her too. Plans for their future. He'd seen a new flat in Tadderly, a modern one on the ground floor, not far from the primary school. But it would be a train journey for Florence to get to Odile's café each day. Adam wondered about the idea of another baby, a brother or sister for Elsie. The thought of two toddlers playing together made him smile.

The sound of a car engine idling brought him from his dream. He turned to see a silver Porsche Boxster, a man with his elbow hanging out of the window, his jacket sleeves casually turned up.

The man said, 'Hello. It's Adam, isn't it?'

Adam forced himself to be calm. His first instinct was to feel defensive. Florence had told him about Darryl when Elsie was born. Adam wasn't a man who naturally felt anger; he wasn't violent. But he was wholly loyal to Florence and Elsie. And the natural animosity he felt towards Darryl was unavoidable. He scowled as Darryl offered a false smile.

'You don't know me, but I've been hoping we could have a chat.'

'What about?' Adam felt his heart accelerate and his fists became hard knots.

'I'm a solicitor in Charlbury. I've heard you and your father are accountants in Tadderly. I was wondering if I could put some business your way. A client of mine asked me to recommend someone.'

Adam looked into Darryl's eyes and he didn't believe him. The story was a concocted lie so that he could speak to him. Adam's breath was coming quickly now; he was sure Darryl had ulterior motives, to do with Florence and Elsie. He said, 'You must know an accountant in Charlbury.'

'I'd like to use someone from Middleton Ferris. I like the village. I have connections here.' Darryl's voice was treacle smooth. 'Let me give you my card.'

Darryl handed Adam his business card. It had his phone number on it and his name, Darryl Featherstone, LLB. Adam stared at it.

'Give me a call some time and we'll talk business,' Darryl said with a smile. 'Maybe we can get together in the local hostelry for a drink. I'm sure we can find a lot of things to talk about. We have a lot in common. You know what I mean.'

Darryl's words hung in the air as he accelerated away, turning the corner, disappearing towards Orchard Way. The cloud of smoke and horsepower roar that was pure testosterone.

Adam stared at the card. He was shaking. It was clear as daylight what had just happened. Darryl Featherstone hadn't meant a word about sharing business interests. He'd stopped for an entirely different reason. It was a veiled threat.

The smug voice still rang in his ears: 'We have a lot in common.'

He meant Florence. And Elsie.

It was a direct challenge. Darryl Featherstone was a solicitor, so he'd be clear about paternal rights. He intended to ruin everything for Adam and Florence. He wanted access to Elsie.

Adam promised himself that he'd say nothing to Florence. It would hurt her too much. She'd worry. No, he'd find a way to protect her.

Elsie was his daughter, not Darryl's. He'd do whatever it took.

30

Josie, Lin, and Cecily sat in The Sun, watching Neil chatting to Dangerous Dave and Dickie Junior at the bar. Cecily said, 'You've all got Minnie's message on the WhatsApp group. We can't let Tina sell her house to Darryl Featherstone.'

'Dave thinks Darryl's his new best friend. It's obscene,' Lin said sadly. 'And I was there when Jimmy was talking about Tina's house, telling him how we were such a welcoming community. And Darryl said, "I know," as if he was talking about Florence. I was nearly sick.'

'Do you think Darryl wants a relationship with Florence? Or is it Elsie he's after?' Josie whispered.

'He hardly seems the type to step up as a father,' Cecily said. 'But he could be the sort of man who'd get pleasure from upsetting a happy little family.'

Lin glanced towards the bar. 'He has Jimmy in his pocket, and Dave. Neil's really stuck between a rock and a hard place: he'd love to say something to Dave but he can't.'

'Does Florence know that Darryl's trying to move here?' Josie asked. 'Does she know that Dave's friends with him?'

'I hope not,' Lin said.

'Minnie's fobbed Darryl off until next weekend,' Cecily said confidentially. 'So that gives us time to come up with something.'

'She won't let Tina sell to Darryl,' Lin said.

'Probably not. I expect he'll want to get it at any price. I remember that lovely nurse, Sophie, telling me he spends his money foolishly. But Darryl needs to back off,' Cecily said. 'He has no real interest in a relationship with the child, I'm sure. Where has he been through Florence's pregnancy and Elsie's first nine months?'

'With other women, by all accounts,' Lin said.

'We just need to keep Florence safe.' Josie sipped from her glass.

'Oh, yes. If Darryl starts making demands, it could be a real shit storm.' Lin put a hand over her mouth. She was on her second gin. 'What? It's the best way to describe it. Poor Florence and Adam.'

'It won't come to that,' Cecily said. 'Come on, ladies, drink up. The next round's on me.'

'All right.' Josie reached for her elderflower pressé. 'So, we have a lot to discuss as the Silver Ladies. Let's meet at Odile's next week.' Josie smiled. 'I want to bring Poll Toomey to our next lunch. You'll like her. She's quite shy in her own way, but she comes across as a bit blunt. She's lovely though, and she's a dab hand with a screwdriver.'

'She sounds wonderful,' Cecily said. 'And we need to support Minnie. Jensen has taken himself off to India. She's missing him.'

'Minnie? That woman's had more lovers than she's read books. Well, maybe not quite that many.' Lin squeezed her eyes closed. She'd definitely drunk too much.

'So, that's Florence and Minnie who need our help. And you, Josie,' Cecily said. 'You have a hot date on Tuesday. How can we support you?'

'I'm petrified,' Josie admitted. 'I'm still not sure I'm doing the right thing.'

'See what happens,' Lin chuckled. 'And we want all the gory details.'

'There won't be any,' Josie said, alarmed.

'It's my turn to ask for support. I have an announcement to make,' Cecily said.

'Oh, do tell,' Lin leaned forward on her elbow and promptly slipped off the table. She heaved herself back.

'Is it about Eddie?' Josie asked, her face a picture of compassion.

'It is. I've made a decision,' Cecily explained. 'I wrote all my feelings down on paper, as if I was writing to him. And I found out that I blamed him entirely for what happened to Joyce. I blamed him for letting me down. I put it all at his door and I decided I wouldn't have anything to do with him ever again.'

'Oh.' Lin was genuinely sad. 'I was hoping it would work out like a dream.'

'Then I changed my mind.' Cecily sat up straight. 'I want to have it out with him once and for all. I want to ask him to his face why he let me down and let himself down at the same time. I want to hear it from his lips.'

'Good for you,' Josie said. 'Minnie will be delighted.'

'We all are,' Lin agreed.

'And I want to know if he still loves me. If he has always loved me, like I love him still. And if he does—'

'Yes?' Lin was on the edge of her seat.

'What then?' Josie asked.

'Then, and only then, I might forgive him,' Cecily said

firmly. 'But I need to know. So I'm going to take you up on your offer to drive me to his house, Lin. And I want you to come too, Josie. And Minnie.'

'Oh, definitely,' Lin said.

'So, that's my decision.' Cecily stood up. 'We'll discuss this further at Odile's next week.'

'I'll arrange it on WhatsApp,' Josie offered.

'Good. I'm going to wave to Dickie to tell him I need another round brought over. Decisions like this don't happen every day. So – my round. Drinks, ladies?'

'Mine's a gin,' Lin said as she leaned towards Josie and whispered, 'So, what about Minnie's plan to make Eddie the perfect birthday present for Cecily?'

'On track.' Josie put her thumb up and whispered back, 'Watch this space.'

* * *

On Monday morning, Florence came downstairs in a happy, dreamlike state. Elsie had slept through for two nights running. She and Adam had enjoyed a wonderful meal together on Saturday night, completely uninterrupted. He'd told her he loved her even more often than usual.

On Sunday, Rita and Linval had taken Elsie up to the farm for the day to see the animals. Adam had driven Florence to Evesham and they had been on a rowing boat together. Adam had pointed out a pretty little cottage that was for sale; he'd even suggested moving from the village, which Florence was less than keen about, but Adam's eyes had gleamed when he'd talked about a house with a garden, and how nice it would be to have two children so close together. They had ended the evening in each other's arms.

She'd never been more contented. He was a keeper.

Downstairs, Adam was feeding Elsie breakfast, tempting her with a milky cereal. She was sitting in her high chair, wanting to play. Adam was wearing his smart clothes, trying to avoid the creamy blobs of porridge Elsie was dribbling; he was due in the office at nine.

Florence set to toasting bread. She said, 'Dad's in the bathroom. He's taking longer over his grooming nowadays.' She gave Adam a worried look. 'He's still hoping Mum'll come home.'

'But you don't want her to?' Adam asked, pouring coffee.

'No, she causes trouble.' Florence sat down and accepted a steaming mug of coffee. 'It broke everyone's heart when she left. She'll do it again.' She forced a smile. 'Dad seems happy though. He's had a new bloke in the garage a few times to fix up his racy car. Now Dad says he wants to buy a four-by-four. He needs a family car, apparently.'

Adam froze. 'Did your dad say what sort of car it was?'

'No. He was banging on like he'd found a new best friend and I missed what he was saying because Elsie started yelling.' Florence shook her head. 'Why? Are you after a sports car?'

'No.' Adam gulped coffee and a troubled look passed over his face.

'So what's happening at work?' Florence asked.

'Bobby and Hayley are in today, and Natalie's in for a meeting tomorrow. It's make-or-break time.'

'Are they selling the fields?'

Adam plonked a plate of toast on the table. 'I've put some numbers on paper and there are two options, sell or branch out. George Junior thinks it might be better to sell, but Bobby and Natalie are keen on investing.'

Florence handed a piece of buttered toast to Elsie, who gnawed it eagerly. 'You're a great accountant, Adam.'

His gaze met hers across the table. 'It's for our future. Me and you and Elsie. I don't want anything to spoil our happiness.'

Florence took his hand. 'Nothing will.' She noticed the expression in his eyes. 'What's worrying you?'

'Things are almost perfect, me and you.' Adam passed a hand across his forehead. 'I just don't want the past to rear its head.'

'The past?' Florence's brow knotted.

'Well.' Adam thought about what was worrying him and he chose the second option, the lesser of two evils. 'Your mother, what if she came back and tried to interfere? Or...'

'Or?' Florence shook her head to dispel the image of Darryl watching her outside Odile's café.

'We'll be fine.' Adam grinned. 'So, what are you up to at Odile's?'

'Same old,' Florence said. 'Josie's booked a table for Wednesday. They're all having lunch, Cecily, Lin, Minnie.'

'That's nice.'

'Malia texted that she's coming home soon with her new man.'

'Malik. That's all she can bang on about.' Adam made a face.

'Natalie met someone while she was out clubbing. A young farmers' type. He's called Anthony.'

Adam chewed his lip thoughtfully. 'Florence, can I ask you something?'

'Anything.' Florence met his brown eyes. 'What's worrying you?'

'I just need to ask. Well, Natalie's out clubbing, Malia's in London and here's you, stuck in Middleton Ferris with a baby, living at your dad's.'

'And?'

'Don't you feel you're missing out?'

'No, not ever.' Florence held her toast in the air, a half-moon bite mark in the bread. She looked around the kitchen. 'I do worry sometimes though.'

'What do you worry about?'

'That you must find me boring.'

'No way!' Adam exclaimed. 'You're the most beautiful—'

'At night during feeds, I'm sitting on the bed in my old dressing gown, covered in baby dribble, dark rings round my eyes.'

'I wouldn't change a thing.'

'I worry sometimes.'

'About what?'

'Elsie. You being her dad. People say stupid things.'

'Such as?'

'Such as...' Florence took a shaky breath. 'I was at Geraldine's picking Elsie up the other day, and Geraldine was joking about her baby, saying that Arthur was the image of his father.'

'And?' Adam didn't need to ask. He knew already.

'She just blurted out what everyone in the village's thinking. She said, "Elsie looks nothing like Adam. She's got such light skin." I felt awful.'

'She's ours, Florence. I don't care what people say.'

'But what if it leaked out? What if he – Darryl—?'

Adam took her hand. 'Forget him. He's nothing.'

'But suppose he did something awful, like get a court order for a DNA test or something?'

'Don't think that. He's not going to bother us.' Adam's face clouded. He hated lying to Florence.

The knot appeared again in between Florence's eyes. Then the puckered skin relaxed. 'I'm so glad we have each other. Imagine if he came back.'

'He won't,' Adam insisted.

There was a loud ringing of the front doorbell. Both Florence and Adam jumped. Their eyes locked.

Dangerous Dave shouted from the hall. 'I'll get it.'

They sat, staring at each other, listening to Dave's friendly tone. 'All right, mate. Yes, another week at the grind. Ah, no. You must get a lot of exercise in your line of work though...'

'The postman,' Adam mouthed.

They heard the door clunk and Dave appeared holding three letters. He leafed through them.

'Junk mail, junk mail, and—' he held out a pink envelope '—this one's addressed to you, Florence.'

Florence glanced at her father as she took the letter. He had toilet roll stuck on a cut on his chin. Another shaving accident. She said, 'It's from Mum.'

'Open it,' Dave said. It was all he could do not to tear it from her hands. Florence glanced towards Adam, who was watching her. Elsie was dribbling toast. Florence ripped open the envelope, tugged out the letter and scanned the contents. They were brief.

'Mum says...' Florence took a deep breath. 'She missed the train last Friday. She was held up at home. Unforeseen circumstances. She's sorry. But – oh, that's rude.'

'What?' Dave's face fell. 'What does she say?'

'She says if I'd given her my phone number like she asked in the first letter, she could have texted me and...' Florence was unimpressed.

'And what?' Dave asked. 'Is she coming to see us?'

'She's given me her number. She wants me to send her lots of photos of Elsie in pretty clothes so that she can show her friends.'

'She has friends?' Adam said under his breath.

'And she's going to come on Friday, on a later train.' Florence heaved a sigh. 'At least I won't need another afternoon off. I can finish at three.'

'I'll meet her,' Dave offered.

'I might be able to get home early on Friday,' Adam said.

'Oh – hang on. She said not to wait for her at the station. She said she'll come up here for tea at half four.'

'She's staying for tea?' Dave said excitedly.

'Here's what she put. "I'll stay for tea and get the seven forty-five train back afterwards. A takeaway might be nice, and wine." Same old mum.' Florence shook her head sadly.

'But she's coming. That's good,' Dave said. 'Florence, give her your phone number.'

'All right,' Florence said tiredly. 'At least she can let me know when something goes wrong again.'

'What if she lets you down again?' Adam asked.

'She'll come,' Dave said optimistically. 'Right, I'll pop into Tadderly on Thursday and get a haircut. And what do you think about that pink shirt I got for Christmas, Florence? Adam, you're a young bloke – what should I wear?'

'Whatever you want.' Adam shook his head in disbelief.

'Steady on, Dad,' Florence said anxiously. 'It's just tea. Don't set your heart on anything more.'

'Florence is right, Dave,' Adam said loyally. 'Maybe wait until she gets here before you start making plans.' He kissed Florence's cheek. 'I'd better get off. I'm running late.'

Florence held Elsie up to him and said, 'Elsie. Give Daddy a kiss.'

'Bye, sweetie.' Adam pecked the baby's petal-soft cheek and turned to go.

At that moment, the image of Darryl swam in front of him, the revving car, the false smile. His intention had been clear –

he wanted Elsie. What else could he possibly want? He intended to ruin everything Adam and Florence had. Tears filled his eyes.

Give Daddy a kiss.

Daddy.

The conversation with Darryl hit him again like a sucker punch. More than anything in the world, he wanted to be Elsie's father, Florence's partner. His worst fear was losing them both.

He couldn't let Florence know he'd met Darryl. Or what that man wanted.

31

The last half an hour had been nerve-wracking. Josie watched the minute hand crawl down from ten o'clock to half past. Mike was late. Perhaps he wasn't coming. She hurried upstairs for another glance in the full-length mirror in her room. Her hair shone. She looked neat and fresh in a jacket, T-shirt and capri pants. She was dressed for walking, sightseeing, having lunch. Ready for anything.

The digital bedroom clock said it was 10:32. Josie was dismayed to feel her heart pumping hard. Her breathing was shallow. Mike Bailey still had the ability to trouble her emotions. She glanced through the window and saw his Audi turn the corner too fast, the engine snarling, the top down. It seemed moments since he'd done the same thing on his Triumph as a teenager, roaring through the estate towards her parents' house in a cloud of blue smoke. She hurried downstairs to the front door and opened it, inhaling musk and vanilla.

'I'm sorry I'm late.' Mike was all apologies. 'I took the car to the garage to get it washed and sort out the air in the tyres—' He noticed her properly. 'You look gorgeous, Josie.'

Josie thought he looked good too. He wore a stylish leather jacket, a cap, and those tight jeans. Josie had a question. 'Are we driving with the top up or down?'

'You decide.'

'Down. Will I be cold?'

'I've brought blankets. But you might want to bring a hat and a scarf.'

'I'll fetch something.' Josie felt a sudden surge of excitement, picturing herself cruising through the countryside in a sporty car. She dashed upstairs and came down with two scarves and a choice of three styles of hat: a cap, a bucket and a floppy straw one. She grinned. 'I thought I'd be prepared.'

'You'll look stunning,' Mike said easily. 'Shall we go?'

'Where are we going?' Josie asked as she locked the front door.

'Down Memory Lane,' Mike said enigmatically, leading her towards the car.

He pulled on a pair of sunglasses and they drove through the village, along Orchard Way, where Gerald Harris was busy in his garden. Mike blared the horn and Gerald stood up, waving. He accelerated along Newlands, past Odile's café, towards Tadderly Road and away from the village.

Josie pulled her bucket hat down over her ears and pushed sunglasses on. 'Why are we driving through the village?'

'Because I want everyone to see I'm out with you.' Mike smiled.

'But Bomber – Gerald – will tell everyone.'

'I've told him already,' Mike said smugly.

'Told him what?'

'That I'm going out with the most wonderful woman.' Mike raised an eyebrow. 'Josie, this is just like old times.'

Josie closed her eyes behind the sunglasses. 'It is.'

She asked herself how she felt as the car engine purred beneath her and the wind pushed strands of hair across her face. She waited to feel guilty, to be filled with that sinking feeling that she was letting Harry down, but the feeling didn't come. Instead, she thought that Harry wouldn't mind her seeing an old flame. He'd understand that she was lonely, she was alive, and taking time out to enjoy herself. It didn't mean that she hadn't loved Harry, that she didn't love him still. There was room in her heart for Mike too. Perhaps.

The Audi took a bend at speed and Josie opened her eyes. They were driving along the A361. Josie knew the road well. She couldn't help smiling.

'We used to come along here on your bike. Do you remember the time I had a long skirt on? I kept trying to hold it down. The wind lifted it up like a bell and my legs were freezing.'

'I felt like Brando in *The Wild One* with you clinging to me. It was the greatest feeling in the world,' Mike said and Josie could hear the emotion in his voice. 'Those were the best times.'

'They were good times,' Josie agreed.

'They can be good again,' Mike replied.

Josie watched the scenery flash past and breathed in cool air. Stretches of emerald fields, squatting tall trees, clouds overhead in a blue sky like curled lambs: it felt good to be driving along through the countryside next to Mike in a fast car with the heating on. Her face was cool and her legs were toasty.

She smiled. 'Are we going where I think we're going?'

'We are.' Mike turned to her briefly before he focused ahead on the open road. 'The place where I first told you how special you were.'

They drove through familiar villages, Wigginton, Swerford, then Mike made the sharp right turn to Rollright. He slowed down and brought the car to a halt. There was one other car parked nearby, an old Jeep. Josie clambered out and Mike closed the roof. They paused by the signpost for donations, where Mike placed a ten-pound note in the box. He guided Josie along the little path, through the opening in the woodlands, following the sign that said 'The Kings' Men.'

Josie and Mike emerged from the clearing and stared at the Rollright stones. Josie said, 'We came here that evening in June – how many years ago?'

'Fifty something?' Mike smiled.

They stood together and Mike took her hand. A circle of weathered ceremonial stones stood before them, some straight, some leaning to one side, some taller than others. From a distance they looked like pieces of gnawed wood.

'They're as beautiful as ever,' Josie said.

Mike turned to her and she knew what he was thinking. He said, 'They've been here since around two and a half thousand BC.'

'We could never count them.' Josie smiled at the memory. 'Seventy something. But every time the number would be different.'

'Shall we sit?' Mike indicated the rug under his arm.

'All right.' Josie nodded and he led her to the centre of the circle. There was no one around as they sat down on the rug. The wind made a low sound as it funnelled through the limestone circle. Josie adjusted her sunglasses and glanced around at the stones, jagged like old teeth, weathered with yellow blotches. Mike said what was in her mind. 'This place was special.'

'It was,' Josie agreed. 'We'd come here on the bike and there'd be families, kids running around, they'd leave at teatime and there would just be us.'

'We'd lie on a rug and watch the sun set. You'd be in my arms.'

Josie remembered. 'I never wanted to be anywhere else.'

Mike was quiet for a moment. He said, 'I never loved anyone like I loved you.'

Josie turned to face him. 'What about your wife? Caroline?'

'Ah.' Mike shook his head slowly. 'You know how you have an awful experience and you get amnesia to numb the pain? That's how it is with Caroline.'

'It can't have always been so bad.'

'Perhaps it wasn't, at first. She was the daughter of one of the officers. I was an ambitious young pilot. I've no idea what made us think we could make it work. We were so different. But it ended badly.'

'She left you.'

'Not soon enough. She'd been having an affair. She denied it. Then I found out.'

'That's awful,' Josie said and Mike gave a hollow laugh.

'It hit me hard. I'd never been right since I did active service. I was given a desk job because of the nightmares.'

'Nightmares?' Josie frowned.

'PTSD. I was really shaken up. When I came home, it was obvious that Caroline and I were finished. But we had a nice house, a good lifestyle. And she had the best of both worlds: a husband with a good pension and a boyfriend she could spend time with when I had one of my turns.'

'Turns?' Josie was filled with pity. It came to her keenly that she didn't know the man he'd become. So many years had passed and left a gap between them.

'I lost my temper a lot in those days. The doctor gave me meds, but I'd end up having nightmares, sweating.'

'Because of your life as a pilot?'

'It changed me, Josie. I was a long way down a rocky road. But I turned it round.'

'How?'

'Time heals.' Mike took in the circle of stones. The wind blew his hair. 'I had to rethink the person I was.'

'And now?'

'Caroline's gone and the bad times have gone with her.' Mike took Josie's hand again. 'I came back to Middleton Ferris. I've never forgotten you, Josie. We used to come here, our hearts full of love and hope. And now—'

'Now?' Josie felt sorry for Mike. He'd been through a stressful time.

'Just being here, remembering how we'd lie on a rug and make plans, I feel a better person.'

'I'm glad,' Josie said encouragingly. 'So, what now?'

'Now?' Mike asked hopefully.

'I mean, what shall we do now?' Josie asked. Mike had spent a lot of time thinking about the past. But she wanted to leave it behind now and focus on the present. 'We could wander round the Whispering Knights and the King Stone.' Josie clambered up and held out a hand. 'I remember the view from the Whispering Knights. Those three stones look like a giant doorway facing down the hill. And you can see all the fields for miles.'

Mike stood up. 'I remember being here with you, looking out over the countryside. It felt like we had the future at our feet.' He smiled. 'Perhaps we still do.'

'One day at a time,' Josie said carefully. It was only their first date.

'You're right. Let's take a walk, then we'll drive to our favourite pub in Hook Norton and I'll buy lunch.'

'The Horseshoe?' Josie said. 'I haven't been there for a long time.'

'I checked the menu online. It looks great.' Mike's fingers linked through hers. 'Come on, let's go and say a quick hello to our old friends the Whispering Knights, then I'll whisk you off. This afternoon, the world's our oyster.'

* * *

The Horseshoe was an old pub with a stone floor and cob walls, a wooden-clad bar and sepia photos of the local brewery in the eighteen hundreds on the walls. A sweet-faced landlady pulled half-pints of golden craft ale from hand pumps and took their orders from the menu. Josie chose smoked aubergine and walnut tagliatelle and Mike picked the pan-fried sea bass and saffron risotto. Their heads were close throughout the meal as they sat side by side, and afterwards they shared a dark chocolate and orange mousse. One dish, two spoons.

Over coffee, Josie told Mike about the Silver Ladies, how important her friends were, and he related the story of his best friend, Oliver, who'd died from combat injuries. His voice cracked with emotion as he explained how he had sat at Ollie's bedside and waited for the end, and how he'd cried when Ollie finally closed his eyes.

'You had such a hard time.' Josie leaned over to Mike and brushed his cheek with her fingers.

'It could just as easily have been me in his place,' Mike said in a hushed voice.

'I'm glad it wasn't.' Josie smiled warmly and their lips met for a moment. Josie realised that the pub was full of diners and people were staring at them. She laughed to cover her awkwardness: she hadn't seen the kiss coming.

Her cheeks tingled. 'They don't expect to see older people kissing.'

'Forget them. There's just you and me,' Mike whispered and he kissed her lightly again.

The sunshine was honey-thick and warm on their faces. Mike took the long route home, via the pretty stone houses of Stow-on-the-Wold and on to the beautiful Georgian town of Woodstock. They paused for a while to look at antique shops and galleries, strolling hand in hand to tea rooms where a waiter served them with tea and cake.

They drove home, Josie's head resting against Mike's shoulder. He stopped the car outside Josie's house. The sun was low in the sky, a beautiful plum-coloured sunset.

'What time is it?'

'It's past seven.' Mike exhaled pure happiness. 'Time's flown by.'

'It's been such a lovely day,' Josie said.

'It has,' Mike agreed. 'Can we do it again?'

'I'd like that.' She'd enjoyed herself more than she'd thought possible. Nervously, she found herself blurting, 'Do you want to come inside for a bit? I could make us something to eat.'

'That would be nice,' Mike said. 'I'm not ready to go home yet.'

'I know,' Josie agreed. 'It's hard living by yourself.'

'It's not something I'll ever get used to.' Mike's face clouded. 'Even when I was a pilot, being alone was terrifying. And later, it was even worse.'

'Later?' Josie felt a shiver go through her, a premonition. There was something Mike wasn't telling her. She made no move to get out of the car.

'The worst part. Worse than the nightmares and the PTSD.' Mike shifted awkwardly in his seat. He couldn't meet her gaze.

'What happened?'

'I suppose I ought to tell you.' Mike put his hands to his head. 'That was the toughest time for me.'

'What was?'

'When I was in prison.'

Josie thought she had misheard. 'Prison?'

Mike's voice was low. 'I was in prison for three years.'

'Why?' Josie said, hardly able to believe his words. 'What did you do?'

'I killed someone,' Mike said. 'It was manslaughter.'

'Oh.' Josie felt herself sway a little. So much had happened to Mike in those years since she'd loved him. Suddenly, she felt she hardly knew him at all.

'It's a sound I never got used to, a grown man crying,' Mike whispered. 'Some nights it was me.'

'What happened?' Josie wanted to take Mike's hand but for some reason she couldn't. She glanced towards her house and wished she were inside. On her own. Then she felt unkind.

He met her eyes. 'It's hard to tell you.'

'You don't have to.'

'You deserve to know.' Mike looked as if his heart might break. 'You might hate me for it...'

'Just tell me.' Josie's voice was a whisper.

'It was years ago. I was in a particularly bad way. My head was all over the place and my marriage was on the rocks. We were rowing. Caroline was goading me, calling me names, saying I was a loser. She left and I followed her. She drove to a pub in Stanton Fitzwarren, two miles away. I watched her go in. Then I followed her and she was with a man, younger than me. They were sitting together, laughing. His arm was round her. Of course, I lost my temper and challenged him and he said something nasty. I can't remember what it was.'

'Go on,' Josie urged. She shivered, although it wasn't cold.

Mike stared at his hands. 'Well, he was throwing his weight about, shouting, and he pushed me. So I hit him. He fell back, smacked his head against the bar and then he was on the floor. He didn't get up.'

Josie caught her breath. 'Oh, Mike.'

'Of course, I admitted it in court. It was my fault. There were extenuating circumstances. I did my time, came out and...' He placed a hand over Josie's. 'Does this change things between us, Josie?'

'I'm not sure.' Josie wriggled away from him instinctively. She hadn't intended to. 'It's hard to take it in.'

'We've had such a lovely day. I didn't want to tell you, but I had to. It's best you know if we're...' Mike put an arm around her. 'Josie, we were so happy.'

Josie didn't move. 'It's a shock.'

'I thought we'd be able to pick up where we left off.'

'Mike.'

Mike's lips brushed hers tentatively. Josie smelled the warmth of his skin, but she felt cold. Empty. He said, 'I suppose you need time now.'

'To take it all in, yes.' Josie put her hand on the door catch. 'I'm sorry – it's all a bit sudden.'

'Do you want to go inside? Shall I go home?'

'You're a lovely man.' Josie didn't move. 'I just need a day or two to get my head around it.' She shuddered. 'It's come as a shock, from nowhere.'

'I understand, really, I do.' Mike's face was etched with sadness. 'Will you ring me?'

'Just give me a few days?'

'Of course.'

Josie clambered from the car and hurried towards her front door. She half turned to wave, but it didn't seem appropriate.

She had no idea how you behaved when a man you'd spent a wonderful day with dropped the bombshell that he had killed someone. Her hand shook as she pushed the key into the lock.

Inside the house, she closed the door behind her and leaned against it, closing her eyes, her mind racing. Perhaps she should have invited Mike in, talked things through. But she needed time to herself first. She needed to compose her crashing thoughts.

It had been a beautiful day. Full of hope. She'd almost fallen for him again. But now things had changed.

And Josie was numb. She had no idea how she really felt.

32

Josie was still worrying about Mike when she met the Silver Ladies for lunch the following day. She'd texted him to thank him for a nice day out. It all sounded a bit formal. But she had no idea how to behave. It might be better to put a stop to things now – she'd already started to become fond of him. But he wasn't the same Mike she'd loved when she was eighteen. How could he be, after everything that had happened?

Florence weaved in and out of the tables with a tray of soup. It was the lunchtime rush and the café was full. Bobby Ledbury and Natalie had been and gone, Dangerous Dave too, but Jimmy and Kenny, Gerald and Margaret and other people from the village were seated, sharing food and banter.

Minnie was scrutinising the faces around the table. Josie had hardly touched a mouthful. Cecily was sipping soup daintily. Lin was dunking bread and Poll had almost finished every scrap. She licked her lips. 'Not bad scran.'

'Good,' Minnie said. 'And it's lovely to have you along, Poll. Now, this is a bit of an unusual lunch. We have various things to resolve. I'll go first, shall I?'

'Go on.' Lin was still chewing.

'I've had a couple of texts from Jensen. He's still in India. He sent a photo of a theatre company – he was on stage with them, wearing a dhoti.'

'Did you reply?' Cecily met her eyes directly. 'Or are you just too proud?'

'Of course I replied. With a kiss,' Minnie said. 'Although he didn't even say "Wish you were here".'

'He must be missing you or he wouldn't have sent the photo,' Lin protested.

'Unless it's his way of saying, I'm enjoying myself and you can get lost,' Poll said cynically. 'Some blokes are like that.'

'Oh, no, he loves her,' Lin said loyally. She was glad she'd been warned about Poll's directness.

Poll seemed satisfied. 'What do you think, Minnie? You're clever.'

'I'm determined I'm not losing this one. He's a keeper. Once he's back from India, I'm going to lay my cards on the table. He won't be able to resist.'

'Good move,' Poll agreed.

Minnie continued. 'Meanwhile, Tina's had an offer on the house from you-know-who.'

'Who's that?' Poll asked.

Cecily smiled gently. 'I'll fill you in later.'

'It's a good offer. She's thinking it over,' Minnie said. 'But I'm taking matters into my own hands.'

'What will you do?' Lin asked. 'You can't let Darryl buy it.'

'Watch this space,' Minnie said, looking pleased with herself. 'Over to you, Josie.'

'Well – Mike.' Josie put her head in her hands. 'To be honest, I wish I hadn't gone out with him. I'm so mixed up.'

'Perhaps you should stay away,' Lin said worriedly. 'After what you told me. What if he has tantrums or mood swings?'

'The poor man has PTSD,' Cecily said. 'He's a war hero, not a criminal. Talk to him, Josie.'

'I should.'

'They should give him a medal,' Poll said. 'Poor Mike didn't mean to punch that man's lights out.'

'It's serious though. Life changing.' Josie looked sad. 'You're right though; I'll talk to him.'

'But not until you're ready. Take your time,' Minnie said. 'Now, Cecily, when are we going to see Eddie? Let's sort that out.'

'We should.' Cecily looked around the table, taking in each hopeful face. Her expression was determined, but her hands quivered at the thought. She had no idea how she'd react to seeing him again.

'Let's go on Sunday. The roads will be quiet,' Lin suggested. 'And if you're not going to tell Eddie you're coming, he'll probably be in on a Sunday afternoon.'

'You should tell him.' Poll rubbed her hands. 'He'll get nice cake in.'

Cecily made a soft nervous sound: after a lifetime of dreams and hopes, everything was becoming scarily real.

'We'll wait in a café nearby. Or a pub,' Minnie said.

'Are we all going?' Poll said excitedly. 'I can't wait. I think you're so brave, Cecily, seeing your bloke after seventy years.'

'I don't know what to expect,' Cecily said quietly. 'But I need closure. And I expect Eddie does too.'

'You might fall in love with him all over again,' Lin said.

'It sounds to me like these blokes are giving you a lot of grief, except for Lin here. And you're all old ladies, so you haven't got forever.' Poll swigged tea from her mug. 'It's about time you got it sorted out.'

'Well said, Poll,' Cecily agreed. 'I'm so glad you've moved here. That's exactly the sort of straight talking we appreciate.'

'Oh, Fergal likes me to say what I think. He says it makes him smile.' Poll winked. 'So, what's next on the agenda?'

'Cecily's birthday,' Josie said.

Lin clapped her hands. 'Yes. We wanted to make this one special.'

Cecily held her hands up modestly. 'I've had so many birthdays. And we've all been so busy.'

'All the more reason to celebrate,' Poll said.

'So,' Minnie said firmly. 'I've booked the venue and invited guests. That's hush-hush. I'll arrange drinks.' Minnie looked pleased with herself.

'When is it? I love a party,' Poll said.

'August the second. A week on Saturday,' Lin said. 'I've sorted the entertainment, but you mustn't ask, Cecily, because we want it to be a bit of a surprise.'

'I'll do a cake,' Josie added. 'If that's all right, Cecily?'

'I'm thrilled.' Cecily looked relieved not to be talking about Eddie.

'Your birthday,' Minnie said emphatically, 'will be the party of the year.'

'What can I do to help?' Poll asked. 'I can chuck any troublemakers out, or I could help with the music. I can sing.'

'Thanks, Poll,' Minnie said. 'Why don't you come to Lin's now to talk about it? Cecily, I'm sorry to say you're not invited. We're making plans and talking presents.'

'I'll stay and have a piece of Odile's cake.'

Cecily stared around the café. Jimmy and Kenny were shuffling out, waving their hands and calling out, 'See you, Miss Hamilton.' Most of the other diners had already gone.

Minnie brushed Cecily's cheek with her lips as she rose to

leave. Lin and Josie clambered up and Poll followed them, reaching out to grab the piece of bread that Cecily hadn't eaten, pushing it into her mouth.

'Nice bit of cob,' she said.

'Are you sure you'll be all right by yourself, Cecily?' Lin asked.

'The Flying Plum's outside. I'll be fine.'

'We'll meet soon. I'll come round for a cuppa. I need moral support,' Josie said.

'Don't we all?' Cecily replied. She was already anxious about meeting Eddie next weekend.

As the door clanged and Josie, Minnie, Lin and Poll left, Florence appeared from the kitchen through the colourful plastic strips. She glanced towards the door. 'Oh, I thought that was someone coming in.'

'No, it was a mass exodus. Minnie, Lin, Josie, Poll. They've gone to plan my birthday bash. But I'm still here. Florence, might I have a cup of peppermint tea and a slice of cake? What do you have today?'

'Rhubarb drizzle or ginger and lemon.'

'The rhubarb, please, and a blob of cream,' Cecily said sweetly. 'How are you, dear?'

Florence glanced at the clock. 'Not bad. Another hour, and I can fetch Elsie from Geraldine's and go home, start cooking. Adam's going to be late tonight. He's got a meeting.'

'Oh? Is he busy?'

'He's working on the Ledbury farm.'

'I heard George Junior wants to sell. The village grapevine says that Henry Turvey will buy the entire farm.'

'He's made an offer, although I can't say any more.'

'That was always the Ledburys' farm,' Cecily said.

'Bobby and Natalie want to keep it,' Florence said. 'I'll get your cake.'

'Thank you,' Cecily said, watching her disappear back to the kitchen.

The café was suddenly quiet. The only other person there was a woman with a small child at the other end of the room. The woman was on her phone and the child was copying with a toy one.

Cecily stared at her hands. They'd once been fine hands, tapered fingers, long nails. Hands that played the guitar, that guided smaller ones to write. Hands that comforted, active hands, talented ones. Now the skin was loose and paper thin, with liver spots. She examined her bare ring finger and remembered the diamond Eddie had slipped on there. She'd offered it back to him, but he'd told her he wanted her to have it. She remembered the tears in his eyes. 'Keep it and remember us.'

It had been the best he could afford. It was in a wooden box in a drawer, back at Tadderly Road.

She never looked at it now. Everything it had meant was buried forever.

Cecily put her hands to her eyes and her mind drifted back through the years. She and Eddie were sitting in his car, his face miserable.

'I have to tell you something awful. And I'm to blame. I've let you down, Cecily. Joyce is—'

Cecily remembered how his eyes filled with tears as he took her hand, the one with the engagement ring on. She'd worn a green and white polka-dot dress. It was late. They'd been to the cinema and Eddie had been preoccupied all evening.

The exact moment she realised the truth of what had happened was locked in her memory. She'd known from Eddie's expression that something was horribly wrong.

Her voice had been a whisper. 'Joyce?'

'She's having a baby.'

'Joyce is—?'

'A baby. It's mine. Cecily, my love, it was a mistake. It happened when I gave her a lift home, after I dropped you off. Just once.'

Cecily remembered watching Eddie's lips move as the words tumbled out. She couldn't hear for the blood that pounded behind her eyes.

'I didn't mean to. I mean, she offered it on a plate and I said no and then she – well, one thing led to another and it was over in seconds, and I looked at her and couldn't believe what I'd done. In seconds, Cecily. My love, I—'

Cecily's world changed for ever in that moment. Like a breaking piece of glass, the small cracks showed first.

'You and Joyce?' Cecily asked in disbelief.

'But I love you, Cecily. I swear. It won't change anything between us. I mean, Joyce had done it before. She knew what she was doing and – well – I couldn't help myself.'

'Eddie – you and Joyce – made *love*?'

'Well, it wasn't love, we—'

The cracked glass had shattered. In two. Cecily's world broke in half. She tugged her hand away and covered her face, as if not seeing would take it all away.

'No, Eddie. The baby is yours? How can that be? No. I can't believe Joyce is pregnant. If she is, then – there's only one thing you can do. The right thing.'

'I'm sorry, Cecily. I'm so sorry.'

Cecily took her hands from her eyes and her face was covered in tears. Eddie's voice echoed in her memory as if it were yesterday.

Florence was back with a tray containing a china cup and

saucer, a teabag in water, a slice of cake covered in cream. She placed it in front of her.

Cecily smiled bravely, wiping the last tear away. 'Thank you, Florence.' She glanced at the clock. 'It's quarter past two. It's quiet now.'

'We'll get a few passers-by. That should take us up to closing time.' Florence smoothed her apron. 'Andrew Cooper usually comes in later on for a coffee. And Jill and Rosemary, Henry Turvey's sisters, like to pop in.'

'This is delicious cake, I must say.' Cecily licked her fingers.

'That new man was in here yesterday, Mike Bailey. He was talking to Fergal over a cup of coffee.'

'Oh?' Cecily was interested. 'Was Josie's name mentioned?'

'Probably.' Florence gave a short laugh. 'I heard Fergal say he'd never understand women. He couldn't live with them and he couldn't live without them.'

'Poll's nice. Direct. But honest. The world could do with more like her,' Cecily said. She heard the café door chime behind her. 'I think she and Fergal are well suited.'

'They are,' Florence began. The doorbell clanked almost inaudibly. Then Cecily saw the colour drain from her face as she stared at someone beyond Cecily's shoulder.

Cecily twisted round. Darryl Featherstone stood by the door, arms folded. She could smell expensive cologne. He was dressed immaculately. He would have been incredibly handsome but for the sneer on his face.

'What do you want?' Florence's voice was barely audible.

'You might be nicer to me. Fetch me a coffee to go.' Darryl didn't sit down.

Florence continued to stare. Cecily could see her body shaking with fear.

'A coffee?' Florence repeated. She was fixed to the spot.

'Or we could have a chat instead, if you prefer,' Darryl said. His tone was unfriendly. 'Did your boyfriend tell you I had a little word with him the other day?'

'No.' Florence sounded worried.

'I offered him a bit of business. I'm surprised he didn't mention it. Then we talked about something else.'

Florence's voice was a whisper. 'Is this about Elsie?'

'The kid? The one your dad keeps showing me photos of?'

'Does he?'

'It just annoys me.' Darryl's lip curled in a snarl. 'You're walking around the village I used to live in, pushing her about in a pram. But she's mine, isn't she?'

Cecily watched him, unnoticed. Florence gripped the back of the chair nearest to her. 'She's mine.'

Darryl hadn't finished. 'You go around like butter wouldn't melt, pretending to be a big happy family, and no one knows who the father is. I've asked a few people on the quiet, Jimmy, Kenny. No one has a clue. But everyone wants to know, don't they? Perhaps I should tell them. If she's my kid, I want everyone to hear it. I might even want to take her out, get to know her. What's her name – Elsie? And if she's not mine, then, well...'

'Then what?' Florence could hardly speak.

'Well, she clearly isn't Adam's, is she? Look at him. He's Afro-Caribbean. So just for the record – am I the kid's father or—?'

'Or?' Florence's knuckles were white against the chair. Her knees were buckling.

'Or are you just a dirty slag who's slept with half the village?'

'You stop right there, young man.' Cecily's voice boomed, just as it had in the classroom fifty years ago. 'I hardly think you have the right to ask that question.'

Darryl glanced at Cecily and back to Florence. 'Who's this old bag? Your gran?'

'Now, listen to me.' Cecily drew herself up to her full height. She barely came to Darryl's shoulder. 'Don't you dare talk to Florence about that child.'

'I have rights.' Darryl smirked.

'Rights? What rights do *you* have?' Cecily met his eyes, her own hard as bullets. 'You're nothing at all to that little girl. Or to Florence and her family. Where were you when Florence was pregnant? Or when she gave birth? Where were you during the long nights when she was up feeding?'

'That's hardly the point.' Darryl couldn't care less.

'It *is* the point,' Cecily insisted. 'You invite Florence to your house, to your room, when your wife is away. You lie to her; you pretend you care for her and you pressurise her into having sex with you. Afterwards, you show your true colours and tell her you're married and that she was just a bit of fun.' Cecily placed her hands on her hips. 'Not very commendable. Not exactly good father material.'

'Is that what she told you?' Darryl looked as if he had been slapped.

'Florence has been the soul of discretion. She's more interested in the future of that little girl. All you want is bragging rights about paternity. And while we are talking about rights...' Cecily took a deep breath '...men who coerce women into sleeping with them and run around like a rooster afterwards are nothing more than cockroaches. In fact, as far as I'm concerned, coercion and rape go hand in hand.'

Darryl was stunned. 'How dare you? You old crone.'

'I've lived a long time, it's true. And I've kicked men into touch who are a hundred times better than you,' Cecily said, her voice calm. 'But I promise you this. If you breathe a word to anyone, in the village or beyond, that you have anything to do with Florence or Elsie, I will personally see to it that your name is dragged through the mud for the obnoxious sexual predator that you are. And—' Cecily was ready with her knockout punch '—I know a sweet little nurse by the name of Sophie Lamb from Tadderly who will agree with everything I say.'

'How the hell do you know about—?'

'As I said, I've lived a long time.' Cecily sat down again and picked up her fork. 'Now go home, please, Darryl. You're spoiling my appetite. Despicable lounge lizards who fancy themselves as gigolos always leave a nasty taste.'

Darryl muttered a word beneath his breath that might have been 'bitch'.

A voice of thunder came growling from the entrance to the kitchen. Odile stood in her apron, her face furious.

'You get the hell out of my café, you hear me?' She glared. 'You're not welcome. If you set foot in here again, I'll phone the police and tell them you're threatening my staff. Now get your ass out and don't you ever come back.'

There was a moment's silence. Darryl stared around the café, at Odile, Florence, Cecily, and finally at the woman with the child, both clutching phones and gaping open-mouthed. He said, 'You can keep the brat.' Then he slunk away. The doorbell chimed behind him.

The woman with the child was busy all of a sudden, finishing her tea, packing things away, rummaging in her bag.

Odile said, 'Are you all right, Florence?'

Florence nodded. Her shoulders were hunched.

Odile wrapped an arm around her. 'His sort are all mouth and trousers, but they're weak inside. You've seen the last of him.' She turned to Cecily. 'Can I get you more tea? That one must be cold. And another slice of cake.'

'I've hardly finished this,' Cecily began, but Odile was beaming.

'Cecily Hamilton, you were magnificent. You told him exactly where to get off. I heard you from the kitchen. You called him a despicable lounge lizard. I just wanted to cheer.'

'Thank you, Cecily,' Florence said, her voice tiny.

'He had it coming,' Cecily said grimly. 'Men like that—'

'Indeed. I'll get us all a strong tea. Florence, you look like you need one,' Odile insisted. 'Sit down. I'll bring cake too. You need the sugar. It'll give you time to recover. And don't you worry, not a word of what happened will pass my lips.'

'Thank you.' Florence looked at Odile with grateful eyes. A tear glistened on her cheek.

'We'll all sit down.' Odile offered Cecily a wide smile. 'Cecily, I want to hear all about all the men you kicked into touch who were a hundred times better than Darryl.' She hugged Florence again. 'And later, you go home to Adam and Elsie and enjoy your sweet little family, and don't you worry about that toad ever again.'

33

Minnie was in a bad mood. She'd been listening to Stravinsky's *The Rite Of Spring* all morning and she felt irritated. The piece was about a girl chosen to dance herself to death to celebrate the start of spring. New beginnings. And endings. Minnie turned the music off and pulled on her boots. Tina had gone out first thing to see Gary. Jensen hadn't messaged for three days. His last text said that he was leaving India.

She shrugged a jacket over her dress and decided she needed to be outdoors. Yes, she was definitely feeling miffed about something. She pushed her bicycle into the street. Above her was an iron sky. A cold wind funnelled between the houses and made her shiver. She was certainly fed up. Lunch in The Bear was what she needed. As she cycled past Brasenose Recreation Ground, she wondered if she should have phoned one of her friends and suggested they join her. Company over lunch was always good. But Minnie didn't feel much like socialising. She was definitely out of sorts.

She pushed harder on the pedals, increasing speed as she passed Holy Rood Church and crossed the Thames via Folly

Bridge. Her grey curls lifted in the wind and Minnie's head cleared. She wasn't annoyed. She was sad. She'd tried twice to contact Jensen and hadn't been able to reach him. She had her speech ready. She was going to tell him she didn't want to be without him a moment longer, and that was that.

An old song came to her, one that they were made to sing in primary school when Terrible Thomas had been their teacher. He'd wielded the cane and growled through gritted teeth, 'Sing, you buggers, or I'll make you sing.' This was long before Miss Hamilton and her guitar had come along and they'd sung their hearts out for fun. Terrible Thomas had made them sing a song called 'On Top of Old Smokey'. Minnie recalled the lines.

I lost my true lover
For courtin' so slow

As a kid in plimsolls and patched clothes, she'd often wondered what it meant, courting too slow.

She knew now. Perhaps Jensen had lost patience. She'd call again later. This time, she'd get through. She'd tell him how much she loved him.

Minnie cycled along St Aldate's, turning right into Blue Boar Street, glancing towards the museum, the ornate carved stone frontage and the striking glass and iron roof. She'd been there so many times as a student herself, examining Roman pottery. Securing her bike, she grabbed her bag and hurried towards The Bear, a majestic white building with a black sign and gold letters.

It was impossible to count the number of times she'd drunk beer in The Bear, from when she'd been an awestruck student at St Hilda's right up to being a professor. She'd sat in the bar and eaten lunches, listened to live music, started relationships, ended them, cemented friendships. But today she was going alone to think.

It felt like a second home.

The pub was already half full, students, chattering groups of tourists, even in July. Minnie bought a pint, ordered a pie with gravy and settled down at a table. She took a deep sup of ale and told herself that she had her books, her house, her friends, her health. She didn't need Jensen.

But she knew she was wrong.

Tina was well again, independent, able to function by herself. It was exactly the right moment for Minnie to go to New York. Or invite Jensen to stay. She should have made it clear that she was desperate to be with him. But it was difficult over a Zoom call. And Minnie was, by nature, phlegmatic, while Jensen was romantic and demonstrative.

She wondered if she'd blown it. No. She'd try again. And again.

The pie arrived and Minnie tucked in. She had no intention of going off her food now. She'd speak to Jensen later. And the pie was good. Instead of fretting, she started to plan for the day. Thursday. The bookshop was calling to her. Browsing and sniffing the scent of crisp new books always lifted her spirits.

But she was in love with Jensen. It had to be said. She'd call him when she got home. She'd say those three little words out loud.

There was a clatter in the doorway and someone called her name. Minnie glanced up and saw Tina in denim dungarees, grinning for all she was worth. The man who stood next to her was the same height with a white beard and white hair, an honest face. Tina rushed towards the table and the man followed her, leaning slightly to one side, limping. Tina sat next to Minnie and said, 'You weren't at home. I thought we'd find you here. This is Gary.'

Minnie held out a hand and stared into his round brown eyes. 'Hello, Gary. Pleased to meet you.' She liked him immediately.

He plonked himself at the table. 'Hello, Minnie. I've heard so much—' Gary's handshake was firm.

'I'll bet you have,' Minnie said. 'Can I buy you both lunch? The pies are special.'

Tina shook her head. 'No, we can't stay. We're off to the Botanic Gardens. We've got the tour booked.'

'Thanks for organising it, Minnie,' Gary added.

'We're meeting Sue and Mark for dinner afterwards.' Tina's face shone with enthusiasm. 'We just wanted to tell you. Gary's asked me to move in.'

'Oh, well done.' Minnie hugged her sister and said, 'You certainly can't be accused of courting too slow.'

'Pardon?' Tina's brow knitted, but Gary was smiling.

He said, 'Perhaps you'd like to come round for lunch once Tina's moved in. We're going to celebrate new beginnings.'

'New beginnings,' Minnie repeated. 'That's wonderful. Of course, I'll make myself available.'

'And our vegetables are growing like there's no tomorrow,' Tina continued. 'I'll bring you some courgettes and kale.'

'Fabulous,' Minnie said.

'We ought to get going, love,' Gary said to Tina. Minnie registered the word *love*, the easy affection between them, and she smiled.

'We ought to. Glad we found you, Minnie.' Tina was still beaming.

'It's brilliant news.' Minnie was genuinely happy for them.

'See you later.' Tina had an arm through Gary's. They were

heading towards the door as she called over her shoulder, 'Don't wait up.'

'I won't.' Minnie watched them go.

She was alone with her thoughts. She had achieved her goal: Tina was independent, she'd found herself a new direction. A new friend, or whatever Gary would become. Now she was free to do as she wished.

There was only one thing she wished for.

Her phone buzzed and Minnie picked up. There was a message from Jensen. Minnie smiled; if she'd been a New Ager or a Roman oracle, she'd have said she'd manifested it, or summoned him by the magic of their love. It read simply:

> What are you doing now?

Minnie was puzzled. She replied.

> Having lunch at The Bear. Then I'm off to the bookshop.

She paused, wondering if he'd reply again. Just as she was about to give up, another text came in.

> Think of me if you find a copy of Scene by Edward Gordon Craig. I never replaced the one I lost.

Minnie was puzzled.

Was he asking her to buy him a book? If so, this was the perfect opportunity. She'd cycle to Westgate and see if she could get him a copy. She'd send him a photo of it with the words 'I love you'.

She imagined jumping on a plane to New York and taking it to him.

Minnie was on her feet, paying for her food, rushing towards her bicycle, cycling as fast as she could along Speedwell Street, hair flying, laughing at the appropriateness of the name of the road. She reached the bookshop, secured her bike and hurried inside.

She paused fleetingly to inhale the books, the dust of ancient tomes, the new perfection of unread novels. Her feet propelling her forward, she searched for the book. Edward Gordon Craig. English modernist theatre practitioner from the twentieth century. Minnie racked her brains to remember what she knew of him. He controversially said that actors were no more important than marionettes. He patented movable screens for the Moscow Art Theatre production of *Hamlet*. The book Jensen wanted would be in the Arts section, in Screen and Stage.

Minnie bustled through the shop, turning corners, passing shelves of books. Philosophy... Social Sciences... Stage and Screen...

Then she stopped dead.

A man was browsing alone by the bookshelf, reading a book, holding it up. He peered through gold-rimmed spectacles beneath a cloud of white hair. Then he turned and gave a broad smile, warm with recognition.

'Hi, Minnie.'

'Jensen.' Minnie was stunned.

'I told you I'd take things into my own hands,' he said. 'So here I am.'

'And here you must stay.' Minnie grinned.

She rushed at him, leaped, flung herself into his arms, wrapped her legs around him and was kissing him. He kissed her back, easing her onto her feet, grinning. 'Is this the way senior academic ladies behave in England?' He circled her in an embrace. 'People will be shocked.'

'I couldn't care less,' Minnie replied and she kissed him again.

***

Josie sat in the back garden at Barn Park with Lin and Neil, gazing towards the Ledburys' field. The sun slid behind a pale cloud and she shivered. 'I can't make my mind up, Lin. I don't know what to do.'

Lin was all sympathy. 'Mike cares about you.'

'And that's the problem.' Josie exhaled. 'For a while, when we were out, we were teenagers again. I think I might have been falling for him. He told me about what he'd done and I realised how much time had gone by. We're not the same people. Too much has happened.'

'But he's the same bloke.' Neil turned from where he was hoeing weeds in the garden. 'He talked to us all about it in The Sun. He's been through hell since he left the RAF. He was a pilot who served his country.'

'Have you spoken to him since, Josie?' Lin asked gently.

'I've texted him a few times, asked him how he is.' Josie made a sad face. 'I've fobbed him off when he asked me to come round. I'm playing for time.'

'Perhaps it's just better if you tell him you don't want to go out with him,' Lin said. 'It would be kinder in the long run.'

'But I enjoy being with him. After all this time, after Harry —' Josie heaved a sigh. 'It was so nice to have company.'

'Meet him and talk to him about how you feel,' Lin suggested.

'But how will I get over him having killed someone?' Josie

asked. 'Every time he holds my hand, I'll know that was the hand that killed a man.'

'It must be very confusing for poor Mike.' Neil leaned on his hoe. 'One minute he's fighting for his country, a pilot, expected to kill people, congratulated when he does, a failure when he doesn't. Then he comes home, all mixed up in his emotions, and the rules have changed.'

'That's true,' Lin said. 'And his wife was awful to him. I don't condone killing, but he didn't mean to do it.'

Neil said, 'It was a mistake, a bad one, but he's paid for it. He needs to look forward, Josie, not back.'

'I suppose so,' Josie said. 'But it's a big thing. I'm not sure I can just move past it.'

'Oh, look.' Lin pointed up the field. 'It's Nadine. And George.'

Josie smiled. Nadine was leading the way, trotting along towards the fence, George behind her, waving a hand. Neil shouted, 'Hello, George. How's tricks?'

Nadine flopped over on her side and George placed a pig's treat beneath her snout. She snaffled it up. 'Pretty good, I reckon,' George said.

'Are you selling the field?' Lin asked. 'Is it being developed into a quarry?'

'I'm selling a couple of big fields to Henry Turvey to raise some cash: the big ones on the other side of the house. But I have plans for this one – well, Bobby has. He and Hayley have been applying for grants and Natalie has found funds for herself. It's all thanks to Adam Johnson.'

'Oh?' Neil moved towards the gate. 'What's happening, George?'

'This is a rural area.' George shoved his hands in his pockets. 'We meet the criteria.'

'What criteria?' Lin asked.

'We're going to "promote the social welfare of inhabitants of rural communities by advancing education and leisure". That's what Adam said. We have a business plan and we'll get funding.'

'How will you do that?' Neil asked.

'Well, Bobby and Hayley are planning to set up a petting farm in this field. Hayley's going to run it, advertise it and organise more animals, rescued donkeys, llamas, furry things – and Nadine's going to be the star.'

Nadine blinked up adoringly and George gave her another treat from his jacket pocket.

'Hayley's very switched on. She'll do a gift shop and cakes and tea. And Natalie wants to set up riding stables. She's going to get local kids to come. There's a school in Tadderly for partially sighted kiddies, and they're keen to get involved.'

'Well.' Neil smiled. 'It's all happening on the farm.'

'It is. George Junior and Bobby will do the day-to-day management, the animals and the agricultural side. I'll wind things down a bit so that I can spend more time with—' he handed Nadine a third treat '—Penny. It's about time.'

'It is,' Lin agreed.

'So, Josie, I hear you're making a big cake for Cecily Hamilton's birthday. Dickie said there's going to be a do in the pub and we're all invited. Ninety-two.' George's bushy eyebrows shot up. 'That's a good age. I hope we all last that long.'

'So do I,' Neil agreed, glancing towards Lin.

'Mind you, she's on her own. It must be hard on your lonesome. I'm not sure I'd like that, especially at ninety-two.' George leaned against the fence. 'It would be horrible, not having anyone to talk to, just the four walls you live in.'

'It is,' Josie said. She was at home every day, without Harry.

'Lin, Josie and Minnie are taking Cecily out on Sunday to cheer her up,' Neil said. 'She's going to look up an old mate.'

Lin and Josie exchanged glances. They both wondered how the visit to Eddie would work out.

George rubbed his chin. 'Do you remember when Miss Hamilton first turned up? We were all in love with her. We thought she was the best thing since sliced bread. Who'd have thought she'd still be living here now? I mean, we're old, but she's ancient.'

'She's marvellous,' Lin agreed.

'But time waits for no man – or woman,' Neil said. 'Cecily said something recently, after Dickie's funeral. It was a quote by someone called Lorca. He was a clever chap. He said, "Those who are afraid of death will carry it on their shoulders."'

'He's right.' Lin met Josie's eyes. 'Life's for the living, as they say.'

'Exactly, even if you're Cecily Hamilton's age,' George chuckled.

'Right.' Josie tugged her phone from her handbag and pressed the screen.

'Who are you ringing?' Lin asked, but Josie was already speaking.

'Mike, where are you?' She listened a moment. 'Having coffee at Odile's? Who with? Oh, on your own? That's good. Could I join you? Yes, now. No, I'm at Lin's. It's just – we need to talk.' Josie listened to Mike's voice for a moment, taking in the anxious tone. She said, 'No, I was thinking, let's take things really slowly, and see what happens. But I wondered – if you'd like to accompany me to Cecily's party a week on Saturday.' She listened for a moment; a smile spread across her face. 'Yes, I'll be five minutes. Ask Florence to get me a hibiscus tea.'

34

On Friday afternoon, Florence, Adam and Dangerous Dave were sitting at the kitchen table. It was laid for four people and spread with a variety of food. There was salad, ham, eggs, tomatoes, potatoes, sausage rolls from Odile's – not the takeaway Elaine had asked for, but Florence had done her best. Elsie was wearing a pretty dress, a small ribbon in her hair. She was sitting up on her playmat, surrounded by toys, oblivious of the tension in the room.

Florence said, 'Does anyone want a cup of tea?'

'Let's wait for Elaine,' Dave said. He had left work early, showered and doused himself in powerful aftershave. He was wearing a tie.

Adam glanced at the clock. 'It's twenty past four. If we have a drink now, she's bound to turn up and want one. I'm thirsty.'

'I'll make us a cup,' Florence said. 'I need to be doing something, I'm shaking.'

'I bet she hasn't changed a bit,' Dave said. 'I loved the way she'd do her hair, up with all the dangly bits.'

'Well, let's see what happens when she gets here,' Adam

said. Florence hoped her mother would behave herself. It would be typical of Elaine to harp on about Elsie not looking like Adam. Florence felt her pulse quicken. The awful encounter with Darryl had left her bruised. She'd said nothing to Adam about it. It would hurt him.

It was easier to clank cups, boil hot water, make tea.

Florence returned to the table with teas all around. Elsie reached for her water cup and was guzzling. It was four twenty-eight: time was crawling. Adam looked nervous. Dave was chewing his fingernails.

He said, 'She should be here any moment. Did you send her photos of Elsie, Florence?'

'I sent her two.' Florence cupped her tea in her hands. 'She didn't reply.'

'Not even to say thanks?' Adam frowned.

'Nothing,' Florence said. It was half past four. 'Shall we eat at five?'

'I hope she gets here soon. She has to get the seven forty-five train back. I can walk her down to the station. Mind you, if she wants to stay on, I can run her back to Blisworth.'

'Dad, no.' Florence shot him a warning look. 'Just, no.'

'I'm just saying, it's only forty minutes by car.' Dave started on his thumbnail, chewing the skin. 'She might want to make it a regular thing, tea every Friday.'

'Steady on, Dad, you'll be moving her back in next, and we don't want that. I certainly don't,' Florence said and Dave's face was guilty.

It was almost twenty-five to five. It was typical of her mother to be late. It was typical of her mother not to come at all.

Dave picked up a piece of ham and tore a shred from the end. 'Only the fatty bit – she doesn't like those bits.' He chewed for a moment, then pushed the whole slice into his mouth. 'I'm starving. We've got plenty.'

Adam stretched his arms above his head. 'It's been a long week.' He meant it had been a tough one. It was still tough now.

'It has. But you've had a good one,' Florence said. 'The Ledburys.'

'That went well, yes.' Adam found himself thinking about meeting Darryl and pushed the memory away. 'We had a nice takeaway, and we spent some time together.'

'You'll be after your own place soon,' Dave said.

Adam glanced at Florence. 'We've got the deposit. The flat fell through but—'

'You'd miss us if we weren't here,' Florence teased. 'You'd miss Elsie's night feeds and my cooking.'

'You need your own space.' Dave leaned his chin on his fist. 'A young couple need privacy. Besides, Elaine might come back.'

'That's not likely, Dad,' Florence said quickly. 'Please, don't pin your hopes on Mum.'

'But what if she's on her own? What if her bloke has left her and she realises that all along she wanted to be here with me?' Dave looked miserable. 'Do you think she'll come, Florence?'

'Honestly?' Florence blew air from her cheeks. 'She's late.'

'You don't think she's got lost?' Dave tried again.

'Of course she hasn't.' Florence would have been angry but she'd started to feel sorry for her father.

'Shall I go for a walk, see if she's on her way?' Adam offered.

'I could go.' Dave stood up.

'Or we could just start on the food and to hell with her,' Florence suggested.

Elsie caught the sharpness of her tone and dropped her water cup, her face alarmed. Adam made a low clucking sound and picked her up. He said, 'We're all on the edge of our seats. Where is she? She's fifteen minutes late.'

'You know what trains are like,' Dave said hopefully. 'She'll be here any minute.'

Florence examined her phone; her thumb moved across the screen. 'I've messaged to ask where she is.' She exhaled, a little irritable. 'She made me exchange phone numbers. I might as well make the most of it.' She stared at her message. 'Come on, Mum, answer.'

'Ring her,' Dave said. 'Perhaps her phone's in her bag or something.'

There was a sharp knock at the front door. The bell rang. Dave was on his feet. 'It's her.' He took off into the hall at a fast pace, almost falling over the rug. The door opened and Florence heard voices, a woman's light voice, a man's, joking, friendly. She turned to Adam. 'That's not my mother.'

Dave came into the room, followed by Natalie and Bobby Ledbury, his girlfriend Hayley and the two small children. Natalie was holding a huge bunch of flowers. She handed them to Florence. 'Here. These are for you.'

Florence took them, puzzled. 'Why?'

'For lending us Adam when he was working late.' Natalie turned to Adam. 'We wanted to say thanks.'

Bobby handed Adam a wicker basket. 'It's a hamper of stuff – food, drink, just to say how grateful we all are.'

'We're so thrilled about the farm,' Natalie gushed. 'I'm going to expand the stables and Bobby's taking over the management. Hayley's starting a petting farm.'

'Lily and Alfie are excited.' Hayley knelt down to her children's level. A long fringe fell over her eyes. 'Say hello to Florence and Adam and Dave.'

Alfie looked away and Lily pushed a finger up her nose and

said, 'Hello. Mummy, can I stay and play with Elsie? Elsie came to our house with Adam.'

'We want to have you over for a meal,' Bobby said. 'To say thanks.' He turned to Dave. 'You too, you'd be welcome.'

'I can babysit,' Dave protested.

'Or Josie can. She promised to,' Florence remembered.

'No, bring Elsie. We'll let the kids spend time,' Hayley said.

'And I'm going to bring Anthony, my boyfriend. He's got loads of horses,' Natalie added.

'We're so grateful.' Bobby shook Adam's hand. 'What you've done to help our family. You've been brilliant.'

Florence was still hugging the flowers. 'Do you want to stay and have something to eat? We've got too much.' She noticed it was past five now.

'It's a nice spread.' Bobby was eyeing the potatoes.

'Wanna sausage,' Alfie spoke up. 'Mummy, can I have—?'

'Is it all right?' Bobby took two sausage rolls from the plate and gave one each to the children.

Dave followed suit, cramming flaky pastry into his mouth. 'Oh, what the hell.'

Florence's phone made a low sound and she tugged it from her pocket. Adam moved closer to her, Elsie in his arms. 'Is that your mum?'

Dave's mouth was full, but he spluttered, 'What does she say? Where is she now?'

'It's not her. It's Minnie Moore,' Florence said. 'Adam, she says her sister, Tina, is selling the house in Harvest Road. And she wants us to have first refusal.'

Dave grinned. 'Would I be able to pop over from the garage for lunch?'

'Of course. Imagine having a house in the village.' Florence was amazed.

'Can we afford it?' Adam couldn't help smiling as he wrapped an arm around her, Elsie in the other.

'We'll talk to Tina and Minnie.'

'Right,' Dave said firmly. 'I've got a few cans in the cupboard. I might even have a bottle of something a bit fizzy. Sit down, tuck in. Let's make an evening of it.'

'We could,' Bobby said.

'Anthony's picking me up at half seven but—' Natalie sat down '—the potato salad looks nice.'

'Well.' Dave spoke from a cupboard. His head was inside searching for beer and his backside stuck out in the air. 'Let's have a few drinks and some food together. My wife has stood me up. Ex-wife.' He emerged with a pack of beer in one hand and a dusty bottle of Prosecco in the other. 'I can't say I'm not upset. She's broken my heart again. And I expect there will be a pink letter on Monday morning with a lot of excuses. But it makes me cross that she's let my princess down again. Both my princesses.' He lifted the cans. 'Let's have sausage rolls and drink to the future of the farm. Can you have a small one, Florence, love? To better times.'

* * *

It was an overcast Sunday morning as Cecily clambered into the front seat of the Sharan, Josie and Poll seated behind her. She was wearing a pretty dress and coral lipstick. Her whole body was trembling. 'I'm not cold, Lin. I'm absolutely petrified,' she said.

'What are you frightened about? Are you worried you might not fancy Eddie any more?' Poll asked bluntly.

'What if he's not in?' Josie wondered. 'What if we go all that way for nothing?'

'It's an adventure though.' Poll grinned.

'We're picking Minnie up in Oxford. She'll calm us all down,' Lin said. 'And guess who's coming with her?'

'Tina?' Josie asked.

'Jensen,' Lin said cheerfully. 'He turned up in Oxford, out of the blue. They're both all loved up again.'

'Oh, that's splendid!' Cecily watched Lin turn the heating up. 'Thank you. I'm just so nervous. Would you believe it?'

'I'd be in bits,' Poll agreed. 'Seventy years without seeing the bloke you love? Mind you, he'll probably have a seizure when he sees you, Cecily. You'll have to give him the kiss of life and then it'll all turn out hunky-dory.'

Lin pressed her lips together trying not to smile as she accelerated along Tadderly Road. 'It's less than an hour to Minnie's, and another forty minutes to Benson. I think we should arrive around eleven-thirty.'

'Oh dear. Do you think I should have told him we were coming?' Cecily's face was anxious. 'What if he's cooking Sunday dinner for one and I turn up?'

'It'll only be a ping meal,' Poll said with a shake of her hair. 'He can bung another one on for you.'

'Minnie's found somewhere the rest of us can have lunch,' Josie said. 'There's a pub that looks out on the Thames. It serves food all day. Sunday roast, bar snacks.'

'Oh, we'll be all right, then,' Poll piped up. 'And if you've gone off Eddie, or he's boring you to death, just give us a bell, Cecily, and we'll bring you to the pub with us and we'll all drown our sorrows together.' She gave a short laugh. 'Fergal's down The Sun with Neil and Jimmy and Kenny and that nice fella, Mike Bailey.' She nudged Josie suggestively. 'They won't miss us if we stay on a bit.'

Cecily closed her eyes and let the rumble of the engine

soothe her. She tried not to let her overactive imagination worry her. But she played the scene over and over again. Her first thought was that Eddie would be a little shrunken man with a walking stick and she'd be sorry she came. Her second worry was that he wouldn't recognise her, or he'd tell her he'd changed his mind and didn't want to see her after all. Her third was that he'd have a house full of friends, watching the sport. And her final fear was that he wouldn't answer the door, or simply would not be in, and she'd go home without meeting him, feeling more empty than she ever had.

She dozed for a while and her fears became dreams. Eddie unrecognisable. Eddie not interested, unapproachable.

In Oxford, she was still half asleep when Minnie and Jensen climbed in behind her and she heard Poll say, 'It's a good job this car has seven seats, Lin. It's a nice little bus. Are we getting off to that other place now? I'm starving.'

She dozed again. In her final reverie, Eddie was twenty-four and ruggedly handsome. James Dean. He came to the door with a baby in his arms, a glamorous blonde film star hanging on his shoulder, and dismissed Cecily with an abrupt, 'Who are you? I don't know any old ladies.'

She woke as the car slowed down in a small terraced road and Lin said, 'We're here, Cecily. Woodbury Close. Number seven is the one with the green door.'

Cecily felt fear leap into her throat. It was as if her heart were being squeezed in a giant fist. She gasped aloud.

Minnie leaned forward. 'Do you want one of us to come with you?'

'No. I have to do this by myself.' Cecily heard the tremor in her voice.

'We'll be at the pub just down the road,' Lin said gently. 'We won't come unless you message us. Or we'll come at four if you don't.'

'You'll be fine,' Josie soothed. 'Good luck.'

'I think you're so brave,' Poll said. 'I don't think any of my exes would want to see me again. And I'd run a mile if I saw any of them.'

'Shall I help you to the door?' Minnie offered.

'No, no, I'll be fine.' Cecily eased herself from the car.

Jensen was next to her in a flash, supporting her arm. 'There you go.'

'Thank you, Jensen.' Cecily gave her bravest smile. 'Wish me luck.'

'Good luck, Cecily.'

The chorus came from the car and Cecily called, 'Emily Dickinson said, "Fortune befriends the bold."'

She heard Poll ask, 'Isn't he that orange man who did *Bargain Hunt* on the telly?' The Sharan pulled away and Cecily was on her own, facing a green door with a white bell and a brass knocker.

35

Cecily rang the doorbell for the second time and waited. Perhaps Eddie was hard of hearing now. Perhaps he was slow on his feet. He'd earned the right: he was ninety-four.

The silence continued, and she rang the bell a third time. Cecily shivered inside the thin dress. The sun had come out, the air was warm, but her skin was gooseflesh. Her legs were shaking with fear.

She knew it was him before he answered the door. She could see his shape through the frosted glass. Smaller, a little bent over, but it was definitely him. Cecily took a deep breath.

The door opened and Eddie was looking at her, his face full of recognition. His expression froze, as if he couldn't believe what he was seeing. His dark eyes were amazed, filled with tears. Cecily thought he looked older, of course, but in some ways he looked no different.

His hair was white, the skin on his face sagged a little around the chin, but he was still Eddie Blake. There was the same ruggedness, the serious eyes and strong cheekbones, the easy grin, the way he arched an eyebrow. He said her name as if it were a prayer. 'Cecily.'

'Yes, it's me, Eddie.' She didn't know what else to say.

'I've heard that voice so often over the years, in my thoughts. It hasn't changed. You haven't changed.'

'Oh, I have.'

'Please, come in. Come in.' Eddie's smile was still charming. Cecily followed him through a carpeted hall into an open-plan lounge and kitchen. She looked around at white walls, a plush pale rug, a leather sofa. Cecily was glad to sit down before her legs became any weaker. She glanced at the framed photos on the wall of a man wearing a gi – a white cotton jacket and loose black pants tied with a black belt. He was fighting, in various positions, practising a martial art. Cecily leaned forward; it was Eddie, throughout the years. In the first photos he was sturdy and strong, dark haired; in later ones his hair was white and he was more sinewy. He saw that she was looking.

'I did a lot of aikido. I got to third dan. I taught it a little bit.'

'So you were a sensei?' Cecily asked.

'Yes, it means—'

'Teacher. Or keeper of the way. Or the one who was born before.'

Eddie didn't move. 'Over the years, I needed to do something that would make me a better person, a fitter one. Aikido suited me.'

'The way of harmonious spirit.' Cecily knew the meaning of the word.

'I found aikido calmed me down and gave me discipline. It helped me cope.'

'It suited you. I can see that from the photos,' Cecily said politely.

'You were a teacher too.'

'All my working life,' Cecily said.

'I knew you moved away and took up a post somewhere in Oxfordshire. I bet you were a wonderful teacher. But did you never marry? I notice your name is still Hamilton – Sammy told me when she looked you up on social media.'

'Eddie.' Cecily met his eyes and their gaze held. She said, 'Could I have a cup of tea? Or water?'

'I'm sorry, of course.' Eddie stood up. 'What would you like?'

'Do you have green tea?'

'It's all I drink now,' Eddie said; he moved to the kitchen area and filled a kettle. Cecily looked round for clues about his past, for photos of Joyce, of Elizabeth. She found one on the windowsill and she narrowed her eyes to see it better. She could make out Eddie, probably in his fifties, flanked by two women. One was young, twenties or thirties, holding a baby: it was Elizabeth with Sammy. The other woman must be Joyce but Cecily hardly recognised her. She looked much thinner, shrunken, and behind her smile she looked unbelievably sad. Cecily eased herself from the chair and went over to examine the picture. In it, Eddie's arm was around his daughter. Cecily could see the resemblance between them. Joyce stood a little apart, her hand against Eddie's shoulder for support. He was leaning away from her, grinning into the camera, but his eyes were filled with unhappiness.

The photo told the whole story.

Eddie brought two cups over and placed them on the low coffee table. He sat next to Cecily and said, 'I'm so glad you came.'

'I thought about it very carefully after Sammy gave me your address,' Cecily admitted. 'I almost didn't.'

'Tell me about yourself.' Eddie's face took on that eager expression she knew so well, the same expression that had attracted her to him so many years ago at The Orchid Ballroom. She remembered listening to him speak over a lemonade; he'd been drinking shandy. She had watched his mouth move for a long time before she had found her voice.

'I was a teacher in Oxfordshire. I live there now.' Cecily reached for her tea. 'And no, I didn't marry.'

'Why not?' There was a hopefulness in Eddie's voice.

'I didn't see the need,' Cecily said firmly. She wanted to say that she had been let down once and wouldn't risk being hurt again, but she couldn't bring herself to say it, certainly not yet. So she said, 'Teaching was fulfilling. It became my life.'

'I remember how ambitious you were, how determined we both were, how we planned our future…' Eddie's voice trailed away. He glanced down at his hands that held the cup. 'I had a garage. My own business. I ran it for a while and employed a couple of blokes. It was quite successful. Joyce—'

Eddie looked up and Cecily nodded, encouraging him to go on.

'Joyce wanted to stay at home with Lizzie as she grew up. Then she wasn't well, off and on.'

'Oh?'

'We stayed together for Lizzie. We weren't close. She had her own friends, belonged to a reading group. I had my martial arts.' Eddie took a breath. 'We were good parents. Lizzie was a happy child; she went to college, did well, we gave her the big wedding she wanted. We helped her financially a bit, bringing up Sammy.'

Cecily shook her head. 'Weren't you happy, Eddie? You and Joyce?'

'Not really.' Eddie took a deep drink. 'I wasn't what you'd call a loving husband. We neglected each other. Joyce became angry with me, frustrated; she took tablets for depression. Then her health went downhill.'

'What a waste,' Cecily said, and she heard the bitterness in her voice. 'And all because you made one mistake.'

Silence filled the room and hung there. Eddie exhaled, a sigh of someone whose life had been filled with regret. 'I thought of you every day.'

'That makes it an even bigger tragedy,' Cecily said.

'I heard you'd got a job in Oxfordshire. It was pure coincidence, but a garage business came up in Wallingford and I moved us all down here when Lizzie was a toddler. Joyce wasn't keen. But I hoped we'd meet again.'

'And Joyce?'

'I did my best to make her happy. But there was nothing between us, no love. We did the family things with Lizzie, holidays, and when she grew up Joyce and I drifted apart. She had asthma, heart problems and finally cancer. I looked after her. I owed her that. I made sure she had everything she needed.'

'Apart from love.'

'Yes,' Eddie said sadly. 'I never loved her. And I don't think she loved me either.'

'Poor Joyce. I remember her as someone who was so full of fun. All she wanted was to settle down with a family.'

'That's what I wanted too.' Eddie looked up from his cup. 'But not with Joyce.'

'And what about you?' Cecily changed the subject. 'You look well.'

'I look after myself. I had a bit of a problem with narrowing arteries, and I got a couple of stents put in. That was a few years ago. I'm fine now.' Eddie put his cup down. 'And you?'

'I'm independent. I have some wonderful friends.'

Eddie smiled; his expression was still one of disbelief that

Cecily was sitting in his house. 'It's so good to see you. Cecily, can I offer you lunch?'

'You can,' Cecily said. 'But first, there is a question I have to ask you. It's one that has been bothering me for so many years.'

'I know what it is,' Eddie said. 'I've been asking myself the question since the day I let you down.'

'And what is the answer?'

'I don't know.' Eddie exhaled loudly, resigned. 'Times have changed, Cecily. In those days, things were different. The roles of men and women weren't what they are now, and the rules about sex were very black and white. You were the woman I wanted to marry, and Joyce was—'

Cecily's temper flared immediately. 'Joyce was the sort of girl you used? Is that it, Eddie?'

'No. I've been ashamed of what I did, every day of my life.' Eddie ran a hand through his hair, a gesture Cecily remembered, and it made her heart ache. 'You know what happened that night. The three of us had been out – Albie had broken up with Joyce and we took her along with us so she wouldn't be left out. I drove you home, and afterwards I said I'd see her home safely.'

Cecily remembered as if it were yesterday. 'We'd been dancing and she'd had a couple of drinks. Snowballs. Joyce always said they went to her head.'

'I drove her to her house. It wasn't far from yours. She was pretending to be tipsier than she was. She asked me to help her to the door. She wanted me to take her inside the house. When I got in, I discovered there was no one else at home. Her parents were out. She threw her arms round me and her hands were all over me. I stood there while she took off some of her clothes and she was tugging me to her bedroom.'

'You should have said no.'

'I should.'

'So why didn't you?'

'I was stupid. I did try to put her off at first, but she was persistent. I had a moment's weakness and I thought, oh, what the hell, why not?'

'Eddie.' Cecily caught her breath.

'I've never forgiven myself. Cecily, I let you down. I let Joyce down. I ruined my life. For one moment, for sex, for nothing. So that I'd feel like a man. And do you know? Afterwards, I felt really bad.'

'What did you do?'

'I apologised to Joyce for what I'd done. I told her I didn't love her, I loved you. And she was crying. So I tucked her up in her little single bed and I left as quick as I could. I was shaking.'

'Why?'

'Because I'd done something terrible. How could I tell you, Cecily? Joyce was your best friend. I was your fiancé. I knew how you'd feel. I despised myself, my stupidity. But I paid the price.'

'We all did,' Cecily said miserably. 'You, Joyce, me.'

Eddie looked down at his hands. 'Things could've been so different.'

'They could.'

'I wanted to marry you. We'd have had a family. We were good together.'

'Oh, we were, Eddie.'

'Did you ever wish things might have been different?'

'Every day.' Cecily found it difficult to speak. Tears pricked her eyes. 'Never a minute went past that I didn't love you.'

'What a fool I was.' Eddie shook his head in disbelief.

'I'm glad I came to visit. I'm glad we talked things through.' Cecily touched her cheek and realised it was wet.

'You must hate me.'

'Not at all. The complete opposite. But I was angry with you. For years, I blamed you.'

'I deserved it.'

'But not now, Eddie. I forgive you. I...' Cecily held out a hand. 'I want us to be friends.'

Eddie moved to sit next to her and took the hand she offered. 'Can we? Can we mean something to each other again?'

'If we've loved each other all our lives and we can't heal the past, what chance is there for the rest of the world?'

Eddie brought her fingers to his lips. 'I remember I placed a ring on this finger.'

'I still have it.' Cecily smiled. She saw his lip tremble.

'Can I visit you?'

'I think so.' Cecily leaned against him and he wrapped an arm around her. 'I think we can put the past behind us and move forward. Today has been good. We've talked, we've listened. And we've found peace with each other.'

'We have,' Eddie said, and he kissed her lips.

36

The following week was a flurry of preparations for Cecily's party. Lin and Neil were handling the invitations, phoning friends in the village to check who was coming, liaising with Dickie Junior over tables and chairs. Josie was making the cake, a classic sponge decorated with a pink guitar and pale green flowers. Florence and Odile were preparing food and Minnie was orchestrating buffet food from her living room in Oxford, arranging for dishes to be sent to The Sun in advance.

Poll Toomey had relatives in Birmingham who were apparently a dab hand with 'decking out a room'. Late on Friday evening, after closing time, Poll and two of her sisters-in-law snuck into The Sun and transformed it. Inside, colourful balloons hung from the ceiling along with strings of heart-shaped fairy lights. The three women heaved tables into a long square shape, covered them in red cloth, placed fresh flowers in vases, scattered coloured electric tealights. They arranged a huge banner on the wall that read 'Happy birthday, Miss Hamilton'. By midnight, the bar in The Sun was ready.

On Saturday, Lin spent time with Cecily, giving Josie,

Florence, Dickie Junior, Neil and Odile a chance to organise the food and drink. Jack Lovejoy and his folk band, Glyndŵr, arrived fresh from a gig in Worcester and began to set up in the corner. Minnie, Tina, Jensen and Gary turned up and there was some excited whispering before Sammy Pearson arrived with her grandfather. Cecily had no idea that Minnie had arranged for Eddie to come.

The evening sunshine was soft and hazy as lemon curd outside The Sun as Cecily stepped from the Sharan, holding onto Lin's arm. Her hair was newly styled and she wore a glittery party dress and her favourite coral lipstick. On the third finger of her right hand, she had placed Eddie's engagement ring. She promised herself that she'd phone him later and arrange to meet. She'd thought of little else for a whole week.

Cecily frowned, noticing all the cars in the car park. 'You said there would just be a handful of guests, Lin. All these people can't be here for my birthday.'

Lin smiled. 'It's your special day, Cecily. Quite a lot of people want to help you to celebrate.'

Inside The Sun, everyone was in their designated places, waiting for Cecily. Kenny Hooper and Jimmy Baker had pints in their hands already. Gerald Harris and Margaret Fennimore sat next to them in their finest clothes and Odile and her husband, Ronnel, were wearing their brightest summer attire. The vicar, Andrew Cooper, was sitting with Henry Turvey from Charlbury and his family. Janice and Geoff Lovejoy sat next to the Ledburys, who crowded around the table. George and Penny were laughing and joking with their son and his wife, although Nadine hadn't made an appearance, much to Dickie Junior's surprise. Natalie had brought Anthony, a fair-haired young man in a tweed jacket, and Bobby was seated with Hayley and the kids. Even Dr Müller had turned up with her partner. The next chairs were occupied by Linval and Rita Johnson, Malia and Malek, Tina and Gary.

Florence was busy putting Elsie in the high chair Dickie kept out the back for families who brought babies. Little Elsie's face was lit up with excitement. Adam whispered, 'Florence, your mother doesn't know what she's missing.'

'Are you talking about the letter she sent on Monday?'

'The famous pink envelope,' Adam said. 'Do you think she'll write again?'

'I doubt it. After telling us that her boyfriend didn't want her to visit. But could I send more photos of Elsie.' Florence shook her head in disbelief. 'No, she won't come now.'

'Do you think your dad's all right?' Adam handed Elsie a little cup of water, glancing towards the bar where Dangerous Dave was buying a round of pints.

'He seems better now that he knows how the land lies. At least he's not hoping for the impossible. He wants to go round to Tina's house and look at what decorating needs doing. He thinks he's going to be renovating a château.'

'That's another accident waiting to happen.' Adam kissed Florence's nose. 'Our own house, though.'

'I can hardly believe it,' Florence said.

'She's here,' a voice called. It was Minnie, sitting next to Jensen, Josie, Mike, Fergal and Poll. Neil was installed next to an empty seat reserved for Lin; there was a spare one for Cecily. Eddie was seated next to where she would be, smiling and dapper in a suit and tie, his granddaughter Sammy beside him.

Cecily wandered in clutching Lin's arm and everyone stood up and clapped. Jack and Glyndŵr, from the corner, began to play 'Happy Birthday' and everyone joined in a rousing chorus. Cecily couldn't move, she was so surprised. Tears glinted in her eyes. 'I was expecting half a dozen people. Not the whole village. And, oh – look how beautiful the place is.'

Poll grinned as if she'd won the lottery. 'That's bostin! We wanted to make it nice.' Fergal wrapped an arm around her proudly.

Minnie called, 'Come and sit down, Cecily. Dickie's got champagne.'

Cecily glanced towards the empty seat and caught her breath as she noticed Eddie, suited and booted and smart. She couldn't move. His eyes shone as he clambered to his feet.

'Eddie,' Cecily said, the words stuck in her throat. 'You came.'

'I couldn't miss your birthday.' He stood up gallantly, holding out a hand. 'Cecily.'

She took it and they faced each other. The moment seemed to hang on the air as their eyes connected and they were lost in thought. Then he whispered, 'Please, let's sit.' He guided her to her chair and handed her a small parcel. 'This is for you.'

Cecily's lips trembled with more emotion than she could cope with. 'What is it?' She fumbled with the little package, conscious that her fingers shook, that everyone was watching. She tugged out a box. Inside was a gold chain, a locket, a single word engraved on it.

Love.

Cecily closed her eyes as Eddie wrapped it round her neck and fastened the clasp. She turned back and both their faces were wet with tears.

She kissed his cheek. 'This is such a special day. All these wonderful people, just for me. And you're here, Eddie. At last I have you here with me.'

Dickie was at her shoulder, filling glasses with champagne.

Music burst from the corner; Jack and Glyndŵr were playing 'Who Knows Where the Time Goes?'.

Cecily noticed the spread on the table. 'Oh, what a beautiful buffet. Who's done all this? Just look.' She indicated plates piled with food. 'All these dishes.'

'We all chipped in,' Minnie said with a smile. 'Odile made the stewed beef and dumplings and the soursop ice cream.'

'Minnie ordered takeaway from the village,' Jensen said.

'And Josie made cake,' Lin added.

Dickie was at Cecily's shoulder, pouring champagne into her glass. 'And this is from me, Cecily. To say thanks. To say how much we all loved our time at Middleton Ferris school. To say how special you are.'

'Hear, hear,' Minnie agreed.

Voices from around the room cried out, 'We love you, Miss Hamilton.'

'Can we dig in now?' Jimmy Baker shouted and Dangerous Dave laughed.

'I already have. Sorry. These fondant potatoes are a bit moreish.'

Champagne bubbled in glasses and forks clanked against plates. Elsie was alternately chewing at a piece of celery held in one hand and a fondant potato in the other. She threw the celery on the floor. Dishes were passed and low sounds of enjoyment mixed with bubbling conversation. Cecily turned to Lin. 'This is so kind of you all.'

'Happy birthday, Cecily.' Lin grinned.

'You're the best teacher.' Josie leaned over with a smile.

Jensen was impressed. 'What a feast. I think I might stay in the UK.'

'I might imprison you here forever,' Minnie whispered in his ear.

Dickie was back with glasses of champagne, buck's fizz, elderflower pressé. 'Who's for a top-up?'

'Me.' George Ledbury held out his glass.

Tina leaned over to the Johnsons. 'Do you want to come to the house afterwards? Florence and Adam are having a look round, and Dave's coming. I know they want you to be there.'

'Oh, we'd love to.' Rita grinned.

Glyndŵr were singing 'Like a Rolling Stone'. Everyone was singing along or deep in conversation. No one saw the door open. A handsome, impeccably dressed man wandered to the bar, leaned against it and said, 'Did someone forget to invite me?'

Jimmy Baker looked up. 'Hello, Darryl. Good to see you, mate.'

Dangerous Dave was on his feet, clambering towards the bar. 'I'll buy you a drink.' He turned to Florence. 'Darryl's been my best customer these last few weeks.' Florence froze. Adam took her hand beneath the table. Dave said, 'It's all right if Darryl joins us, isn't it, Cecily?'

'No, it is not,' Cecily said, her tone like ice. The music stopped. The whole room became silent.

Minnie said, 'Go home, Darryl. You're not welcome. You know why.'

'But he's a good customer.' Dave was confused. 'He brings his Porsche in. He used to live here once.'

'Used to,' Neil spoke up. 'You need to go, Darryl.'

'I don't get it,' Dave said. 'Can't he at least have a drink with us?'

'That's not a good idea, Dave,' Minnie said quietly.

'What's the poor bloke done?' Jimmy Baker was on his feet.

There was a pause. Then Darryl laughed, a low, unpleasant snicker. 'I wouldn't want to drink with any of you. I just came to have a look at all the village idiots sitting together, swilling at the same trough.'

'There's no need for that.' Fergal's voice was a warning.

'There's every need,' Darryl said. 'I have a job in Cumbria now. I'll buy a house there and I'll be made welcome. Not like this dump.'

'Have a drink,' Dave said again, baffled. 'I'll get you a pint.'

'I wouldn't drink with you,' Darryl said, his face full of disdain. 'You've no idea, do you, Dave? Why don't you ask your little slapper of a daughter why I'm not hanging around?'

'Don't you dare.' The words escaped Adam's lips. Florence was pale and shaking.

'Look at the kid she's got there. It looks nothing like its so-called father,' Darryl sneered. 'That's because he isn't the father. I am.'

There was a moment's stunned silence. Minnie said, 'That attitude's nothing to be proud of.'

'No, but I'm going to set the record straight. So you all know what a little slag she is.'

Dave turned to Florence, his face creased with disbelief. 'Florence?'

Florence couldn't speak. Adam wrapped a protective arm around her. Elsie was on his knee now.

Darryl was centre stage. He was enjoying himself. 'I picked her up outside the café and invited her back to mine. I didn't need to ask twice. She was all over me, not bothered if I had a wife or not. There was only one thing she was after.'

Florence's lips moved but no words came out.

'She got her kit off and dragged me upstairs like the tart she is.' Darryl's voice became louder. 'It was all right. Not the best shag I've had, but there you go. She told me she was on the pill, that she'd slept with half the men in the village.' He glanced around, his smile triumphant. 'Bobby Ledbury, the Toomey boys – their dad.'

Fergal clambered to his feet. 'You're a lying little gobshite.'

'But not you, Adam. You're left holding the baby like a pathetic wimp, while your missus runs around screwing anyone with a spare half-hour on their hands. So, Dave.' Darryl turned smartly. 'That's why I won't have a drink with you. I'm not interested in the kid. Who knows? It might not be mine anyway. But I just thought I'd let you know, before I go, what a cheap, trashy tart you have for a daughter.'

Dave stared at Florence in disbelief. Her face was covered in tears. He grabbed Darryl by the shirt. There was a tearing of material.

'You bastard.'

Kenny Hooper's voice could be heard saying, 'This ent right. There's gonna be trouble.'

Dave lifted a fist, his face seething red. 'You bastard.' He launched a hard punch towards Darryl. Someone caught his arm in mid-air.

'Don't, Dave. Don't. He's not worth it.'

Everyone watched as Dave turned in slow motion, his face snarling, his fist still raised. Mike Bailey was next to him, holding his arm fast.

'Don't hit him. I know he deserves it. He deserves for you to punch his lights out. But you're the bigger man. Sit down, Dave. Sit down and I'll get you a drink.'

'But the bastard said my Florence was a—'

'I know what he said. But it's lies. Nobody believes him. He's just a jealous man with an axe to grind.' Mike was out of breath, sweating, panting. 'Come on, Dave – sit down.'

Fergal and Bobby were on their feet, one either side of

Darryl, shepherding him towards the door. Darryl shouted, 'If you lay a finger on me – I'm a solicitor.'

'No one would lay a finger or anything else on you, you feck,' Fergal said angrily.

'And don't you dare speak about Florence again, or come anywhere near her,' Bobby spat between gritted teeth.

'You're not welcome here,' Fergal snarled.

Darryl looked furiously around the bar, taking his time. Then he broke from their grasp and rushed out into the street, slamming the door behind him. Fergal addressed the room. 'That's the last we'll see of him. Are you all right, Florence?'

Florence nodded slowly. She couldn't speak. Adam's arms were around her.

'No one says things like that about my friends and family without getting a thick ear,' Fergal added. 'He was lucky today.'

Dave was back in his seat, a pint in his hand, breathing heavily. Florence whispered, 'Dad? Are you all right?'

Dave took a moment to compose himself. His face was covered in tears. 'Don't you worry about him, Princess. He's nothing. Nobody believes him.'

Mike reached over and shook Dangerous Dave's hand. 'Well done, mate.'

'No, thank *you*.' Dave was still quaking. 'I totally lost it, after what he said about my girl.'

Mike understood. 'I was glad to help.'

Josie took his hand and leaned over, pecking his cheek. 'Well done.'

Glyndŵr started playing 'Ramblin' Boy' and Dickie was back with refills. George Ledbury leaned across the table. 'Can we have cake now, Josie?'

Josie glanced at Cecily, asking permission. Cecily stood up slowly and raised a hand. 'I want to say a few words, please.'

The band stopped playing. Everyone was listening.

'Thank you.' Cecily gave a little cough. 'Thank you all for this tremendous party. I consider myself truly blessed to be sitting here breaking bread with so many people I love and admire.' Her eyes swept the room, taking in Minnie, Josie, Lin, Florence. She reserved a special smile for Eddie and continued. 'As you know, I was a teacher here some hundreds of years ago.'

There was light laughter and Kenny yelled, 'It wasn't that long, Miss.'

'I learned a lot from my pupils,' Cecily said, her eyes misty. 'And I'm still learning. When I first started teaching, I wanted you all to aspire to be the best. The best reader, the fastest runner, the quickest at reciting tables, the smartest speller. Now I think the best that we can be is kind, considerate and full of forgiveness.'

Andrew the vicar could be heard at the far end of the table, mumbling, 'Hear, hear.'

'The past has gone.' Cecily's voice grew stronger. 'We need to learn from it, not rake it up and dwell on it. I'd like to quote the wonderful writer Zadie Smith out of context, just to make my point, and suggest that, "The past is always tense, the future perfect." What happened in here today...' her eyes met Florence's '...means nothing at all. It's something we never need to think of or talk about again. It was the ranting of a weak, jealous man. Don't let's look back, or dwell on bad things. Let's live now, love now, believe that today is the best of us.' Cecily took a deep breath. 'I have wasted time thinking about my past mistakes – and the mistakes of others – and wishing we hadn't made them. I imagined these errors to be huge, but in fact they were tiny. They are gone now. And I know some of you have things you wish you'd never done, Mike... Eddie... Dave. But we're not the sum of our faults. We're telling our own story even now. We're who we are, who we will be, not who we once were.'

Eddie took her hand, the one wearing his ring, and kissed it.

'Hear, hear,' Jensen yelled and started to clap. Everyone else joined in, cheering, applauding.

Cecily's tiny voice could be heard saying, 'And now, let us eat cake.'

Glyndŵr struck up the opening bars of 'Teach Your Children'. Cecily lifted a knife and began to slice the iced sponge into equal pieces.

EPILOGUE

It was Monday in Odile's café, almost two o'clock. The lunchtime crowd had been and gone but the Silver Ladies were still there. Cecily, Minnie, Josie, Lin and Poll sat with their heads together, oblivious of the time, talking and drinking tea.

Cecily smiled. 'I seem to spend my life drinking tea and having lunch.'

'It's not a bad way to grow old,' Lin suggested.

'I'm going to grow old with my Fergal,' Poll said into her cup. 'Did you see how manly he was the other day, how he escorted that yuppy bloke out of the pub?' She sniffed. 'If he hadn't done it, I would've. After what he said about Fergal and Devlin and Finn. And Florence. He was out of line.'

'He's a minimus, a nothing,' Minnie said. *'Stultus est.'*

'What does that mean when it's at home?' Poll cackled.

'The man's an idiot,' Cecily explained. 'I could find a more appropriate word, but I won't give him another second of my time.'

'I just hope Florence and Adam don't dwell on it,' Josie said.

'I don't think they will.' Minnie stirred her tea. 'Tina showed them round her house after the meal. They want to buy it. They've made an offer.'

'That's good,' Poll said. 'They're a nice little family.'

'We're a good family too,' Lin said. 'A village family. I'm proud of us.'

'I've got an announcement.' Josie leaned her head on her hands. 'I'm going out with Mike tonight. We'll take it slowly, see how it goes. But we have a date.'

Minnie laughed. 'I can trump that.' She leaned forward confidentially. 'Jensen's moved in. For how long I don't know. But we're together. And I'm not taking it slowly, Josie. I'm going to throw myself right in at the deep end.'

Lin thought for a moment. 'I'm married to the handsomest boy in the class. Neil and I have been together for nearly fifty-one years. Doesn't that trump everything?'

'Fergal's bum's pretty spectacular,' Poll mused. 'That trumps everything as far as I'm concerned.'

'I can trump you all,' Cecily said. 'I'm thinking of asking Eddie to come and stay with me in the bungalow.'

'Stay?' Lin's eyes danced. 'For the summer?'

'For ever?' Poll asked.

'I have no idea,' Cecily laughed. 'We'll take things day by day and enjoy our time. Twilight years. After so long apart, I think we have a lot of lost time to make up.'

Poll said, 'No one would believe you're ninety-two. You're just bostin'!'

'She's marvellous, isn't she?' Minnie agreed.

'I love the man.' Cecily smiled. 'I can't help how I feel.'

The plastic ribbons that led to the kitchen flapped and Florence emerged carrying a tray with five bowls of soup. Lin inhaled. 'Mmm. I can smell the spice.'

'Vegetables, ginger, garlic, miso, chilli and a dollop of good tahini,' Florence said. 'Odile's Monday creation. Enjoy.'

She turned to go and Josie called, 'What's the news about the house move?'

Minnie added, 'Has Tina definitely accepted your offer?'

'She messaged me this morning – and yes.' Florence smiled. 'It's just what Adam and Elsie and I need. A place of our own.'

'And you'll only be a few doors down from me,' Lin said. 'Oh, I'm so glad, Florence.'

Florence hesitated. 'I ought to thank you – you've all been so wonderful to me and Adam. And thanks for what you said in the pub, Cecily.'

'Any time. Don't mention it. You're a token Silver Lady.' Cecily had her spoon in the air. She had already started on the soup. 'Oh, do tell Odile this is delicious.'

'I will.' Florence took a few steps away before she turned back. 'Adam's taking me out into Tadderly on Saturday night for a meal. We're going to celebrate.'

'The house move?' Minnie asked.

'Just being us, being together.' Florence smiled dreamily. She was about to go, then she said, 'Josie, I don't suppose you'd babysit Elsie?'

Josie looked horrified for a moment. She said, 'Well, I did offer a while ago, didn't I?'

'You did,' Florence agreed. 'I'd ask Dad but he's hopeless. He falls asleep and doesn't hear her crying. And he'll probably want to go down The Sun.'

'Well, I suppose I could. On Saturday?' Josie was unsure. 'I'm not really good with babies, but yes, I'll give it a go.'

'Why don't we all babysit Elsie together?' Poll said. 'I'll bring a few beers round and some bostin' board games, and we can do a bit of gambling for pennies.'

'We'll tutor Elsie in the ways of unrighteousness.' Minnie laughed. 'I'm up for it.'

'I'll come. I'll get Neil to make us a drizzle cake,' Lin added.

'And I'll bring my guitar. We can teach Elsie a few Buddy Holly songs,' Cecily said.

'It'll be just like old times.' Josie smiled. 'Ah, it's so good that you have my back. I was terrified of babysitting alone.'

'We're not alone, any of us,' Cecily said firmly. 'As long as we have each other, we can face the world.'

'Do you remember what you used to tell us when we were in primary school, about friendship, Cecily?' Lin asked.

'What did she tell you?' Poll was fascinated.

'A good friend is like a four-leaf clover,' Josie began.

'Hard to find and lucky to have,' Minnie finished the sentence.

Poll's face clouded and she banged the table with her fist. 'Oh, I'll kill that Fergal Toomey.'

'Why?' Cecily wanted to know. 'What's Fergal done now?'

'He said those exact lines to me on the day he proposed. He told me he'd made them up himself, and I thought I'd met the man of my dreams.' She burst out laughing. 'Now I find out he got them from his teacher.' She looked from face to face and shrugged. 'Ah, well, what does it matter? Life's too short for arguing, and anyway, the soup's going cold.'

* * *

MORE FROM JUDY LEIGH

Another book from Judy Leigh, *The Golden Gals' French Adventure*, is available to order now here:

https://mybook.to/GoldenFrenchBackAd

ACKNOWLEDGEMENTS

Thanks to Kiran Kataria and Emma Beswetherick, whose warmth, professionalism and kindness I value so much.

Thanks to the team at Boldwood Books; to Amanda and Marcela and Wendy and Nia, to designers, editors, technicians, voice actors.

And special thanks to Sarah Ritherdon.

To Rachel Gilbey, to so many wonderful bloggers and fellow writers. The support you give goes beyond words.

To Martin, Cath, Avril, Rob, Tom, Emily, Tom's mum, Erika, Rich, Kathy N, Julie, Martin, Steve, Rose, Steve's mum, Jan, Rog, Jan M, Helen, Pat, Ken, Trish, Lexy, Rachel, John, Nik R, Pete O', Chris A, Chris's mum, Katie H, Shaz, Gracie, Mya, Frank, George, Fiona J and Jonno.

Thanks to the Haytor Vale WI for their hospitality. To all at the LLPP.

To Peter and the Solitary Writers, my writing buddies.

Also, my neighbours and the local community, especially Jenny, Laura, Claire, Paul and Sophie, Niranjan and all at Turmeric Kitchen.

Much thanks to Ivor Abiks at Deep Studios and to Darren and Lyndsay at PPL.

Love to family, to Ellen, Hugh, Jo, Jan, Lou, Harry, Chris, Norman, Angela, Robin, Edward, Zach, Daniel, Catalina.

So much love to my mum and dad, Irene and Tosh, who I miss more than words.

Love always to our Tony and Kim, to Liam, Maddie, Kayak, Joey.

And to my soulmate, Big G.

Warmest thanks always to you, my readers, wherever you are. You make this journey special.

ABOUT THE AUTHOR

Judy Leigh is the bestselling author of *Five French Hens*, *A Grand Old Time* and *The Age of Misadventure* and the doyenne of the 'it's never too late' genre of women's fiction. She has lived all over the UK from Liverpool to Cornwall, but currently resides in Somerset.

Sign up to Judy Leigh's mailing list here for news, competitions and updates on future books.

Visit Judy's website: www.judyleigh.com

Follow Judy on social media:

- facebook.com/judyleighuk
- x.com/judyleighwriter
- instagram.com/judyrleigh
- bookbub.com/authors/judy-leigh

ALSO BY JUDY LEIGH

Five French Hens

The Old Girls' Network

Heading Over the Hill

Chasing the Sun

Lil's Bus Trip

The Golden Girls' Getaway

A Year of Mr Maybes

The Highland Hens

The Golden Oldies' Book Club

The Silver Ladies Do Lunch

The Vintage Village Bake Off

The Golden Gals' French Adventure

The Silver-Haired Sisterhood

The Silver Ladies Seize the Day

The Morwenna Mutton Mysteries Series

Foul Play at Seal Bay

Bloodshed on the Boards

The Cream Tea Killer

BECOME A MEMBER OF THE SHELF CARE CLUB

The home of Boldwood's book club reads.

Find uplifting reads, sunny escapes, cosy romances, family dramas and more!

Sign up to the newsletter
https://bit.ly/theshelfcareclub